2/25

merger

sanjay sanghoee

merger

A Tom Doherty Associates Book
New York

MERGER

Copyright © 2005 by Sanjay Sanghoee

This book is printed on acid-free paper.

A Forge Book
Published by Tom Doherty Associates, LLC
175 Fifth Avenue
New York, NY 10010

www.tor.com

Forge® is a registered trademark of Tom Doherty Associates, LLC.

Library of Congress Cataloging-in-Publication Data

Sanghoee, Sanjay.
    Merger / Sanjay Sanghoee.—1st ed.
        p. cm.
    "A Tom Doherty Associates book."
    ISBN 0-765-31112-7
    EAN 978-0-765-31112-2
    1. Consolidation and merger of corporations—Fiction. 2. Corporations—Corrupt practices—Fiction.
3. Chief executive officers—Fiction. 4. Investment bankers—Fiction. 5. New York (N.Y.)—Fiction. 6.
Wall Street—Fiction. I. Title.

PS3619.A567M47 2005
813'.6—dc22

                                                                                    2004066427

First Edition: July 2005

Printed in the United States of America

0 9 8 7 6 5 4 3 2 1

For my parents,
Saroj and Subhash

acknowledgments

When I first sat down to write *Merger*, I thought that creating a novel was a one-man show.

It is not.

Writing is one thing, editing is quite another. The latter deserves a medal of honor. The man who earned this reward is my editor, Bob Gleason, whose insightful suggestions and valiant efforts to ensure that my ravings at least resembled a work of fiction are the reason that bookstores will carry my novel. A similar thanks goes to Tom Doherty, Roy Gainsburg, and Eric Raab, all of whom took the time to comment on the manuscript and guide me through the remarkable maze that is the publishing world. Of course, none of this would have come to pass without the efforts and belief of my fabulous agent, Elizabeth Winick. Her generosity and patience made the process almost unfairly easy. Thanks also to Henry Williams, who, on more than one occasion, kept me from self-destructing, and to Tracey Adams and Melinda Boothe, who got me into the game.

And those are just the professionals.

No acknowledgment for this novel would deserve to get past the first page without a very special thanks to my friend and mentor Josh Steiner. More than anyone else, he has taught me how to be a professional, encouraged me to quit smoking (I'm almost there), and come to my rescue on way too many occasions, including for *Merger*.

The funny thing about writing is that you can't do it without food or electricity. Words seem inadequate to describe my gratitude to and respect for David Lee, Jeffrey Libshutz, and Peter Leibman, whose selfless support has quite simply given my dream of writing a fighting chance. The same applies to Nancy Nouel and Linette Paladino, those lovely ladies without whom life at LLJ could never quite be the same. They all put up with me day in and day out, and for that alone they deserve Purple Hearts.

The third leg of my holy personal trinity is Nash Madon, who kept believing in my work even when I didn't. A great boss but an even better friend, it is scary to think how all this could have turned out if he hadn't kept me together. . . .

Another mentor whom I'd like to thank is Professor Robert Willens, who tried very hard to teach me something useful at Columbia Business School but ultimately realized I was a better writer than a banker.

A thriller has many many moving parts and it would be impossible to put one together without the constant aid and attention of seasoned literary experts. Since I did not know any, I relied on my father and my friends. For the most part I took their suggestions, but sometimes I did not. In the cases where their changes did not make it into the manuscript, it was because they are not seasoned literary experts and should not meddle in things they know nothing about.

Seriously, though, the following people contributed their time, energy, and technical expertise to this book and for that I will always be grateful: Garth Symonds, Scott Johnson, my father, Todd Rubsamen, Jacob Weinberg, my father, Jessica Rohm, Elisabeth Rohm, my father. Yes, I know I mention my father several times, but I have honestly never met anyone who has so many comments on so many things. . . . It's almost unbearable.

Which brings me to why I wrote this and to the real reason for doing anything. Love. I receive lots of it (most of it undeserved) from Pam, Sonu, Suman, Sushma, Veena, Ashwani, Rakesh, Ranjan, Samir, Sudesh, KK, and all my family here and in India. A special inductee into this hall of fame is Linda Meehan and she knows it. . . . Their love is a gift and may I never forget it.

Per Eric's instructions I need to wrap this up, but not without some very special thank-yous: Serena Reisyan for her love and support; Marco Walker and Dan David, who have literally housed me for the past few years; Christian Blechinger, who gave up his living room table and peace of mind for the sake of my novel; Susan Kroll Smith, who always treats me with a rare kindness; Susan Haack, who humored my paranoia by safeguarding the manuscript; Adele Morrissette and Pat Tipton, who employed me while I wrote the first draft.

One person I don't need to thank is Gary Stuart, who already knows how grateful I am.

As with all acknowledgments, it is inevitable that some people who should be mentioned are not. The reason has nothing to do with the relative size of their contribution but with the limitations of my brain. You may have slipped my mind, but not my heart.

Well, it's time now for me to go and for you to enter the world of *Merger*. Watch your back.

Sanjay Sanghoee

merger

prologue

The tortured man slipped in and out of consciousness. The stench of charred flesh was overpowering, but the two men standing over him hardly noticed. They were used to it. Besides, it would all be over soon. The victim had given them the information they needed, and now all that remained was to kill him and dispose of the body.

While his captors were preparing for the grim finale, the tortured man thought of his family. He could see them in his mind's eye, like a home movie running in slow motion. They were the best thing in his life, and they were beautiful. He apologized inwardly for leaving them. He hoped that God would forgive him too.

The last image in his brain was of his child, and if his tired face would have permitted it, he would have smiled. Then the bullet ripped through his head like a high-powered drill piercing balsa wood. The next two bullets expanded the damage. The point blank range caused his brains to splatter obscenely onto his shirt, but by then he was already dead.

The corpse was badly decomposed by the time it was found. Of course, the people who had left it there hadn't bargained on it being found at all, which is why it was wrapped carelessly in garbage bags and wedged in behind the wheel of a broken-down Oldsmobile in a junkyard. Neither of these factors were particularly conducive to the preservation of the body.

Since it was virtually impossible to recognize the rancid mass of decaying flesh and bones as a human being, let alone a specific individual, the caretaker of the yard had spent a few minutes surveying the mess with justifiable horror and confusion. He had been carrying out a routine checkup of the place when he had chanced upon his discovery, and whoever this was lying in his yard, there was no doubt in the young man's mind that it was a harbinger of trouble.

He debated whether to leave the body where it was and simply load the Oldsmobile into the industrial-strength compressor that was used to dispose of the junk that found its way into the yard. The compressor would erase the problem quite efficiently. Given the circumstances in which he had found the body, it was unlikely that someone would come looking for it. He didn't even want to speculate on who was responsible for the corpse.

Had the young man been as conservative or as experienced as his father, he would have followed this course of action.

However, in spite of his concerns, and despite his unglamorous profession, José Rodriguez was a romantic at heart. When he wasn't taking care of the yard that his father could no longer run, he wrote sonnets about nature. He hoped one day to be a famous poet, and write for a living. The junkyard business held no interest for the young Hispanic, and he would never have accepted his current responsibilities if not for the fact that his father was ailing, and needed his son's help to keep the business alive.

Had he asked his bed-ridden father for advice, the old man would have told him not to get involved. In almost thirty years of running the business, he had seen many strange things and learnt first-hand that junkyards were a preferred venue for the disposal of things never meant to be found. In the scheme of things, it was always best to look away. It wasn't as if anyone would complain.

But José didn't ask his father for advice, and was loath to dispose of the body in such a cavalier fashion.

He thought back. A few weeks ago, he had found a hole in the chain-link fence surrounding the yard, where someone had clipped through the metal wiring and created a circular opening about two feet wide. José had initially thought that it was the work of hooligans looking for the television sets and stereos that occasionally found their way into the yard and could sometimes be repaired and sold illegally for a minor profit, but he now guessed that it was done to transfer the body through the fence.

After calling the police, he waited by the Oldsmobile, clipping his nose to keep out the stench of the corpse, but unable to walk away from the revolting spectacle inside the car. Some part of him was fascinated at the sight of the carnage, and he felt ashamed of his voyeuristic tendencies. The same romanticism which enabled him to write such beautiful poetry in his spare time was now expressing itself as a macabre curiosity about death and violence.

Rotted though the corpse was, he suspected that the victim was a man. He wondered who he was. *Did the dead man have a family? Had he been murdered, and if so, how and by whom? Was he tortured before he was killed? Why was he killed? Would the cops be able to find the killer? What were the man's last thoughts when he was dying?*

These were the thoughts of José Rodriguez as he waited for the police to arrive.

The police detective who had been assigned the case had just received the name of the dead man.

They had had a hell of a time finding it, since the body had been badly decomposed and the victim's face had been bludgeoned to a pulp by the killers. Luckily, the assailants hadn't been too good and had left traces of the dental work intact, which had been used to make the identification.

There was no doubt that it was a homicide. An autopsy had revealed that the victim had been shot thrice in the head with a large caliber handgun. Moreover, the man whose name the detective now held in front of him had been punished. The method of the torture was particularly gruesome.

Sighing, the detective dialed a number of his desk phone, and within a few minutes had the information he wanted. Putting on his jacket, he walked out of the station.

Most of his job was crappy, but this was the worst part. He had to go tell the widow of the dead man that her husband had been brutally murdered and dumped in a junkyard. To add to it, there was a teenage daughter, and the detective wished fervently that she wouldn't be home when he delivered the bad news.

Later that day, the police would search the apartment of the dead man for clues.

. . . .

That same evening, the name and photograph of the murdered man were released to the news outlets, in time for the nightly news and the next day's papers.

Unbeknownst to José Rodriguez or the police detective, the discovery of the homicide had set in motion the final act of a saga of greed, corruption, and mayhem that began almost three months earlier, under the guise of a corporate merger.

part 1
the setup

one

TriNet Communications was a monster. With holdings in cable, entertainment, technology, fiber optic networks, and long-distance telephone services, the fifteen-year-old company had become a juggernaut in the world of media and telecommunications. Wall Street liked monsters.

The conglomerate had started as a technology provider for cable companies. As the cable operators upgraded their systems through the '90s and prepared for the convergence of voice, data, and video over their pipes, TriNet's share price rocketed to reflect the growth potential of its business. Taking advantage of Wall Street's bullishness, the company had used its strong equity and the surplus cash on its books as currency to make a series of rapid-fire acquisitions, putting it in the uppermost echelons of media players in the United States.

Vikram Suri was the CEO of TriNet. Like the company that he helmed, Vikram, or Vik as his friends and the press called him, was the epitome of success. Tall and thin, with pleasant features and an intense gaze, he cut an ambiguous figure—elegant, magnetic, and calm; yet aggressive, unpredictable, and dangerous. Educated at Oxford and Harvard, Vik was an exception both within the world of CEOs, which was dominated by silver-haired white men, and within his own community. Few Indian men had attained public-figure status in the Western world, and fewer still were regarded as glamorous.

All the same behind the self-effacing charm and chic media image, Vik was as ambitious and ruthless as any of his old-world counterparts. He had a large appetite for risk, and an even larger one for acquisition. Having taken over the leadership of TriNet six years earlier, he had initiated the firm's aggressive merger spree.

Right now, Vik was seated at his desk, reading a report that he had received earlier in the day. The document consisted of thirty foolscap pages, with an unmarked black cover and simple spiral binding. There was no name or other information to identify either the author or the intended recipient of the report.

Though unassuming in its appearance, the document was a loaded gun.

After about an hour, he was frowning heavily. Making some notations on a pad lying on his desk, he tagged a page with a neon-colored sticker and shut the folder. He stared at his notes, picked up the phone, then changed his mind. Putting down the receiver, he tore up the paper with his writing, and tossed it into the trash.

Reaching into a humidor on his desk, he pulled out a Cohiba. Warming it slowly near the flame, but never touching it, he slowly puffed on the Cuban to light it. A bright orange flame erupted at the end of the cigar and an aroma of luxurious decadence quickly filled the room. Most corporate chieftains considered fine cigars to be one of the essential accessories of success, and Vik was no exception.

Staring vacantly out of his office window atop a skyscraper in downtown Manhattan, Vik let his mind wander. This was the way he did his best thinking. The report was more than he had expected, a lot more. Even as he felt the excitement building up inside him, his logical mind meditated carefully and unemotionally on the facts that he had just learned. He deconstructed the document methodically, and reorganized the intelligence into a clear but detailed map in his head. With this mental picture, he set about examining the possible courses of action that could be taken.

A few minutes later, he stuffed the report into a leather attaché case and left the office.

Downstairs, a black limousine waited expectantly in front of the building. A uniformed chauffeur snapped to attention as Vik stepped through the revolving doors, and rushed to open the car door for him. The CEO nodded his thanks and got in. As the limousine snaked its way through Manhattan traffic to its destination, Vik continued to think.

By the time he arrived at his apartment building, he knew what he was going to do.

At the same time that Vikram Suri was deciding what to do with the confidential report on his desk, a nineteen-year-old computer genius at UCLA was making a huge mistake.

Corey Meeks, affectionately known to his friends as "his meekness," was trying to disprove the moniker that had been the bane of his young existence. In short, he was showing off to his friends.

Holding court in the cafeteria, he was telling a congregation of geeks about his sexy new job. As the openmouthed four-eyed mutants stared at him in awe, Corey described in vivid detail how an anonymous corporation was paying him the big bucks to hack into computer systems and conduct electronic surveillance on their rivals. It was, as Corey expressed it, the corporate equivalent of a "black op"—with state-of-the-art computers and an unlimited expense account! Corey seemed justifiably proud of his latest gig and was clearly impressed with his own talent that had won him the position.

Ordinarily, this gathering of the meek and the ugly would have ended in a beer guzzling fest at a private apartment where all the guys would sit around talking about how they would "do" Pamela Anderson, and all the girls would be nonexistent. . . .

However, today Corey had work to do, and so after regaling his audience for a while, he took his leave. As he did, one of the members of his fan club, a street-smart eighteen-year-old named Adam, whose geeky exterior was really an act that he used to good advantage, went down the hall to a pay phone and dialed a number. He talked rapidly and then hung up, staring back in the direction of his friends. As the sounds of crude guffawing emanated from the assembly, Adam groaned. *What a bunch of losers! If only they weren't so useful at finals time. . . .*

When Corey arrived at his workplace, called "The Center," he received the surprise of his life.

A hand clapped firmly over his mouth and he was lifted physically off the ground by a powerful pair of arms. The two men then carried Corey to a computer table that had been cleared of all its equipment. Laying him on top of it, one of his assailants drew a knife; a large hunting knife of the kind that Corey had seen in countless slasher films. The man then proceeded to unzip Corey's pants. The nineteen-year-old hacker stared at him with a look of abject fear in his eyes, and groaned deeply. He tried to struggle but the man holding him down was too strong.

The first man then pulled down Corey's pants and placed the knife strategically near his private parts. The geek nearly fainted.

"I consider my profession an art, Corey," said the assailant, moving his knife around Corey's groin in a menacing circle. "And like any artist, I look for new and creative ways to practice my trade."

Corey could feel himself blacking out. His mind simply couldn't handle the reality of his situation. His captors, however, weren't here to cut up an unconscious man, and someone cracked a vial of smelling salts near his nose. Despite his ardent desire to faint, Corey had no choice but to stay in the moment. He groaned again.

The man with the knife now placed its tip suggestively on a *very* sensitive spot.

"All right, Mr. Meeks. Let's cut to the chase. We're here because you were talking a bit too loudly this afternoon, specifically about your 'new job.' Now what did I tell you the first time we met, eh? Let me remind you."

The man moved his knife back up to Corey's groin and made a tiny incision. Corey went insane, bucking violently and almost driving himself full tilt into the waiting knife. The man pulled away the knife hurriedly.

"Settle down, you idiot!" he said gruffly. "We're not here to kill you, but if you move, you'll kill yourself. . . . Game time's over. First rule of The Center, *it doesn't exist,* you got that?"

Corey nodded dumbly, not even hearing the words at this point. His mind was in a whole different place now, and it was all he could do to keep from tumbling over the edge into full-blown insanity.

"Keep your mouth shut, show up on time, and do your job," continued the assailant. "We're paying you well and expect you to follow our rules unquestioningly. You break the code and next time we rape your nerd ass, kapeesh?"

This time Corey didn't even respond. He was too far gone to worry about rape at this point. Compared to his present torture, it might almost have been pleasant.

The man with the knife now brought it back down to Corey's body. The tip of the metal felt icy cold, and the geek flinched in spite of his fear. The assailant just shook his head in disbelief.

"I tell you, and you still won't listen. *Don't move!* For a smart kid you're pretty stupid, you know that, Corey? Lucky for you, we're going to give you a souvenir that will remind you of our little chat. . . ."

At this, Corey started to strain against the man holding him down, trying to shout, bite, and generally break his captor's grip.

"Cut him already, Chad! This kid's a lot stronger than he looks," yelled the man struggling with the frantic nineteen-year-old.

With a deft stroke of his blade, the man with the knife did just that. As blood spurted everywhere, Corey bit insanely into his captor's hand, drawing blood. The man cursed and pulled his hand off. Corey started to scream, wailing like a newborn baby.

"Dammit! Shut him up, will you?" said the man with the knife, dumping the extracted testicle into a garbage can and cleaning his hands with a cloth. "He'll wake up the neighbors a mile away with that whining."

At that, a brutal hand swept across Corey's face, and this time he did black out.

The doctor who stitched up Corey's remaining testicle chided the assailants.

"How many times have I told you guys not to cut too deep? One of these days you're going to kill someone who *shouldn't* be dead, and then you'll get it in the neck from the boss. . . . And don't expect me to save your sorry asses, either."

Chad Rollins, the one who had performed the partial castration, just shrugged. "It's not a science, Doc. Things happen. Will the kid be all right?"

"Of course. Lots of people survive on one testicle. He can go home in a couple of hours."

"Great, we need him back at work soon. This time we *know* he'll keep his mouth shut."

As the men left the doctor's office, Chad pulled out a disposable cell phone. His partner looked at him inquisitively.

"Gotta update the boss," explained Chad. "Goddamn Indians always want updates. . . ."

───────── two

Tom Carter always hated these nights out with "the boys." Of course, the boys were no longer just boys, and included the women in his firm as well, but the whole thing was pretty stupid. A bunch of socially inept investment bankers would go out drinking and dancing (badly) all night, and finally try to hook up with each other. It was almost a rite of passage for young female analysts, fresh out of college, to sleep with associates, and in some cases vice presidents and managing directors as well. It was a terrible idea, but people never seemed to learn.

The night club was loud and raucous when Tom walked in, and right away he knew that he wanted to leave. He almost turned around when he was stopped by a hand on his shoulder. It was Robert Darlington III, the senior partner at Morgenthal Winter (MW)—Tom's boss.

Robert was an old-world banker, who despite having inherited a fortune from his British-born parents had worked hard to establish his own name in the business. He was one of those rare scions who had surpassed even his own pedigree. At MW, he was regarded as shrewd but fair. Sixty-five years old, he was a mild-mannered man who rarely participated in these events. Tom was surprised to see him here.

"I thought you hated these things."

Robert smiled. "I do, but you have to go out with the troops once in a while or they think you're unapproachable. I certainly don't understand any of this," he said, indicating the night club environment, "but I figured a few minutes with the crew would be encouraging for them. I want to bridge the gap between the old guard and the young Turks."

"I know how you feel," said Tom, feeling much older than he was.

"How are things going at the office?" asked Robert, even though he knew exactly how they were going.

"I'm just wrapping up the Phoenix Mobile memo and we should be ready for committee in a couple of days," replied Tom.

"Good to hear that. Steve's been raving about your work and the partners think highly of you. You're on a fast track, son," said Robert, clapping Tom's shoulder for the second time. It was his trademark gesture.

Tom beamed. In any profession, being told that you were on a fast track was ear candy, but hearing it from the senior partner was a real treat.

Robert looked down at his watch and winced. "I've been here too long. My daughter Elaine will be furious. I'd promised to spend some time with her tonight, discussing her latest boyfriend. . . ."

He rolled his eyes, as if to say "I hate all her boyfriends . . ." Tom laughed.

After his boss's departure, Tom hung out with the rest of the crew, which included eight analysts, five associates, and three vice presidents. All of them were drunk out of their minds even before he arrived. The evening was pleasant, if pointless, but finally Tom decided to call it a night.

As he was about to get up, he felt a hand stroke him beneath the table. He turned slowly in the direction of the touch, and saw one of the female analysts, Melissa, staring at him with the strangest eyes he had ever seen on a woman, drunk or sober. Tom, who only had a couple of beers in his system, was alert enough to recognize the signs and gently tried to extricate the girl's hand from his leg.

Melissa, however, was well past the point of backing away from anything that night and moved her hand up to Tom's crotch. As the investment banker froze, the young analyst started rubbing him through his pants, hard. Realizing this was getting out of control, Tom rose abruptly and announced that he was leaving. He dared not look down, hoping that his embarrassment wasn't showing through his pants.

Before he could make it out of the club, however, he was slammed to the wall by a tiny but ferocious Melissa, who had decided she wanted a piece of the handsome vice president. They were in a dark corner now and she started rubbing him again and breathing hard. She reached down and unzipped his fly.

By now Tom had recovered some of his balance, and grasped Melissa firmly by her arms. He pushed her away and looked her straight in the eye.

"You're tired and very drunk, Melissa. Go home and get some sleep. I'll forget this ever happened, all right? Just go home," he said kindly but firmly.

Melissa looked at him in confusion. She was young and very attractive and had never been rejected by a man before, least of all an older man. *What was this guy thinking, giving up an encounter with a hot twenty-two-year-old?!*

Rocking a little on her feet, she looked at Tom suspiciously and then finally responded. "Are you gay?"

Tom almost laughed. He stared at the cute little blonde for a few seconds, then just shook his head.

"No, I'm not. And you're a very attractive young woman. But you're also an analyst who works for me. This is wrong, and tomorrow morning you'll thank me for it. Now just say goodbye to everyone and then *go home. . . .*"

Tom left the nonplussed Melissa standing there and walked out of the night club, shaking his head. He had no doubts that Melissa would go home with one of the associates that night, but at least *he* hadn't taken advantage of the young girl. It was sad, he reflected, that someone so smart and so beautiful allowed herself to get caught up in the twisted games of her male colleagues. But he also understood that these kids worked really hard and had no time for a social life.

Everyone had to get laid once in a while.

As Tom was looking for a cab, he realized that he was very turned on. Melissa's advances had aroused him much more than he had realized, and now he *did* need some action. . . . For a second, he looked back at the club and thought of the perky young blonde just waiting for him to take her. Tom blushed. He felt ashamed. He shook the thought from his head and turned back to the street.

He supposed he could go to some bar and try to pick up a woman, but at this point, he wasn't in the mood to work for it. It would take too long and he wasn't sure if he could last out the courting ritual.

With a sinking feeling, Tom realized that tonight, like so many other nights, would be spent practicing the maxim of "love thyself."

As he got ready for bed, Tom stared at his reflection in the bathroom mirror.

He was six feet tall, with wide shoulders and a strong build. Some female advice and months of self-training had taught him to square those shoulders back and lift up his chest to take full advantage of his frame. Even though he didn't possess the picture-perfect looks of a fashion model, his face was nonetheless handsome. A firm jaw line, a blunt but well-proportioned nose, warm eyes, and lustrous brown hair gave him a distinctive look, one that was equal parts masculine and urbane.

He looked like Hollywood's version of a banker—too edgy to be a banker but too corporate to be anything else.

Part of that was genetics, the rest was circumstance.

His father, Harry Carter, had been a junior investment banker with a premier firm in New York City when he married Claire Tipton, an attractive young brunette who was studying economics at a small college in Connecticut. Three years later, they had their first child, a girl.

When the baby reached the age of five, Claire had decided to go back to work, landing a job in the lending department of a large commercial bank. She was smart and seemed to understand finance instinctively, and was soon promoted to a managerial position overseeing the bank's flagship location near Grand Central Station.

Tom's father, too, had climbed rapidly up the corporate ladder and had attained the office of managing director at the then-enviable age of thirty-nine. The Carters were making good money and had eventually moved to an expensive apartment on Park Avenue, where Tom was born.

From an early age, Tom had shown a natural aptitude for mathematics and the sciences, often scoring the highest marks in his class, and participating successfully in national competitions. He had received the best private education in Manhattan that money could buy and was on a fast track for the Ivy League. But unknown to his doting parents, Tom's secret interest wasn't academics. It was sports.

In addition to being tall and muscular, he was also extremely agile and had excellent hand-eye coordination. During his first year at Harvard University, he had caught the eye of the football coach, who enticed him into playing for the school as a quarterback. Soon Tom was pouring all his energy into football and spending less time on his studies.

The result was academic probation.

Harry and Claire, who had grown increasingly conservative over the years, were horrified and had pleaded with their son to give up his athletic ambitions and focus instead on school. Being stubborn, Tom had told them what they wanted to hear but in reality had continued on his personal path, finding himself even more alienated from intellectual pursuits than before, and immersing himself in what he considered the *art* of football. Had Tom stayed on that track, he would have wound up as either a national football hero, or an embittered cipher with head concussions and no college degree. He didn't get the chance to find out which.

During a particularly rough game later that year, Tom sustained a painful knee injury, which left him with a limp for the next two years of his life, and ended all hopes of becoming a professional football player. Secretly, his parents had heaved a sigh of relief, and encouraged their distraught son to refocus his energies toward that which he had neglected for so long—his academics. Having nothing else to do and no other outlet for his considerable frustration, Tom had complied.

As a testament to his intelligence and determination, he had rapidly pulled himself out of academic probation and taken summer classes to make up for the course material that he had ignored and the credits that he needed to graduate. His faculty advisor and professors were duly impressed and had gone out of their way to provide him with support and praise for his efforts. Two years later, Tom Carter graduated Harvard with high marks and a degree in economics.

Following in his father's footsteps, he had applied for and entered the financial analyst program at Kidder, Peabody & Co. The world of investment banking seemed heady and glamorous for a kid straight out of college, and Tom had quickly embraced the attitude and lifestyle of the white-shoe firm. Within a year, he was spending far more than he was making and soon found himself turning to his parents for help.

Harry was a pragmatic man and understood only too well the ease with which an impressionable young man could fall into the debt trap, especially with the temptations of Manhattan; and was willing to settle his son's debts if he promised to be more circumspect in the future. Claire, however, was a commercial banker, and looked at money the old fashioned way: what went out couldn't be more than what came in. In spite of her love for her son, and probably because of it, she decided that it was time for him to learn a valuable lesson in life and blocked her husband from bailing him out.

Tom had gotten his first taste of reality, and he wasn't amused. Having been born into a silver-spoon life, he had assumed that there was a natural abundance of wealth in the world, and had never envisaged a lack of it. As the harsh light of day hit him, he began to work harder and more conscientiously at his job, for the first time aware of the actual demands of investment banking rather than just the accompanying lifestyle. It was an experience that would shape the rest of his life.

Tom still regretted not being able to pursue a sports career, but the world of investment banking had offered enough challenges to make it worthwhile. The intricacies of deal-making, the byzantine nature of the negotiation process, the strategic maneuverings of corporate giants, the arcane language of analytics; all held appeal for the overactive mind of Tom Carter. Had this not been the case, he would have found it difficult to channel his nervous energy and to build himself a new dream—one that he felt was worthy of his ambitions.

From high-profile initial public offerings (IPOs) of companies that would one day become household names, to mega-mergers that created some of the largest and most powerful corporations in America, Tom got to witness, and in some cases participate in, some of the deals of the century. With each transaction and learning experience came a sense of satisfaction and power for the young man. In some ways he was still playing football, just on a different playing field.

Following the analyst stint at Kidder, he had returned to school to enhance his knowledge of finance and learn the disciplines that dovetailed with investment banking. While earning his MBA at Wharton, Tom applied himself to subjects ranging from capital markets and venture capital to business strategy and marketing. In order to be a good banker, it wasn't enough to be knowledgeable about money and valuation; it was equally important to understand the business processes that drove those valuations and generated that money.

Business school had molded Tom as much into a businessman as an investment banker, and two years later, he was ready to hit the ground running. His first offer had been from Shearson Lehman Brothers, a firm known for its survivor mentality and a penchant for aggressive deal-making. It was the ideal place for the smart young graduate, who took advantage of his environment by taking on responsibilities far above his station, and quickly. In no time, Tom was sitting at negotiating tables and contributing his input discreetly to his bosses. His talent and drive didn't go unnoticed, and he had been promoted rapidly to the position of vice president.

As is common in the world of finance, less than a year had gone by in his new title before he was recruited by a headhunter for a similar position at Morgenthal Winters. In spite of his competitive nature, Tom had never entertained the notion of being accepted into the tiny but powerful firm that a columnist in *Forbes* had once dubbed "a haven of some of the sharpest minds on Wall Street." To the young banker, and even his father, it was like winning an Oscar.

The group that had proposed hiring him specialized in mergers and acquisitions in the red-hot media and telecommunications sectors. It seemed like the best of all worlds. Grateful and eager, Tom had taken the opportunity as a trust, and worked hard to establish his professional reputation.

Even though he lacked the cutthroat mentality that made people into rising stars in the business world, he made up for it in ability: he was well-organized and meticulous; had a good head for financial analysis; boasted both depth and breadth in his knowledge of the markets; and had strong execution skills. During this time, he had also cultivated a large Rolodex of contacts in the media space—something that would be essential for his climb up the corporate ladder.

There was no doubting the discipline and ambition of the newly minted vice president, and in the eyes of his superiors, it was evident that he would go places. The only question was, *how fast?*

Harry had often told his son that it wasn't the speed with which he rose through the ranks that would matter the most in his career, but the strength of his reputation and contacts when he reached that station. Tom didn't fully agree.

While he was committed to being excellent at his job and loyal to his clients and the firm, he had a burning desire to make his mark in the world, and having been thwarted once in his ambitions, he wasn't about to be slowed down a second time in his life. Since his first day at MW, he had made it clear by his relentless work ethic and consistent initiative that he was there to be noticed. After three years in the trenches, he hadn't failed in that endeavor.

No one guessed the secret insecurity that drove him or the football injury that had raised the stakes for him both personally and professionally.

But then, no one really cared. As long as Tom Carter continued to use his skills effectively and profitably for the firm, he would make managing director. That was where the real gravy lay—the gold mine of the banking world. And if Robert Darlington's words meant anything, it would happen sooner rather than later.

Now all he had to do was not screw up.

─────────── three

Steve Brandt swiveled around in his chair and looked up from *The Wall Street Journal* as Tom walked into his office. A cup of coffee and croissant lay untouched on the wide desk in front of him, accompanied by neat piles of paperwork, stationery items and a flat-screen computer. Seated comfortably in the climate-controlled office in an expensive pin-striped suit, he conveyed the image of the quintessential investment banker.

"Morning, Tom. How are you?"

"Good. Your coffee's getting cold," replied Tom, pointing to the cup.

"Never touch the stuff, but the aroma wakes me up," grinned Steve.

Tom sat down and pulled out a file.

"I have the fairness opinion memo on Phoenix Mobile. Do you want to review it now or later?" he asked. Phoenix Mobile was a Florida-based wireless service provider that MW had been retained to sell.

Steve put down the newspaper. "Let's do it now. I may have some changes."

Tom nodded. "I thought you might, so I asked Lee to come down."

Lee Kang, a Chinese-American whose parents had migrated to the United States nearly two decades earlier, was an associate at MW. In the chain of command, he worked under Steve Brandt and Tom Carter. As if on cue, he stepped into the office, dressed sharply in a powder-blue shirt with French cuffs, silver links in the shape of knots, and a Hermes tie—a signature accoutrement for most investment bankers and high-level corporate executives.

As always, Tom surveyed him with a mixture of mild amusement and outright irritation. Although a business school graduate and former associate himself, he still found Lee's air of self-importance annoying. It was as if an MBA had deep fried his brains and left him with a crust of unwarranted superiority. What made it even more disturbing was that Lee was not alone. Every damn associate coming from the Ivy League now had the same attitude. *A first-semester course in getting-your-ass-kicked would do them some good,* thought Tom.

After nodding curtly to his bosses, which in his mind was the way that powerful people said hello to each other, Lee settled himself next to the vice president, smirking for no reason. Tom glared at him.

"Did you bring a pad?" he asked, staring at Lee's empty hands.

The smartass look left the associate's face immediately. "N–no," he stammered. He got up to fetch it. Tom stopped him.

"I've got an extra one. Try to pay attention, all right?" he said, not at all pleased by Lee's gaffe. A stupid oversight like this made the vice president look bad in front of *his* boss. Steve kept discreetly silent, but Tom could tell he was angry. They were paying these morons six-figure salaries to walk into meetings without a writing pad!

As Lee took the proffered pad awkwardly and tried not to look up, Tom leaned forward and handed Steve a copy of the memo. The managing director read through the document carefully, stopping to make notations with a red pen. He addressed Lee, "Did you update the comparables for yesterday's stock prices?"

Lee nodded, happy that he hadn't forgotten that, at least.

Comparables, in term-of-art parlance, were the trading multiples of public companies used to determine the valuation of the target company. Based on those, and other benchmarks, investment banks determined if the price tag for a company was "fair." The fairness opinion memo was an internal document prepared for presentation to the bank's fairness opinion committee, which would debate the details of the transaction and then decide whether the bank's analysis was correct.

Three quarters of an hour later, Steve handed back the memo with red marks all over it, and Tom and Lee walked out of his office.

. . . .

Back in his own office, Tom gazed at the picturesque view of Central Park before him. The offices of Morgenthal Winters ran between the thirty-third and fortieth floors of a Sixth Avenue office building in Midtown Manhattan. It was a posh location, and the offices reflected both the stature and financial success of the firm.

MW was a white-shoe investment bank. While the firm employed only 350 professionals, some of whom were involved in trading and sell-side research, it competed fiercely in the mergers and acquisitions advisory space with the bulge bracket firms, most of which employed more than ten times that number of people.

The firm's reputation as a leading player had been established in the '80s through a series of high-profile deals that were executed by small teams of brilliant bankers. The place was still lean and mean, and the people employed within its doors were among the best in their profession.

The corporate culture was one of respectful indifference. Everyone knew what they were doing, seldom exchanged advice with their peers, and didn't give a damn about anyone personally. It was simply a well-oiled deal machine.

Another rule at MW was that you did what you were told, without argument and without delay. If a managing director told you to come in at three in the morning and leave six days later without sleeping in the middle, you either did it or could find yourself another job. It was the only way for a boutique firm to maintain its lead in a cutthroat market.

Indeed, MW was often ranked in the top three by Securities Data Corporation in its annual "league tables" of mergers and acquisitions advisors—the Winston Cup of investment banking.

The day was sunny and bright, and the Great Lawn in Central Park would soon be filled with people enjoying the mild spring day. Traffic was lined up on Central Park East all the way up to the zoo, where a police car and an ambulance had blocked the right lane.

Tom turned away from the window and returned to his work. There was a pile of research reports on his desk and a copy of the financial model for Phoenix Mobile. He pushed away the research reports and began poring over the model. He had gone through it before, but wanted to make *sure* that it was correct. MW, like all other banks, put accountability front and center in their corporate culture, and even minor mistakes could damage a banker's career.

As soon as Lee had processed the changes to the fairness opinion memo, they could distribute it to the committee members. A first-year analyst would be sent for this job, running from office to office to make sure that each person received it prior to the meeting.

The committee found the valuation to be fair.

Now Steve's team would have to finalize a presentation to the board of directors of the client company, most of which would simply come from the fairness opinion memo. This was a cookie-cutter process and Steve wasn't overly concerned.

Steve Brandt was a managing director at MW. Like most of his peers at the firm, he was a career investment banker. He had worked at some of the top Wall Street banks in the media sector prior to being hired by MW to head their media practice. In addition to his knowledge of the long distance telephony, cable, and Internet service provider arenas, Steve had brought an extensive Rolodex of high-level contacts to the table. The managing partners of MW had realized that Steve could be a revenue generator.

Owing to his reputation as a rainmaker, Steve's compensation had risen rapidly. Being one of the few major private investment banks, MW didn't disclose its income to the public and discouraged internal discussions regarding individual pay; but within its closed doors, it was rumored that Steve had an annual income in seven figures.

With the status and money came influence in New York high society, political connections, and media exposure. Steve was often quoted in the major financial publications and was occasionally invited to comment on the market or specific deals by CNN.

Steve's phone rang. He picked it up.

It was his secretary. "Mr. Vikram Suri on the line for you."

Steve was silent for a second. Then he said: "Put him through."

four

There was a knock on Tom's door. Julie, Steve's secretary, poked her head in. "Steve wants to see you—right away."

Tom wasn't surprised. Managing directors always wanted to see you "right away." It was all part of the karma of Wall Street.

Steve was on the phone with his back to the door when Tom entered his office. Turning slightly, he waved the vice president to a chair. A minute later, he put down the receiver and turned with a broad smile on his face.

"I hope you got plenty of rest last night, Carter. We got a live one in the hopper!"

"I figured as much. What is it?"

"TriNet Communications wants to make a bid for Luxor Satellite."

Tom's eyes lit up. "How much do you suppose Luxor is worth?"

"Based on unofficial numbers, approximately eighteen billion."

Tom whistled. This could be the biggest deal that MW had ever managed. He did some quick math. The standard investment banking fee for something like this was 0.3 percent—that meant a merger fee of more than $50 million.

"How tight is this going to be?" asked Tom.

"Very. They want to make the bid by the end of next week, which gives us about ten days to do our due diligence, prepare the valuation, and deliver a fairness opinion."

Tom frowned. "Why so quickly? Is Luxor in play?"

"Not yet, but I bet Vikram Suri has good reason to expect it will be. He spoke with Craig Michaels, the CEO of Luxor, and he's eager to make the deal. Suri probably wants to nail this thing before Michaels changes his mind."

Tom knew that "sweetheart" deals like this were fairly common, particularly in transactions of this size. Rarely did companies merge with other firms solely on the basis of price. Strategic concerns, even the personalities of the CEOs, were major deciding factors in the success of a deal.

Steve pulled out his Palm organizer and tapped on the screen with the stylus. "I have a meeting out of the office at four, but I should be back by six-thirty. Get the troops ready for a strategy meeting at seven P.M."

Tom nodded. The "troops" meant Lee Kang and a financial analyst, who would be working for Lee. The analyst would be chosen from a pool of eight who rotated among different deal teams.

It was 3:00 P.M., Day 1.

five

Having filled his team in on the priorities, Steve turned to the last but most important topic on the agenda.

"What names should we use for the deal?" he asked, looking pointedly at the analyst.

Chris Back, whose foreseeable life had just crumbled in front of his eyes upon hearing the to-do list, tried courageously to smile. It was a strained, pathetic expression, but one that everyone in the room knew well, mostly through personal experience. As an analyst, Chris was the lowest banker on the team, and hence was there only to process and be generally abused. He hadn't slept in about nine months and had just lost his first few hairs from the stress of tight deadlines and demanding bosses.

Picking code names for a transaction was one of the few enjoyable parts of his job. Most merger assignments in investment banking were referred to by code names to minimize the chances of inadvertent leaks, especially by administrative staff.

The code names would be used only for external presentations and memos. Internal briefings almost never involved them. Even so, it was the one assignment where the analysts were actually encouraged to use their brains.

"How about Project Lens?" suggested Chris. Project names at MW were based on the first letter of the name of the target company, in this case Luxor.

Tom shook his head. "Too obvious."

Chris was about to suggest "Project Liquor" but reconsidered.

"How about Project Line with TriNet named as Triangle?"

Steve chuckled. "Suri should like that. Luxor Satellite will definitely add an additional line to TriNet's business. All right, settled. We have a meeting with the Luxor management tomorrow morning. Tom, can you send me a draft of the due diligence questions later tonight?"

Tom nodded. He would need to bring himself up to speed on Luxor's assets over the next few hours and compile a list of information items that TriNet and MW would require to determine the purchase price.

"Who's representing Luxor?" asked Tom.

"Bradford." Steve smiled thinly.

Bradford Associates was one of MW's competitors in the mergers and acquisitions arena. Although the firm's performance was respectable, it lacked the blue-chip pedigree of Morgenthal Winters and hence was viewed as a second-rate citizen. It was an unavoidable snobbery.

Tom shrugged his shoulders. "I guess someone has to represent them."

On his way out of the office, Steve was accosted by Julie, who handed him a sheet with a list of names. He glanced at her inquiringly but then read the title: *List of Possibles for SB.*

The "possibles" in question were a series of eligible young women who were part of a luncheon club. Julie was in charge of setting up her boss on a date with one or more of them.

Steve scanned her face for signs of ridicule, but there were none. Her careful nonchalance was a study in discretion.

It was no secret to her or any of the other administrative staff that their bosses were lonely people, and led remarkably boring personal lives. The stresses of their job and the conservative nature of their profession usually made the bankers dull company for anyone, including themselves. It was true that some of the managing directors and vice presidents were married, but even this cadre of lucky individuals had little more to look forward to at the end of each day than the hollow shell of a Norman Rockwell painting, or as it was affectionately known amongst the analysts, a "Normal" Rockwell life.

Another huge part of the problem were the long work hours. Unlike many other professions, where people worked hard but not around the clock and not incessantly, investment banking demanded the complete and unrelenting commitment of its soldiers. As a result, even senior bankers often spent inordinate amounts of time at the office; checking and rechecking analyses, obsessing over changes to presentations and memos, and constantly trying to stay one step ahead of the competition through an endless barrage of ideas and pitches, day after grueling day.

It was no wonder that Steve Brandt needed his secretary to find him a date.

Each name on the list had a brief description of the woman with a series of likes and dislikes, and background. It seemed more like the credentials of the Playmates of the Year rather than the potential social calendar of an investment banker.

After crossing off a few names, Steve handed the page back to Julie. "Set them up."

Julie nodded without a word and took back the list. Some part of her wanted to smile knowingly, but she knew that doing so would be hurtful to her boss, who was after all a nice enough man, notwithstanding his inability to find a woman on his own.

Tom donned his jacket and shut off the lamp on his desk. He had spent the last few hours educating himself on Luxor Satellite. Most of the information had come from satellite industry reports.

Luxor, which had started as a small fixed satellite services (FSS) provider in the late '80s, had been acquired in the mid-'90s by a large diversified conglomerate. With a healthy balance sheet behind it, the company had proceeded to grow its FSS operations and expand into direct broadcast satellite (DBS)—satellite television.

Eventually the CEO of Luxor, Craig Michaels, had arranged a management buyout, or MBO, with the help of a major bank. The bank had loaned him the money to buy out the conglomerate, using the assets of Luxor as collateral. Currently, Craig owned the majority of Luxor, with the bank and other senior management making up the rest.

This was also probably why Vikram Suri wanted to buy the privately held company.

Purchasing Luxor would be relatively easy since there were only a few shareholders to negotiate with, and TriNet could probably obtain it at a reasonable price. By taking it public in a few years when the market improved, the gains could be substantial.

As Tom walked out of MW's Midtown offices and hailed a cab, his mind was sifting through the information that was now crammed into his briefcase.

DBS seemed to account for the bulk of Luxor's business, which was fortunate due to the low costs of maintaining existing satellites and the ability to add additional subscribers with little incremental cost. On average, it cost about $250–300 million to construct, launch, and insure a satellite. However, once the "birds" were up in space they could be used to serve a large consumer base for twelve to fifteen years without replacement. The introduction of new services such as high-speed Internet and interactive television could drive up profitability for the company.

The cab arrived at the apartment building. The doorman greeted Tom as he stepped into the lobby.

"Good evening, Mr. Carter. This arrived for you in the afternoon," said the doorman, lifting a basket of flowers from behind his desk.

Tom frowned. *Who could have sent him flowers?* He picked it up, thanked the doorman, and went upstairs. In his apartment, he pulled out the card from the bouquet and read it.

It was from his ex-girlfriend. She wanted to have dinner and "patch things up."

Tom sighed. Their breakup hadn't been an amicable one. Although intense in the beginning, the relationship had lost most of its steam in a few months. He had grown tired of her constant independent-woman posturing and the need to dictate every nuance of their personal lives.

It wasn't entirely her fault, Tom realized. Most women in New York were caught up in the confusion between the need to maintain control over their personal and professional lives and the inevitable loss of control necessary to maintain a stable relationship. Compromise was viewed as a weakness, yet no relationship could be sustained without some push and pull on both sides.

Tom had given her the benefit of the doubt for a while, but nothing had changed. In the end he had walked away, sympathetic but disappointed.

Despite his reticence, he went toward the phone. He didn't want to be rude, and what damage could a phone call do?

At the last second, his common sense kicked in. He put down the receiver.

Like Steve, he was a lonely man and neither the fancy apartment nor the hefty paychecks could possibly make up for his inadequate social life or his reliance on self-gratification. Still, he wasn't about to be sucked back into a bad relationship, no matter how tempting the fruit.

Putting it out of his mind, he focused again on Project Line. Based on his research, he had drafted a preliminary list of questions for the due diligence meeting in the morning, and sent it via email to Steve. He had also spent an hour with Lee and Chris reviewing the financial analysis that needed to be prepared. Now all he needed to do was get a good night's sleep.

Before going to bed, Tom put the flowers in a vase. He was, after all, a sensitive man.

────────────────── six

The white stretch limousine arrived at its destination shortly after 9:00 P.M. The tires crunched on the gravel as the car pulled up to the head of a semi-circular driveway.

A lone passenger alighted from the rear and stood still to survey his surroundings. Tall and broad-shouldered, he was a rugged looking man with thick-set eyebrows, deep brown eyes, and a considerable mustache, which he was now stroking thoughtfully. A rich mane of dark hair was combed back from the creased forehead, accentuating his craggy features. Overall, he had the look of a man not to be taken lightly.

This was true.

Craig Michaels was an imposing personality. A heavy smoker and drinker with a booming voice, a penchant for gambling, and general indifference towards everyone, he was Nick Nolte in a good suit.

Hailing from a wealthy West Coast family, Craig had spent the early part of his professional life working in Hollywood. By roping in some of his college buddies to invest in a fund for movies, he had set about producing a string of small independent films in the '60s and '70s. However, making movies was an expensive business, and since none of the movies had gotten noticed by critics or audiences, Craig was soon burning his personal fortune to pursue a passion that he didn't seem to have a skill for.

In the late '70s, on the advice of his father, he had finally dropped his production activities and entered into the cable business, working as a programming officer. In this capacity, he was responsible for negotiating deals with up-and-coming cable networks. As the cable industry grew rapidly in the '80s, so did Craig's fortune. His success at inking lucrative deals with the top networks in the country, coupled with his reputation for hardball deal-making, had propelled him to the position of COO. Even so, Craig's ambition was to run a company, not be part of someone else's team.

Having been on the content side of the business, he understood that the real money lay in distribution. The long-term potential of satellite services was apparent, and when Luxor Satellite had approached him to helm the firm through its growth, Craig had seen it as the perfect platform to make his mark.

His fierce negotiating skills and take-no-prisoners attitude had proved to be invaluable as he took the company through its paces. As a result, Luxor's profitability had improved dramatically under his leadership, and eventually Craig had convinced a bank to help him buy out the company.

Being aware of his talents and reputation, he was also commensurately egoistic, running his company like a personal fiefdom. No one questioned his authority at Luxor and almost all senior executives and even board members were his personal picks. Consequently, Craig had earned the nickname "Lord Michaels" or simply "The Lord," which was amusing enough unless you happened to work for his Lordship.

The party in the Hamptons had begun an hour earlier and guests were crowding in through the front door of the house, being greeted by a fully accoutred butler and a coat check girl. Outside, a team of valets was on the ready to park the guests' cars, or direct the chauffeurs to the parking spaces at the right of the house.

The "house" was actually a mansion, and was huge. Even with his less-than-modest standards, Craig Michaels was impressed by the sheer size of the building. Sitting in the middle of a large and immaculately landscaped garden, the house towered above the expansive property, four stories high and spanning a hundred yards on either side of the expansive porch. Powerful spotlights illuminated the castle-like structure.

Behind the princely mansion was a sandy beach that stretched out for a few miles on either side, and a long, curving boardwalk leading to the sea. From the front of the house, Craig caught a glimpse of the well-lighted walkway as it snaked around to the right before disappearing toward the moonlit water. People were standing on the boardwalk, chatting and laughing, with drinks in hand.

As he entered the mansion, he was equally awed by the opulence of the foyer. A floor made of pink marble, exquisite paintings in gilded wood frames, tapestried chairs, and gold candelabra adorned the high-ceilinged room. At the far end of the room was a large, sweeping stairway carpeted in crimson. *If this was just the foyer,* thought Craig amusedly, *then the stairway must lead to heaven.* On either side of the entrance were tall oak double doors that had been thrown open to allow the guests to walk through the house.

The uniformed servant led Craig to the right and then returned to his post at the front door. Craig was no stranger to luxury, but what he witnessed took his breath away. The room he had entered was the main ballroom, and although sparsely furnished to retain its purpose, its grandeur was irrefutable.

Every wall of the room was covered from floor to ceiling in the most exquisite tapestries he had ever seen. A gigantic crystal chandelier with gold trimmings hung high above the room, bathing the guests in a warm shower of golden light, and tantalizing anyone who happened to glance above with its brilliant sparkle. The polished wood floor might have been a sheet of ice, so fluid were the waltzing couples in the center of the ballroom.

An army of efficient but unobtrusive waiters flitted smoothly through the guests, offering drinks and hors d'oeuvres and whisking away empty glasses and napkins. Against the left wall was a set a small stage, where an orchestral band played a Viennese waltz. The acoustics of the room were such that one could hear the music clearly and yet converse in a normal tone of voice.

If Craig had been a literary man, he would have thought his milieu to be a scene from *War and Peace*. But despite his lack of cultural erudition, he had been around enough opulence to distinguish between the elegant and the garish.

There was nothing tawdry or nouveau riche about this setting—it was simply *regal*.

The Sun King himself was busy playing the perfect host, a role he enjoyed tremendously. Dashing and handsome in a dark dinner jacket, he walked around the large ballroom, smiling and shaking hands with his guests and occasionally stopping to exchange a word or two with a senator or a Fortune 100 CEO. His intense gaze, elegant features, disarming smile, and of course the unmistakable air of wealth, all contributed to his impact on the room.

Even if he had not been a public figure and generous party-thrower, Vikram Suri would have commanded any room he walked into. Like the bombshell aware of men's sexual desires and her resulting control over them, Vik knew well the power of his charisma and wielded it like a saber fashioned out of ego and sharpened by success.

He liked to think of himself as a modern-day Napoleon. The liberal American perspective on Napoleon failed to acknowledge his many accomplishments and usually painted him with the same brush it used for Hitler and Stalin, a comparison that caused Vik incessant heartburn. He waited eagerly for the day when America would decide to learn some history. Most people schooled in the European system, as were most Indians, had a markedly different vision of the emperor. Vik considered Napoleon a hero; one whose life had mirrored an epic novel and whose intense talent, magnetic aura and powerful destiny had carried him to heights mere mortals could only dream about.

Like his French idol, Vik viewed life mostly in terms of merit and rewards. That was, after all, the American dream.

Gliding smoothly through the crowded room, he spied Steve Brandt a few feet away, speaking with a congressman. He smiled broadly and walked over.

"Steve, glad you could make it! Congressman Reynolds, I see that you have had the chance to meet one of the finest bankers on Wall Street."

Congressman Reynolds, a wizened old man in his eighties, simply grunted a response. He was too busy drinking to care much about who he was meeting. Unfazed, Vik kept talking. "Good job on the gun control bill. It's about time we had some people with guts up there calling the shots."

Once again, Congressman Reynolds made a sound. He didn't like discussing political issues at parties, especially where there was free alcohol. He had had three heart surgeries in as many years, and God only knew how long he would survive. His primary concern right now was to ply his ailing body with as much liquor as it could sustain, and thus die a happy man.

Steve put on his best ass-kissing smile. It was a well-practiced expression. "You really are the king of parties, you know that, Vik? I think I saw Gene Hackman around somewhere!"

Vik chuckled. "Yes, he's an old friend. Hollywood loves the Hamptons, particularly on someone else's dime." Leaning forward confidentially, he added: "I wanted to be a movie star once."

In his own mind, of course, he was one.

"How are things going at headquarters?" asked Steve, referring to Project Line.

Congressman Reynolds had walked away in search of the bar, and Vik resumed in a more serious vein. In deference to the public nature of their conversation, Vik referred to Luxor by its investment banking code name.

"My team is working to vet the numbers we received from Line this morning. We'll get them to you by nine A.M. What about you?"

Steve tried to look casual. "Everything is on track. We should have the comps and deals done by tonight and can start on the financial model tomorrow. The CFO of Line will fax the debt covenants to my office later tonight."

Debt covenants were the conditions imposed by lenders on a borrower, such as restrictions on excessive future expenditures, to ensure that their loans were protected.

Vik nodded and dropped his voice to a stage whisper. "Good. We would like to get a fairness opinion in three days, and can start drafting the definitive agreements at the same time. We would like to get our board to approve the bid by early next week and then make the offer to Line by the end of the week. Think you can manage that?"

"I don't see why not," Steve replied confidently. It was easy to be confident when you had a team of grunts at your disposal. "For a 0.7 percent success fee, we could lasso the moon if you wanted."

Vik laughed unpleasantly. Steve felt a small twinge in his stomach. It was a condition spurred by too much ass-kissing. He looked awkwardly at his guest. Vik clapped Steve on the shoulder to put him at ease. "Relax. The fee is well-deserved. We like to keep our friends happy."

The word "friend" was dropped casually into the conversation, but it was enough to get the banker salivating. Vik smiled inwardly. He was a master of the carrot and the stick, and bankers made the best donkeys.

Having dispensed with business, Vik now switched gears. "Walk with me," he said, spotting someone across the room and moving in that direction. Steve followed, scanning the passing crowd for more movie stars.

A few feet away, he saw a distinguished man with iron-gray hair speaking to a group of young women, all attractive. He seemed familiar, but Steve couldn't quite place him.

The two men made their way to a corner of the room, past a small group of people sitting on a plush sofa, talking earnestly about something. If trust fund babies could be identified by looks, this group was wearing a neon sign proclaiming inheritance. They looked up for a second, waved to Vik, and went back to whatever they were talking about. The CEO of TriNet suddenly stopped walking. Steve looked at him quizzically.

"I want you to meet someone. She's an old friend of mine," explained Vik.

No sooner had he said that than Steve was startled by the presence of a woman standing next to him. He had no idea how she had gotten there without him noticing. Vik made a cordial introduction.

"Steve, this is Laura Briggs. Laura is a political consultant. And this is Steve Brandt, managing director at Morgenthal Winters."

Laura smiled brightly and extended her hand. Steve shook it and said hello. His eyes were riveted to the striking beauty in front of him.

Vik put his hand on Steve's shoulder. "If you'll both excuse me for a while, I need to tend to something. Glad you could make it, Steve."

Vikram Suri shut the door behind him.

Craig Michaels settled himself in a cushioned armchair in front of a wide desk. He took in the room with mild surprise. It was in direct contrast to the opulence outside. The oak desk and three walnut chairs were the only pieces of furniture in the room. Bookcases lined the walls and the only window was in an alcove behind the desk. It was a haven of privacy.

The carpeting was deep burgundy, and thick. Walking into the room, Craig had barely felt the floor beneath him. He smiled to himself. In spite of his own hubris, he had to admit his host was in a league of his own.

For most Americans, the common reference points for Indians were Gandhi or Manhattan cab drivers. Wall Street and Silicon Valley had changed that, but only slightly. Vikram Suri, however, had managed to skate around all those stereotypes and craft an image for himself that was both glamorous and enigmatic. What Craig didn't know was how difficult it had been and what it had done to the man in the process.

Seating himself behind his desk, Vik beamed confidently. In this house, in this room, and behind this desk, he was master of his domain more than ever. In an amusing piece of legerdemain, a leather cigar case appeared in his hand out of nowhere, and he pulled off the cover like a magician revealing a rabbit inside a hat. Withdrawing two cigars, Cohibas, he proffered one to Craig.

Like his counterpart from TriNet, Craig was an ardent aficionado of fine cigars and wouldn't touch anything but a Cuban. He accepted the cigar, then watched his host reach inside a drawer and pull out a jewel-encrusted egg-shaped object. With a flick of his thumb, Vik broke the top off the egg, which swiveled backwards on golden hinges. Craig frowned. *Could that be . . .*

Only half-answering the unspoken question, Vik activated the lighter inside the egg. A slim finger of fire shot up from the bottom half and the Indian leaned forward to light his guest's cigar with it.

"That's a mighty fine lighter," puffed Craig, still wondering if his original assessment was correct. He was almost too scared to ask.

Vik noticed his questioning stare and laughed. "You are wondering if this is a Fabergé egg," he said, lighting his own cigar and snapping shut the oval-shaped case. "As it happens, it is. A genuine twentieth-century ruby- and diamond-studded egg by the famous House of Fabergé. This particular piece is among the last ones he created for Czar Nicholas II before the revolution. Only about fifty of these glorious creations have survived."

"And it contained a lighter?" asked Craig, finding it hard to believe that Easter eggs, at any time in history, could be used for such a purpose—although with those damn Russians anything was possible.

Vik grinned perversely. "Of course not. I had the lighter installed after I bought it. You cannot imagine how difficult it was finding a jeweler willing to tamper with a Fabergé egg."

"I can, actually," said Craig dryly.

"Anyway. It is mine now and I choose it to be a lighter," stated Vik, obviously reveling in the fact that he could modify even a priceless masterpiece like a Fabergé egg to his own specifications. It mirrored the way he dealt with everything, including people.

To indicate a change of subject, Vik slapped the table lightly, then leaned back in his chair. "So, Lord Michaels, what did you think of the due diligence session today?"

While Craig hated being referred to as "Lord" by the press, he didn't mind it from his peers. Subordinates did not dare use the term in front of him.

"Productive," replied Craig, meaning he couldn't care less about mundane details like that. "I think we can pull together the information you need, provided of course your boys don't keep adding more questions to the list. The darn things seem to grow all the time!"

"Of course they do," responded Vik patiently. "Along with the investment bankers' fees. They have to earn their pay somehow, Craig."

One of the best kept secrets of investment banking was that in deals of this size, most bankers were simply brought in to serve as rubber stamps on the deal, more to enable the boards to exercise their fiduciary duty than to provide any real strategic or financial advice. As both men knew, most deals happened like this, in rooms like these; and the CEOs often knew the purchase price and terms well before their bankers did.

"Even so, I think things will go smoothly," offered Craig, puffing on his cigar with relish.

"I have no doubt," said Vik, with a self-assuredness that would have given a lesser man than Craig Michaels the chills.

"Vik, maybe this is a good time to discuss the number, so I can prep our boys for it. Wouldn't want the board rejecting your bid," laughed Craig.

Vik gave him an amused look, then went back to contemplating his cigar, which he was turning slowly between his slim fingers. "Your boys don't matter much, Craig, you and I both know that. You own the majority stake, which means you have everyone by the balls."

Leaning his cigar against an ashtray, Vik steepled his hands in front of him like the Godfather. "So what really matters is you."

"Well, I certainly intend to make this as painless for you as possible," confirmed Craig, spreading his hands magnanimously.

Vik stood up and walked over to a small bar to the right of the desk. Through the closed door, he could hear the faint sounds of the party. The band had switched from classical to jazz. He stared quizzically at Craig, who shook his head. Shrugging his shoulders, Vik poured himself a glass of cognac. Returning to the table, he sat down and dipped one end of the cigar into the glass.

He gave the spirit a few seconds to sink in and then took a long puff, watching the smoke curl up into the air. He looked back at the Luxor CEO.

"We're going to bid ten billion," he said softly.

Craig nearly dropped his cigar.

"Are you crazy? You know damn well the company is worth *at least* fifteen billion, and that's before a premium!" Craig retorted hotly.

In a reaction bordering on schizophrenia, Vikram Suri's expression changed. His face hardened and the superficial friendliness faded. Reaching into a drawer, he pulled out a document and threw it across at Craig Michaels. It struck him in the chest and fell to the floor.

Craig, a hot tempered man at the best of times, was about to jump over the table and lunge at his host, but then checked himself. Years of deal-making experience had taught him to keep his emotions under control. Pursing his lips, he picked up the document from the floor.

"What the hell is this?" he demanded.

"A report. Take a look," invited Vik, his eyes gleaming like a panther's in the dark.

For the next few minutes Craig read the report silently, flipping rapidly as he skimmed through the text. His face was inscrutable, a skill he had mastered during his days in Hollywood. But when he finally looked up, he had gone pale.

"What do you want, Suri?"

"As I said, we're going to bid ten billion."

Craig digested the statement quietly. He wasn't an easy man to intimidate, but the information in the report had floored him. The possible ramifications of the document becoming public were unthinkable, and he knew enough about powerful men to realize that Vik wouldn't simply allow him to walk away from the deal. Apparently Hollywood was no match for Wall Street.

With none of his earlier bravado on display, Craig demurred. "All right. I'll accept the bid and convince the board to go along with it."

Vik laughed. "That's exactly the problem."

Craig was dumbfounded. "So what *do* you want?"

Vikram Suri took another puff of his Cohiba, and grinned broadly.

"I want to make a deal."

Steve Brandt and Laura Briggs got along very well. Although she seemed a bit guarded about her experiences as a political consultant, he wasn't entirely surprised by that. Much like investment bankers, political consultants were often hesitant to discuss their clients or activities since most of their work was confidential, and any verbal slips could easily wind up in the hands of the press, where they would make good copy.

Laura was a woman of diverse interests and understood Steve's line of work much better than most non-banking people did. Part of being a political consultant, he supposed, involved keeping abreast of a variety of topics, including the financial markets.

From city councilmen to senators and even the President of the United States, the mantra for the past ten years had been "it's the economy, stupid." The most recent downturn in the market had only changed the color of the spotlight on Wall Street, but in no way diminished the public's or the politicians' interest in the arcane workings of the financial world.

Laura had known Vikram Suri for almost six years and thought very highly of him. Steve didn't discuss his professional relationship with their host, and she didn't ask.

For the rest of the party, they spent most of their time together, and at the end of the evening he offered to drive her home. It turned out that she was staying with a friend a few houses away and had walked to the party.

"I'm staying at the Enclave Inn in Bridgehampton. Would you like to join me for a drink at the hotel bar?" asked Steve, staring expectantly at the tall, graceful woman as he helped her with her overcoat.

She looked at him, hesitated for just a second, then said: "I would like that."

As they were walking out of the Suri mansion, Steve once again spotted the gray-haired man that he had seen earlier in the evening. This time he recognized him.

It was the chairman of the Securities and Exchange Commission, better known as the SEC.

seven

On a beautiful spring day, there's no place on earth like Midtown Manhattan. Clean and bright, the well-paved sidewalks, elegant luxury goods stores, exclusive hotels, plush office buildings, and expensive condominiums that line Fifth Avenue form a foundation of extravagance that remains nonpareil anywhere on the globe.

To the north of this polished haven of opulence lie Central Park and the residential palaces of the Upper East Side. To the east lies Madison Avenue, home to the advertising world and itself a shopper's paradise—for the discriminating buyer, of course. On the west, the commercial monoliths of Sixth Avenue, which house corporate giants like McGraw Hill, UBS, and General Electric, gradually give way to the theater district on Broadway and the unapologetic glitz of Times Square. To the south of Midtown lie the wonderfully bohemian locales of the Village and SoHo, the ethnically-oriented Chinatown and Little Italy, the not-so-radical world of Wall Street, and finally the prosaic and officious environs of City Hall and the courthouses.

In this way, Midtown Manhattan forms the crossroads to multiple worlds, all of which are contained within a few square miles of metropolis. It was through this neighborhood that Tom Carter now walked, heading to his office from the subway stop at Fifty-first Street and Lexington Avenue.

Even at this early hour, when native New Yorkers were rushing to work with strained looks on their faces or no expression at all, the area was crowded with tourists—walking shoulder to shoulder up and down Fifth Avenue, chatting and gesturing at the shops and buildings, stopping occasionally to take pictures and then moving on in their pilgrimage—completely oblivious to the stresses and concerns of the city. It was often jokingly remarked that you could always tell a New Yorker from a tourist—the tourist would be smiling.

The most crowded area, as usual, was Rockefeller Center, where people congregated in impossibly large groups around floral displays, car exhibits, NBC show tapings and other activities of interest at this time of year. As Tom attempted to circumvent a set of Swedish high-school girls who were rapidly piling out through the revolving doors of the NBC Studio, he bumped into an older group of tourists who were waiting to cross the street to Radio City Music Hall for a tour of the legendary theater. An old woman that he had nearly shoved into incoming traffic glared angrily at him. Muttering a hasty apology, he continued on his way.

Once he reached Sixth Avenue, the crowd thinned out a bit and he was able to breathe.

A few minutes later, Tom stepped through the revolving glass doors of the MW building and walked to the elevators. He was dressed fashionably in a charcoal gray three-button suit, a white shirt with French cuffs, a black silk tie, and polished black shoes with buckles. He cut an impressive figure, and was aware of numerous stares directed at him, mostly from women. He smiled, returning the looks from some of the more attractive females.

As he rode up in the elevator, he went through a mental checklist of the tasks that needed to be completed that day.

Luxor's management had delivered their operating financials to Tom early in the morning, and he had forwarded them to Chris to "clean up" so that they were easy to read.

That afternoon, Tom would vet Luxor's numbers to ensure that the margins, growth rates, and other drivers of the company's projections made sense. Target companies usually overstated their projected revenues and profit potential—in the hopes of obtaining a higher price in the transaction, and it was up to the investment bankers for the acquiror to make sure that the numbers used in the valuation were reasonable.

Later that night, probably around 4:00 A.M., the merger model would be completed and placed on Tom's desk. While the vice president would thankfully not be there to receive it, he would be in the office again by

7:00 A.M. to check the model. Lee and Chris would most likely go to sleep at their desks at around 4:30, and would be woken up by Tom at 7:15. Steve would be in by 10:00 A.M., at which time the managing director and the vice president would discuss the numbers in preparation for a conference call with TriNet later that day.

One way or another, Tom knew, the team at Morgenthal Winters had to finish the valuation by tomorrow night. They would have exactly half a day after that to prepare and deliver the fairness opinion, and then the weekend to finalize the board presentation. By next week, TriNet would make a bid for Luxor.

It was 8:45 A.M., Day 3.

While Tom Carter was walking to his office, Vikram Suri was jogging downtown on Third Avenue, twenty blocks away. It was part of his morning routine. He would usually leave his Murray Hill apartment at 8:00 A.M. and jog down towards Gramercy and then cross-town to Chelsea. The apartment, albeit a penthouse, was nothing more than a place to "crash" whenever Vik stayed in the city. It was near the Thirty-fourth Street helipad—and a short chopper ride to the Hamptons. As usual, he was wearing a plain hooded sweatshirt and sweatpants.

After the call with Steve Brandt three days ago, he had started mobilizing his forces at TriNet in order to prepare for the merger. The internal deal team at the company as well as outside consultants would be responsible for crafting and finalizing the details of the transaction. Vik's job would be to provide approval for all high-level decisions as well as handle personal negotiations with the CEO of Luxor—as he had done the night before.

Of course, the discussion last night with Craig Michaels was strictly "off the books" and would remain that way. Other than two other people who knew selective details of that conversation, no one but Vikram Suri was privy to the deal that he had cut with the rough-hewn Californian, and if things were managed correctly, no one ever would. Although the report that he had in his possession could destroy Craig's career and possibly land him in jail, Vik had scant interest in either outcome. He was more interested in his personal agenda from the merger, and *that* was the purpose that his blackmail tactics had served him last night.

Vik turned right on Twenty-third Street and began to head west. He was jogging rapidly, pausing occasionally to catch his breath, but for the most part running on with the stamina and speed of a professional athlete. Despite his relatively sedentary profession, the CEO of TriNet Communications was in excellent physical shape. His body was finely toned with not a stitch of fat anywhere on his person. If people could be aerodynamically designed, Vikram Suri would have been a stealth bomber.

As was his habit, he hardly noticed the people that he passed, intensely focused on his workout and, more importantly right now, on the merger. Even more than the conversation with Craig Michaels, his mind was preoccupied with a discussion that he had had a few days prior to his call to Steve Brandt. He had arranged the meeting through an intermediary in a private suite of the Waldorf Astoria after receiving the confidential report. The American, who was the other party to the meeting, had been given the room number by the intermediary and had come straight up to Vik's suite without informing the reception desk.

The meeting had been brief but risky. Knowing the consequences of failure, Vik had prepared meticulously for the discussion, covering all bases and lining up enough ammunition to ensure that the American, who was in a position of considerable authority, would bite. If he had refused to cooperate, Vik would have had to walk away from the Luxor deal, having tipped his hand—and there were other risks as well.

In the end, however, Vik's gamble had paid off and the American had agreed to become his "silent" partner. With him on board, Vik knew that the chances of success were exponentially higher and the price for his cooperation would be well worth it. Vik hoped fervently that there were no press people at the Waldorf that night. . . .

Since Vik was lost in his reverie, he didn't see a couple walking in the opposite direction, and collided head-on with a large man in his mid-thirties. Due to his momentum, both Vik and the man were propelled to the sidewalk in a jumble of arms and legs as they struggled to keep their balance. The woman issued an exclamation as the two men fell to the ground.

It was a few seconds before Vik regained his composure. He checked to see if he could stand up, and satisfied that he could, he looked over at his partner in the accident. The man, dressed in an expensive three-piece suit, also rose from the pavement and brushed himself off. He checked his jacket carefully for tears.

"Are you all right?" asked Vik good-naturedly.

The man continued checking his suit and didn't respond. The woman came up alongside him and touched his arm in earnest. "Honey, are you okay?"

The man nodded silently. He turned to glare at Vik. "Are you fucking blind?"

"I'm really sorry. I just didn't see you in front of me . . . ," explained Vik, sounding apologetic.

"What the hell do you need, a neon sign?" hollered the man. "You could have hurt me or my girlfriend, you idiot!" Passersby slowed down to watch the spectacle.

Vik remained calm. "I said I'm sorry. It was an accident," he said, stressing the word "accident" as if explaining it to a child.

"You almost ruined his suit!" responded the woman angrily.

Vik stared amusedly at the couple, who were white. *She was more concerned about the suit than the boyfriend! Must be WASPs,* he thought.

"Fine, I'll buy you a new suit," said Vik, meaning it. If you could buy your way out of dumb arguments like this, it was worth every penny.

"You know how much this suit costs? Probably more than your annual salary," the woman scoffed, completely sure of herself.

If you only knew, thought Vik. "All right, let's end this now. If you will accompany me back to my apartment, I will give you the cash for a new suit," he said politely.

"Why not give us the money now?" asked the man, challenging him.

"Because," Vik explained patiently, "I don't carry my wallet when I jog." He wanted to strangle these people!

The woman laughed unpleasantly. "Forget it. You look like some kind of—delivery guy." There, she had said it. Now she felt a lot better.

Vik stared in amazement. He had dealt with stereotyping before, but this was ludicrous. He responded sharply: "And just what about a person's appearance makes him *look* like a delivery guy?" His voice rose by several decibels when he said this, and almost immediately an audience gathered around them. It was the ultimate New York pastime.

The couple exchanged a confused look. Then recognition dawned on their tanned faces. The man turned back to Vik. "I know what you're trying to do—paint us into a couple of racists. You immigrants are all alike. First sign of trouble and . . ." he trailed off, the unspoken conveying much more than words.

Vikram Suri felt like he would explode. But as much as he wanted to nail this bastard to the sidewalk, he was the CEO of a major media company and street fights weren't part of the corporate agenda. He started walking. Just before he was out of earshot, however, he caught one last comment.

"Frigging Mexicans."

If it hadn't been so funny, Vik was sure he would have turned back and started a fight. It wasn't so much that they didn't know the difference between Mexicans and Indians or that they were racist jerks that offended him, but the fact that an exchange like this could take place on the streets of New York in today's day and age.

Like any immigrant, Vik knew that racism wasn't just an unfortunate relic of the past. It lived and breathed in every crack and crevice of society, from the embattled streets of Harlem to the palatial boardrooms of corporate America. Since the civil rights struggles in the '50s and the explosion of multiculturalism in the '70s and '80s, the disease had gone underground. It was no longer the gruesome evil that had once haunted so many, whites and non-whites. It was now an insidious virus that mutated almost as fast as people caught up with its latest incarnation.

In other words, bigotry had learnt discretion.

Through his college years in London and early work life in the United States, Vik had always imagined himself to be assimilated with his well-bred white colleagues from privileged families, but had gradually discovered that he wasn't really "on the inside." He was rarely invited to weddings, family outings, or dinner parties that his paler brethren seemed to attend regularly. He was an oddity, the token Indian that the Europeans and Americans liked to brag they knew, the one they turned to for recommendations about chicken curry.

At first he had blamed himself for the situation, convinced that perhaps his personality or habits made them uncomfortable, but soon realized that the social exclusion was more a matter of subtle, if mostly subconscious, prejudice on the part of his Caucasian friends. They simply didn't consider him a part of their community. Of course, adding to his misery was the fact that his ambition and cunning *did* cast him as an outlier, which had alienated him not just from white society, but other ethnic groups as well.

This would become the bedrock for a deep and deadly complex.

It started as mild irritation, a chronic impatience with the world. Before long, however, Vikram Suri graduated to full-blown paranoia and volatility. He was developing his *own* brand of racism—him against everyone else. It was a frustrated man's defense. The infamous glass ceilings of corporate America did nothing to improve the situation, and Vik began to think of himself as a victim.

Of course, the only logical response to this mostly phantom threat was for him to become richer, more powerful, and more famous than anyone else; and it was this desire that fueled the unrelenting drive and ruthless guile that he now carried with him like life-support. What made him particularly dangerous, however, was not the chip on his shoulder, but the fact that he knew how to hide it. Over the years, he had mastered the art of disguising his complex under an impenetrable veneer of urbanity and charm, and in the rare event that someone broke through, they experienced the full brunt of a desperate man's fury.

Vikram Suri the struggling Indian had turned into Vikram Suri the media baron, and no one was going to rob him of his crown.

Craig Michaels was the sort of man that Vikram Suri loved to hate.

Having grown up with a healthy dose of prejudice and a massive superiority complex, he represented everything about Caucasians that was offensive to anyone who was not, and even many who were. Unlike his counterpart at TriNet, however, Craig's racism had been forged not from resentment but by an utter lack of acknowledgement or understanding of any ideas, beliefs, customs, or lifestyles that weren't his own. The fact that he was born and bred in the one nation on earth that truly espoused multiculturalism as a virtue and bore it as a badge of honor did nothing to dissuade him from his viewpoint. To him, America was the perfect land, and non-European immigrants were just a lapse of judgment that could, and would, eventually be corrected.

After Vik's party in the Hamptons, he had gone back to his home in Connecticut drunk, and in a foul mood.

His exchange with Vikram Suri had left him seething and confused. In the face of Vik's threats, he had felt cornered and powerless, and knew that he had no choice but to go along with the man whom he hated not just because of the blackmail but because of his race. It was the ultimate insult for a man who would have gladly subsidized the activities of the Ku Klux Klan were it not for the fact that his professional ambitions would have been crushed through such an inopportune association.

Nevertheless, he *had* done what he had done, and now Vikram Suri had a report in his hands proving it. Even in his inebriated state, he could clearly remember the motivation for his actions. A few years after the buyout of Luxor Satellite, in which Craig Michaels had personally wound up with 62 percent of the company, he had initiated a series of initiatives aimed at packaging the company for a future sale. Some of those initiatives had been of an unorthodox nature and accordingly, he had covered them up.

The long-term plan had always been to sell the company for a hefty profit, and when Vikram Suri had first approached him with the idea of the merger, he was enthusiastic. But the price that the CEO of TriNet had suggested was considerably lower than what Craig expected to receive for his troubles. Ordinarily he would have told Vik to go to hell. After all, he could probably obtain a much higher value for Luxor in an auction.

But the report changed all that. As long as Vik had the document in his possession, as long as he even *knew* about its contents, his threat was credible, and deadly. If the information became known to Luxor's other shareholders, it could mean jail time for Craig Michaels, or at the very least the end of his career.

Muttering incoherent obscenities against the civilized world under his breath, he had pulled back the covers on his vast bed and dropped onto it with a force that bordered on punishment. Even as the first vestiges of sleep had begun to intrude upon his angry consciousness, Craig Michaels began to dream.

He was in a dark cave—correction, it was a semi-dark cave, for there was a faint illumination in the rocky chamber that outlined the dirt-covered walls with a relief that would have been impossible in the physical world with only a smattering of light. It was one of those convenient illusions that are a luxury of inhabiting an imaginary world. Somewhere in the far distance, Craig could hear the wind howling. Or was it some demonic creature circling the environs of the cave, hoping for a bite to eat? Craig decided it had to be the latter, since this was obviously going to be one of those needlessly scary dreams and it would naturally end with him being eaten alive in the most gruesome way imaginable; or worse still, the dream would end in some common inanity like him falling indefinitely into space. He wished fervently it wouldn't be the latter, for one thing that he couldn't stand was a lack of originality.

He waited and waited, until finally he decided that the cave was beginning to get boring, and if this dream, or nightmare, or whatever it was, was going to go anywhere, he would need to take the initiative and do something. So, seeing the world as through the lens of a movie camera, Craig made his way to the entrance of his subterranean prison, moving slowly to avoid stumbling over the rocks which would inevitably be strewn carelessly around the floor (*Why the devil couldn't they clean these sets up?*), and gradually reached the mouth of the cave. Outside it was pitch black, and Craig snickered at the lack of logical consistency—*How could there be light* inside *the cave when it was completely dark outside? The set designer should have been fired for* that *mistake.*

Hello, what was this? There was someone else in his dream. A woman, sitting cross-legged on the floor of the cave, near the entrance. Her back was to Craig, and he could hear chanting. A few seconds later, the woman bowed her head to the ground, and stayed that way for a full five minutes, to the extreme curiosity of her onlooker. Craig advanced toward her, wondering what she would look like. When he reached the woman, he touched her shoulder. The head moved up slowly from the floor, and in the moment before she turned, Craig wondered if he had made a mistake. Who knew what hideous gargoyle lurked on the other side of that head, and then he would have no choice but to jump screaming from the cave, and do the damn falling thing. . . .

But the woman on the floor turned out to be the most beautiful that he had ever seen. She was young, with short cropped brunette hair that seemed to accent her youth. Her face was perfect, with a liquid loveliness that could only be possible on the airbrushed cover of *Vogue,* or in a dream. Craig smiled broadly, suddenly quite happy with his situation. This could turn out to be a pretty good deal, if all went well. He couldn't remember—did one actually have to charm a girl in a dream, or could he simply jump her, given the fact that it was his show?

He didn't wonder for long, for the girl on the floor stood up quickly upon seeing him, and without uttering a word, dropped the ankle-length robe that she was wearing, exposing her naked form to him with a lack of shame that could only have been termed lascivious. A fairly lewd man by nature himself, Craig knelt down on the floor and started to eat her with pleasure. She moaned fantastically as his tongue entered the deepest recesses of her body, and ground her pubis into his face recklessly. Reaching behind her, Craig slapped her firm buttocks, and her writhing grew even more frantic. Fully aware of his carte blanche in this situation, he took hold of her arms and pulled her roughly onto the ground. Her head hit the stone surface of the cave, but somehow made no noise, and taking his cue from the fact that the laws of physics could obviously be bent in this wonderful place, he grasped her lower body and pushed it up and over her abdomen violently. Now she was twisted impossibly over her torso and her lustful moaning grew louder, echoing hauntingly in the cavernous surroundings. Craig was now more turned on than he could ever have been in the waking world, and began to spank her with a rare enjoyment, stopping only briefly to admire the deepening redness on her hips that he had caused with his beating. The girl did nothing to stop him and only issued guttural sounds that he was happy to construe as acquiescence, if not downright pleasure.

Within a few minutes, he decided he was through playing around and began to have full-blown sex with his ethereal partner. Even in a dream, he could feel and taste and smell the carnal pleasures of the woman's body. As his animal frenzy mounted, he shut his eyes tightly, which of course produced a result no different than in the physical world, and got ready to climax.

In the moment of consummation he opened his eyes, much to his regret.

Vikram Suri smiled up at him wantonly.

To Craig Michaels' wretched horror, Vik's eyes carried in them the unmistakable glaze of a satisfied lover. In a wispish, silvery voice, the Indian said: "Mind if I get on top next time?"

Craig screamed, and began to fall. . . .

eight

At 5:00 P.M. the Project Line team, including Steve Brandt, Tom Carter, Lee Kang, and Chris Back, assembled around a long conference room table with a speakerphone in the middle.

Tom dialed a number at TriNet. Three members of the TriNet team—Mark Pearson, the CFO; John Cohen, head of corporate development; and Helen Mosbacher, Vikram Suri's personal deputy—introduced themselves and the call began.

For the next hour Steve and Tom walked the TriNet team through the numbers, stopping to answer questions and note changes.

"How soon can you get us the revised valuation?" Helen asked at the end of the call.

"We can email you the new numbers in an hour," said Tom.

"Good. We also need to go over the structure of the deal. Can we talk at nine, Steve?" asked Helen.

Steve glanced at his watch. It was 6:15.

"If you like, we can discuss the structure right now while our analyst runs the numbers," he offered.

There was an awkward silence at the other end. Then Mark's voice came on.

"Thanks for the offer, but John and I need to run another meeting. Helen will coordinate it."

"That's fine, but since we're rendering our fairness opinion tomorrow, we'll need to make some decisions—" responded Steve, wondering what was going on.

Helen cut him off. "We know the timetable," she snapped.

"Of course. I'll speak with you at nine," said Steve hastily, ending the call.

Steve walked back to his office, slightly flustered. He was usually a good judge of corporate protocol but had made a critical error a few minutes back. He should have realized right away that Helen Mosbacher wasn't simply there to keep Vikram Suri informed. She was a messenger. And whatever message she had to convey couldn't be done on a conference call with four other people. Hence, the ploy to schedule a later call with him alone.

As he sat down behind his desk, he put on his reading glasses and began to look through the merger analysis again.

One of the most important considerations in determining the structure of a merger was the tax treatment of the deal. Steve had determined that the TriNet deal could be structured as a tax-free reorganization, as long as the company paid for Luxor in stock rather than cash.

There was a knock on his office door.

"Come in," said Steve.

Tom stepped inside with a pile of papers in his hand. They were the revised numbers. He presented a copy to Steve and sat down to wait. The managing director looked them over carefully and then put down the pages.

"Fifteen billion. I can't say that I'm crazy about the new projections, but then it's not the mid-nineties anymore. Our client has a right to be cautious."

Tom smiled. "Fifteen billion is still a pretty respectable number. Even if the forecasts weren't cut, I doubt that Vikram Suri would make an acquisition at the going rate; he's too smart for that. I'm sure that Craig Michaels is expecting some hardball on the bid."

Steve was about to ask Tom what he thought about the awkward exchange with Helen, but then checked himself. It was partially his own fault and he could never let a subordinate see that. In their own tiny world, managing directors were Supermen.

"All right," commanded Steve, "send it to Helen."

—————————nine

While Steve was waiting for Helen to call him back, Amanda Fleming was getting ready for bed. It was still early, but she was tired.

Putting out her cigarette, she walked to the bathroom to change into her nightclothes. She slipped on her pajamas, then brushed her teeth and washed her face. Returning to the bedroom, she slipped in between the covers and shut off the light.

In the silence of her apartment, she could hear noises from the street. People chatting and laughing outside a bar; the honking of taxicabs as they raced through the intersection; a car alarm, probably a malfunction. These were the night sounds of Manhattan and they were usually comforting, dependable sounds.

Tonight, however, they did little to soothe Amanda's nerves. She was feeling extremely restless and had no doubts that her angst would prevent her from falling asleep for hours. Right now, she was thinking about Jack Ward.

Jack was a field agent for the FBI, and she had been dating him for about six months. At first things seemed to be going well. He was smart and attractive, and they shared many common interests, including a passion for music and skiing. He was considerate and made every accommodation for Amanda's unpredictable schedule. But lately none of this seemed to be enough. While the relationship worked on a practical level, it lacked the elusive chemistry that Amanda had always desired and believed in.

She was mature enough emotionally to realize that fairy tale romances rarely, if ever, existed, and that all relationships were more the result of extensive compromises and hard work than the magical spark of destiny. Yet this clinical assessment didn't help Amanda, whose dreams were strong and whose quest for the truth in her professional life in no way tainted her ability to chase that which was probably a mirage.

She sighed as she realized that this one too would have to be let go. Breakups were always hard and she had no reason to believe this one would be any different. They said it took *twice* as long to get over a breakup as the relationship itself. She was living testament to that fact many times over. . . . She would do it tomorrow, when she would meet him for dinner after work.

Work. Her mind turned quickly to the other mainstay of her young life.

Amanda was a staff writer for the business section of *The New York Times.* Her beat consisted of brief reports on the mergers and acquisitions activity in the market, and occasionally an exposition piece on a particular deal.

It was a desirable job that rarely required much digging or legwork, since most companies and sources were only too happy to provide information in exchange for coverage in one of the top newspapers in the country. On the rare occasion when a deal had negative implications, the vast resources and formidable reputation of the *Times* made it fairly painless to get the right quotes and information.

Sometimes, Amanda wished that it wasn't so easy.

Since graduating from the Columbia School of Journalism, she had held jobs with the financial desks of *The New York Post, Daily News,* and even the ABC network news. While she had enjoyed her experiences and worked with highly respected journalists, she had never gotten the true feel of "guerilla" journalism.

Part of the problem was that financial news was rarely as dramatic as political news. In the heyday of Michael Milken and Drexel, there had been plenty to write about. Now, however, the worst that ever happened was a bad earnings report. For the aggressive young reporter, it felt like a dose of Valium.

When she finally drifted off to sleep, Amanda dreamt of satellites.

In the morning, she would think it odd.

· · · · · · ·

Helen Mosbacher was a tall, statuesque redhead with a striking figure. She was thirty-five and smart as a whip. As Vikram Suri's right hand person, she functioned as a mix between a personal assistant and a chief of staff. While not officially in charge of the Luxor acquisition, she was intricately involved in every aspect of the proposed transaction, and the rumor at the firm was that she had the authority to act on Vik's behalf on all matters concerning the deal. So far, her role had been primarily one of observer, and she hadn't stepped on anyone's toes.

That had changed a few hours ago, at the end of the conference call with MW. Until then, Mark Pearson and John Cohen had been the "point" people for the Luxor acquisition, coordinating the financial and strategic efforts of the TriNet team in formulating a bid for the satellite operator.

In a private exchange, out of earshot of the speakerphone, Helen had made it clear to the two men that she would "decide on all matters" concerning the structure or valuation of the deal. In non-corporate speak, this meant that the CFO and the head of corporate development were to keep out of any high-level discussions or negotiations unless specifically invited to participate.

Most senior executives at public companies would have been livid at such a suggestion, but Mark and John were experienced hands who understood the realpolitik of business. The first commandment at TriNet was never to question Vikram Suri. The second was never to question his deputy.

Helen had just finished going through the revised numbers from MW. Even though she wasn't pleased with the results, she wasn't entirely surprised either. Most of this had been expected. The real challenge was managing the process, but then that was her forte. Picking up the phone, she dialed Steve Brandt.

When the banker came on the line, she dove right into it. "We want to do a cash-option merger, Steve."

A cash-option merger was a form of tax-free reorganization in which the shareholders of the target company were given the option to receive either equity or cash for the sale of their shares.

"Do you have that much cash?" he asked with surprise.

"Yes," came the curt response.

"For how much?"

There was a long pause. Then another voice came on the line.

"Steve, we want to bid seven billion," a cultured voice informed him.

Steve frowned. It was Vik. What was he doing on the call? But then, of course, it was his deal.

"Hi Vik. I see your guys have come up with a better deal than us," he said jokingly.

"I'm perfectly serious," said Vik calmly.

Steve took a second to think this new development over, then stated: "As your investment banker, I have to tell you that seven billion is too low—"

"Thanks for your input, but that's what we're bidding. I take it you'll be ready to deliver the fairness opinion tomorrow?" asked Vik, sweeping aside the banker's judgment.

"We will, although I need to make sure I understand the seven billion number," replied Steve, frustrated.

"Well, then, make sure you do," answered Vik quietly.

Even though it was a cryptic remark, Steve understood its hidden message perfectly.

For one thing, it meant that Vikram Suri didn't intend to discuss TriNet's reasoning behind the valuation, and Steve was being encouraged to leave the issue alone.

Secondly, it meant that it was the investment bank's job to find a justification for a $7 billion valuation. In other words, Steve and his team would need to modify the numbers so that a $7 billion result could be reached in the end.

Steve knew that this type of "reverse engineering" wasn't exactly ethical from the standpoint of the client's shareholders. However, it wasn't illegal either, and as long as it was being done to pay a lower, and not higher, price for Luxor, it wouldn't hurt TriNet's interests. It was simply a financial and legal *game* . . .

Of course, if the bid was rejected, it would mean the expense of more time and money for TriNet to "up" the offer—which would eventually come out of the shareholders' and customers' pockets.

But who really cared?

"We'll get moving on it right away," promised Steve. "Helen, I'll have Tom Carter call you later tonight to finalize the numbers; is that all right?"

"That's fine," responded Helen sweetly.

"Sounds good," said Vik, and hung up.

As soon as Steve hung up with Vik, he sat back in his chair to think. He had to get his vice president moving on the numbers, but he had to do something else first.

He had to cover his ass.

It was 11:15 P.M., Day 4.

────────────ten

Laura Briggs was dressed in a sheer black nightgown, her tall, elegant body outlined suggestively beneath the flimsy fabric. Her long black hair fell around her shoulders untidily, accentuating her sultry look. She had soft, sensual features, sparkling blue eyes, and full lips. Her eyes were lit with desire for the man in front of her.

Steve moved toward her and took her in his arms. His lips pressed against hers and he kissed her passionately. He held her body tightly against him with an urgent sense of arousal. Pulling her head back by the hair, he began to kiss her face, brushing his lips against her cheeks, lips, and forehead. Their tongues met in another frantic kiss and she reached down into his shirt, running her long, delicate fingers over his chest.

Lifting her up gently, Steve carried her to the luxurious king-sized bed in the middle of the bedroom. He laid her down and pushed her nightgown up above her waist. Kneeling, he began to kiss her thighs, exploring her creamy white skin with his tongue and hungrily edging upwards. She sighed with pleasure as his hands moved up beneath her dress and grasped her full breasts, squeezing them.

She was in heat now, and reaching down, pulled the nightdress up and off her body, revealing her beautiful naked form to the man making love to her. Steve looked lustfully at the sight before him and quickly moved his mouth up to Laura's breasts, licking and sucking on her hard nipples. She was clearly in ecstasy and he found her moaning and shifting incredibly exciting.

One hand moved below her waist and began to rub her in a slow, circular motion. She gasped at his touch. After a few minutes, she pushed him away and proceeded to remove his clothes. Thoroughly aroused and too impatient to wait any longer, she pulled him on top, guiding him inside her.

After it was over, Steve and Laura held each other in the darkness.

"That was incredible. I can't even describe the sensation," confessed Steve.

"I know. I've never been so aroused. You're definitely the best lover I've ever had," Laura responded, giggling.

"Oh, and how many other lovers have you had?" asked Steve playfully.

Laura laughed. "Good try. How is the deal with Vikram going?" she asked.

Steve was startled. "How do you know about that?" he asked, a little too gruffly.

"Take it easy. I don't know anything except that you guys are working together. Vik and I are old friends, so I know how to read him."

Steve relaxed. He was being paranoid. It was part of being an investment banker. A lack of confidentiality could kill the biggest and best deals, and pillow talk was particularly dangerous.

"I know how bankers work, Steve, so we don't need to talk any more about this, all right? I just want to be with you. I don't care what deals you work on," said Laura, nestling close to him.

Steve pulled her closer still. "I'm sorry, darling. I was being a little crazy."

"Yes, you were," responded Laura in mock hurt.

Steve marveled at the chemistry between them. They had met only a few days ago, but already he had had the most intense physical experiences of his life. It was as if their bodies were made for each other. To add to the intimacy, their thoughts, their personalities, everything seemed to mesh perfectly.

After the party at Vikram Suri's mansion in the Hamptons, Steve and Laura had gone back to Steve's hotel for a drink. He was staying at The Enclave Inn, a chic motel in Bridgehampton designed by Martha Stewart's daughter. Over glasses of wine, they had curled up in front of the television to watch the news. A few minutes later, he kissed her. After a brief hesitation, she kissed him back. They had wound up in bed and made love till early the next morning.

Tonight was their second night together. Laura had a modest but comfortable apartment in the Gramercy area, and Steve had come straight to her after the meeting with Tom. He had needed to see her particularly badly after the surprises of the day. In her arms, he felt calm and oblivious to the pressures of his job.

Just as he was about to fall asleep, he felt Laura's hand reach down and stroke him. The banker moaned.

After an hour-long meeting in which the fairness opinion committee found the valuation of Luxor Satellite to be fair, Tom headed back to his office. His secretary handed him a slip of paper with a message on it. He smiled to himself as he sat down behind his desk. The old man never failed to call.

For the past ten years, even after Tom had graduated college and entered the professional world, Harry Carter had made it a point to call his son once every day, sometimes even two or three times, to find out how he was doing and to give unsolicited advice that usually turned out to be annoyingly correct. Tom had always been close to his father, but of late their relationship had grown even deeper, entering a spiritual phase that had less to do with the parent-child dynamic than a significant friendship.

Tom picked up the phone to call his father. When the old man came on the line, his deep and experienced voice was like a soothing balm on the stress of the day.

"Hello, Dad. How are you feeling?"

Harry coughed briefly. "I'm fine, son. How are things at your end? Doing any big deals?"

Tom suppressed a chuckle. Every day his father started with the same question, even though he had gotten the complete lowdown on Tom's work just twenty-four hours earlier. All the same, he always humored him.

"Just the satellite deal that I told you about. I can't discuss the name, you understand. But things are going well. We went to the fairness committee today and got their approval."

"You mean the rubber-stamp committee," opined Harry cynically. "When are you coming to see me?"

That was just like the old man, thought Tom. He had a habit of changing the subject abruptly, especially when it came to asking that question. Tom fidgeted uneasily. He hadn't seen his father in a month, and with all that was going on with the TriNet-Luxor deal, he wouldn't be able to get away for a while. He knew that it wasn't his fault, but he felt guilty nonetheless.

"With everything that's in the hopper right now, Dad . . ."

Harry cut him off gently.

"I know, I know. Don't worry about it. I just miss you, son, that's all."

Tom chatted with his father for another ten minutes, then hung up the phone. He felt drained. Even though he looked forward to hearing Harry's voice every day, and even though it gave him comfort to know that he was all right, it was a stressful affair. It wasn't the unsolicited advice or the occasional jabs of guilt that the old man directed at him that made him tense.

It was the fact that Harry Carter was dying.

─────────── eleven

The helicopter took off from the heliport at East Thirty-fourth Street at 7:00 P.M. on Saturday. It was a clear evening, and the passengers could see the red, white, and blue cascading lights of the Empire State Building recede gradually into the distance as the pilot maneuvered the chopper expertly over the Manhattan skyline, heading out towards the Hamptons.

All three passengers had been on this trip before, and hardly paid attention to the breathtaking view. Instead, they were busy discussing the TriNet-Luxor merger. Seated to the left of Vikram Suri was Helen Mosbacher, and to her left, against the window, was George Lomax.

George was a director of TriNet and one of its most influential board members. As the former head of a "big-four" television network and then a major Hollywood studio, he had established himself as a formidable figure in the media world through a long career spanning five decades and almost every medium of distribution, including radio, television, cable, and the Internet. His in-depth knowledge, experience, and formidable network of contacts—including corporate CEOs, Wall Street financiers and marquee names in entertainment—had made him one of TriNet's most prized commodities. He had been instrumental in bringing several large pieces of business to the conglomerate since joining its board in 1998, and consequently carried considerable sway with the other board members, as well as TriNet's management.

Vik was trying to convince George to approve the merger in the board meeting on Monday. George's support was critical, since most of the other board members would look toward him for his opinion, as well as his imprimatur. While the other directors of TriNet were all accomplished people in their own right, none could boast the reputation or contacts that George Lomax brought to the table.

Vikram Suri was the chairman of the board, and as such, his word carried a lot of weight. But without George's support, the vote could be tight and there would be a lot more difficulty in getting it passed. Early on, and despite his natural egomania, Vik had been smart enough to realize that someone like George Lomax could be a great asset to TriNet, but also a potential threat if handled without care. Hence he had established a close relationship with the man—to ensure that they were on the same page on major issues. On the few occasions they had disagreed, Vik had yielded to the elder board member.

Tonight Vik hoped that the media magnate would return the favor.

The sound of the rotors made it difficult to hear or be heard, and soon the three passengers gave up trying to shout over it. The discussion would wait until they landed.

Forty-five minutes later, the lavish houses of Southampton came into view, the lights gleaming brightly in the near distance. One of the few helipads in the Hamptons is on a short boardwalk on the southern tip of Southampton, on the side opposite the beach. It is little more than a block of concrete and is reflective of the glorious nonchalance of the extremely rich residents.

Despite the small landing area, the chopper landed without incident. The passengers disembarked, bending their heads to avoid the wind from the whirling rotor blades. A limousine was waiting for Vik and his guests, and within minutes they were at his mansion. George Lomax was having dinner later in the city, so they decided to have cocktails by the poolside.

"I've already told you the strategic rationale for the merger, George. This deal is very good for us. The addition of another distribution medium to our holdings is worth its weight in gold. And Luxor is the perfect property!" enthused Vik, sipping a martini.

George Lomax was a short, pudgy man, with an overall appearance that belied the tremendous power and influence that he carried. While a multi-millionaire several times over, he dressed very simply and rarely showed off his wealth—in his personal or professional life. He was a strong family man and deeply religious. His suburban lifestyle and humility had marked him out as an "odd cookie" in the brash, glamorous worlds of television and Hollywood. Even so, his winning combination of street smarts, hard work, and patience were hard to beat.

Seated on a deck chair, he took a taste of his scotch, staring thoughtfully at the large, well-lit pool. He could never quite adjust to Vikram Suri's over-the-top lifestyle and trappings of wealth and power, but then he was also tolerant of others' preferences and would never voice his opinion openly, especially to a colleague.

"You mentioned that the real value of Luxor's assets is ten billion?" he asked.

"With very conservative assumptions. In a more realistic scenario, the value could be as high as fifteen billion. So basically, anything south of that is a steal," replied Vik, staring George in the eye.

"And we're sure that we're not getting a lemon?"

"Positive. Our lawyers have been through the liens and are drafting an ironclad legal agreement. Luxor's satellites are relatively new and in great shape," answered Vik confidently.

"I don't know, Vik. I'm always leery of anyone who tries to sell something at less than its worth," objected George.

"I agree with you, but the value of something depends largely on the condition of the market. It's a buyer's market right now," Vik pointed out.

"Then why not go after one of the publicly traded satellite operators? After all, it's always a safer bet than a private company," George asked shrewdly.

The CEO of TriNet shook his head. "Too expensive. The public companies in this space are not cheap, and have constant access to the capital markets—even if the market is tough. A private company, on the other hand, is more vulnerable."

George thought this over silently. Vik's reasoning made sense.

"How do we know there won't be a bidding war once we make our offer?" he asked eventually.

A bidding war could create a circus, spiraling the value of Luxor skyward. Many great deals died for precisely that reason. Corporate mentality being what it was, even companies that had no reason to bid for a satellite operator would get into the game, afraid that they would miss some biblical boat—even if there was no flood.

"There won't be. Craig Michaels assured me of that. They're not in fire-sale mode, George. This is just a logical deal for both parties," replied Vik, finishing his drink and signaling the waiter standing quietly nearby.

"So if we're in sync with Michaels, then why are we low-balling them on the purchase price?" asked George, referring to the seven billion dollar bid.

Vik grinned. "What's a deal without a little negotiation, George? I want to see how Luxor reacts. If they want ten billion, we'll give it to them. But if they're willing to accept a lower bid, then who are we to deny them the opportunity?"

George was irritated at this last statement. He had played his share of hardball in life, but only when necessary. He believed in simplicity. Part of being street-smart was in knowing when not to be *too* smart.

But he also saw the wisdom in Vik's approach. For good or bad, it was a smart bargaining tactic. In this case at least, the game might just be worth it.

He consulted his watch. He needed to get back to Manhattan soon. His daughter and her husband were in town, and would be coming over for dinner. He hadn't seen his little girl since they moved to Denver four months ago, and couldn't wait to get going.

"All right, Vik. I'm almost there. But explain to me why you want to offer a cash-option merger? If there's so much value in the combined company, why not just offer stock?"

Vik accepted a fresh drink from the waiter.

"Craig Michaels wants cash for his sixty-two percent of Luxor. This way we can give it to him and still do a tax-free deal. Our balance sheet is clean, so we can borrow the money from the bank."

"And what if we need to pay ten billion?"

"Then we borrow the remainder against an ESOP," replied Vik, smiling like a man who had thought through every possible contingency.

An ESOP, or employee stock ownership plan, was an employee benefit plan, similar in theory to a 401(k) or other pension plans, but with certain benefits that most other plans lacked. An ESOP allowed companies to borrow money from a bank against shares allocated to the employees of the company. These shares would be held in an escrow account, from which they would be released periodically.

Due to tax advantages over other kinds of debt, ESOPs were an attractive way for companies to finance growth or to repurchase shares.

George was impressed. He stood up and buttoned his jacket.

"Great work on this, Vik. You have my support," he said in an upbeat voice.

Vik rose and shook hands with the older man. "Thanks a lot for coming down here, George. I know we could have done this over the phone, but I wanted to make sure you were completely comfortable with it."

"I am, and I'll speak to the other board members before the meeting on Monday. Now if you'll excuse me, I must get back to the city," said George hastily.

"I appreciate your support. My driver will take you to the chopper," smiled Vik.

George said good night to Helen Mosbacher and left.

Helen, who had been discreetly silent through the conversation, lay back in her pool chair and smiled at Vik.

"It looks like you did it," she said, impressed.

Vik sipped thoughtfully at his drink. "It's not over yet."

"I know, but at least we're not going to have any problems with the board."

Vik nodded, staring out at the beach behind the house. The lights around the pool had been dulled and the moonlight reflecting off the sandy beach radiated a bright glow in the distance. A cool evening breeze made its way from the water to the people seated by the pool, and carried with it the sound of the waves lapping gently against the shore. The lights of a boat gleamed on the far horizon, then suddenly blinked out, as if embarrassed at being caught.

It was a very relaxing milieu and Vik soaked in the beauty of the scene with eagerness. In the high-flying corporate world, each day was more stressful than the last, and the ability to release the tension in a luxurious setting was what kept people like him sane. To Vik, this wasn't opulence, but a necessity, and the knowledge that most of the world didn't live in this splendor didn't worry him in the least. His success was due to his own hard work, courage, and brains, and whatever he got he heartily deserved. If some people didn't like his lifestyle, that was their problem.

Turning to Helen, he admired her beautiful form, reposing gracefully against the body-length cushion on the pool chair. She was wearing a simple floral dress that hugged her magnificent figure and reached down to her knees. Her perfectly round breasts rose and fell rhythmically under the thin material. As George had noticed with some discomfort, she wasn't wearing a bra. Her ruby-red hair was pulled back in a bun, accentuating her strong, aquiline features and showcasing her sparkling blue eyes. The wavering light from the pool danced suggestively over her long body, ending in stabs of burgundy highlights from her hair.

The ruthless businesswoman of the day had been replaced by a sensual Greek goddess, Vik noted with awe. It was exactly that mix of unrepentant cold-bloodedness and unrestrained feminine charm that had prompted the TriNet CEO to appoint Helen as his confidante and chief deputy. On more than one occasion she had used both those qualities to generate substantial business for TriNet, and to convince CEOs, financiers, politicians, and celebrities to endorse Vikram Suri's ideas and plans.

His eyes fixed on Helen's, Vik rose and walked over to her. Kneeling down by her chair, he worshipped her long, beautiful legs with his mouth. His hands reached up and undid the buttons on the front of her dress.

part 2
the execution

twelve

It was just after 11:00 A.M. when Amanda Fleming put on her sunglasses and walked out of the high-rise apartment building. The entrance was on Columbus Avenue and underneath the building were a series of high-priced garment stores, catering to the hip and affluent young crowd which permeated the Upper West Side of Manhattan.

Walking over to Broadway, she hailed a yellow cab and asked the driver to take her to the Plaza Hotel. It was pleasant outside and the reporter rolled down her window, pulling out her pack of Marlboro Lights. As she was about to light up, the Pakistani driver turned irately and gesticulated at the "No Smoking by Law" sign on the partition in the cab. Amanda hastily put back her cigarette and lighter, grumbling audibly to the indifferent cabbie. This city was becoming more and more fascist every day.

The cab drove down Broadway, past Columbus Circle, where the new AOL Time Warner building was being built and promised to overshadow the garish Trump International Hotel nearby, and along Central Park South. Scores of New Yorkers and tourists were walking on the pavement next to the park, taking pictures and moving along slowly, enjoying the lovely weather. It had been a long, harsh winter, and people were exceptionally pleased at the sea change in the climate. Rollerbladers weaved in and out of the crowd, heading into Central Park through the numerous entrances along Fifty-ninth Street.

As the cab pulled up in front of the posh Plaza Hotel, Amanda snapped shut the compact she had taken out to adjust her makeup, paid the driver, and got out. The stairway to the hotel was appropriately covered in a rich crimson carpet, and a uniformed doorman ushered in guests ostentatiously through the Fifth Avenue entrance. Amanda was elegantly dressed in a lime-green Chanel suit, and her soft blond hair fell neatly around her slim shoulders. She was strikingly beautiful, and seemed to fit right in with the men and women in expensive couture walking through the revolving doors.

In reality, of course, she was *not* one of the high society "dames," and had no desire to become one.

Unlike the women around her right now, Amanda had had to work hard to make ends meet after her father left her mother when she was sixteen. Unable to afford the luxury of socializing and going on expensive vacations like most of her friends, she had instead spent her college years (including holidays) doing part-time jobs to supplement her mother's inadequate secretarial income. Despite her financial handicap, she hadn't yielded to resentment or frustration; instead she had focused on developing her journalism skills by reading and writing voraciously in the little spare time that she had.

While her friends spent most of their time bar-hopping and exploring the considerable night life of Manhattan, Amanda had penned various articles on political and business issues and submitted them assiduously to various publications, hoping to be noticed by the editor of a major magazine or newspaper. After a number of rejections, she had finally had an op-ed piece published in a minor newspaper. Using the clipping as a marketing tool, she had compiled a sample portfolio of her writing and forwarded it to practically every East Coast publication that she knew of.

Eventually a female magazine editor who was a year away from retirement at a major publication had invited her for a meeting. The old woman was looking for new talent to mentor, and Amanda was eager to learn. Soon Amanda was working as a staff writer for the magazine and covering a decidedly unintellectual, but fun, social beat. It wasn't exactly Pulitzer Prize work, but Amanda was able to develop her sense of dress, speech, and style through the extensive socializing, and create a network of high-level contacts—mostly with successful corporate women—that she knew would be essential in furthering her career.

Along with her personal skills, Amanda had also honed her writing talents, turning the otherwise racy gossip column into an elegantly-styled story medium, following the lives and careers of the people in her column in detail and weaving a thread of continuity through the weeks and months of social events. It was an unusual and creative way to present an otherwise underrated section of the magazine, and soon readers were writing in to express their appreciation of the humorous, clean, and informational style of the young columnist.

Even her accent had changed, going from the unimpressive and flat tone of most young New York women to the cut-crystal accents of the higher class.

Amanda's mentor had taken note of these changes and improvements, and advised her to apply to the Columbia School of Journalism, which was noted for its excellence and widely recognized as a training ground for future editors and anchormen and women.

At Columbia, Amanda had discovered something that had long been missing from her life—men. With her hazel eyes, blond hair, and Anglo-Saxon looks, she had no difficulty in attracting trouble, and had dated numerous well-heeled corporate executives, bankers, lawyers, and journalists, and even a handsome millionaire. Despite the challenging curriculum, she had found plenty of time to go out, party, ski, sail, and explore the adventurous side of life that had been denied her in her college years.

However, while most of the men had been white Anglo-Saxon protestants, or WASPs, and close to her own cultural mores, she had found their social circles rather dull and uninspiring. Being a creative person by nature, she had chafed at the inevitable conservatism of the New England culture and what she perceived as a deeply ingrained coldness in their interpersonal relationships. As a moderate feminist and a Democrat, she was deeply critical of the forced "family values" amongst the WASPs, which she considered hypocritical given their generally adulterous lifestyles.

The other aspect of New England culture that intrigued her was the Anglo-Saxons' control over money and power in America. From the White House to Wall Street and the boardrooms of corporate America, they had long held the keys to the political and financial locks of the country, stemming from the early twentieth century creation of vast financial empires to the more recent permeation of politics and business by the graduates of Harvard, Yale, Princeton, and Columbia. While it was true that the Jews exerted an equal, if not superior, amount of influence over the financial machinery of the United States, it was less so in the sphere of politics.

As a journalist, Amanda had felt that in order for her to examine and criticize the power structures in America, it was necessary for her to keep a personal distance from the people that exerted that power. It was true that she was a staunch supporter of free enterprise, but she was also concerned about the social impact of capitalism, and often found herself taking an anti-corporate stance on political and economic issues. This inevitably brought her into conflict with the Ivy League crowd, which supported big business almost fanatically, and widened the ideological gap even further. As a result, she had gradually moved away from her active circle of friends and sought company elsewhere.

Which had brought her to the FBI agent. As she walked through the hotel lobby to the house phones at the far end, she reflected on her breakup last week.

It had been less emotional than she had thought it would be, and Jack Ward had handled her words with aplomb, if not exactly understanding. He had tried to talk her out of it, but she had been adamant about parting ways, and after an exceptionally long silence, he acquiesced. Amanda suspected that he had seen it coming and had prepared himself for it. Her suspicions were confirmed when he accepted her hand of friendship without a fuss. Both of them knew that couples seldom survived as friends after a breakup, but Jack was a good man and Amanda still wanted him in her life—just in a different role.

Pulling a slip of paper out of her purse, she dialed the room number written on it. A man's voice answered.

"Hello. Mr. Chandler, this is Amanda Fleming with *The New York Times*. I'm here for our interview. Would you like me to come up or wait for you in the lobby?"

"Thanks, Ms. Fleming. I'll be down in a minute," came the pleasant reply.

Amanda waited by the reception desk, checking her dictaphone for batteries and tape. She was interviewing the CEO of a book publishing firm on the recent acquisition of an electronic book company by their chief competitor. She had spent the weekend learning about the electronic book market and how it would impact the publishing business, including her interviewee. That was the Wall Street version, now came the real thing. In point of fact, she knew it would be exactly the same. . . .

Although Amanda was good at reading between the lines and often directed difficult questions at her interviewees, she rarely attempted to "trip them up." *The Times* was as well known for its conservative journalism as for its liberal bias. While the newspaper often carried exposés on political issues, it hardly ever ventured into controversial territory on the business side—that was the domain of *The Wall Street Journal.*

Amanda had been offered the job at the *Times* through the generous intervention of a dowager she had networked with early in her career. She had known going in that it was a plush assignment, enabling her to interview senior executives at Fortune 500 firms, network with research analysts and investment bankers on Wall Street, get invited to industry conferences and corporate parties, and never really have to uncover any smoking guns.

It was the sort of job that was a blessing for journalists who regarded themselves as chroniclers of news, but a curse for those who wanted to *find* the news. While Amanda was certainly the latter, she realized that in order to pursue her dream of being a groundbreaking reporter, she first needed access and pedigree in the business, which the *Times* could provide.

Amanda's interviewee came downstairs a few minutes later, and the two walked into the hotel lounge. The CEO was extremely cordial and answered her questions in detail. On some competitive issues, however, he sidestepped her, issuing platitudinous statements for the press's benefit. She could have pushed for more, but there hardly seemed to be a reason. It was not as if the fate of the world hinged on the electronic book market.

After thanking him for his time, Amanda departed for her office. Between the interview and her research, she now had enough to write the piece. *Great,* she thought cynically. *What a coup.*

As she entered a cab outside the Plaza Hotel, her cell phone rang.

While Amanda was conducting her interview at the Plaza Hotel, Tom Carter was reading the morning paper with his feet up on the desk. He was killing time while TriNet's board of directors met to approve the bid for Luxor Satellite.

Late last night, he and Lee Kang had put the finishing touches on the board presentation, and Steve Brandt had approved the final version for binding around midnight. A few minutes later, Chris Back had run down with the book to the copy center a few floors down, where a skeleton crew was waiting to copy and bind the books.

Early this morning, a car had delivered the presentations to Vikram Suri's office at TriNet. Steve and Vik had already gone over the substance of the presentation over the weekend, and the TriNet CEO glanced only briefly at the book before going down to the conference room where the board meeting was being held.

The meeting went on for about an hour and a half, with most of the board members already being aware of the transaction and the details. By the time Tom reached the international section of his paper, the board had already voted on the Luxor bid, and approved it.

Helen Mosbacher parked her car and walked over to a pay phone at the end of the street. She picked up the handset and dialed the Manhattan number. After three rings, a pleasant female voice came on the line.

"Good morning. *The New York Times* business section. How can I help you?"

"I need to speak with one of your staff columnists—Amanda Fleming," said Helen.

"Sure. Let me connect you to her line."

Helen was put on hold for a few seconds, then a male voice came on the line. "Hello. This is Amanda Fleming's office."

"I need to speak with her, please."

"She's out of the office right now. Can I take a message?"

"That won't be possible. It's urgent that I reach her. I have some valuable information for her," said Helen, glancing around to see if anyone could overhear her.

There was a pause at the other end of the line before another voice came on. "Hello, this is Christine Peters. I'm a columnist with the business section as well. Is there something I can help you with?"

"I said I want to speak with Amanda Fleming. I have an important lead, and it's for her ears only," Helen maintained adamantly.

In truth she had picked Amanda's name only because she had read some of her work and thought it was fluff. Someone like that would be hungry for a real story.

After a contemplative pause, Christine said, "I understand. I'll have our receptionist patch you through to her mobile phone, all right?"

Helen relaxed. "Thanks. Nothing personal, you know."

"No problem. Just hold on."

Ten seconds later, Helen heard a faint ringing as her call was transferred to Amanda's cell. On the second ring, someone answered.

"Hello," said an elegant voice.

"Is this Amanda Fleming?"

"Yes, it is. Who's this?"

"Never mind that. I have a valuable lead for you. Do you have a pen and paper?" asked Helen.

Amanda fumbled around in her purse for her pen and notepad. As a reporter, she carried them with her wherever she went. Cradling the phone between her left ear and shoulder, she pulled off the top of the pen and flipped open the notepad.

"Shoot," she said in a curious but professional tone.

"TriNet Corporation is going to make a bid for Luxor Satellite on Wednesday."

"For how much?"

"Seven billion in a cash-option deal."

"Who are you?" asked Amanda again, knowing full well that she was unlikely to get an answer.

"As I said earlier, never mind. Do you want the story or not?" asked Helen tersely.

"Of course I do. But I still need to know how *you* know all this?"

"Let's just say I'm close to the deal, all right? That should give you the quote you want."

Amanda smiled. The quote in question was "from a source close to the deal" and it was one of the most common tools employed by journalists to avoid naming their sources without using less credible quotes such as "from an anonymous source" or "based on a tip."

"What more can you tell me about the deal?" she asked, her pen at the ready.

Helen went through some details related to the merger, including the names of the banks representing TriNet and Luxor, and the likelihood that Craig Michaels would want cash for his lion's share of the satellite operator. Amanda jotted down everything verbatim, and at the end of the call went back over her notes to see if she had missed anything. Despite this source's caginess on some issues, she was surprisingly willing and able to share information, thought Amanda. Most leaks were furtive and the details they gave sketchy.

On the other end of the line, Helen was on autopilot, having done this before a number of times, anticipating most of the questions that the young journalist was throwing her way. She knew exactly how far to go and what not to say that could reveal her identity in any way, either now or later.

"Have you called any of the newswires or Internet sites with this?" asked Amanda. If the story was already with the newswires, it would be old hat within the hour.

"No, just you. I'm prepared to give you an exclusive," assured Helen.

Of course, *The New York Times* also had an online presence, but if this source didn't intend to share the information with anyone else, it might be a bigger coup to run an "exclusive" in print the next day—something that didn't happen too often nowadays.

"Why the *Times* specifically?" persisted the reporter.

"I think you already know that, Ms. Fleming."

She was right, of course. Amanda knew perfectly well why she wanted the story "broken" by the *Times*—an article in the *Times* carried with it the stamp of credibility.

Whoever this woman was, thought Amanda, she wanted to make sure that the TriNet-Luxor story would be taken seriously by the market and not dismissed as a rumor.

The only real competition in this regard (for financial news) was arguably *The Wall Street Journal*. Amanda wondered briefly whether her source intended to call the *Journal* as a backup. She asked her.

"No, I don't. You and I both know this story is too large for you to turn down. So let's move on, all right?" replied Helen irately.

Amanda ventured one final question. "*Why* are you doing this?"

"My agenda is none of your business," snapped Helen. There was a ring of finality in her voice.

Amanda took the hint. "I need to get a corroborating source and run this by my editor, but it should be on the front page of the business section tomorrow."

"Good," said Helen, and put the handset back in its cradle.

Amanda dialed her office and asked to be put through to her editor. When the editor of the business section came on the line, she relayed the news to him. After listening carefully, he gave her permission to delay the piece on electronic publishing and focus on the breaking story. But first the reporter had to find a corroborating source.

As Amanda rang her editor, Helen picked up the phone again and dialed an unlisted number at the office of Vikram Suri. It was a private line that he used for communicating with close friends and high-level business associates.

Vik was sitting at his desk when the phone rang. After the third ring, he picked it up and punched in his private security code, which enabled him to receive the call. If he hadn't been around to answer, the phone wouldn't have taken any messages and no one else would have been able to take the call. The TriNet CEO had chosen this system to ensure that his most private communications would stay that way.

When Helen heard her boss's voice on the other end, she identified herself. Vik acknowledged her but kept deliberately quiet. Even though this was a scrambled line and anyone listening into the conversation would have heard a lot of undecipherable encrypted nonsense, he wanted to minimize his own exposure by saying as little as possible.

Helen knew this and just said a few words: "The thing we discussed is done."

"Thank you," said Vikram Suri tersely, and put the phone down.

thirteen

News leaks could occur due to a simple mistake on the part of someone connected with the deal, or because of the deliberate actions of someone who stood to gain financially or strategically from a public circus. This last group could include competitors, disgruntled employees, senior management, or even board members of the merging companies—basically anyone who wanted to influence the outcome of the deal.

While Amanda was certainly curious about the motive behind this leak, she was more concerned right now with putting her piece for tomorrow's edition together. Given the tight timeframe in which the story had to be written and finalized, she knew that she would have to hustle.

The first order of the moment was to confirm what she had just heard from her "source." The *Times* did not dabble in "speculation"; which meant that Amanda had to find a credible source to corroborate her information. The more detailed the story, the more sources her editor would demand.

The business desk was one complete floor of the *Times'* building, and Amanda occupied one of the hundred or so cubicles on the floor. Settling herself down behind her tiny desk, she pushed away the reams of research reports and magazine articles that covered its surface, and piled them into a corner.

Having organized herself, she pulled out her notes from the call and read through them again. While the woman on the phone had certainly been forthcoming, there were still plenty of blanks that needed to be filled in. Only after some intensive research would she have enough material to write a piece.

After handing out some of the grunt work to an eager intern, she turned her attention to the more difficult task of finding a corroborating source.

The big problem with finding someone to talk about a leak was that the confidant could potentially leak it to someone else, which would ruin the exclusivity of the story. The only way around it was for Amanda to call someone that she knew personally and whom she could trust to keep her confidence.

She picked up the phone and dialed the number of a friend who was a satellite analyst at Merrill Lynch.

When Josh Porter came on the line, Amanda told him very briefly about her situation, and asked if he would mind asking his buddies in the industry if they had heard anything about a possible acquisition of a satellite company, or even if any of them were rumored to be on the selling block. She didn't mention TriNet or Luxor, Josh was tactful enough not to ask.

He promised to do his best and get back to her within the hour.

Now that TriNet's board had approved the bid for Luxor Satellite, the team at MW was busy drafting the bid letter. The letter, which would be the official document used to make the bid for the satellite company, would have to be ratified by the legal team and then delivered to Craig Michaels, the CEO of Luxor. Once the letter was received, Luxor's board would meet to discuss the bid and vote on it.

While the bid letter was being drafted, the law firm of Rohm, Forrester & Carruthers (RF&C) was busy finalizing the legal agreement that would be forwarded, along with the letter, to Luxor's management. As part of the due diligence process, the team at RF&C had received various liens and other asset-related documents from Luxor. These had been pored over in detail to determine the status and condition of the assets owned by the target company.

Caroline Brown was going through one such document. She was one of the partners at RF&C who was representing TriNet in its proposed merger with Luxor. Dennis Cunningham and Richard Forrester were the other partners on the team.

Sitting in her spartan office in Rockefeller Plaza, the fifty-five-year-old woman frowned as she read through the highlighted sections. After cross-checking some details against other documents on her desk, she called in her associate, a plain looking young man with short cropped nut-brown hair.

"James, could you make a copy of this and give it to Dennis and Rich?"

The associate nodded with the glass-eyed look of someone who has gone too many nights without sleep, took the document, and walked out of the office. A few minutes later, he popped his head in and confirmed that he had done as he was told. Caroline smiled her thanks and James retreated, closing the door after him.

Picking up the phone, she called the other two partners to discuss the document they now had in front of them. After discussing it for ten minutes, they agreed that Caroline's concern was valid and that she should call someone at TriNet about it. She thanked them for their input and returned to her reading.

Caroline Brown, a short, kindly woman with a matronly air about her, was well-liked by her peers and the staff at RF&C. After getting a degree from a generic law school, she had spent most of her career at two firms, RF&C being one of them. The first law firm had been second-tier due to her lack of a degree from a prestigious institution, but she had worked hard and risen fast at a time when women were still given short shrift in Corporate America. Despite her humble disposition, Caroline was a shrewd "player" in corporate politics, and in many instances had managed to outsmart and outmaneuver her testosterone-filled male colleagues through her understated personality and non-confrontational attitude. In a world and time where women usually had to sleep or sue their way to the top, Caroline Brown had done it the right way.

Fifteen minutes later, she placed a call to the general counsel of TriNet Communications. The general counsel was the internal lawyer for the company, and in this case was also a woman. Caroline was always proud of other successful women in her field, since she knew how hard it was for them to succeed in the male-dominated arena of corporate law.

After exchanging brief pleasantries with Helen Mosbacher, Caroline voiced her concern. Helen asked if Caroline could fax her the relevant pages.

A few minutes later Helen had the fax in front of her and read through the marked sections quickly. Caroline waited patiently on the other end of the line.

"I see your point, Caroline, but we've gone over this internally and don't think there's a real risk."

"Maybe, but I would feel a lot better if we had more supporting documentation, or at least different language," insisted Caroline, taking off her reading glasses and putting them on the desk.

Her eyes were weary from all the reading over the past few days. Ruefully she noted that her age was beginning to show.

"Fine. Let me speak with Vik and get back to you," promised Helen.

She called back half an hour later.

"You'll have a new set of documents by this evening. Oh, and you should, of course, get rid of the *old* documents to avoid any confusion," Helen said quietly.

Caroline didn't need to be reminded, since most law firms made it a practice to shred any unnecessary documents. This wasn't really done to avoid confusion, but to avoid having to produce them in lawsuits. Even a straight-shooter like Caroline couldn't argue with this policy.

She assured Helen that the documents would be disposed of "appropriately."

Josh called Amanda back forty minutes later. He was apologetic.

"I'm afraid there was nothing on the grapevine. I asked some friends in the satellite business and analysts at other firms, but no one seems to have heard anything, not even rumors. I'm sorry, Amanda—I know that isn't what you wanted to hear."

"That's all right, Josh. Thanks a lot anyway."

As she put down the receiver, she bit her lip pensively. Josh was one of her best sources for this kind of information. If he couldn't find anything, it wasn't a good sign. She flipped through a mental Rolodex of contacts to determine who else might be able to help her. As a journalist with the *Times* she knew a lot of influential people, but they would be curious and quiz her in detail before doing anything. She couldn't risk giving up her competitive advantage.

While waiting for Josh to call back, Amanda had had time to digest the implications this story had on her career. To be able to break a major story like this in a prestigious newspaper would be a real coup for her; with the appropriate follow-ups and analysis pieces, she could turn this into a major asset. She was determined to find a source.

Just then the young intern showed up with the research that Amanda had requested. He had pulled a fair amount of information and done a good job organizing it. Everything was tabbed and highlighted so that Amanda could jump to the relevant sections without wading through pages of public documents, articles, research, and database reports. She thanked him for the work and complimented him on his thoroughness. He'll make a good journalist someday, thought Amanda. He left her alone and went off eagerly to his next assignment.

Putting aside the research, Amanda picked up the phone and made two more calls, one to a senior investment banker whom she had interviewed a few months back, and the other to her broker at Salomon Smith Barney. This time she cooked up a story about doing an article on the cable and satellite industries.

While waiting for them to call back, she sifted through the research that the intern had compiled for her. In less than an hour, she had drafted an outline for the Luxor story, striking a balance between the current merger and historical perspective.

When the calls came, the news wasn't good. Although her contacts provided her with plenty of information about other deals, there was no mention of TriNet or Luxor. If there was something going on, mused Amanda, the lid was on tight. Either that or her anonymous source had lied . . .

Sighing, she stood up to go downstairs. It was time to do some serious thinking, and smoke a cigarette.

James picked up the documents to be shredded from Caroline's office, and walked them over to his desk. Securing the pages with a rubber band, he placed them on the floor among other piles of paper. He would shred them later.

If he hadn't been as tired and sleep-deprived as he was, he would probably have remembered to do just that. However, his eyes were burning and his body felt like it would fall apart from sheer exhaustion. Additionally, he had to read through a 400-page legal document with red ink all over it, and compare it to a revised draft—page by page.

After what seemed like an eternity, he shut the original, satisfied that all the changes had been made, and threw it down on the floor. The document landed on top of Caroline's pile.

Due to his immense workload, and because the documents were now hidden from view, James would forget to shred them. Eventually his secretary would file them away in the miscellaneous drawer.

Amanda had an idea, and waited impatiently outside the editor's office for an audience.

Ten minutes later, the silver-haired man summoned the young woman into his room. After relaying the events of the past few hours and in particular her attempts to confirm the Luxor story, she presented the elderly editor with her plan. He listened attentively and nodded his head. It was a risk, but under the circumstances, the most logical choice. Making calculated gambles was part and parcel of being a journalist.

Returning to her desk, Amanda dialed the number for TriNet Communications. When the receptionist answered, she asked for the CFO's office. A minute later, Mark Pearson's secretary came on the line.

"Mark Pearson's office. Can I help you?"

"Yes, this is Amanda Fleming from the business section of *The New York Times*. I'm researching a story on a possible acquisition by your company, and I was wondering if I could speak to Mr. Pearson regarding the same," said Amanda, putting on her most professional but innocent voice.

There was a brief silence at the other end of the line and then: "Please hold."

As the background music kicked in, Amanda felt anxious. She wondered if she should have been so direct. *Would the CFO refuse to take her call?*

She was counting on the shock value of her overture to get her a statement from the company. A more tactful approach would have been safer but most likely would have yielded nothing more than a polite "no comment."

A few minutes later, she hit pay dirt. A professional-sounding voice came on the line.

"Hello, this is Mark Pearson, Ms. Fleming. How can I help you?" His tone was cordial and cooperative, but guarded.

"Thanks for taking my call, Mr. Pearson. We have reason to believe that TriNet may be planning an acquisition. I thought you might like to comment on it." Amanda didn't mention the fact that this was her last resort and without a statement from the company, her editor wouldn't publish the story.

There was a brief pause as Mark digested the journalist's request. He could have simply said no comment and slammed the phone down, but that would have aroused suspicion. The best course was to play along and see where this led.

"What exactly are you referring to, Ms. Fleming?"

"The Luxor deal. Would you like to tell me about it?"

"Why don't you give me some more details first?" said Mark smoothly, trying to bait the journalist.

But Amanda had played this game before and was equally adept at it.

"Mr. Pearson, I would like to stress that this is merely a courtesy call. We already have the details we need for our story, but would prefer to involve TriNet for reasons of professionalism. Either way, the article *will* run with or without you."

Mark pursed his lips in anger, and then quickly calmed down. He knew from years of dealing with the press that if the *Times* did have what they needed, they would happily print it without an official quote from the company. But he also knew that an official quote gave the story a much stronger backbone.

Given the tight lid on the proposed merger, there must have been a leak from someone on the deal team. He hadn't heard any rumblings from his friends in the analyst community and there were no rumors floating around in the financial newsletters. If the *Times* had the story, then there was a high probability that they had gotten it from an inside source—and probably had enough details to run an exposé.

"When are you planning to print this?" he asked curtly.

"Right away, actually; online," lied Amanda.

"Give me your number and let me call you back," snapped Mark, sounding flustered.

Getting off the phone with Amanda, Mark walked over to Vikram Suri's office. The CEO was in a meeting, but Mark asked that he be interrupted. When Vik came out to meet him, Mark gave it to him straight. "We have a leak. I just received a call from *The New York Times* regarding Luxor. It could be a problem."

Vik thought it over calmly.

"Even if it's just a blurb in the news, once it's out we'll need to do a press release to comply with the SEC's disclosure rules," he said finally.

"Precisely. I'm not thrilled about it, but if this *is* going to come out, we might as well make sure it's our version," suggested Mark.

"Fine. Do a release through the *Times* if they are willing. If so, give them an exclusive, but *not* for immediate release; for tomorrow morning's print edition. Get Lucinda Brightman to coordinate with the reporter on a draft."

"Why not release it today?" asked Mark, puzzled.

"First of all, I want time to inform the board personally so they don't get caught by surprise. More importantly, the market is closed for the day. We don't want to give people a full extra night to think about this.

After it comes out, the market analysts will take at least half a day to digest the deal and start speculating about it publicly. That buys us some time. The bid letter goes out tomorrow and I don't want to have to revise it because our stock seesaws on the announcement."

"But the Luxor board will still take days to vote on the deal, Vik," Mark pointed out.

"Sure, but the Fed is expected to cut interest rates next Monday, which should divert the attention of the market for at least a couple of days. By the middle of next week, the arbitrageurs will have made their money and gone home, most people will have forgotten about us—and our stock will normalize."

"And if it doesn't?"

Vik shrugged. "The Fed's action will make it difficult to determine if our stock price is inflated due to the interest-rate cut or the Luxor announcement. Since our bid expires at noon next Thursday, there won't be much time for Luxor's board to debate the issue."

Mark was impressed. What had seemed like a crisis a few short moments ago was now no more than an inconvenience—thanks to Vikram Suri's unerring ability to cope with contingencies.

What Mark did not know, as he headed back to his office, was that his icon had in fact precipitated this contingency, and far from being surprised by it, was counting on it.

When the CFO of TriNet informed Amanda Fleming that there would be "no further discussion" unless certain terms were agreed upon, most notably that the story wouldn't be run until tomorrow's print edition, the *Times* reporter was elated. Without revealing that the story wasn't scheduled to run until tomorrow anyway, she "agreed" to it in exchange for an exclusive, including background, quotes, and deal numbers.

Amanda spent the next few hours on the phone with Mark Pearson and Lucinda Brightman, the communications director of TriNet, drafting and polishing a full-page story on TriNet's proposed bid for Luxor. She was amazed at how much more information and insight they were able to provide compared with the public research that she had lying on her desk. Predictably, an article written with an inside source had a distinct, richer flavor. For the young journalist, it was the flavor of success.

By the time she was done, it was 8:30 P.M., Day 8.

———————— fourteen

Tom Carter was seated at a long conference room table, across from the CEO of Trademedia Publishers. The short, stout man was chewing on a half-smoked cigar, scowling menacingly at the team of investment bankers facing him. A managing director from Morgenthal Winters went through a fifty-page "pitch book," highlighting and expanding on various strategic opportunities that the bank had identified for Trademedia.

The magazine and trade book publisher had not retained MW to come up with any ideas, but the bankers had prepared the presentation in the hope that the company would be impressed by their work and hire them for a future transaction. This was standard industry practice and investment bankers spent a substantial portion of their time making such pitches as an essential form of "face-time."

In the middle of preparing the board presentation for Project Line, Tom had eked out enough time to compile the fifty pages now in front of him. Behind each potential acquisition target or divestiture opportunity, there was a page of "quick and dirty" financial analysis, detailing the potential impact on Trademedia's income statement and cash flows.

Tom knew that the CEO of Trademedia could chew as many expensive cigars as he wanted and glare as hard as his eyes would permit at the bankers, but after the team from MW left, the management of Trademedia would pore over the pitch book in detail and examine the bank's recommendations carefully.

By the time the meeting wrapped, the CEO had warmed to the bankers and shook their hands vigorously as they walked out the door, promising to be in touch soon. Tom felt good. In the end, the relationship with the CEO, and not necessarily the ideas, would determine whether MW would be hired.

When Tom stepped into his office, he realized that he had forgotten his morning newspaper. He had woken up late and rushed out to hail a cab, neglecting to bring *The New York Times* with him. Walking downstairs to the newsstand in the lobby of the building, he picked up a copy. As he rode up in the elevator, he pulled out the business section, as was his habit.

His mouth fell open in surprise.

The circus began at about 10:30 A.M. on Tuesday. Initially, the market didn't react to the *Times* announcement of TriNet's $7 billion bid for Luxor, being unsure of the implications of the deal. However, as the news began to sink in, the shares of TriNet started to move.

At first, the movement was desultory and sporadic, as some investors viewed the news as positive while others expressed their disapproval. It was a well-known fact that more than half of all mergers did *not* result in an increase of shareholder value, and an acquirer's stock almost invariably went down as a result.

However, as the news hit the major newswires and Internet news sites, an army of analysts and financial pundits began to evangelize about the suitability of the merger, validity of the purchase price, and the odds of the bid's success. Gradually, the price of TriNet's shares began to inch upwards.

At first blush, the merger seemed like a great idea. The sex appeal of adding satellite to TriNet's cable holdings was apparent and easy for investors to grasp. Moreover, most analysts considered the assets of Luxor undervalued at $7 billion, which made the deal all the more attractive to the market.

As more buyers rushed into the market, afraid to miss out on the opportunity to buy the stock, a frenzy ensued, causing the price to spiral upwards at a breakneck pace. At the same time, short sellers rushed into the market, betting that the stock price of TriNet had nowhere to go but down at these unrealistic levels, and selling shares that they didn't own at inflated prices. Later, when the price went down, they would buy enough shares to fulfill these sales, and make a profit on the spread.

By market close, the shares of TriNet were up almost 20 percent from their opening price—a fifty-two-week high—and there would be even more activity in after-hours trading.

The New York Times article appeared on the front page of the business section and covered most of the page. It detailed the proposed transaction, its time frame, and the parties involved. Official quotes from the senior management at TriNet confirmed the information in the article and provided meaningful insight into the potential synergies between the companies as well as post-merger strategic plans. It was a full-blown exposé and a major coup in business journalism for the *Times*. The newspaper promised a series of follow-up pieces, including a special pull-out section on the satellite industry, in the next few weeks.

Tom whistled slowly as he put down the paper. This changed everything. Even though the bid letter was ready to go out at the end of the day, he wondered if TriNet would delay it to evaluate the impact of the news leak.

His question was answered an hour later when Steve summoned him to his office. He motioned the vice president to a chair and filled him in briefly.

"Is it worth asking where the leak came from?" queried Tom.

Steve shrugged. He looked stressed. "You know how these things work, Tom. . . . It could have been practically anyone and it's nearly impossible to trace these things. Either way, Vikram Suri was furious!"

Tom nodded sympathetically.

Steve folded his hands in front of him and placed them slowly on the table. Some of the color seemed to return to his face. "The good news is that the bid letter is going out as planned. Vik believes that all this will die down by next week when the Luxor board is supposed to vote on the deal. The terms will remain the same."

"Despite the run-up in the stock price?" Tom asked skeptically.

"Artificial. It will even out. The folks at TriNet figure the Fed interest rate cuts will take most of the blame in the short term."

"How did Luxor react to the announcement?"

"That's why Vik was angry. He called Craig Michaels to discuss the article and got an earful about *our* sloppiness in maintaining confidentiality. Craig was probably just trying to jockey himself into a stronger bargaining position, but we were the bait. . . . In the end, the two doyens of industry kissed and made up," said Steve, sighing.

Tom laughed shortly. He could only imagine what the exchange between Vikram Suri and Craig Michaels must have been like. As two of the hardest-nosed men in American business, they must have been like two Roman gladiators, circling each other with swords drawn, looking for an opening to lunge at each other. After realizing there was no way to win, they must have thrown down their swords and opted instead for the brotherhood of killers.

"It's a dirty job, but I guess someone's got to do it, right?" continued Steve, giving his vice president a thin smile.

Tom concurred. Sometimes, he reflected, being an investment banker was a bit like being a punching bag.

Steve was justifiably nervous about the incident. It wasn't the stock price fiasco that bothered him—that would go away. The thing that worried him was the reverse engineering that he had done to meet Vik's demands. To justify TriNet's preferred bid, Steve's team had had to stretch the truth. As long as no one found out, the managing director couldn't care less.

But what if the source of the leak also knew about the banker's little secret? Would there be any reason for him or her to reveal that?

Of course, Steve had been careful to cover his tracks. He had made sure that any exchanges between him and his team were over the phone or in person. There was nothing in writing, nothing to intimate that Steve Brandt knew anything about the reverse engineering.

At worst, he could play the patsy and claim that his vice president had not apprised him of all the details. After all, if you couldn't trust your vice president, who could you trust?

Tom Carter, on the other hand, had sent emails and memos. Several of them. Some of them were to his managing director, updating him.

Steve had saved every last one of them.

The bid letter went out as planned, and the Project Line deal team kept its fingers crossed as TriNet's stock price continued to fluctuate.

Situations like this were an arbitrageur's dream, and plenty of activity ensued in the stock, including large "block" trades by brokers at the behest of institutional clients. More than seven million shares of TriNet were being traded per day, about three times its regular volume.

Nevertheless, having surged, dipped, and surged again, the stock no longer had a clear direction; it was anyone's guess where it would go next.

fifteen

Lunch arrived expeditiously, which was just as well, since both Tom Carter and Larry Milton were famished.

Larry was a buy-side equity analyst for a major institutional investor and had attended business school with Tom. Even though Larry had since married and his wife was expecting, his friendship with Tom hadn't waned a bit since school, and the two often confided in each other about their problems, hopes, and plans.

It was Monday afternoon, and one of those rare days when Tom could get away from the office during work hours. Accordingly, they had met for a quick game of squash at the New York Athletic Club, and then headed over to Fresco's for lunch.

As soon as the waiter had served the food and left, they began eating.

"Do you think the Luxor bid will be accepted?" asked Larry between mouthfuls of salmon.

Tom nodded, but didn't say anything more. It was understood that he couldn't discuss MW's clients or deals with Larry, and any inadvertent slips would stay between them. Investment bankers were prohibited from talking about their deals with anyone until closing, particularly buy-side analysts who worked for large institutional investors, since their buying and selling actions could affect the market for a stock.

"I'm sorry, Tom. I know you can't talk about your deals, but I have to tell you this one's got me curious. Seven billion for a company that's worth at least fifteen? I don't get it," continued Larry, ignoring his friend's glare.

Tom remained taciturn.

"The word on the street is there's something very strange about this deal," Larry pressed on, hoping to elicit a response from the investment banker.

Tom put down his fork resignedly. "What do you want me to say? Everything *I* have seen so far is on the up and up." He laid particular emphasis on the word "I." It didn't go unnoticed.

Larry looked him in the eye. "My gut tells me there's something rotten in Denmark."

"You should try reading his other plays too. Maybe you'll find new clichés," answered Tom dryly.

"You should watch your back," cautioned Larry, unfazed at his friend's sarcasm.

"I appreciate that, but you can relax. I'm comfortable with the numbers, and if there's something else, it's not my job as an investment banker to worry about it. You know the drill: we do the numbers and our client makes the decisions."

"Sounds cozy," observed Larry cynically.

"And what the hell is *that* supposed to mean?" countered Tom hotly.

Larry sighed. "I'm just being a friend, so quit biting my head off. I've met a lot of people who don't even realize when they've crossed the line, and it's usually because of something someone else did. Just be careful."

Tom nodded absently, and the two men resumed eating.

Larry changed the subject. "How's the filet mignon?"

"Good," murmured Tom, finding himself thinking about what Larry had just said. "How's the salmon?"

Fishy, mused Larry to himself, *just like the Luxor deal.*

The board of directors of Luxor Satellite met on Tuesday morning. The deadline for the bid was Thursday at noon, but Craig Michaels and the other board members had discussed it informally over the weekend and the decision had already been made. The purpose of the meeting was to ratify that decision.

Craig made a brief presentation to the members, with a secretary taking the minutes of the meeting, and then opened the floor to questions. A couple of directors asked for clarification on some points and Craig dispatched the queries rapidly and efficiently. A few minutes later, the board voted on the merger with TriNet Communications.

The bid was rejected unanimously.

It was 11:00 A.M., Day 16.

sixteen

Since Amanda Fleming did not have an exclusive arrangement with the management of Luxor Satellite, the news was announced through a traditional press release to multiple media outlets. First, the newswires picked it up, followed shortly by the online news sites, and eventually by radio and television. The papers that had late city editions were next. *The New York Times'* story didn't appear till the next morning.

Unlike the news leak on the proposed merger a week before, this latest announcement impacted the markets immediately and more dramatically. TriNet's stock plummeted as sellers flooded the market on the bad news. The Luxor board's rejection of a bid that had been perceived as overwhelmingly positive by the market was a blow to the stock of the spurned suitor.

Fueling this fire were the short sellers who in the days before had sold TriNet stock that they didn't have, on the gamble that the price of the stock would go down. These fine men and women now greedily snapped up the shares being sold at increasingly lower prices in order to fulfill their commitments. These "long" shares in turn were put up for sale by their new owners who wanted to stop their losses. Also buying were the bargain seekers and the bottom feeders.

The net result of all this was that buyers and sellers supported each other, pushing the price downwards at a rapid clip.

Eventually, the panic selling in TriNet began to infect other blue chip stocks as well. Even though the bad news was endemic to TriNet, that didn't stop investors from projecting their pessimism onto other media stocks, which was the equivalent of innocent bystanders getting shot during a gang war.

By 2:00 P.M., the Dow had plunged 6.5 percent, and by 3:00 P.M., it had declined by 8 percent from its open. Nonetheless, it was still within the limits prescribed by the SEC and trading continued unabated. Had the Dow dropped by 10 percent before 2:30 P.M. that day or by more than 20 percent at any time, it would have triggered a shutdown on the New York Stock Exchange (NYSE) and necessitated an announcement by TriNet to "clear the air"—in the general interests of the market.

At 4:00 P.M., the NYSE rang its closing bell. Ten minutes later, Amanda, who was on the phone with an institutional analyst trying to get a newsworthy quote for tomorrow's story, punched in the ticker symbol for TriNet Communications on *CBS MarketWatch*. The screen took a couple of seconds to refresh and then the data appeared. TriNet's stock had closed down 24 percent—slightly below its price level before the news leak a week ago.

At the same time that Amanda was scrambling to submit her piece for Wednesday's business section, Vikram Suri was on the phone with George Lomax, the influential TriNet director, discussing the implications of the day's events.

"So what happens now, Vik?"

"We up the bid to ten billion and finance the remaining debt with an ESOP."

"I don't know if the board will approve an ESOP. When you first brought it up it seemed like a good idea, but the dilution from an ESOP would be substantial on such a large chunk of debt," argued George, sounding concerned.

"We can address that. The ESOP shares will be issued gradually, so the actual dilution will be limited—particularly if we repurchase shares along the way. The ESOP has tax advantages and allows us to benefit our employees at the same time," responded Vik coolly.

He didn't mention to George that, in addition to the sum required for the merger, the ESOP loan would also include a smaller amount for the repurchase of shares from Vik's personal holdings. Even though it was perfectly normal for TriNet to buy back the CEO's shares via an ESOP, it was less normal for such a repurchase to "piggyback" on a merger. But there was no reason for the board to know that at this stage.

"Let me think about it," said George. "Did you know we closed down lower than before the initial announcement of the bid?"

"Yes. But that was only to be expected. Speculators always drive up the shares to ridiculous levels, and then any bad news hits the stock that much harder."

"Sure, but the market is up almost five hundred basis points from the Fed interest-rate cut, so logically our stock shouldn't be down by *that* much," objected George.

"I agree; but you and I both know this is only temporary . . . and a successful merger with Luxor can only help us," Vik reasoned.

"But that's nearly twelve billion in value we lost today, Vik! I think that making such a low bid was a mistake, and what makes it worse is that I went along with it!" countered George, his tone getting heated.

Vik tried to soothe the older man.

"I'm not arguing with you, George. I'm simply trying to manage this process so we come out ahead. I realize the seven billion bid was a gamble and we lost, but in the overall picture, it was a risk we had to take. It's our duty to our shareholders to ensure that we pay the lowest possible price for Luxor."

"Which is?" asked George, perplexed.

"Ten billion."

"How do we know that?"

"Because I had an informal chat with Craig Michaels and that's what he told me," replied Vik, only half-lying.

"Why didn't you have that discussion with him before making the bid?" demanded George.

"I did, but he was more ambivalent about the number then. These guys know how to play high-stakes poker too. They wanted to see what our floor was before upping the ante. For all *they* knew, we could have bid fifteen billion," Vik pointed out.

George considered this for a moment, and realized that the CEO was right.

"Fine, assuming that we did do the right thing with the bid and that it makes sense to raise it to ten billion, what guarantee do we have that they won't reject our bid again, or start courting other suitors?" he asked.

"We don't. But I intend to get the new bid ready by tomorrow afternoon, convene our board by the day after and get this in Craig's hands by Friday. This time I'll give him till Monday evening to decide. It's not enough time for some other bidder to get serious, and if Luxor really wants to sell, they'll be hard-pressed to walk away from ten billion.

"Besides, the only companies that can afford to make a higher offer are the other satellite operators who can enjoy cost savings through economies of scale, but our market intelligence shows that none of those players are likely to be buyers at this time."

"And if they accept the offer and *then* go back to the dance?"

Vik laughed. "At a five-hundred million termination fee, they can go home with anyone they want. I'll be happy walking away with an easy half-billion dollars."

George finally conceded. "I'll try to speak with the other board members before our meeting."

"And the ESOP?" asked Vik delicately.

"Is that your recommendation?"

"Absolutely," answered Vik confidently.

George sighed, but not unpleasantly. He was impressed. He had been systematically worn down by the aggressive CEO, and that didn't happen too often to George Lomax.

"All right, Vik. You win."

After getting off the phone with George Lomax, Vikram Suri dialed an unlisted number in Maryland. A phone rang in the private den of a very powerful man—the same one Vik had cut a deal with prior to the merger. The distinguished American, who was playing with his three-year-old grandson when the call came in, handed the child to his wife and went into his den, closing the door behind him.

Without bothering with any preliminaries, Vik related the gist of his conversation with George Lomax.

"Will he stick to his word?" asked the American gruffly. He didn't like being disturbed at home with business, particularly when he was spending time with his family. Also, he didn't trust anyone—least of all business people.

"Don't worry, he'll come through. I've known him for a long time, and he's a straight-shooter," Vik assured him.

"And we know how this will turn out?"

"Bet on it."

"I'm not a betting man," rasped the American. "*Don't* screw this up. . . . I agreed to come along for the ride as long as everything is fine. But *one* thing goes wrong and I'll bail out faster than you can blink, you got that?"

"Take it easy; nothing will go wrong. I'll make sure of it. Now go back to your family and I'll keep you updated," said Vik soothingly.

The Indian shook his head as he put the phone down. He hated giving updates to anyone, most of all *this* guy. At the same time, he needed someone to watch his back, and in that regard, the American was pure gold.

seventeen

On Wednesday afternoon, Tom Carter was busy preparing the board presentation for a $10 billion bid. TriNet's board was scheduled to meet the next day and the CEO had requested an updated book for the meeting.

Most of the changes were cosmetic, yet others involved extensive rewriting of key sections. All the while, he was careful not to contradict anything said in the earlier presentation; in the event of a shareholder lawsuit, the two presentations could be compared and the investment bankers on the deal would be questioned on any inconsistencies. It was perfectly acceptable for TriNet and MW to rethink their initial assumptions, but any suggestion that the original assumptions were wrong would be an invitation for trouble.

While Tom was busy preparing the board book, TriNet's stock continued to nosedive.

The primary driver for the downward movement of the stock was the speculation that another bidder would soon emerge for Luxor Satellite, raising the bar for TriNet if they decided to bid again. What had seemed like a steal at $7 billion now promised to become a horserace in the high teens and possibly in the low twenties of billions of dollars. Investors delivered their verdict on the situation by selling their holdings as rapidly as they could.

The only ones buying now were the arbitrageurs and the hedge funds, whose bread and butter lay in betting against the market.

One of the buyers was a broker in Tennessee. A young man, with a crop of curly red hair and a sunny disposition, he stared at his computer screen, paying special attention to the ticker for TriNet. When the stock reached his target price, he executed an order to buy 100,000 shares. He could have waited another hour and the price might have fallen even further, but his orders were clear. As a broker, his job was to follow his clients' instructions to the letter, not showboat on their behalf.

Some of these shares would be used to cover short sales from a week ago; yet others would be held longer. At the bargain basement prices that the shares were purchased, there was nowhere for them to go but up.

A few minutes later a slightly older broker in Chicago executed a similar order for similar reasons at a slightly different price.

Over the next twenty-four hours, similar trades would be executed by brokers in New York, Massachusetts, Maine, Washington D.C., Florida, Texas, New Mexico, Minnesota, Idaho, Ohio, Nebraska, Georgia, Maryland, Virginia, Louisiana, Arizona, Alaska, Hawaii, and California. All of this was the sort of activity commonly seen after a failed attempt at a merger.

In this case, however, it was anything but common. . . .

Exactly five hours later, the board presentations were ready, and a messenger was sent to deliver them to TriNet's offices. Vikram Suri took one copy with him to read at home and locked the rest in a filing cabinet in his office.

At 10:00 A.M. the next morning, the board would meet to vote on a revised offer for Luxor Satellite, and Vik would make the case for a $10 billion bid.

Julie, Steve Brandt's secretary, was sending out some letters that her boss had dictated earlier in the day. She could have left them for tomorrow, but there was always the risk that something was urgent. Steve could sometimes forget to indicate that and then there would be hell to pay. It was Julie's job to save him from his oversights.

One of the letters was a bill that she had to pay on his behalf, but he had not left her a check.

Stepping inside the managing director's office, Julie went over to his desk and used her personal key to unlock his private drawer. Inside were several papers and some personal effects. But no checkbook. Sighing, the dedicated secretary pulled out the stack of papers and laid it on the desk. She had been through this drill before. Rummaging through the pile, she soon found what she was looking for, ensconced between some letters and folders. The top check was signed, as Steve always left it for occasions such as this.

Julie tore off the signed check and replaced the book in the drawer. Lifting the stack of papers from the desk, she put those back as well. Without her realizing it, the folder at the bottom of the pile remained on the table.

Julie looked down at her watch. It was getting late and if she didn't hurry she would miss the next train to Bronxville out of Grand Central. The following train wouldn't be for another hour, and it was a pain to wait for it.

She locked the drawer and hurried back to her desk. The folder remained where it was.

Before leaving the office, Tom decided to drop off a copy of the board book on Steve's desk. He might come in early and would want to read it.

The managing director was gone for the day and his secretary had left minutes earlier. The security staff had yet to make their rounds of the building to lock empty offices, so Steve's door was open. Tom stepped inside.

He placed the presentation on his boss's desk and was about to walk back out when he spotted something. It was a folder, lying near the edge of the desk. Tom walked over and picked it up. He frowned as he read his name, scrawled in Steve's handwriting, on the cover.

Despite his misgivings about doing so, he opened it. Inside were all the memos that he had drafted for Steve on Project Line. Beneath the memos was a pile of emails, again sent by Tom and related to the merger. None of this was unusual, given that Steve was working on the deal. It was only natural for a managing director to keep copies of memos and emails to refresh his memory.

But what made Tom uncomfortable was his name on the cover of the folder. *Why his name? Why not the name of the deal?*

As he stood above Steve's desk, thinking about this, he was suddenly aware of a creeping sensation. Tom glanced around nervously. It felt like he was being watched. He had not bothered to turn on the overhead light and in the faint illumination from the hallway, the vice president imagined that he could see the shadows in the office *move.* They seemed to be joining hands and groping toward him, trying to box him in. It was as if in this room, in this darkness, the firm, the *real* Morgenthal Winters, was coming alive.

Dropping the folder back on Steve's desk, Tom walked hurriedly out of the office.

Shortly before the meeting in which the TriNet Communications board approved the $10 billion bid for Luxor Satellite, Steve Brandt delivered a revised fairness presentation to the fairness opinion committee at Morgenthal Winters.

This valuation too was found to be fair.

There were four messages on his desk when Tom stepped into his office on Friday afternoon. After hanging up his suit jacket, he reached for the phone, ignoring the message slips lying next to it. He dialed Steve's line.

Steve was out of the office, but Julie informed him that the bid letter had gone out this morning, along with an amended purchase agreement. She asked him if he wanted to reach the managing director on his cell. Tom hesitated. He wanted to ask Steve about the folder on his desk, but that would look incredibly stupid, not to mention insulting. What the hell was Tom doing snooping around his boss's desk, anyway?

Voting against his paranoia, Tom demurred.

There was nothing left to do now but wait till Monday, thought Tom, and turned his attention to the calls that he had received. There was a message from Lee Kang stating that the magazine publishing comps for Trademedia would be done over the weekend. Larry had called to find out if Tom was up for a game of golf on Sunday, and Tom's sister had called to inform him that she and her husband were going away to Cancún for a couple of weeks.

The last message was from an Amanda Fleming at *The New York Times.* Tom thought the name sounded familiar but couldn't place it immediately. Then he remembered—she was the reporter who had broken the story of the TriNet-Luxor merger a week and a half ago. She wanted to discuss "future bids" by TriNet and had left her number.

While it was commonplace for journalists to track down the investment bankers on a deal to get the inside scoop, most bankers avoided the temptation of being quoted on a pending merger. Even if nothing proprietary was revealed, it could be considered a violation of the client's confidentiality and wasn't worth the risk.

Tom balled up the message and threw it away.

He was about to call his sister back, then stopped. For some reason, he decided to call his father instead.

Harry Carter was probably in his garden, tending to the plants that were his only real company since Tom's mother had died in a car accident a year ago. Tom was convinced that his father had never really recovered from that incident and it had accelerated his aging process immeasurably. It was something that he tried to hide from his son, but the strain around his eyes and the rapidly thinning hair told a different story.

The phone rang five times but no one answered. Tom frowned. Harry usually carried the cordless phone around with him wherever he went. By Tom's request, he even carried it to the bathroom, just in case. *Where could he be?* Perhaps he was sleeping.

Tom put down the phone and consulted his watch. If he left now, he could be at his father's place in an hour. After his wife's death, Harry had insisted on moving out to a small house in Long Island. Even though he had made a good sum of money during his days in banking and invested wisely, he had lost most of his savings during the bursting of the stock market bubble in 2000. As much as the investors who had unwisely placed all their money into Internet stocks, the blue-chip investors had been burned by the overall downturn in the market, and Tom's father was no exception.

As a result, Harry had decided on downgrading his lifestyle to avoid burdening his son with the expenses. At first Tom had objected, being worried that he would be unable to respond to him quickly if there was ever an emergency, but eventually he had given in. Besides, having a garden had done the old man some good, giving him something to do with his time, and the quiet suburbs were good for his nerves.

Tom opted to take the company car. It was one of the perks of being a vice president that he could take a car on the company's expense anywhere during the day or night, as long as he didn't abuse the privilege too often, and didn't take the car to California. The driver, a Russian, greeted the banker courteously and drove off as instructed.

As the Lincoln Town Car headed towards Queens and Long Island, Tom settled back in his seat and tried to relax. The traffic was sparse, and with luck they would be at Harry's place in a little more than thirty minutes. He tried him again from his cell, but there was still no answer.

With time on his hands, Tom began to remember. The memory of it was as painful as when he had first realized it six months earlier. It had happened when he had paid his father an unexpected visit one Sunday afternoon. The old man had been sleeping when he had arrived, and the doorbell had woken him.

He had come out to greet his son in his pajamas, and Tom had seen the bloodstains instantly. They were small, but fresh and clustered around the middle of the nightshirt. Tom had asked his father where the blood had come from, but the aging patriarch had simply shrugged, genuinely confused by the question. It was then that Tom had noticed the deepening lines across the temples and the dark circles underneath the eyes.

The doctor had stated flatly that Harry Carter was dying. The stress of his wife's untimely death had hit the erstwhile banker quite hard, and some part of him had simply decided to stop living. Even though he took great pride in his children, and especially in Tom, his primary *raison d'être* seemed to have vanished, gone up in a plume of smoke from a fiery car wreck. Physically, he wasn't so much ailing as falling apart, and it was only a matter of time, the doctor had informed Tom sadly, that his body would no longer be able to sustain the strain of having to go on without the cooperation of the will.

Tom had been devastated at the news. Since he could remember, his father had been a pillar of strength and survival whom he had sought to emulate. To the young man, Harry was forever. In truth, Tom knew that his father was aging and that some day he would have to say goodbye to the man who had given him life, love, and everything in between. But the speed of Harry's decline had frightened him.

As the car pulled into the driveway of the house, Tom stiffened. His heart was beating quickly now, and a deep sense of unease had gripped his mind. He would have been in a daze if not for the alertness brought on by extreme nervousness. Something had made him pick up the phone and call his father that afternoon. Coincidence? Paranoia? Intuition?

Reaching for the handle of the screen door, Tom pulled it open. Tremulously, he pushed the doorbell. He could hear the musical sound of the bell echoing inside the house. No one answered. He waited for a few seconds and then pushed the button again.

Trying to contain his panic, he pulled out the spare key that he always carried, and pushed it into the lock. It turned smoothly.

He entered the house silently. Standing in the middle of the foyer, he looked around. The house was small, but neat and uncluttered, the way Harry liked it. There was no sound from anywhere. Tom yelled out, but there was no response.

He decided to check upstairs. He sprinted up the brief stairway and towards the master bedroom.

The door was ajar.

In that moment, he realized just how much his father meant to him.

eighteen

On Monday morning, Vikram Suri woke up early. He had stayed the night before in his Murray Hill pied-à-terre, and was flying out to a meeting in Boston at 10:00 A.M. The apartment was large and airy, and double-glazed picture windows stared out over the city from a vantage point high above the surrounding buildings.

Vik was seated at an oblong dining table, sipping his coffee and reading the morning's edition of *The Wall Street Journal*. He paused to add some more milk and sugar to his coffee so that it was practically undrinkable, a habit common among Indians and stemming from their tea-drinking days under British colonialism. Some habits died hard.

At half past seven, the doorman rang up to inform him that the car driver was there. Putting on his suit jacket and picking up his attaché case, Vik walked out of the apartment, switching on his burglar alarm before he left. Downstairs, a black limousine was waiting in front of the building and the driver greeted him as he came out. Getting into the back, he pulled out the rolled-up *Journal* from his bag and resumed reading. The car proceeded to La Guardia Airport.

While one part of his mind was concentrating on his reading, the other portion was whirring away in preparation for the next few hours.

The meeting in Boston was with a major bank to discuss obtaining an ESOP-backed loan for his company—the one that would be used to finance a portion of the merger consideration for Luxor Satellite. Due to the favorable terms of such a loan, the banks always imposed stringent requirements to ensure that their money was safe. In a merger situation, there would inevitably be dozens of questions about the profitability of such a deal for TriNet Communications and the fairness of the valuation.

Vik would present them with the fairness opinion delivered by Morgenthal Winters and copies of the financial model to address these concerns. In addition, Mark Pearson, the CFO of TriNet, had prepared a summary of the credit ratios both before and after the deal, highlighting TriNet's considerable capacity for debt, due to its reasonably clean balance sheet, and the leveragable capacity of Luxor's profits.

However, the real problem wasn't the present, but the future. Vik knew that if the bank in Boston agreed to the loan, it would almost certainly impose restrictions on future debt raises by TriNet. At the same time, the issuance of shares for the ESOP would make future equity issues prohibitively expensive. As long as cash flows remained positive, there would be no problem, but if the company ran into trouble in the near future, there would be nowhere to turn. Without the ability to raise cash through debt or equity, TriNet Communications could wind up in bankruptcy.

When the car arrived at the airport, Vik's private jet was fueled and waiting for him. He greeted the captain and crew and then made himself comfortable in the main cabin, which on Vik's personal wishes was part office, part luxury den. An attractive young hostess brought him a drink.

Although private jets rarely flew out of La Guardia—Teeterboro being a more common venue—Vik preferred the cachet of flying out of a major airport. Some part of him imagined that the common folk in their uncomfortable economy class seats were staring jealously at his sleek plane that, unlike the commercial carriers, was a haven of luxury. Of course, most economy class passengers were too busy cursing their seats and trying to stretch their legs to notice or care how he was traveling.

As the Gulfstream taxied for takeoff, the CEO of TriNet gazed through the tiny window of the plane with unseeing eyes. As far as he was concerned, the remote possibility of insolvency wasn't a good enough reason to abandon a merger that made so much sense. For this and other reasons, he was willing to overlook the dangers of taking on an ESOP-backed loan.

The hard part, of course, would be convincing the bankers in Boston to take the risk. But then that was what Vikram Suri was best at—making the impossible happen.

Like most people who have suffered the death of a loved one, Tom was struggling to find meaning in his father's death. But there was no meaning to be found, not within the philosophical walls of religion nor in the practical realm of science. It was not in the death, but the life of Harry Carter that the answer lay.

As he gazed at his father's picture on his desk, Tom realized with astonishment that as long as he had known him, Harry had *always* taken the high road, both in life and in his career. Even though he had enjoyed plenty of success on Wall Street, he always valued ethics over success, defeat over stolen victory. He had worked hard at his profession not just to make money, but because he believed in what he did, in the value that he could add to society and his family through his efforts.

In a moment of cynicism, Tom ruminated on how different the profession was becoming now. Harry's high ideals seemed nowhere to be found in the new crop of single-minded drones coming out of business schools who would be the bankers of tomorrow. *Was it a matter of generation? Would ethics become a relic of the past? What about his own beliefs and values? Did they compare to his father's or were they simply a cheap imitation?*

Tom wondered if he could ever be the man that his father was.

Later that day, the board of Luxor Satellite approved the merger with TriNet Communications.

The CEO of Luxor, Craig Michaels, picked up the phone and called his counterpart at TriNet to inform him of the decision.

Vikram Suri was in a meeting with a bank in Boston when his secretary patched the call through to his cell phone. Excusing himself, he stepped out into the hallway to receive it. He came back into the conference room a minute later with a triumphant look on his face.

A few hours later, the two companies issued a joint press release stating that they had signed a definitive agreement to merge, and that the deal would now go into regulatory review by the Federal Trade Commission and the Department of Justice as per pre-merger notification requirements of the Hart-Scott-Rodino Antitrust Improvements Act of 1976.

It was 7:30 P.M., Day 22.

part 3
the investigation

nineteen

Suzie Goldwater was new to the SEC. After graduating from Vassar, the twenty-year old had worked for a year at an advertising firm before cajoling her one and only daddy to land her this job. As with all such things, it was a nepotism-based position created solely to appease a big political contributor, and carried little in the way of responsibility.

Nonetheless, sexy Suzie, Vassar party girl and daddy's little angel, was thrilled at being able to walk the corridors of power at such a tender age. In her mind, it was only the first step to much bigger and greater things. She watched *Legally Blonde* dutifully every day . . .

Today was only her fourth day, but Suzie was eager to impress and wanted to do something that would showcase her initiative and considerable potential to her superiors. That was, after all, the way all famous people had reached the top.

Ever since the Enron and WorldCom scandals, the SEC had received a facelift, both for the public and in practice. The new mandate for the market watchdog was to make sure that abusers of the system were not only caught and penalized, but also nipped in the bud. In other words, the SEC had gone from being primarily an enforcement agency to a preventative body.

Accordingly, Suzie received a list on her desk of all major deals that had been announced publicly over the past month. A brief but unfortunately worded memo on top encouraged all employees to "keep a watchful eye" for any potential abuses related to these transactions. One of the mergers on the list was TriNet-Luxor.

The memo was a legal formality and all regular employees knew that it was not to be acted upon. The only actions that the SEC undertook were those authorized by senior officials.

Blissfully unaware of any such restriction and glowing with pride at her important role in the United States government, the naturally blond and adoringly stylized Suzie picked up her shiny new phone.

Tom Carter nearly dropped his coffee when he heard that the commission was calling.

Picking up the phone gingerly, he took a call from a Ms. Suzie Goldwater. In her most cultivated voice, the powerful Ms. Goldwater explained to the banker that the TriNet deal was on the SEC's watch list and would Morgenthal Winters like to share information with them that might save everyone a lot of trouble later?

Nervous at her accusatory tone, Tom did what any good banker does when confronted with an awkward question—he said he would call her back.

Steve Brandt was in his office when Tom walked in and informed him of the problem. Frowning, the managing director called the general counsel.

The general counsel in turn called Ms. Goldwater back to find out what the hell was going on. Upon being asked the exact same question that Tom had, he told her he would call her back.

Next, the general counsel at MW called the general counsel at TriNet, as per protocol. The general counsel at TriNet promised to take care of the matter and promptly referred it to Vikram Suri's office.

Half an hour later, Suzie was summoned to the office of the chairman. The Commission's head honcho wanted to see her. Fully expecting to be promoted to deputy chairman of the SEC by lunchtime, she walked confidently into her boss's office.

She came out five minutes later in tears. Things had not gone well for the earnest young blonde, and they had given her only fifteen minutes to clean out her desk. Apparently her daddy's pull did not extend *that* far.

As she packed her things, she thought about her next move. Obviously politics was not in the cards for the moment. *Then what?*

By the time Security had ensconced her safely outside the building, much to everyone's relief *in*side, Suzie had made up her mind. She would go to medical school. The thought of having people's lives in her hand warmed the cockles of her heart.

Having performed her small but vital function in the wheels of government, she was ready to move on.

Amanda Fleming rolled over in bed and hit the alarm clock on its head, groaning at being woken up at the ungodly hour of 8:00 A.M. The beeping of the clock ceased almost immediately, much to her relief. Sitting up groggily, she shut her eyes against the bright sunlight streaming into the room. She felt like she was floating, but it wasn't a pleasant sensation.

Then the headache hit her. Clasping her forehead, she lay back down, groaning again. She had been out drinking and dancing till 4:00 A.M. and was now paying the price for it. After a few minutes of lying very still inside the pink bed sheets, she decided to administer some medicine to her suffering.

Pushing herself up on her elbows, she reached over to the bedside table and groped around for what she fervently hoped would be where she had dropped it last night. It was, and heaving a sigh of relief, Amanda lit her cigarette. She knew that smoking first thing after waking up was the surefire sign of an inveterate smoker, but she didn't give a damn right now. Her head was pounding, her nasal passages felt congested, she needed more sleep, and she had to be at work at nine. Something that might give her lung cancer thirty years from now was the least of her problems.

Ordinarily, the young reporter was no lightweight when it came to partying, and seldom suffered from hangovers or sleep-deprivation. But the last few days had taken a toll on Amanda—she was getting increasingly bored and restless with her job. The cushy interviews at posh hotels, after-the-fact pieces on cloyingly friendly mergers, and a general lack of activity in the markets, had all contributed to her pulling her hair at the sheer sameness of it all.

Nor did it help that, since her big story two weeks ago, Amanda had been unable to get an interview with anyone at TriNet, Luxor, or with their investment bankers. It seemed that everyone connected with the deal was respecting some sort of gag order and she couldn't even get Mark Pearson on the line, who had been so forthcoming with information the first time.

Over the past few weeks, the *Times* journalist had learnt first-hand that you were only as good as your last story. While her breaking story on the TriNet-Luxor merger had attracted a lot of attention, and she had been toasted widely among her colleagues for scooping the newswires and Internet sites, the flames had gradually died down. It was painfully obvious that the intrepid Ms. Fleming had no other aces up her sleeve. Although the young reporter had combed her contacts for new information and even staked out TriNet's offices for a couple of days, she had discovered absolutely nothing.

The straw that broke the camel's back, however, was when the revised bid was accepted by Luxor Satellite. The fact that she hadn't known about the new offer in advance wasn't looked upon favorably by her editor, who reacted by handing her the assignment of opining on the future of pure dot-coms. Amanda had accepted the "filler" piece dejectedly, knowing that the most use anyone would get out of it was for wrapping fish at Fulton Street.

It seemed that her rising star had fallen even before it made it above the horizon.

Sighing, she lifted herself out of bed. Despite her troubles, she was certainly not going to solve them by remaining hidden in the sheets. The reporter showered, got dressed, picked up a cup of black coffee from the corner deli, and jumped into a cab. Leaning back in the rear of the car, she planned out her strategy for the rest of the day.

While she pretended to do her research on the dot.com story, she would once again try calling the bankers at Morgenthal Winters to get the scoop on post-merger preparations—which almost certainly were under way by now, and the status of the antitrust review.

So far, neither the managing director on the deal, Steve Brandt, or the vice president, Tom Carter, had called her back. A long time ago, she had interviewed Robert Darlington III, the ranking partner at MW, in connection with a deal that he had closed. He was very gracious then. This time around his secretary had politely intimated that he couldn't comment on a pending transaction, and declined to put her through.

The reporter even tried the old trick of calling them before 8:30 A.M. or after 6:00 P.M., when the secretaries had left for the day and bankers usually answered their own phones, but she either wound up speaking with temps or chatting with the voicemail. It seemed that the bankers had gotten smarter over the years.

It was ironic, mused Amanda, how her initial success had set her up to inevitably disappoint, and even more ironic that she had done absolutely nothing to unearth the original story and had simply filled in the blanks. She wished right now that she knew how to reach the woman who had leaked it to her.

As Tom Carter had predicted, the management of Trademedia Publishers had pored carefully over the bank's recommendations from the first meeting and called them back for a follow-up. The company was particularly impressed with the idea of acquiring its second biggest competitor in the trade book space—which was currently trading below market, thanks to the exciting personal lives of some executives.

Upon receiving the call-back from the CEO, Hal Reardon, Tom had assigned an associate the task of preparing a detailed analysis of a hypothetical merger between the two companies.

Since most of the foundation had been laid by Tom, and the CEO had called the vice president directly, the managing director had given Tom permission to lead the deal, offering his help if and when needed. It was a golden opportunity for Tom to prove his mettle to Robert Darlington, and so he attended the meeting alone.

"It seems like a no-brainer to me, Tom," drawled Hal in a thick Texan accent, chewing on his ever-present cigar.

Tom smiled. "I agree. The synergies are obvious; and with this acquisition, you can leapfrog your biggest competitor by a mile."

"Are you sure the multiples don't reflect something other than the CEO playin' around with lil' boys?" Hal asked with his inimitable subtlety.

"It's a public company, Hal, and we've done our homework. The company is doing better than ever, but the scandals have done a lot of damage to their credibility," explained the vice president.

Hal returned to the financial analysis that Tom had handed him at the start of the meeting. He didn't need to flip through the nearly ten pages of the model, since everything he was interested in was summarized on the top sheet. After a few minutes, he switched the cigar to the other side of his mouth and resumed chewing.

"Hmmm, interesting. You think we can use our stock for the deal?"

"Absolutely. Despite the recent performance of your stock, the fundamentals of your business are pretty strong. With this acquisition, your stock is bound to rise to levels more reflective of your *true* potential . . . ," Tom responded tactfully.

The CEO threw his head back and laughed. He pulled his cigar out of his mouth and surveyed the investment banker with amusement, as one would stare at a circus attraction. To him they were all circus attractions, but this one had potential.

"Well put, Tom. I'm sold. Let us do a final powwow internally and we'll let you know if we want to proceed. Thanks for coming."

The pudgy Texan rose to indicate that the meeting was over. The banker stood up as well and shook his hand heartily. This had turned out better than he had expected, and he guessed (correctly) that it was mainly because Hal Reardon had taken a liking to him.

It was early evening by the time the meeting ended, and Tom decided to head home. He had some work left at the office, but it could wait till tomorrow. Having led a successful meeting and potentially secured a client for the bank, he could afford to reward himself by calling it a day.

Upon entering his apartment, he took off his jacket and tie, poured himself a drink, and settled down in front of the television. He flipped through the channels, looking for signs of intelligent programming, found none, and switched off the set. Outside, the weather had turned from mild to cold, and storm clouds had moved in, hovering threateningly over Gotham. Predictably, the weathermen had failed to foresee the imminent thundershowers and most pedestrians would get soaked tonight for a lack of umbrellas.

Tom shut his eyes and tried to concentrate on relaxing. Most investment bankers had a hard time unwinding since they were so used to a frenetic schedule, and it took a lot of effort simply not to *make* any effort. Pulling up his feet onto the comfortable couch, Tom lay back and tried to forget the office, Trademedia, Project Line, everything.

For the most part he was successful.

At some point he must have dozed off, for he started awake at the sound of a thunderclap. He sat bolt upright, unsure of what had woken him. Then he saw the rain pelting against the window with flashes of lightning behind it, and relaxed. He slumped back into the couch, resting his head against the cushion. He brought his watch level with his eyes and stared at the dial.

It was two in the morning. He groaned.

Since his father's death, he hadn't slept very well, averaging less than five hours a night. The lack of sleep hadn't really affected his work, *yet*, but Tom knew that if he went on like this, it would eventually catch up with him. He had tried sleeping pills, but those gave him a headache the next morning, and he quickly discontinued them. Tom knew that the only true cure for his insomnia lay in his coming to terms with Harry's demise, but that was easier said than done.

The reality was that he felt guilty; guilty about what had happened, guilty about not having done more for his father when he was alive, guilty about not living up to his father's standards and expectations, guilty about disappointing him in both life and death, guilty about *letting him down.*

Of course, these emotions were natural for someone who was bereaved, and somewhere in the deeper recesses of his mind, Tom knew they were unfounded.

To pull himself back from his nightly abyss, Tom tried to think of something else. He went back over the meeting at Trademedia, his rapport with Hal Reardon, the—

Then he remembered.

He had been waiting for Hal in the conference room when he overheard someone on the Trademedia team remark to a colleague that it must have been a "cakewalk" for MW to advise TriNet on a sweetheart deal. For some reason, the words had swirled around in the banker's head since then.

Sweetheart deals were the dirty little secret of corporate America. Most deals involved some degree of incest, either in terms of interlocking investments, business contracts, board representations, or even personal relationships between senior officers. So it wasn't farfetched that TriNet had received favorable treatment from Luxor in the merger. Nor was it illegal.

Nevertheless, mused Tom, such deals were often unethical. In business school, he had taken a class in business ethics and the professor, a former deputy secretary of the treasury, had challenged the class to determine whether a deal was unethical if the decision makers were the primary beneficiaries of the transaction. The answer, of course, depended on whether there were other parties involved in the deal.

The issue ultimately was of fiduciary responsibility. In the case of a large public corporation like TriNet Communications, it was the legal obligation of the board of directors to ensure that any deal made by the company maximized the gain for *all* shareholders, not just the largest holders or senior management.

That was why investment banks were hired. By bringing in an outside party to scrutinize mergers, companies reduced their potential liability from shareholder lawsuits. In addition to helping their client negotiate the best possible deal, an investment bank would also take the responsibility of opining on its fairness. From a legal standpoint, this latter service provided corporations with a "Get out of Jail Free" card, enabling them to redirect shareholder wrath away from themselves and toward hired guns. For this privilege, corporate America paid Wall Street handsomely.

Having spent the brunt of its fury, the storm outside seemed to have abated. Tom rose and walked over to the living room windows. He pulled them open, letting in a cool breeze. The rain had cleansed the air and the city seemed brighter, clearer. His thoughts returned to the comment that he had overheard.

Ethics aside, the team at Morgenthal Winters had done nothing wrong. They had followed the instructions of the client, respected the wishes of the CEO, and analyzed the numbers as per standard banking practices. While Tom could recall that there had been some disagreement between Steve Brandt and Helen Mosbacher about the projections and valuation, that was simply par for the course in any merger. In the end, they had been able to justify the numbers to the fairness opinion committee and that's all that mattered.

But the call from Suzie Goldwater had rattled him.

Although the general counsel had assured him that it was a gaffe and nothing more, Tom felt uncomfortable. In the present climate, the SEC was becoming unusually belligerent about prosecuting companies—and their bankers—for decisions that only a few years ago were considered "business as usual." Tom knew that most such investigations led to nothing, but even the smallest hint of scandal could kill a deal before it made it to the dotted line. Not to mention ruin careers.

Of course, he had seen it all before. A mega-deal, press coverage, and conspiracy theories were the Marx Brothers of capitalism. Freak incidents like the Goldwater affair were part of the game and nothing to get alarmed about. Public paranoia, though powerful, didn't necessarily translate into criminal probes.

The problem was his own suspicions.

It was like a high-grade counterfeit bill.

On the surface everything seemed fine, but somewhere beneath it lay a seamy undercurrent that resonated with his innermost instincts. It was as if a crucial aspect of the deal was being hidden from view, something that went beyond the scope of deal structure, valuation, or market issues. *A skeleton in the closet, or a hidden agenda perhaps?* The truth was he didn't have the foggiest notion of what it could be, or even whether there really *was* anything at all.

He was still in his shirt and pants, and headed to the bathroom to get ready for bed, stripping off his clothes as he went. The warm water against his face soothed him, and he held his wet hands to his cheeks for a long moment, cherishing the heat.

His reflection in the mirror told him that he needed rest. His handsome face was drawn, his complexion pale. There were bags underneath his eyes and his lips felt parched and weightless. Tom Carter was astonished at the change that had come over him in such a short time. It was as if he had aged ten years since Harry's death. He needed to sleep.

He dried his face and went into the bedroom. As he slipped under the covers, his mind was still restless.

After tossing and turning for ten minutes, he finally gave up. *This is crazy*, he thought. *He was driving himself insane. Harry was dead and nothing would change that. If the feds came knocking again, nothing would change that either.*

The question was whether he himself had done anything wrong. Propping up against the headboard, the vice president went back over what his role had been on the deal so far. The initial valuation, the conference call with TriNet, the instructions from Steve to revise the numbers—all done by the book. Then why was he worried?

The folder he had found in Steve's office, the one with his name on top.

As the middleman on the deal team, Tom Carter had been responsible for executing all the changes required by the client. That meant memos and emails, both internal and external. The revelation came like a knife through the heart.

He had left a paper trail.

Was he being set up by his own boss?

Unlikely, reasoned Tom, since a scandal would hurt Steve as badly as himself. Besides, he had known the managing director for a long time and trusted him completely.

But Steve wasn't the firm.

The firm was an impersonal entity, devoid of loyalty or feelings of any kind. In public, they were a white-shoe investment bank. In private, they followed the law of the jungle. Unless you were an owner, the firm's interest in your personal welfare was nonexistent. You did your job and you collected your dues. That was it, that was all. If you got in the way, heaven help you. Tom now recalled his experience in Steve's office the night he had discovered the folder. He had felt the shadows, the office, the building itself moving in towards him, *trapping* him.

It was not as if Robert Darlington or the other partners were criminals, or that the vice president had any reason to suspect betrayal. It was only a matter of survival. Tom Carter was merely a functionary, a simple brick in the wall. *He* could not bring down the entire edifice, so *he* could be sacrificed. . . . In the event of a crisis, MW would have no choice but to throw him to the wolves. Tom's fear escalated.

What if Suzie's mistake sparked off a real investigation at the SEC? Who would they come looking for? Was he vulnerable? Had he broken the law?

The truth was, he might have.

The RICO statutes were pretty broad, and even unethical activities could be considered a breach of the law, especially when there were politicians willing to make a cause out of it. Corporate America was under fire to be sure, and investment bankers were a favorite scapegoat for Washington.

How would Harry have reacted to his son being taken away in handcuffs by the feds? What would happen to Tom's future if his face was plastered all over the newspapers as a criminal?

The old man would have been sick to his stomach and Tom would be finished.

Investment banking was a tightly knit industry and a person's reputation was his only real asset in the game. Once that was tarnished, nothing short of an act of God could turn back the clock.

Even if he dodged the bullet, Tom would be finished professionally, his hopes of a promotion shattered, his credibility among clients destroyed. If he went looking for another job on Wall Street, his black mark would follow him. If he looked outside of finance, his shredded reputation would still dog his heels. The bank would make sure of that.

For most people, it would have been scary. For Tom Carter, it was hell and damnation. Having been thwarted once in his ambitions, he wasn't sure that he could handle it a second time. The memory of his foiled sports career still haunted him, and he was acutely aware of his need to compensate for that disappointment.

He needed to find out just how counterfeit the bill really was.

twenty

In 1890, the United States Congress passed a law forbidding any contract, scheme, deal, or conspiracy to restrain trade. This law, which formed the basis of all American anti-monopoly laws, came to be known as the Sherman Antitrust Act.

Two decades later, the government established the Federal Trade Commission (FTC), which, together with the antitrust division of the Department of Justice (DoJ), is responsible for keeping American business competition "free and fair."

The FTC may undertake special investigations on the orders of Congress, the president, or on its own initiative. However, many companies provide only partial access to their records, making it difficult for the commission to develop its case. Moreover, a decision by the Supreme Court declaring that access to records of private business, except where substantial proof is submitted as to a specific breach of law, is a violation of the Fourth Amendment of the Constitution, makes the FTC's job all the more difficult.

In order to enable the FTC and the DoJ to do their due diligence, the government enacted the Hart-Scott-Rodino Antitrust Improvements Act in 1976, or simply HSR. The act requires parties that enter into transactions of $50 million or more to submit filings with the FTC and the DoJ before completing the transaction. The parties must wait thirty days after the filing before they can legally close on a merger. During that period, the antitrust agencies determine if the proposed acquisition is likely to be anti-competitive.

In the event that the government submits a request for additional information, the companies must wait an additional thirty days after compliance for approval. All in all, it can take sixty to ninety days for a merger to close successfully.

Since Luxor Satellite was a private company, TriNet Communications wasn't required to file complete information on the acquisition. Accordingly, Vikram Suri had directed his team to focus on the competitive positioning of the two companies both before and after the merger, which was what the FTC and the DoJ were after, and provide only minimal information on the underlying financial assumptions behind the deal.

If the government asked for further information, Vik's office would provide it selectively, albeit under the veneer of complete cooperation. Without a specific legal basis for blocking the merger, Vik knew there was little that the FTC could do.

In any case, he wasn't in the habit of rolling over for gutless bureaucrats.

The main thing now was to figure out how he could probe further into the TriNet-Luxor merger without putting his head into a noose.

It wouldn't be easy. Tom wasn't a managing director, and so had limited access to information, both within and outside the investment bank. In the hierarchy of the deal, any questions directed at the management of TriNet would have to go through Steve Brandt, and that was a risk that Tom wasn't prepared to take. It was entirely possible that he was chasing phantoms, and voicing unfounded suspicions to his boss would at best earn him a laugh, and at worst cost him his job.

There had to be a smarter way.

It would have been a simple enough matter to set a few drums beating in the investment community through friends like Larry Milton, and see what turned up. But that had its own pitfalls: even the most discreet of people talked, and Tom was experienced enough to know that eventually such things always came back to bite. His career prospects looked no brighter under this scenario.

So it had to be someone outside the financial community.

Tom mulled this over. He needed someone with whom he could speculate and who would conduct inquiries on his behalf without involving him directly. Of course, that someone could just as easily give away his identity, either deliberately or inadvertently, and he had no idea how to prevent that. Still, he doubted that anyone would take his suspicions seriously on an anonymous basis, and so he would have to take that risk.

The question now was: *who?*

Tom went through a mental checklist. In order for someone to gauge the necessary information, they would need to have access, be able to ask awkward questions without arousing suspicion and without fear of recrimination, be adept at negotiating their way through a maze, and be able to think on their feet.

It sounded like the résumé of a journalist.

twenty-one

Tom was in a pensive mood. He had been sitting on a park bench near the Great Lawn for nearly half an hour, but Amanda Fleming hadn't yet shown. He had asked her to meet him here.

A rollerblader glided by, dropping his torso at an angle and bending his knees to speed up as he negotiated the curving path. A child on a bike rode by in the opposite direction, wearing a crash helmet. Somewhere close by a bird chirped to celebrate the gorgeous spring weather. From somewhere else Tom could hear the twittering laughter of schoolchildren. The sounds of traffic wafted over from Central Park West and reminded visitors to the park that they were still in the big city.

Tom wished that he could enjoy the beautiful day and his rustic environs, but he was nervous about meeting the reporter from the *Times*. When he had finally called Amanda back after her dozen messages, he had told her he wanted to chat off the record. Intrigued, she had agreed to meet with him the next day.

That evening he had gone back over the numbers for Luxor, poring over the assumptions and comparing them with the market research and analyst reports used during the deal. The exercise had been helpful in refreshing his memory regarding some details, but had otherwise proved fruitless. Since he had merely retraced his old steps, he hadn't discovered anything new.

Then he had gone for a long walk along Fifth Avenue, heading past the southern end of the park and onto the posh residential stretch known as Central Park East. Dressed comfortably in a light wool suit and leather moccasins, Tom sauntered uptown at a leisurely pace. Away from the restrictive environment of the office, he was finally able to think.

Whatever ulterior motives lay behind the merger, they couldn't be purely valuation related—this much his gut told him. So in order to find the pattern in the puzzle, he had to detach himself from the details and focus instead on the "30,000 feet" view of the deal.

By the time Tom passed in front of the Metropolitan Museum, he had found at least a partial answer to his questions.

His reverie was interrupted by the sound of a female voice. Tom looked up to see an attractive woman peering down curiously at him. She was of medium height, slim, and very pretty. Her golden blond hair, almost white in its glow, was pulled straight back and tied with a ribbon. Aristocratic cheekbones and a high forehead framed a set of piercing hazel eyes. The eyes were intelligent but teasing, and a modest touch of wine-colored lipstick accentuated a sensual mouth.

Tom sat there for a full three seconds, staring at the elegant beauty in front of him, completely unable to place her or even to recall why he was sitting here in the first place. Used to eliciting this response in men, Amanda took the initiative and extended her hand.

"Amanda Fleming. You must be Tom Carter?" she said perfectly seriously. Her eyes, however, were laughing.

Tom recovered himself quickly and rose to shake her hand, nodding and grinning sheepishly. They sat down.

"I'm sorry. I was daydreaming," he explained, unconvincingly.

Amanda laughed. It was a sparkling, cheerful laugh and very pleasant to hear. After assuring him that it wasn't a problem, she got right to the point.

"You mentioned on the phone that you wanted to talk about something," she said, waiting expectantly.

"Yes, I did. But first let me make one thing clear," began Tom matter-of-factly. "Anything I say is strictly off the record—no 'anonymous' quotes, no speculation, nothing. As I said over the phone, there may not *be* a story here, but if there is, it's yours exclusively—as long as you agree not to write anything without my approval. Do we have a deal?"

Amanda mulled this over. Her face was serious. "Tom, if this is about anything illegal, and if you incriminate yourself—"

Tom waved his hand impatiently. "It's not that. I just want to be sure that my confidentiality is maintained and that we don't create a media circus."

Amanda thought quickly. Even if what this man claimed was true, he was still asking for a lot. She had no doubts that Tom wanted to talk about the TriNet-Luxor merger, and there *had* to be an angle in it or he wouldn't be talking to her right now. But if she agreed to his terms, she might be severely handicapped in her ability to do her job—which was to unearth, and publish, the truth.

At the same time, she didn't have any other leads on the merger and her editor was pressing her for another exclusive. It was a risk worth taking.

Quickly and efficiently, Tom walked the reporter through his thought process of the last few days, taking care to withhold certain pieces of proprietary information. Amanda listened to him with rapt attention, carefully filing away everything he said in a mental data bank. She could have taken out her tape recorder or notebook, but was afraid the banker would get nervous and end the conversation.

As Tom had realized the night before outside the Metropolitan Museum, the thing that troubled him about the merger wasn't the fact that it was a sweetheart deal, or that his firm had put a rubber stamp on the valuation, but that TriNet had put a ridiculously low bid on the table the first time around.

Even as she listened attentively, Amanda was evaluating Tom's remarks from her own perspective.

It seemed evident that the merger had *not* been an arms-length transaction as was represented to the press. Equally apparent was that TriNet's management had to have known Luxor's shareholders would sell at a discount, or else they wouldn't have wasted their time bidding for the satellite company at below its market value. But none of this made it newsworthy. The cornerstone of journalism was conflict, and where was the conflict in what amounted to two companies having consensual corporate sex?

What captured the reporter's attention, however, was the fact that the first bid for Luxor had been summarily rejected. *If TriNet had made the bid based on inside information, then why was it turned down?*

If there was a story here, this was undoubtedly the key. Somewhere in the distance Amanda could smell a smoking gun. But she also knew that finding it would be extremely difficult.

Then there was the matter of why Tom Carter was telling her all this in the first place. She knew a lot of investment bankers, and all of them were company men through and through. For someone at the vice president level to sit in a public place with a journalist and share his suspicions about a $10 billion deal that he had just worked on was unthinkable. Moreover, it could be professional suicide.

"This is all very interesting, Tom. But to be brutally honest, I'm not sure what I can do for you, especially if I can't write about it," she stated matter-of-factly.

It was time for Tom to put his cards on the table.

"Look, I work in a profession where you can get fired for not wearing a suit to a client meeting. . . . In my position, I can't ask too many questions or even express my doubts—they would throw me out in a heartbeat. But *you* can do just that—ask the difficult questions, confront people, dig around, and get to the bottom of this. As an outsider, they won't see you coming."

He paused to let this sink in. It was certainly a compelling argument, but would she bite?

Amanda did bite, but only her lip. "I see where you're coming from, but what if this is just a wild goose chase?"

Tom shrugged. "Could be. But then again, there could be a breaking story here. Isn't that what you do?" he asked pointedly.

Amanda nodded absently. As usual, she was thinking five steps ahead.

"Let's say I was to go along with this. Even if I do find something, my editor at the *Times* will never print it without evidence. Any insinuation against a major corporation would be—"

"Libel, I know," agreed Tom. "Which is why I need your help. If there's evidence out there, they won't let me get anywhere near it. But I may be able to help *you* find it since I know the landscape. You get to make your career and I get to keep mine."

"Yeah, but you already have a career, so why do you want to do this? At best there's no grand conspiracy and you've run a huge risk by confiding in a journalist. At worst we uncover something, in which case you lose your firm and you lose money. If you stay silent, nothing happens, and if you stand up, you're a whistle-blower. I don't get it."

Tom debated whether to tell her the truth. He also wondered what the truth really was.

From the moment he made the decision to approach the *Times,* he had agonized over his true motives. On the one hand, he had a strong desire to live up to his father's standards and Harry's death had driven that point home with blinding force. Harry Carter had taught his son honesty and integrity, and at a level deeper than his pocketbook or career lust, Tom was cognizant of how important those principles were to his life.

But the more important fact was that he was scared. Scared of being framed and scared of getting hurt. Self-preservation was a powerful incentive and, ultimately, the more compelling one. Even more than disappointing his father, Tom was worried about himself. As he recognized, his own role in the merger had glanced the boundaries of ethics, if not exactly the law, and although he was taking orders, he had no proof of that. In the event of a witch hunt, he was defenseless against the firm and the feds, and an easy target. That was the real cause for his concern and his true motive.

He wondered how the reporter would react to that.

"Actually, I could lose a lot by not doing anything. If something *does* go wrong and the deal blows up, they're going to need a scapegoat," answered Tom truthfully.

"And since you're the banker in the middle, you'll be it," finished Amanda shrewdly.

Tom nodded. "I want you to understand. I did not break the law. I did my job the way it's always done, and I did it by the book."

"Then what's the problem?" asked Amanda, confused.

Tom hesitated. "I just don't know if the book itself is fair. The firm's guidelines are to serve the client, and not commit a crime. But there's a gray area sometimes, and we're not allowed to question that. And in the present climate . . . that scares me more than anything else."

"But if the firm asked you to look away, then they're just as culpable, Tom," Amanda pointed out.

"Yeah, but the bank knows how to protect itself," answered Tom grimly. He thought again about the folder on Steve's desk. "Firms never take the fall. Their employees do."

Amanda understood. She was impressed with the fact that he had told her the truth. She had half-expected some kind of Boy Scout answer, and that would have given her pause. His candidness was a good sign—it meant that she could trust him.

"Let me think about it, okay? But *you* need to think about the risk you run by helping me. What if something goes wrong?" she pointed out with concern.

While they had been talking, the Great Lawn had become crowded. Some people were sitting on the freshly mowed grass; others were lying on towels, reading, sunbathing, or sleeping. A woman walked by with a baby in a stroller. A four-year-old boy walked next to her, looking around him curiously and smiling as he caught Tom's eye. The banker smiled back.

"I know the risks, Amanda, but I have no choice. This is the lesser of two evils." A pause. "I can't do this without you."

While Tom and Amanda held their meeting in Central Park, at the headquarters of TriNet Communications, a team of integration experts were busy drafting the post-merger plans for the combined company. The group, termed the "post-merger task force" or simply "the committee," consisted of both senior and junior officers from the corporate and key operating divisions of TriNet and Luxor. The twenty-five-person committee had been assigned the task of determining the synergies and redundancies between the two firms. More specifically, they had to recommend initiatives that would generate cost savings for the combined company.

As with all sizable mergers, post-merger integration was a complicated and time-consuming process, not least of all due to the human factor.

In addition to the imminent layoffs at the corporate level, there would almost certainly be cutbacks in the labor force as well. In the scheme of things, this was a singularly unpleasant and acrimonious task. That was precisely why junior officers and labor representatives were included on the committee: without their involvement and endorsement, the labor unions, the civil rights unions, and even federal and state authorities would make the cutbacks impossible.

In order to make its determinations, the committee, affectionately dubbed the "hack squad," would have to examine in detail the current and future personnel needs of each department, compensation levels, employment contracts and union agreements, pension plans, and a host of federal and state laws restricting the rights of employers to fire their workers.

Next, representatives from the financial planning area would need to analyze and compare the economic costs and benefits of "streamlining" the workforce.

Finally, the committee would need to anticipate the division closings, shutdowns of product lines, restructurings, relocations of manufacturing facilities, and other operational changes that would impact labor requirements. Only after this cumbersome and thankless process would the task force be in a position to make its recommendations.

For these and other reasons, Vikram Suri was glad that he didn't have to be on the post-merger task force; indeed he *could* not be on it—it would have compromised the integrity and fairness of the committee, and most likely biased the integration process in favor of TriNet. In point of fact, that would happen anyway, if for no better reason than the acquiring company would sign all paychecks after the merger. . . . Nonetheless, the appearance of objectivity was essential for the process to succeed.

In the end, of course, Vikram Suri would give final approval for the layoffs.

When Amanda returned to the office after her meeting with Tom, she was in a jubilant mood. The events of the afternoon had been surprising, and very pleasing. She felt elated at the prospect of pursuing a tangible lead—something that would challenge her journalistic skills and investigative instincts.

Sitting down at her desk, she attempted to concentrate on a magazine article about streaming media companies. She had been assigned an industry "wrap-up" on digital content management and some of the companies mentioned in the article were relevant to her piece. However, she stared down at the pages with unseeing eyes. She was still ruminating on what she had heard in Central Park.

On the one hand, she could feel a twinge of excitement inside her at the thought of uncovering a sinister corporate plot to cheat investors or blackmail a multi-billion-dollar company. In terms of pure journalistic fantasy, the story had all the makings of a financial Watergate. But that was in a perfect world.

What concerned her was that all of Tom's speculation could be just that; smoke without a fire.

First off, there was the incontrovertible fact that the merger involved a lot of people, a number of whom were respected professionals in their industries. A cover-up would have been extraordinarily difficult to hide. Most conspiracy theories were based on the notion of a large number of people agreeing to harbor a common secret, and that was precisely why such theories failed. There was far more regulatory oversight today, and someone inevitably talked—for revenge or money.

Complicating matters further was the almost endless stream of insider deals that were transacted on a daily basis across the globe. Even if some of those business arrangements were unethical or illegal, it was impossible for society to track, let alone block, every such instance in a vast economy.

The upshot of all this, realized Amanda, was that there was no story here unless the tracks led to actions that were flagrantly illegal, and unless there was hard evidence to prove it. As she had mentioned to Tom, her editor would never print anything that could open the newspaper to a libel suit, regardless of the sensation value. She could, of course, take any findings to less conservative news outlets, but that would mean the end of her career with the *Times;* and without proof her work would be little more than tabloid journalism. An even more vexing question was how to go about uncovering the truth and compiling the necessary evidence.

If conspiracies were indeed hard to sustain, then any crime that was committed had to be at the very heart of the deal, and would involve people at the highest level—those who had the power to cover it up. The person who had access to that vantage point was Tom, not Amanda.

While mulling this over, she threw some papers—including the unread magazine article—into a shopping bag, and walked out of the building. One of the great things about being a reporter was that no one gave a damn whether you were sitting at your desk or not. As long as you submitted your assignments on time and as long as the assistant editor didn't have to spend all night rewriting them or correcting your facts, you could pretty much come and go as you pleased.

Hailing a cab, Amanda headed down to Chelsea, where she was meeting some friends for an early dinner. Leaning back against the seat, she closed her eyes. She was aching for a cigarette, but didn't want a repeat performance from the last time she had tried lighting up in a cab. Her mind kept whirring away about the merger.

When she arrived at her destination, she pulled out a pack of cigarettes and lit one up, standing next to the stairway leading up to the restaurant. She puffed on it gratefully.

A smartly dressed businessman walked past her into the restaurant, curling his nose in disgust at the acrid smoke billowing into his face. Screw you, she thought. She didn't mind no-smoking zones *inside* buildings, or even smoke-free restaurants like the one she was waiting outside, but they couldn't have the outsides as well.

By the time she finished her cigarette, she knew her answer to Tom's proposition.

Without his active involvement, she didn't see how she could pull this off. It would be a simple matter for her to start asking questions under the guise of an innocuous "puff" piece. But she was certain that anyone involved in the deal would clam up once she started probing into details. Once her cover was blown, she would be put on a watch list and denied access to anyone with internal knowledge of the merger.

It was an impossible situation.

Which was exactly what she needed.

As the committee went about its disagreeable but vital business, gradually and inexorably the names accumulated. These were the people who would be fired after the merger.

Senior managers and deputies; salespeople and researchers; assistants and interns; supervisors and assembly line workers; even janitorial staff and security guards; all were on the list.

Each name was put on a separate row on an Excel sheet. Next to the name were the job title, department, job description, salary, pension benefits, immediate supervisor, phone number, mailing address, social security number, and union affiliation (if any). In the header to the sheet were the words STRICTLY CONFIDENTIAL.

By the end of the second week of the convening of the task force, the Excel sheet had grown to 825 rows, and was still expanding.

Most of the layoffs were at Luxor Satellite, and represented about 14 percent of the existing workforce.

twenty-two

One of the members of the post-merger task force was Frank Wa-chowski.

Frank was an assistant manager with the satellite manufacturing division of Luxor Satellite. His professional duties included the coordination of the labor-intensive assembly process, line supervision of the fabrication plants, and serving as liaison between the senior management and the largely blue-collar workforce. As a member of the committee, his job was to provide an objective assessment of the labor requirements for the fabrication plants and assembly lines.

Luckily for the Polish immigrant, it wasn't his job to speculate on the possibility of increased automation in those departments, or to conduct a cost-benefit analysis of layoffs. That would have been exceptionally difficult for a man who himself had come from the ranks of blue-collar workers.

Despite this minor blessing, Frank knew that he was playing an integral role in the eventual firing of working men and women, and he detested himself for it. Of course, it was a given that no one on the committee would get the axe, but that did nothing to mitigate his misgivings about the situation.

His men trusted him and he understood just how hard it was to make ends meet in the real world. These people had families and many would have no means to feed their children if they got laid off. Most would receive some sort of severance pay, but that would hardly be enough to get them through a few months, let alone tide them over till they managed to get new jobs. Having been laid off himself a couple of times, Frank was sympathetic to the difficulty of finding gainful employment after being downsized.

With a heavy heart, he thought back on the events that had led up to this.

The Wachowskis had emigrated to the United States from Poland in the mid-'70s, having first made their way to London from Warsaw under conditions of great difficulty, and finally arriving in New York on a freighter where Frank had coaxed the gruff British captain into allowing him to cook and clean for the crew in exchange for passage for him and his young wife. As they sailed into New York Harbor, they caught their first glimpse of freedom and a new life in the tall green statue shining like a beacon of hope in the middle of the water.

They had snuck onto shore with the help of the crew, who had hidden them in partially filled crates, lowered the boxes onto the pier, and let the couple out while the authorities were inspecting other pieces of cargo lying on the dock. They had simply walked away from the ship and into the new world with wishes of luck from the crew—even the cantankerous sea captain.

At first, Frank and Uljana Wachowski were shocked at their introduction to America. Since they had landed with hardly any money in their pockets, they had to spend a number of weeks living in squalid quarters near Times Square while Frank went out every day looking for work. He mostly found menial jobs that paid far less than was required to survive in this horrendously expensive city, and without papers, he couldn't go to unemployment agencies or the welfare office for any relief. Besides, he was young and proud and wouldn't even have considered such an option. Consequently, the once-idealistic couple was fast becoming convinced that this had all been a huge mistake.

In the fourth week, Frank got a break. A Polish restaurant owner on the Upper West Side had a sign on his window for a busboy. Frank, who had gone up to Eighty-sixth Street and Columbus to make a delivery, spied the sign and went inside. Almost as soon as the owner realized that this healthy young man was from the old country, he slipped from his broken English into Polish. The old man hired Frank and agreed to pay him just enough so he could make ends meet and move his family out of the crime-ridden neighborhood that they lived in currently. Uljana, who was in constant fear for her life in the drug- and prostitution–infested Times Square area, was greatly relieved when she heard the news. They were still poor, but no longer destitute.

They could have been even more comfortable if Uljana had worked as well, but she was from an old-fashioned Polish family and all she wanted to do was to start a family. Frank, however, wanted to wait.

He hadn't come so far under so much difficulty to be a busboy, and within a short time, had started to help the owner of the restaurant with his books, using the splotchy accounting skills that he had picked up in Warsaw. The young immigrant made up in intelligence and hard work what he lacked in formal training. The old man was impressed with him and slowly took him under his wing, promoting him to cashier and then assistant manager for the restaurant within a year.

When Frank finally informed him that they had snuck into the country illegally and had no papers, he was understanding and merely nodded in silence. A few months later, the old man's lawyer had summoned Frank to his offices on Park Avenue and furnished him with working papers and a social security card. The old man was influential and had pulled a few strings to buy the new immigrant some peace of mind. At least now Frank and Uljana didn't have to worry about being caught and deported as illegal aliens.

Frank had spent the next three years at the restaurant, more out of loyalty to the old man than any real desire to be in the food service business. Gradually, however, Uljana had started to press him about having children, and he had decided to look for a professional job with higher pay. But without the right academic qualifications, he couldn't get such a job, and the couple couldn't afford to spend money on courses. So he decided to stay at the restaurant for a while longer.

If the old man had survived the heart attack, he would have surely made Frank manager of his restaurant and maybe even given him the money to take night courses and get himself a vocational degree. But on the cold night of December 20, 1980 he died; and with him seemed to die Frank's chances of giving himself and his family the kind of life that he had envisaged when he first stepped onto the shores of Manhattan. The executor of the old man's estate summarily sold the restaurant to a major American chain, and the corporation turned the place into a low-scale diner. Since all the hiring was done at the corporate level, the old crew was dismissed with a "Sorry, tough luck" and some small change.

Frank and Uljana had been devastated and decided to delay having a child yet again. Later, much later, Frank would confide to his wife that he had toyed with the idea of suicide, and the only thing that had kept him from killing himself was the thought of his wife having to face this unforgiving city all alone.

By that point it was the booming mid-'80s and new construction was on the rise in New York. As Wall Street yuppies, Hollywood stars, gangsters, and politicians all flocked to the cesspool of sin and excess, new apartment buildings and corporate high-rises were springing up in earnest all over the concrete jungle. With the boom in real estate development came a corresponding rise in employment for construction workers. In his youth, Frank had worked a variety of jobs, including carpenter, builder, and electrician, and now those experiences came in handy as he applied for, and landed, the job of a supervisor at a construction company with sites throughout the city.

Using some of the money that he had saved away while working for the old man, and with plans for a family firmly on the back burner, Frank had gone to night school, taking courses in electronics and telecommunications technology. To his delight and surprise, his lack of a college education didn't hamper him in his efforts to learn a technical trade. He had a good mind for science and math and a passable knowledge of English that was improving every day through his interactions with his classmates. Within a couple of years, the determined immigrant had earned his first degree. Uljana was proud of him and had made him his favorite Polish treats for dinner that night.

Next he had applied for a job as a junior technician at an electronics firm that had its headquarters in Manhattan and an assembly plant for pre-fabricated parts in New Jersey. He was pleasantly surprised at how easily he obtained the job with the piece of paper that he kept carefully in his closet at home—it had cost him a year's salary. The job paid well, almost four times what he had made at the restaurant, and triple his salary at the construction site. An added bonus was that he and Uljana could move out to New Jersey to live since he would be working at the plant. Living in New Jersey would be considerably cheaper than in the city and would enable the happy couple to save some money and realize their dream of starting a family. Eventually, they might even be able to buy a home.

For almost a whole year, the dream seemed to be within his grasp; then suddenly, it was taken away—American style. The company that Frank Wachowski had worked for so gainfully turned out to have a minor problem: the CEO and CFO of the company had been embezzling huge sums from its coffers for years, and finally the money ran out. Due to its capital-intensive line of business, the company had considerable debt on its books and a substantial payroll to meet every week. Without the surplus cash that was often used to service the interest payments on the debt and issue paychecks to employees until the receivables cycle was complete, the company had no recourse but to shut its doors and seek protection under Chapter 11 of the bankruptcy laws.

Frank couldn't believe it.

The CEO and CFO were stealing for years and no one could tell? How could the banks, insurance companies, and suppliers keep transacting business with the company without at least trying to confirm its financial health? Did this entire bloody country function on paper?

Shortly after the scandal broke, the errant executives somehow managed to flee the country to some obscure province in South America, from where they issued inane statements proclaiming their innocence. Despite the open-and-shut case of misappropriation of funds, the press spent a lot of time and energy "trying to understand" the motive for the crimes and even attempting to see "the other side of the story." All this was very new to the horrified Pole and was his first introduction to the glory of American capitalism.

Back to square one, if not zero, Frank and Uljana had taken the money that he had managed to save from the job and moved into a smaller apartment in northern New Jersey. It wasn't the greatest place in the world, but it was half the rent of their previous place and bought Frank a good four months to look around for a new job. He still had his degree and a year's work experience, albeit with a firm that was no longer around and would most likely be recognizable on his résumé only for its infamy.

A month later, Frank had found work as an assistant engineer at a long distance telephone company with technical field offices in and around the Garden State. He had to travel to the different field offices on a regular basis, but didn't mind since the company paid for a car and gas. Besides, a job was now imperative—Uljana had gotten pregnant with her first child and Frank intended to ensure that their child would lead a much better and easier life than either of them. From that point on, it was his only wish, and he and his wife began to squirrel away as much cash as they could spare into an investment fund for the unborn child.

Tracey Wachowski came into the world at 8:12 A.M. on January 3, 1985, and Frank thought that he would die with happiness. He loved the little girl dearly and would spend all his free time playing with her and reading to her. However, the times when he was actually able to do this were rare, for he had to work overtime and sometimes a double shift—first at a field office in New Jersey and then one in Long Island. It was a grueling schedule, but one that he didn't mind as long as he could secure the future for his child.

The first few years had been filled with bliss for Frank and Uljana as they saw their cherubic baby grow into a little girl. Tracey had silky blond hair, which her mother loved tying into cute little pigtails for her. She would scamper around the apartment in her kid-clothes laughing and playing and screaming gaily at anything and everything that amused her. It was an incredible sight to see this fireball of energy and enthusiasm growing up in front of their eyes, and they showered her with love and attention, determined not to miss a single smile, a single mangled word, or a single burp.

Adding to their happiness was the fact that Frank liked his job. He was a line engineer who was sent to troubleshoot wherever there was a problem. While he wasn't brilliant, he was intelligent and careful, and quickly developed a reputation for being the "go-to" guy for certain types of technical problems. He figured it would be only a matter of time before this reputation would make its way to the head office and would win him a promotion, with a better schedule and more pay. Everything seemed to be going according to plan.

Then, in October of 1987, the stock market crashed. At first Frank didn't worry—they needed engineers to keep things running smoothly. During difficult economic times, more than ever, a company couldn't afford to lose its existing customers due to poor service. He seemed to be layoff-proof.

What the simple Polish immigrant didn't foresee was the possibility that his employer might get sold to a large telecom conglomerate, or that it would fire a third of its workforce and shut down some field offices in order to make itself more affordable for the acquiror. So, for the second time since his arrival in the United States, Frank Wachowski was handed a pink slip.

The timing couldn't have been worse, since young Tracey was now three and in another year would start attending school. She would go to public school, of course, but there would still be expenditures, not to mention the psychological impact on the family of not having a bread-winner in the household. It was true that this time Frank had some money in the bank, but that money was for Tracey's college education and a family home. He didn't want to touch it.

So he had started making calls and sending out résumés to firms around New Jersey and New York, hoping to find something that would pay him close to the wages from his previous job and hopefully not involve too much travel—he didn't want to miss these precious early years with his daughter. Throughout this period, he kept up a cheerful front for the sake of Uljana and Tracey, although secretly he was infuriated at being put in this position again by his adopted country. It seemed to him that the land of dreams was actually rigged to stomp the poor and shatter their dreams.

To add to his anxiety, the crash of '87 had caused serious damage to industry, and companies were shutting down operations, scaling back hiring, and initiating severe cost-cutting measures across the board, in-cluding deep pay cuts for employees. Frank found himself staring into the mouth of an abyss. Almost every résumé that he sent out met with a non-committal or negative response and those jobs that he was offered involved very little money and onerous work schedules. It was an em-ployers' market. Scenes of bread lines and rationing from the old country flashed through his mind and he became increasingly worried. This wasn't the life he had envisioned for his wife and child.

Tracey, meanwhile, was reaching that age when children start to be-come demanding, asking for toys she saw on television, video tapes of fa-vorite cartoons, expensive cereals; crying and throwing tantrums whenever her parents couldn't fulfill her desires. It was a perfectly natu-ral process for a child, but one that put tremendous pressure on the fi-nancially strained family. It killed Frank to look into his little girl's eyes and not be able to buy her what she wanted.

It was then that Peter O'Donnell had swooped down from the heavens to save them. At least it seemed that way to the now middle-aged Polish couple.

Peter was a short, fat Irishman who lived with his equally short and fat wife a few doors down from the Wachowskis. He and his wife had been the only people in the apartment complex who had had the decency to welcome Frank and Uljana into the neighborhood, and the two couples often sauntered over to each other's place to spend a pleasant evening chatting and watching television. Peter worked as a foreman at a nearby construction site.

Peter, like Frank, was looking for a technical job. Also like his neighbor, Peter had been sending out his résumés and testing the waters for a number of months, almost as soon as he had started his construction job. A year ago, he had obtained a degree in computer programming from a local community college, and was looking to leverage those skills at a large firm that could provide him with decent pay and job security. He too had been finding it tough going because of the crash.

On the day that Peter first brought up the subject of Luxor Satellite with Frank, he had just returned from the human resources department at the company's Manhattan offices. They had offered him a job as a computer programmer with the fixed satellite services division. His position would entail writing code to monitor the performance of Luxor's satellites, or "birds." It was a good job and Luxor was a growing company.

Peter was thrilled at the opportunity, and had rushed over to the Wachowskis as soon as he got home; both to share the good news and suggest that Frank apply to Luxor as well. Frank knew nothing about satellite technology but figured that his knowledge of electronics would stand him in good stead on the manufacturing side.

If Luxor hadn't been expanding at the time, it was doubtful that Frank would have found his niche so easily or so quickly, but the company needed people, especially technical people, to build its franchise, and was willing to train them. And so it was that Frank spent two months going through a rigorous training program, at the end of which he was hired as a junior engineer with Luxor's fabrication plant on the outskirts of Brooklyn.

With the promise of a stable job and a good salary, Frank had moved his family to Park Slope, from where he could reach work in fifteen minutes. Peter, whose wife was expecting, had done the same, and the two families had moved into brownstones a block from each other. For the first time since coming to the new world, Frank and Uljana had felt a sense of true belonging with a community. There were other people of Polish descent in the neighborhood, and every weekend there was a lively social gathering at a local pub. Uljana had made friends quickly and roped Peter's wife into her circle as well.

Meanwhile, Tracey, who was now a full-fledged teenager, loved going into Prospect Park to rollerblade and ride her bicycle. Having grown up in the United States, she was more American than Polish and shared the American love of the outdoors and athleticism. Frank didn't care if she never spoke a word of Polish or even remembered where she came from. He doted on his only child and all he wanted in this world was to make her comfortable and happy. They had been through a lot over the past few years and he was glad that the storm clouds were finally lifting.

To add to his confidence, the management at Luxor had been observant and appreciative of his technical knowledge and strong work ethic, and hinted to him that he could aspire to becoming a senior engineer at the plant if he kept up the pace.

The only thing that worried him was that most of the money he had made since coming to the United States had either been barely enough to buy food and shelter, or been spent on relocation and carrying them through the periods when he was out of work. The net result was that they had been in this country for more than a decade and yet their savings were inadequate to assure them of a better future. For the proud Polish immigrant it was frustrating.

Adding fuel to the fire were the rising cost of living in New York, Tracey's newly discovered penchant for CDs and clothes, and the daunting cost of a college education. Even though he had a small insurance policy, Frank knew that if something were to happen to him, Uljana and Tracey would be in a tough spot, especially since Uljana had always been a housewife. The thought of his family working desperately to make ends meet broke his heart.

From Warsaw to London to New York, the penniless Polish immigrant had somehow managed to survive and raise a beautiful family. He was determined not to let them down now.

When the serious-looking man in the gray suit had approached him for the first time, Frank was furious. He had just returned from work and was parking his car a few houses down from where he lived, when he saw him. The man, dressed conservatively in a charcoal gray suit, dull white shirt, and black tie, was standing casually on the stoop of Frank's building, smoking a cigarette. His eyes were scanning the street.

Frank frowned as he got out of the car and walked towards the brownstone where he and Uljana had set up their home in a ground floor apartment. The man in the gray suit saw him coming and readied himself. He threw away the smoke and stepped down from the stoop onto the pavement. He waited patiently for Frank to walk over.

The engineer surveyed him warily. This was a decent neighborhood, but nowadays you never knew. Although the man was well dressed, he was still a stranger, and Frank kept his fists at the ready.

When he reached his building, the man in the gray suit stepped forward, extending his hand cordially.

"Mr. Frank Wachowski?" he asked politely.

Frank didn't take the outstretched hand but nodded silently. He wondered how this man knew his name.

"I'm sorry to surprise you like this, but it wouldn't have been appropriate to disturb you at the office. I would like to speak with you about an important matter. Is there somewhere we can talk?" asked the man in the gray suit, trying to force a smile to his wooden face.

"And who are you?" asked Frank suspiciously.

"Oh, I'm sorry, how rude of me. My name is Kevin Renshaw. I'm a . . . business consultant," the suited man explained vaguely.

Frank had been in this country long enough to know when someone was bullshitting him, and he walked past the stranger towards his building.

The man caught him by the arm. Frank whipped around in anger, but the grip was surprisingly firm; and somewhere in it the Luxor engineer felt a hint of danger. He stopped and stared daggers at the man holding him, his left hand balling into a fist as he readied for anything. But the man who had introduced himself as Kevin Renshaw wasn't here to fight, and released Frank instantly, stepping back a couple of inches to indicate that he meant no harm—at least not yet.

"What do you want?" asked Frank irately.

"I have a business proposition for you—a generous one—and it involves very little work on your part. Just a little research. For that you get paid very well."

The engineer's expression changed rapidly. Now he was listening. Although still mistrustful of the stranger, he wasn't about to turn away a chance to earn good money.

Kevin sensed correctly that he had gained his interest, and proceeded.

"I represent a client who needs some information on Luxor Satellite that only you can provide. The data we're seeking is sensitive but we're not asking you to break the law, you understand? We simply want information that you already have access to."

Frank Wachowski, who had always prided himself on his loyalty and honesty, didn't need to hear any more. He turned away quickly and climbed the stairs to the door of the brownstone, withdrawing his house keys. Kevin Renshaw stayed where he was.

"Mr. Wachowski, I really think you should hear me out. If you don't like what I have to say, you can tell me to get lost. But if you listen, you'll find it worth your while."

Frank didn't hear the specific words but he got the general import of the man's remarks and turned around with a fist held up menacingly. Kevin moved back a few steps, but wasn't scared. There was something about him that reminded Frank of a wild animal.

"All right, have it your way. But I'll be back, and then you'll listen. You'll listen because you can make fifteen thousand dollars for a week's work," said Kevin, walking backwards onto the pavement and turning around.

Even in his heated state, Frank still had enough sense to realize that $15,000 was a *lot* of money, especially to him. He hesitated. The man in the gray suit had walked away and was halfway down the block now. Frank thought about going after him, then stopped himself. He would be back. If Kevin Renshaw, or whoever he represented, was willing to pay that much for a week's work, they must want that information badly.

He stood outside for a few more minutes, thinking.

He was still seething at the notion that someone would consider his fealty for sale. But then he could also use the money. His income from work was good, but the family's expenses were growing rapidly. The day-to-day costs of living in New York made $15,000 a very attractive proposition for a man who had struggled to give his family a standard of living they deserved, and one that he intended to maintain.

Besides, the man in the gray suit had assured him that he wasn't expected to do anything illegal. Deep down, Frank knew that it was probably not entirely true. He had enough life experience to know that no one offered you a large sum of money for something that was straightforward or easy to obtain.

Even so, for fifteen grand he was willing to listen.

————————————— twenty-three

Frank stared at the name in front of him in dismay. He was scanning through a stapled sheaf of papers, looking for names that were familiar. Some of them he had recommended himself; others had been chosen by other members of the committee. All of them were people who would lose their jobs after the merger.

The name he was gazing at right now was that of Peter O'Donnell, his friend and neighbor, without whom Frank might not have found his present job. The same Peter O'Donnell who Frank's wife had dubbed an "angel descended from heaven to help them in their time of need."

Frank was about to call up the head of the post-merger task force to demand that Peter's name be taken off the list, but knew that it was futile. For one thing, Frank was too junior to make such a request. For another, the committee would have frowned upon such favoritism and rejected his plea anyway—he couldn't even make a technical case for keeping Peter, since the two men were in different departments.

What made this exponentially difficult for him to swallow was the knowledge that he had unwittingly played a crucial role in this outcome. Of course, at the time he had no way of knowing what the report was for or how it would impact the people that he worked with. And there was no doubt they would have obtained the information from some other source if he had turned them down. But as it stood, he was an accomplice.

For the second time that day, Frank found his mind wandering back over the past.

As Frank had expected, Kevin Renshaw had shown up again a few days later, this time in a dark blue pin-striped suit, cream shirt, and a crimson tie. He had come by in the early afternoon on a weekend, when both Uljana and Tracey were out shopping. Frank had answered the doorbell in surprise, not expecting anyone, and hesitated for just a second before letting him in.

After being seated in the living room of the sparsely furnished but comfortable apartment, Kevin had cut to the chase.

"Have you thought about the offer?" he asked Frank, gazing levelly at him.

"I don't really know much about the offer," professed Frank. "You haven't told me yet what kind of information you want."

Kevin nodded, and in brief but clear terms spelled out the details.

After he finished, Frank was silent. It was obvious that the man in front of him wasn't the brains behind this operation—he seemed to be parroting the technicalities, as if conveying someone else's words. But he was unambiguous about what he wanted.

As the engineer had foreseen, there was a lot more to this assignment than met the eye. Some of the information was completely innocuous; the rest was definitely sensitive. Still, as Kevin had promised the first time around, Frank wasn't being asked to do anything illegal. Everything would be arranged to ensure that.

This was how it would work: Frank would fetch the information from the office and bring it home. The engineer would then leave the documents in his car, from where they would be "appropriated," copied, and replaced—all without Frank's overt involvement. Kevin handed him a list of drop-off points and times that Frank was to memorize and then destroy. He was being offered complete deniability in case something went wrong.

The terms were that he would receive half of the $15,000 up front, and the rest upon delivery of the information, even though Frank would never actually "give" anything to anyone. As soon as Kevin's employers were satisfied that they had received what they were after, Frank would receive a phone call from "Bob," who would give him instructions on how to collect the remainder of his cash.

As Kevin was leaving, Frank asked if there was a number he could reach him at if there was a problem. After a brief hesitation, Kevin handed him the digits.

"Identify yourself only as a friend and don't ever mention the name of your company," he snapped.

Frank nodded dumbly and took the piece of pasteboard with the number.

After Kevin had left, Frank put the $7,500 carefully into an envelope, sealed it, and hid the package behind some boxes in the bedroom closet, where Uljana and Tracey wouldn't find it.

Putting away the list of planned lay offs, Frank picked up the phone. He dialed Peter O'Donnell's number. Just as the line started to ring, he put down the receiver. No sense in raising his friend's hopes until he had the money.

Next, he dialed the number that Kevin Renshaw had given him a few months ago. He hoped fervently that it would still work. Otherwise he would have no way of reaching Kevin, not knowing who he really was or who he worked for. On the latter, Frank had his suspicions, but putting them to the test would be altogether too risky. If he was wrong, he could lose his job and even wind up in jail.

The phone at the other end rang five times, but no one picked up. After two more rings, however, a vaguely familiar voice came on the line. There was an unmistakable hint of guardedness in the tone.

"Hello, who's this?" rasped the voice.

"This is a friend," said Frank, lapsing automatically into the language that he had been advised to use. "I need to speak with you. It's urgent."

There was a momentary silence on the other end and Frank imagined he could hear the man suck in his breath sharply. Then the voice came back on.

"What do you want?" it asked gruffly.

"Remember the little task I did for you?"

No response. Frank hadn't expected one and quickly resumed.

"I didn't realize the consequences of doing that job because I didn't know what it was for. I didn't expect the lay offs. One of my good friends is going to lose his job and I have a problem with that."

"I don't know anything about lay offs or what the hell you're talking about," the voice said smoothly.

Frank persisted.

"I think you do, Kevin. And what's more, I want you to tell your employers that I know who they are and why they needed that information. I'm not stupid."

This time the silence lasted for a full ten seconds. While Frank waited for a response, he fidgeted nervously. He wasn't at all sure how this conversation would go.

"All right. So what do you want?" was the toneless comeback.

"I want more money. Twenty thousand," said Frank, rolling the dice.

"What?!" came the incredulous reply.

"You're putting my friend out of work. I want to give him the money to make it right. It's the least I can do."

"Forget it. There *is* no more money. You already got paid."

"Yes, but that was before I knew what this was all about. I want another twenty thousand," said Frank decisively, trying to bring an edge to his voice.

"You deaf, Polack? I told you there's no money. You got paid plenty for this deal. And I don't give a shit about your friend," the voice sneered.

Now Frank was seething. He wanted to yell into the receiver, but controlled himself. There was nothing to be gained by fighting with an anonymous voice across an unlisted phone line. He was certain now that Kevin Renshaw didn't exist.

"Listen to me, Kevin—or whoever you really are. Either you get me the twenty thousand or I will—"

"You'll do *what*, Polack?" the voice interrupted scoffingly.

"I'll go to the press. I'll tell them all about the information that I compiled and passed along to you."

There was a nasty laugh at the other end of the line.

"You don't even know who I am. The only thing you'll do is put yourself out of a job, and probably wind up getting prosecuted by your company."

"I'm prepared to take that chance. Either way, I blow the lid off this thing and let the press figure out the trail. I may not have any proof, but I have a pretty good idea about where all of this will lead. Is your employer prepared to take that chance?"

There was a thoughtful pause on the other end of the line. Then: "Are you crazy? Do you know what we can do to you?"

"It's you who's crazy. I already told you—I'm prepared to risk my job, but you have a lot more to lose than I do," said Frank, his words sounding hollow and strained even to him.

A flat laugh came over the phone line. There was something sickening about the sound. It was empty and emotionless, as if the voice at the other end didn't belong to a human being at all. Frank stiffened.

"I wasn't talking about your job," informed the voice quietly. "You got a wife and kid, right?"

Frank turned ashen.

The voice continued calmly. "It would be a real shame if that beautiful daughter of yours was to meet with an accident, now, wouldn't it?"

Frank remembered the vague sense of danger that he had felt when he first met Kevin Renshaw. Now the danger felt very real and made him afraid for his family. He didn't know what to say.

"I think you get the picture, Polack. You still want the money?" asked the voice sarcastically.

"No! Of course not. You just leave my family alone, all right?" said Frank fearfully, finding his voice.

"And you'll keep your mouth shut? Not a word to anyone?"

"Yes, yes. I promise. You got nothing to worry about. I'm sorry I called." Frank's voice was quivering now.

The voice at the other end seemed satisfied.

"All right. I believe you. But just remember—one slip, *anywhere,* and you'll regret it," the voice said menacingly.

Frank nodded foolishly, then realized he was on the phone and sputtered a hasty "I got it."

The line went dead.

As Frank headed home that evening, he was thinking about the phone call earlier in the day. Some part of him was frightened at the response that he had received, yet another part was enraged. *How dare they threaten his family?* He couldn't even fathom the evil of men who could conceive of harming a child. Back in the old country, human life had been cheap, but he had never expected that it would be the same here.

Instinctively, he knew that these people—whoever they were—would do whatever they had threatened to do. The only question now was whether they would attempt something despite Frank's assurances that he would keep his mouth shut. That depended largely upon how much damage he could do by going to the press.

What worried him most at this point was that he had been right about the connection between the job that he had done and the merger. Kevin's reaction had confirmed that. As to who exactly had utilized the information and how, Frank didn't know—he had been bluffing over the phone. But he could guess that it was someone at TriNet Communications and that the information had been used somehow to influence the merger with Luxor Satellite. Either way, it was important enough for them to threaten his little girl.

Pulling into a parking spot in front of his home, Frank Wachowski got out of his car, locked the door, and headed up the stairs. When he got to his apartment door, there was a Post-It note near the handle. Frank's heart skipped a beat. Then he recognized Tracey's messy but legible handwriting. It simply said:

GONE SHOPPING. BACK AT 9.
MOM AND TRACE

He smiled and sighed with relief.

After hanging up his jacket on the coat tree in the hallway, he poured himself a drink from the small but well-stocked bar in the living room. The bar was one of Frank's few personal indulgences. He took a long swallow from the glass, and, satisfied with the taste, lay back on the couch to ponder his options. The liquor burned inside him as it made its way down to his stomach. He welcomed the sensation.

The easiest thing, he supposed, would be to deposit the cash slowly into his bank account so Uljana wouldn't notice—it was still in the back of the closet—forget about all this and just go on as if nothing had happened. But now that he had betrayed his hand, he wasn't sure if that would be enough.

He needed some insurance.

Polishing off his drink, he got up and poured himself another one. Somewhere in the distance, the discordant sounds of traffic reached his ears. The dull orange glow of twilight seeped in through the grated living room windows which looked out onto the street. Settling himself back on the sofa, he formulated his plan.

Outside, night had fallen. Frank logged off from his email account and then shut down the monitoring software. He had been working on the computer for an hour and a half, and his eyes felt weary from the strain. Uljana and Tracey would be home soon, and then he would have to act as if nothing had happened.

The monitoring software had programmed his computer to send a message over the DSL line to his email service provider once every three days. The message was a sort of "all clear" signal that instructed the email server *not* to perform certain actions for a period of seventy-two hours. The email server, in turn, had been programmed by Frank to perform those actions automatically every three days, and the "all clear" signal simply superseded that setting.

The combination of the arcane software package and the server configuration enabled Frank to automate the sending of an email message to a specified address upon the occurrence of an event. The trigger event in question was the *absence* of an "all clear" signal from Frank's home computer. If the server failed to receive the signal for three days, it would automatically send an email from Frank's personal account to the email addresses programmed in the system.

Frank, for his part, would need to authenticate the setup at his end once a week, with a password. If he failed to do so, the monitoring software would eventually shut down the system and the "all clear" signal would cease to be sent to the email server. In this way, if Frank disappeared, the trigger event would automatically occur after about seven to nine days, and the email would be sent out as specified.

Additionally, Frank had copied the text of the email and the attached information from his home computer onto the host server, which belonged to the email service provider. Thus, the email's contents were safe even if the files were deleted from his own machine.

Feeling tired but satisfied, Frank went back into the living room and poured himself his third drink for the night. He was a little light-headed by now, but still lucid enough to pick up the phone and dial Kevin Renshaw's number.

On the opposite coast, the hum of servers filled the small room in downtown Los Angeles with a constant background noise. The two people seated in front of large flat-screen panels were used to the sound and hardly noticed it. They were munching on cold slices of pizza and washing it down with generous quantities of Coke. One of them, a nineteen-year-old in a stained UCLA T-shirt, was staring hard at his computer screen.

Corey Meeks put down his slice.

"Take a look at this, Sheri," he said excitedly.

Sheri spun her chair away from her desk and glided over to him.

She gazed at the screen for a few seconds and then whistled softly.

"What should we do?" she asked.

Her colleague answered by picking up the phone and dialing an unlisted number. He got an answer after three rings.

"Hello, this is Corey at The Center. I have something," he said into the mouthpiece.

"What is it?" rasped the voice on the other end.

"It's about that guy you wanted me to keep an eye on. He's been doing some stuff with his email account."

"What kind of stuff?"

Corey told him in guarded terms. He had strict instructions not to discuss things openly over a phone line, and vividly remembered his last warning on indiscretion. He rubbed his groin ruefully. . . .

When he was finished, there was a brief silence.

"All right. Here is what you're going to do," said the voice flatly. "Monitor the account and make sure that we intercept everything he sends. Nothing is to get through until we clear it, you got that?"

"Yep."

"And I want a report every half hour from now on until we tell you otherwise, kapeesh?"

"Yes, boss."

The line went dead.

Corey turned back to Sheri. She was staring at him inquiringly. He filled her in quickly and tonelessly. She groaned.

"Yeah," said Corey, mimicking her feelings. "We'll take turns, but we should order some more pizza and Coke. It could be an all-nighter."

"And I was going to go surfing with my boyfriend," Sheri complained bitterly.

"You, surfing?" laughed Corey. "With the amount of pizza you eat, the only thing you could do on the water is deliver Domino's to ships."

Sheri, who weighed 200 pounds, picked up a stapler and threw it at her irreverent colleague. An office supplies fight ensued, which Corey eventually lost.

Finally calming down, the two college sophomores returned to their workstations.

After adjusting some settings on his computer, Corey settled back to watch. He tapped his pen idly on his desk and wondered what this Frank Wachowski had done to merit surveillance.

————————— twenty-four

Vikram Suri was seated comfortably on his pool deck, reading a book, when the call came. A warm, soft breeze was drifting in from the ocean a hundred yards away. The faint roar of the surf mingled with the sound of light classical music emanating from speakers placed strategically around the pool.

A butler in casual dress wafted seemingly out of nowhere and coughed apologetically. Vik looked up in inquiry.

"There's a call for you, sir," said the butler formally. "It's about The Center." He handed his employer a cordless phone and then retreated back into the shadows—he didn't know who or what "The Center" was and had no interest in finding out.

"Hello," said Vik carefully into the mouthpiece.

"I'm sorry to disturb you, sir, but it's important," responded a voice, without identifying himself.

"What is it?" snapped Vik.

The caller filled him in crisply.

Vik's brow knitted in a frown. He should have foreseen this, he thought, but he hadn't counted on a lackey having the brains to figure out the connection with the merger—especially a Polack. There was, of course, nothing to link him directly to the report or the man who had compiled it, but a press leak could be devastating. At the very least, it would focus an awkward spotlight on the transaction that he couldn't afford.

This situation needed to be neutralized, and fast.

"Are we certain there are no other email accounts that need to be checked?" asked Vik brusquely.

"As far as we can tell. But if he had other plans, he wouldn't have done what he did today. I'm pretty sure he didn't think of this until the phone call this morning."

"And we're sure that we can re-program the server's settings?"

"Positive," came the confident reply.

Vik pondered this. He had never personally been to The Center, but had heard good things about the two hackers who worked unofficially out of the tiny California office. They had performed some jobs for him before and seemed to know their stuff. For one thing, they knew how not to leave a trail, and were dependable in their work. They had good incentive to.

Most of all, they had no idea who they were really working for. They received their generous paychecks and instructions anonymously, and didn't ask questions. Even if something did go wrong, there was simply no tangible connection between The Center and Vikram Suri.

"How do we know that he hasn't already sent the information to someone?" Vik asked at length.

"Why would he? He wants to protect himself and his family, and this was meant to be an insurance policy, not a first strike," the caller reasoned.

"Who is the email addressed to?"

The voice on the line listed a number of names. The last one surprised Vik. He smiled. This fiasco could still be turned into an asset.

"All right, here is what we do," ordered Vik. "Kill all the addresses except the last one. Then edit the text so there's no reference to a threat, and mark it urgent. Send out the email by seven A.M. tomorrow from an anonymous account, and don't accept replies. Can you do all that?"

"I'll have to check with The Center, but I'm pretty sure we can—those kids are smart."

Satisfied, Vik continued. "In the meantime, find me the personal bank account number for the recipient of the email, but I need it before noon tomorrow. Got that?"

"Yes, sir. What about the Polack?" the voice asked hesitantly.

Vik stared out towards the ocean, his eyes bleak. Flecks of white dotted the surface of the water, suggesting inclement weather. His sensitive ears picked up the distant rumble of an approaching storm front.

Deep down inside, he knew he was a criminal. But like most criminals, he didn't consider himself a bad man. In a striking example of self-delusion, he prided himself on doing only what was necessary to achieve victory, nothing more. Part of that discipline, however, was to never let personal feelings get in the way of professional judgment.

Having had to struggle in his own life, he was generally sympathetic with immigrants who had similarly fought to give themselves a comfortable life in the new world. He empathized with their viewpoints, their decisions, and their attitudes. But he wasn't about to be outsmarted by one.

"First find out if he made any copies of the information. Then take care of him, *permanently,*" said Vik, and shut off the phone.

It was raining hard by the time the two men pulled up outside the brownstone. The first man stayed behind the wheel of the car while the second man got out and walked over to the landing of the building. He was wearing jeans and a tan raincoat. His long, untidy hair was hidden underneath a baseball cap, which he had pulled down low over his eyes. The shoes were worn and a waxen gray. Overall, his appearance was unremarkable, and more importantly, forgettable.

The man in the car was watching the street in front and in his rearview mirror, his foot on the accelerator. Even at this time of night and even in this weather there would be people out walking their dogs, and he was watching to make sure that the street was empty. If someone did walk by, he would drive away and around the block. The man outside would simply walk away from the brownstone and pretend to head toward the park. He, too, would double back around as soon as the street was clear.

The clock on the dashboard said 11:00 P.M. Just then, Frank Wachowski came out of his apartment, as he had been instructed, and walked down the steps to the pavement, toward the man in the raincoat. The man behind the wheel smiled thinly, remembering his last conversation with the Luxor engineer. Frank had called him a second time to let him know that he had created an "insurance policy" for himself and his family, and that if anything happened to him or his loved ones, a detailed account of everything would be released to the press and the authorities—automatically.

Thanks to The Center, they knew exactly how.

He had pretended to be impressed by Frank's guts and had told him that his employer had decided to give him the $20,000 he wanted if he promised to keep his mouth shut and never contact them again.

Frank had been surprised, but relieved, and had agreed to meet outside his apartment at 11:00 P.M. for the money. With the email system that he had rigged, they dared not touch him. If they killed him, everything would become public, including his hunch about who "they" were. Anyway, he was confident they wouldn't take the risk.

These were his thoughts as he walked into the rain. The downpour hit him straight in the face as he made his way towards the man in the raincoat. His face was tense and his eyes alert. The liquor had worn off hours ago and the rainwater felt invigorating. He balled his right hand into a fist and held it tightly behind him, ready to swing away in case something happened. Inside, Uljana and Tracey were asleep.

The man behind the wheel watched attentively as his partner stepped forward to meet Frank. Then, quietly, he stepped out of the car, crouching to keep low. Slipping around the back, he bounded across the pavement and into the shadows of the houses. In the protective cover of darkness, he began to creep forward.

The man in the raincoat, whose face Frank could discern only slightly for the shadow of the baseball cap, reached into an inside pocket and withdrew a wad of bills in a transparent plastic bag. He handed it over silently, his narrow-set eyes gazing inscrutably through the semi-darkness and the rain.

Frank took the money and pulled it out of the bag. He started counting it, crouching over it to shield it from the water. There was a loud thunderclap, and then a bright flash of lightning illuminated the street. Frank looked up for a second and was startled. The man in the raincoat had vanished. In the quick flash of light he saw the car standing in the street. The man in the baseball cap was behind the wheel.

He was staring at the car when the blow came from behind. He felt a sharp pain in his head and quickly turned around, his hands extended in a defensive gesture. He dropped the money and saw someone swoop it up from the asphalt. His eyes could barely focus from the pain and the water, but he got a quick glimpse of his assailant. It was Kevin Renshaw.

Before he could react, he felt another sharp pain, this time in his stomach. He doubled over in agony and a small cry escaped his lips. In the inclement weather, the sound was empty and futile. A second later, he was being picked up and dumped into the back of the car. His assailant piled in next to him and the car sped off in the rain.

As warehouses went, this one was extremely small. Located in the heart of Long Island City, and used primarily by a private retailer to store small-ticket electronic items, it was little more than a 900 square-foot container with a door. It was one of six such warehouses that lined one side of the street.

Across the road was a shipping center used for distributing sundry items to a hodge-podge of small shops throughout the New York area. The shipping center was dark at this time of night. Even if there had been people there, it wouldn't really have mattered; both the distribution center and the warehouses were owned by the mob and used to ply their "cover" trades in the metropolitan area, most notably the hundreds of small electronic shops scattered around Manhattan. Occasionally, as tonight, the warehouses would be used by unaffiliated third parties who paid the owners for the privilege of complete privacy.

The rain had been falling for almost three hours by the time the black Ford Taurus pulled up. The driver had had a difficult time navigating his way through the torrential downpour and the heavy traffic from Park Slope to Long Island City. The Citibank Tower loomed high above them, but they could hardly see it through the sheets of rain. Kevin got out first, pulling Frank after him and dragging him toward the shadows. The engineer tripped over the wet, broken sidewalk and felt himself being jerked up impatiently. He stumbled groggily after his captor, still lightheaded from the blow that he had taken a little while ago.

The driver of the car turned off the ignition and walked around the front of the car to the warehouse, pulling out a set of keys from his pocket. He was wet, hungry and in a hurry to get this over with. Fumbling through the dozen or so keys on the ring, he finally located one that had the number 3 etched deeply into the metal head. Groping briefly in the dark, he located the lock on the door, and gripping it firmly to prevent it from slipping in his wet hands, he inserted the key and turned it. There was a loud click, and the lock snapped open. He pocketed the keys and the lock, and swung open the double doors in front of him.

Extracting a pocket flashlight, he switched it on and pointed it into the darkness. The air inside was rank and musty, and smelled vaguely of wood shavings (which were used as fillers in crates), sweat, mold, cigarettes, and garbage—all of which were indeed prevalent on the premises. As the light cut into the thick blackness, the man could see a narrow hallway in front of him, leading up to a set of even narrower stairs. On either side of the gloomy corridor were three rusted metal doors that opened into individual warehouses. This was the main, and only, entrance into all of them.

With Kevin Renshaw following, and dragging Frank Wachowski after him, the man with the flashlight walked down the corridor to the second door on his right and, once again pulling out his keys, slipped one of the larger ones into the keyhole of the door. The lock was old and rusty and it took him some time to open it. With a loud creak, the door swung inwards.

Shining his flashlight in front of him, he marched to the middle of the room, where a thin metallic chain hung from a light bulb on the ceiling. He pulled it, and the room came alive.

Frank squinted at the glare, a small pain shooting up to his temple. His captor had now left his side and gone back down the hall to shut the door leading to the street. The man in the tan raincoat was walking around the room, looking for something. In the middle of the tiny warehouse was a wooden table and four chairs, all in a state of disrepair and with paint peeling off the surface. There were some crates and toolboxes stacked haphazardly against the walls, girlie magazines strewn carelessly on the floor, and a strangely out-of-place cappuccino machine on a large metal cabinet by the door. A can of gasoline and some rags lay on the floor by the cabinet.

Kevin had now returned and he quietly motioned Frank to one of the chairs. Knowing that there was nothing to do but obey, Frank sat down, staring at the two men in front of him and wondering what they were going to do. He was smart enough to know that none of this could possibly end happily for him, but he harbored the secret hope that perhaps all they wanted to do was break a few bones and scare him into keeping his mouth shut. He saw the man in the raincoat pull out a rough fiber rope out of his pocket and advance meaningfully towards him.

"Put your arms behind your back," he said gruffly.

Frank acquiesced without a word. There was no point in resisting.

While his partner secured Frank tightly to his seat, Kevin pulled up a chair across from Frank, and sat down. He gazed levelly at the engineer, but his eyes were inscrutable.

Frank waited tensely for whatever was to come. His mind wandered briefly to his family, then snapped back.

Kevin spoke first.

"You comfy, Polack?" he grinned nastily. Frank didn't respond.

"Don't worry. We just have a couple of questions to ask you, and then we'll let you go," he said unconvincingly.

Even though Frank was smart enough not to trust anything that these men might promise, he was nevertheless under the throes of a feverish hope for his life, and some part of him was relieved to hear the words. He nodded dumbly.

"You really went and stirred up a hornet's nest here, Frank. I still can't imagine what you were thinking. But I guess it's understandable. Twenty thousand dollars is a lot of money for a poor schmuck like you, and I can see how you thought it was worth takin' the risk and asking for more cash. But you see, that's not how we work. We believe in keeping our promises and like to make sure that our friends keep theirs."

The man in the raincoat seemed to have scant interest in what was going on; sauntering over to the cappuccino machine, started to inspect it. His forehead creased in concentration.

"So we find ourselves in a quandary. On the one hand, we were happy with the work that you did and were only too glad to pay you the fifteen thousand. But then you go and threaten us, Frank. It puts a real ugly face on the whole thing, y'know," continued Kevin, staring unwaveringly at his guest.

Frank stifled a desire to say something. Despite his tenuous position, he was getting angry. He was mad for many reasons, but most of all because his captor thought that he had wanted the money for himself—he had wanted it for Peter O'Donnell, *who was going to lose his livelihood because of these bastards.* But common sense prevailed and the engineer held his tongue.

"All right, then. Let's begin. First of all, who else knows about this?" asked Kevin, slipping into a more civil tone.

"No one," replied Frank, shaking his head.

"Are you sure about that? In our experience," said Kevin, indicating his partner, who was still busy trying to uncover the secrets of the cappuccino maker, "there's always someone else who knows, and believe me, Frank, it creates *big* problems. For friends, for *family* . . . "

Frank interrupted him angrily.

"Keep my family out of this. They have nothing to do with it. I wouldn't lie to you—no one except me knows about any of this," he said earnestly.

Leaning forward, Kevin took Frank's chin in his hand.

"I believe you, Frank. That's good. That's real good for you. I don't usually believe anyone," he said, releasing him.

By now, his partner had figured out how to use the coffee machine and had proceeded to make a cup from himself. Turning to Kevin, he asked him if he wanted some. Kevin declined and turned his attention back to Frank.

"Now, as you know, we were prepared to let all this go. We even gave you an incentive to back off, but you wouldn't listen. You come up with this *stunt* about leaking things to the press if we hurt you, and that really makes us mad, Frank. Don't you trust us?" asked Kevin, grinning maliciously.

Fear flickered across the engineer's eyes, and Kevin seemed pleased at that.

"I see you're getting the picture. Good. So why don't you tell us exactly what this 'insurance policy' is and save us all a lot of trouble, eh?"

Kevin didn't mention anything about The Center or the fact that he already knew about the emails that Frank had rigged to be sent out in the event of his death or disappearance. He wasn't here to give information, but to get it.

Frank mulled his captor's words carefully. Despite his fear, his survival instinct was still intact. He knew that telling these men everything was a surefire way of getting himself killed. Once he had spilled his guts, they would have no more reason to keep him alive. And even if they let him go, his insurance policy would be rendered useless, and they would have no deterrent against hurting him or his family in the future.

But if he didn't tell them what they wanted to hear, they could simply torture it out of him and would definitely kill him afterwards.

"I'll tell you everything, but you have to let me go," insisted Frank, knowing full well that any such promise was useless from men like these, but *hoping* nonetheless.

"Of course," responded Kevin coolly. "You have my word. We don't want to kill you; we just want to be sure that our interests are protected. You cooperate with us and we'll make sure you get out of this with maybe just a bruise or two . . ."

Frank nodded despite the insanity of this statement. Carefully, he went through the specifics of the system that he had rigged, starting with the technical details and ending with the list of people for whom the email was intended.

Kevin listened cautiously, observing Frank's facial expressions to watch for any signs that he might be lying. He had already been briefed by The Center, and so was able to compare Frank's version of the story with what he knew to be the facts. Everything seemed to fit.

When Frank had finished speaking, Kevin glanced meaningfully at his partner, who was sitting on a crate against the far wall, sipping a steaming cappuccino and leafing through a girlie magazine. The man in the rain-coat looked up for a second, caught Kevin's eye, and put down his cup. He walked over to the middle of the room and sat down on one of the re-maining chairs, turning it around to lean his chest and arms against the back.

"Did you set up any other rigs like this one?" Kevin asked Frank, try-ing to sound nonchalant. He pulled out a pack of cigarettes from his pocket and lit one up. He offered the pack to his partner, who shook his head.

"No, this was the only one," answered Frank. He was a little calmer now, from all the talking. Relaying the technical details of a computer system had helped infuse a strange sense of sanity to his environment. The possibility of violence now seemed remote, even unrealistic.

"What other 'insurance policies' did you rig up, Frank?" Kevin re-peated tonelessly.

"None. Just the email—it seemed to be the logical way to do it."

"Come on. There must have been something else. A down-to-earth guy like you wouldn't trust a frigging computer with his family's safety, now would you? You must have made a hard copy of the information, maybe put it into a locker or bank deposit box somewhere, or maybe given it to your lawyer to mail out in the event of your death?"

"I'm telling you, no. I never made any hard copies of the informa-tion—I was always afraid that someone would find it by mistake and I would get caught," he explained.

"All right, but where is the original data—on your home computer?"

"Yes."

"Any disks anywhere?"

"No."

"Not a single one, Frank?"

"I promise you, no."

Kevin surveyed him silently for a few seconds, trying to decide if he be-lieved him. Then, suddenly, he got up from his chair and motioned to his associate, who also rose. Picking up the gasoline can by the cabinet, Kevin brought it over to where Frank was tied in his chair. Screwing off the top, he bent down and poured some of the pungent liquid onto the engineer's feet.

Frank, meanwhile, was frozen in fascinated terror as he watched the whole scene. He finally managed to blurt out: "What—what are you doing?"

"Holding your feet to the fire, of course," replied Kevin, laughing raucously at his own joke.

Kevin's partner, who had taken a position behind Frank, leaned forward and smacked him hard across the mouth with a blunt object. Blood poured out of his split lips and trickled down his chin. Fearing another blow, Frank craned his neck away from his assailant. The pain in his head returned almost immediately and somewhere, as if at a great distance, he felt his feet being tied together forcibly. Then there was the sensation of wetness as the gasoline seeped through his jeans above the ankles.

His mirth having subsided, Kevin took a long puff of his cigarette, and stepping back from his victim, threw it onto his oil-soaked feet. The gasoline burst into flames almost as soon as the glowing tip of the cigarette touched it. Within a few seconds, the flames engulfed Frank's ankles.

The scream of agony from Frank's lips was stifled expertly by the man standing behind him. He held the engineer's face in a vise-like grip while Kevin stood back to survey his work. The feet were now a blur of orange, and the stink of burning flesh quickly permeated the room. Hardly noticing the smell, which he was used to, Kevin walked back over to the metal cabinet by the door. To the left of the cabinet and hidden behind a crate was a large bottle of water, the kind used in water coolers.

Hefting it onto his strong shoulders, Kevin brought it back over to the Luxor engineer and slowly poured out the welcome liquid onto his burning feet. As the water struck the flames, they began to die out, and in less than a minute, the only sign of the fire was the steam emanating from the burnt floor, the smell of charred flesh, and a mangled mass of bones and muscles that were once functional.

The man behind Frank slowly released his grip. Frank's first reaction was to gulp desperately for air, and then he began to cry. Not scream, not bellow, but cry. It's a natural human tendency to scream at the infliction of intense pain, but once the pain passes a certain threshold, it no longer lies within the cognitive scope of the human nervous system or the brain;

it simply becomes an ache that causes discomfort, and most of the "memory" of the pain turns into shock.

Sitting back down, Kevin lit another cigarette to replace the one that had gotten burnt in the fire, and gazed dispassionately at his victim. He waited for a few seconds to let the spasmodic weeping subside, and then resumed his interrogation.

"Now then, you know what we're prepared to do. So why don't you tell me what else you cooked up so we don't have to cook *you* again?"

Frank's mind was no longer where it had been a few minutes ago. It was in a dark, foggy place where the normal functions of the human brain couldn't be carried out. Somewhere deep inside this zone, he could see his wife and daughter as he remembered them from last night. Uljana was standing by the stove in an apron, cooking some beef stew, getting plump—but with the same girlish charm that had endeared her to him more than two decades ago. Tracey was sitting in front of the television, polishing her nails and ignoring everyone else in the apartment in deference to Brad Pitt, who was acting his usual buffoon self in a movie.

Vaguely, he heard sounds emanating from close by, but could scarcely make out the words.

Outside, there was a thunderclap, barely muted by the thick walls of the warehouse. Kevin looked irritated at Frank's lack of response; he didn't have time for this nonsense. He repeated his question, more loudly this time.

This time the words were a little clearer, but their import still escaped him. Frank shut his eyes tightly to preserve the vision of his lovely family, the only good thing in his life and his world. It was an invitation to his assailants.

Leaning over impatiently, Kevin punched the engineer in the nose. A gush of blood spurted from the broken cartilage and Frank's eyes flew open in surprise and fear. His mind snapped back to reality. He moved his head feebly toward what looked like a person through the haze.

"Could . . . you . . . please . . . repeat?" he sputtered through the blood covering his nose and mouth.

Kevin smiled and repeated his question.

"No . . . nothing . . . else. I told . . . you . . . just . . . email," whispered Frank sincerely, trying hard to focus.

"All right, Polack. I believe you now," said Kevin, satisfied. He threw the remainder of his cigarette onto the floor and ground it out with his foot.

"It's really a pity, Frank. I was actually beginning to like you. You're just a guy trying to do right by his family and you really don't deserve this," he resumed with mock sympathy.

Frank was past the point of caring. He let his head fall back on the head of the chair and shut his eyes. Uljana and Tracey were still there, waiting for him.

His last thought as the man behind him pulled out a gun was what a beautiful woman his daughter would become one day. Then there was a click, and darkness descended.

The man in the tan raincoat released the safety and fired three shots into Frank's head, standing back to avoid the blood and brains that splattered everywhere.

Frank Wachowski was dead.

The black Ford Taurus stopped outside a junkyard. Kevin and his partner stepped out and walked back toward the trunk. They dragged out the heavy body of the Luxor engineer, which was wrapped in garbage bags, and carried it towards the chain-link fence surrounding the yard. It was still raining hard, and within seconds they were drenched.

One of the men pulled out a pair of pliers and went to work on the fence, creating a hole big enough for him and his partner to get through with the body.

Fifteen minutes later, they had placed the body behind the wheel of a broken-down Oldsmobile on the far side of the yard, behind some other junk, and piled back into their own car. Kevin Renshaw started the engine.

They drove slowly since the roads were slippery and visibility was low. As he squinted to see through the downpour, the driver, whose real name was Chad Rollins and who had once cut a nineteen-year-old's testicle off, cursed under his breath.

Driving in the rain could be murder.

twenty-five

Two days later, a short, plump Polish woman walked into the offices of the local precinct to report a missing person. The sergeant on duty took the details and the photograph, and promised that the police would do whatever they could to find the woman's husband. Secretly, he knew that it wouldn't amount to anything.

Even *if* the guy hadn't simply disappeared on a drinking spree or a whoring binge, it was extremely unlikely that the police would expend a huge amount of time or resources to find him. Most such cases were the result of domestic disputes or misunderstandings and the police department simply couldn't afford to follow up the hundreds of such cases that turned up every year. There was the possibility of foul play, but unless the person's family or associates had a good reason to suspect someone, this case—like most others—would simply get filed away and no action would be taken except perhaps circulation of a photograph to local bars, supermarkets, and schools.

Uljana Wachowski returned home dejected and confused.

Frank hadn't been in bed the morning after the thunderstorm, but she had just assumed that he had left early for work. When he hadn't come home that evening, she had called his office but there was no one there. *He must be on one of his all-night field trips,* she had thought.

The next morning, the people at Luxor Satellite had informed her that Frank hadn't shown up for work that day or the day before. She had called Peter O'Donnell, who had promised that he would ask around the office and in the local bars and pool halls to see if anyone had seen Frank. Then she had gone to the police.

Later that evening, Peter dropped by to give his report. No one had seen Frank since two days ago. No, he couldn't think of any other places that his friend might go. Had she gone to the police yet? What had they said?

After he left, Uljana sat down at the kitchen table and cried.

Amanda Fleming poured some coffee and crossed back to the living room, carrying two cups. Tom Carter was seated comfortably in an over-stuffed leather chair, gazing at the eclectic mix of modern art prints and earthy wall rugs that adorned the room. He accepted the proffered cup gratefully.

She asked him what he thought of the décor.

"It's unique," he replied sincerely. "Interesting but also comfortable."

She smiled brightly, and once again Tom found himself feeling attracted to her. He hoped it wasn't too obvious.

He was right about the décor. The small living room was neatly furnished with two leather chairs, a loveseat, and a coffee table; all space-savers but adequate and pleasing in look. Along one side of the room was a long, thin table, with some magazines, a telephone, and a lamp spaced out evenly on its wooden surface. In a shelf beneath the tabletop were some books and a stereo system connected to large floor speakers placed on either side of the living room. Right now, a muted Chopin was playing. Next to Tom's chair was a short leather-tooled side table with a Tiffany lamp perched on top. The light from the lamp cast a multicolored stained-glass glow on the wall behind.

Amanda settled herself in the loveseat and sipped her coffee. Her bright eyes were sparkling in full reporter mode.

"Thanks. It took me a while to get it this way. The key was figuring out a method to the variety," she said proudly.

"Do you live alone?"

"Yes, why?" she asked suspiciously.

"No reason," answered Tom hastily.

But Amanda knew the reason. He was trying to find out if she had a boyfriend.

She changed the subject. "Let's get down to work. We need to figure out who has the most to gain from this merger. Any ideas?"

Tom considered the question carefully.

"The CEO of Luxor, the board, the majority shareholders, even the employees that will remain after the merger. Of course, only the first three have any real power to influence decisions. Of them, the majority shareholders can sway the board, which in turn can force the CEO's hand."

"So we can count out Craig Michaels?"

"Not necessarily," said Tom slowly. "If Craig was offered a sweetheart deal that favored him over other shareholders, he could have forced his board to accept TriNet's bid since he *also* owns the majority of the company."

"But couldn't that lead to shareholder lawsuits against TriNet?"

"Probably, but those lawsuits are always hard to prove, especially if the deal is structured cleverly," Tom pointed out.

"Which of course is what you do," said Amanda cheerfully.

Tom glared at her. Amanda continued.

"All right, but that still doesn't explain why Craig agreed to sell his company at a bargain price. If he had conducted an arms-length auction, wouldn't he have made more money and also avoided any legal complications?"

"That's right. So we still don't know what motivated Craig's decision, but it's a safe bet he had a good reason for it. He's too shrewd an operator to make a panic decision," observed Tom. His coffee had gotten cold and he put it down on the floor.

"Do you want me to reheat that for you?" asked Amanda, reaching for the cup.

Tom shook his head.

"No, thanks. I've had enough caffeine for today. Let's leave Craig Michaels out of the equation for the moment, even though I have a feeling he's a big part of this puzzle. Let's think about TriNet. Fact number one, someone at TriNet negotiated a sweetheart deal with Luxor. Fact number two, they took a needless risk by making an initial bid that was sure to be rejected. Finally, someone leaked the news to the press. Put it all together and you've either got some bizarre coincidences, or a really smart plan."

"I'll go with the latter," she said with a shrug. "But who stood to profit from all this, and *how*?" asked Amanda, voicing the million dollar question.

Tom bit his lip. He had spent most of his free time over the past few weeks thinking about these questions and had come up with few satisfactory answers. There were too many variables in the equation and he wasn't sure how to solve it. The only way, he supposed, was to pick a theory and proceed with it, until they either hit pay dirt or a dead end.

While he was thinking, Amanda rose to refill her cup. She was dressed simply in a solid blue T-shirt and a white cotton skirt. Her slim, elegant form moved gracefully under the clothes. She returned a minute later with a steaming cup.

"So, have we got our villain yet?" she laughed.

Tom grinned in return. "Can you handle an answer with a question?"

"Shoot."

"What was the purpose of the press leak?"

"On second thought, the press leak *could* have been a coincidence."

"Sure, but let's assume that it wasn't. So what happened once the news was leaked?" Tom insisted.

"At first the acquiror's stock went down as it usually does, but then it rose when the analysts realized what a good deal it would be for TriNet."

"Exactly. TriNet's stock closed up by more than twenty percent on the day of the leak. So several shareholders cashed out and short sellers rushed in to take advantage of the bull market for the shares. But that was only the beginning," said Tom, watching the journalist for her reaction.

Amanda's brow furrowed in concentration.

"When the bid was rejected a few days later, the stock price—which was inflated—plummeted," she finished his thought.

Tom inclined his head slowly in affirmation. Many times over the past few weeks he had been impressed with Amanda's ability to assemble disparate pieces of a story into a logical construct. What took him hours or days of thinking to decipher, she was able to extrapolate in minutes. It was the writer's knack of viewing everything in terms of an unfolding story: each thought, each action, was somehow linked to the next, and the sequence could often be followed like a linear regression.

"The drop allowed the short sellers to make good on their sales, and created an opportunity for bargain hunters to pick up the stock at deflated prices," he said, following through. This was like a dance.

"A week later the bid was revised, but this time the news wasn't leaked. Why not?" Amanda wondered out loud.

"Maybe because this time they knew that the merger would go through. After the announcement of a successful bid, the stock price would go up anyway," replied Tom.

"So where does that leave us?"

Tom rubbed his chin thoughtfully. It was obvious that a number of parties had profited handsomely from the movements in TriNet's stock price, but that was, after all, what the stock market was all about. The only thing that would make the trading suspicious was if one or more parties had been responsible for a large chunk of the transactions. It wasn't illegal for someone to trade actively on market speculation, but it *was* against the law if the party had an inside track on the stock.

"We need to figure out if any of the trading was based on inside information and who was involved," he stated flatly.

"Could it have been someone at the investment banks—either your own or the bank advising Luxor?"

"I doubt it. There is too much supervision at the banks. The compliance department is like an internal police force, monitoring the activities of its employees. Even if something slipped through the cracks, it would have to be minor," replied Tom. "No, it would have to be some senior officer within the company or someone unrelated but close to the top, with a lot of cash."

"So we should start by checking the insider trades," said Amanda, pulling up her legs beneath her.

Tom shook his head. "I already did that. There was the usual exercise of stock options and periodic buying and selling by corporate officers. Nothing big."

"What about non-insiders? Corporations, mutual funds?"

Again, Tom shook his head.

"Anyone holding more than five percent of a company's stock is required to file a statement with the SEC. Mutual funds have to disclose their holdings, by law. Those lists can be obtained from Bloomberg— I checked them and found nothing."

"What if someone traded just below the five percent threshold? Can't we get hold of the names of everyone who bought or sold TriNet's stock during those two weeks?"

"Which would be thousands of people. Only the exchanges have such order books and even those aren't usually organized," cautioned Tom. "Besides, unless you're a law enforcement agency, you wouldn't be allowed to see the books."

"But what if we *could* get the names?" insisted Amanda, her journalistic sensibilities offended at the notion that information could be withheld from the public.

Tom laughed. "It's not that easy, Amanda; and even if you did, you won't find anything."

"Why?"

"Because anyone who is smart will use dummy buyers to spread out the trades. Even the brokers maintain a stash of street stock."

"What's that?"

"Street stock is the name for the shares that a brokerage buys or sells under its own name rather than the name of the client. It's done to enable large clients to trade anonymously."

Amanda rose and stepped to the table alongside the wall. Lying next to the telephone was a pack of cigarettes and a lighter. She offered the pack to Tom, who shook his head.

"Do you mind?" she asked, pulling one out for herself.

"Not really. But you know those things will kill you, right?" said Tom playfully.

She took a deep puff of the cigarette and exhaled slowly, watching the smoke billow upwards toward the ceiling. She looked uninterested in the remark; she had heard it too many times.

"I'm counting on it," she said tonelessly.

Never argue with a smoker or a fool. Tom decided wisely not to engage.

"You said that if a law enforcement agency asked for the order book from an exchange, they would get it?" continued the reporter, refusing to let go.

Tom sighed. "Yeah, but you would still need a warrant from a court."

"I know someone who may be able to help us."

"And who's that?"

"A friend who works at the FBI."

"All right. See what you can do. If we can get hold of some names, maybe we can check them out," relented Tom, but with a faint smile. He was skeptical that Amanda would be able to get any names, but it would be amusing to see her try.

He stood up to leave. "Well, thanks for the coffee."

Amanda walked him to the elevator. She still had the cigarette in her hand.

As they waited for the elevator, Tom stared at the journalist out of the corner of his eye. She cut a strange figure: a simply dressed city girl with the features and air of an aristocrat, standing in a public hallway smoking a cigarette in front of a NO SMOKING sign. There was something incredibly attractive about that.

Screwing up his courage, the banker asked the question that had been on his mind all this time.

"Would you like to have dinner this week? We could compare notes then," he asked, bracing his ego for a hit.

Amanda smiled cryptically. It was the studied look of a woman who had been in this situation many times before and wouldn't give anything away until she was ready.

"I would love to, but let's do it over lunch. The Coffee Shop in Union Square?" she suggested cheerfully.

Tom nodded dumbly. The elevator arrived.

As he rode down, the banker wondered about their exchange. *Was it a brush-off or did she just want to take it slowly? Did she have a boyfriend? How did she see Tom? As a potential lover, or just a friend?*

The latter was almost too horrible to contemplate.

The waitress arrived with two cappuccinos and plopped them unceremoniously in front of Amanda Fleming and Jack Ward.

"Do you want somethin' else or just the check?" she asked disinterestedly. Jack shook his head. She pulled out a pad, ripped off the top sheet and dropped it in the middle of the table. Jack reached forward and pulled it towards him. The waitress walked away.

Without reaching for his coffee, Jack gazed steadfastly at Amanda.

He had been surprised to receive her call the day before. He hadn't really expected to remain in touch with her after their confusing relationship. Although he suspected that it was at least partly his fault, he wanted very badly to blame her for the breakup. For the moment, however, he kept his feelings hidden.

"So, what's up?" he asked in a friendly but wary tone.

Amanda studied his eyes. She had been hesitant to call him for a favor, but had no choice. Like him, she wanted to level blame for the breakup on anyone but herself, but now wasn't the time. Also, she felt guilty—she hadn't told him what this was about.

"I didn't call you regarding *us*, Jack," she said carefully, lowering her head but keeping her eyes fixed on him. "I'm working on a story. It's potentially very big and sensitive. I need some help and I called you because I know that I can trust you."

Jack nodded noncommittally.

Amanda started at the beginning: with the news leak and her exclusive, her calls to Morgenthal Winters, her meetings with Tom Carter, and his suspicions about the TriNet-Luxor merger. She ended with the insider trading theory and her quest for the NYSE order book.

Jack sipped his cappuccino meditatively. He was certainly impressed with the story, but was still not sure why she had called him.

"I need to get those names and the exchange won't release them to me," explained Amanda.

"Don't the investor relations departments at major firms employ outside consultants to track that sort of thing?"

"Sometimes, but it's only for high-level internal planning, and would probably only be available to the CEO or CFO. Besides, I can't run the risk of calling TriNet's IR department and alerting them to the fact that someone is snooping around—it could tip off whoever is involved."

"So what exactly do you need from me?" asked Jack, squinting suspiciously.

"Only a law enforcement agency can get those names from the New York Stock Exchange—which is where you come in," said Amanda hopefully.

Jack shook his head. "First of all, insider trading is the SEC's jurisdiction. Secondly, I can't get the exchange to release the names unless I've got a warrant—"

Amanda interrupted him.

"I know all that, Jack. And I'm not asking you to make a federal case out of this. All I need are a few names to cross-check. You could get those by asking someone at the exchange informally. I'm sure they'll be happy to cooperate with the FBI, right?"

Jack lowered his cup slowly.

"I could lose my job doing something like that. If I get some jerk on the other end of the line who decides to call his boss and tell him that the FBI is sniffing around, they'll call *my* boss, and then I'm up shit creek. If there was a case here, *maybe;* but without it, there is no way for me to justify my actions."

"You could just say that you're checking some facts," persisted Amanda, hearing him but not really listening.

"That's right, about a multi-billion dollar merger. Are you kidding me?" replied Jack sarcastically. "The moment I do that, the NYSE will get suspicious. They monitor their own activities, and they won't like the idea of a government agency finding out what happened before they do."

Amanda thought quickly. Her mind was racing even as her heart was sinking at the prospect that Jack might refuse to do this. She *had* to get that information, and the journalist inside her couldn't take no for an answer.

"I got it!" she said, snapping her fingers.

An elderly man seated in the booth behind them looked up inquiringly. Amanda caught the stare and lowered her voice to a stage whisper.

"You don't target TriNet specifically. You bunch a number of companies into a group and give the exchange a *list* of stocks. That way no single name would jump out, and *most* of the stocks would have been affected to some degree by the merger announcement."

Jack sighed. "Someone could still connect the dots, Amanda. The fact that we're investigating only two weeks of data—two *distinctive* weeks because of the TriNet merger—will give it away."

Amanda racked her brain for the answer. Then it hit her.

"About a week before the news leak, Standard & Poor's lowered its debt rating for Cable Estates, the European cable operator, to junk status," she said, trying to recall the details. "The stock went into free fall as Wall Street expected the company to go into bankruptcy."

"So what?" asked Jack curtly.

"Things like that poison the pool for everyone. All media stocks took a hit that week," explained Amanda excitedly. "So if you give the exchange a wider time frame than just two weeks, the Cable Estates fiasco will hide our tracks for us!"

"You should have been a crook, you know that?" responded Jack cynically.

He stared out of the window next to him. They were seated in a diner on Broadway and people were rushing by with characteristic indifference, noticing nothing and no one around them. It was the New York way.

Across the street, a large Budweiser truck was parked illegally in front of a bus stop, unloading its alcoholic wares to a Chinese deli on the corner. A police car that was driving by stopped behind the truck and an officer in a blue uniform stepped out. As Jack watched, the cop walked into the deli and came out a minute later with two coffee cups in his hand. Leaning down, he handed a cup to his partner. A minute later, the police drove off, taking no notice of the illegally parked truck.

Jack smiled to himself. The NYPD did serve and protect, but only when they were in the mood. . . .

That was why he had joined the Federal Bureau of Investigation. Despite the considerable internal politics of the bureau, the external politicking by department heads and the inevitable inter-agency rivalries, at least the FBI practiced real law enforcement.

As a young law graduate from Georgetown, Jack had decided early on that neither law nor politics would provide him with the personal satisfaction that he sought from his professional life. The legal profession was quickly turning into a money-making racket and the pace of political change in America could be beaten by a tortoise with a limp. Jack Ward wanted to make a difference.

The FBI was an agency devoted to only one thing—putting away the bad guys. As a field agent, he often traveled to various parts of the country on cases ranging from serial murders to kidnapping to cyber fraud. He was an experienced investigator and knew how to obtain information both officially and unofficially.

He offered Amanda an alternative.

"Suppose I call one of my private investigator buddies and have him do some digging? Maybe he can ask around and get someone at the exchange to talk. It wouldn't be official of course, but you might get a few names."

Amanda looked uncomfortable. "But what if he tips someone off?"

Jack laughed. "The guy I'm thinking of dresses like Columbo and lives in a shoebox on Tenth Avenue. The last thing he cares about is stocks and bonds. He's smart as hell though, and I promise you he'll be discreet."

"How long will it take?"

"Probably a week. If he can't get the information by then, he can't get it."

"And his fee?" asked Amanda.

"I give him some paying business sometimes, so I'm pretty sure he'll do this one for free—unless, of course, he needs to grease some palms at the exchange. I don't expect that would run more than a couple of hundred though," answered Jack, thinking.

Amanda nodded. It wasn't ideal, but it was better than nothing. At least Jack hadn't refused to help her, and he was willing to cash in his own chip with the private eye to get the information. Once again, she felt a pang of guilt at having called him. She was taking advantage of their prior relationship and she knew it.

"Thanks so much for doing this. I really needed your help," she smiled warmly.

Jack looked like he was going to say something, then changed his mind. As he placed some dollar bills on the check, Amanda reached for his hand and squeezed it.

"I'm sorry it didn't work out, Jack," she said, staring earnestly into his eyes.

Jack was excellent at hiding his feelings, but some things could get the better of even a seasoned FBI agent. He gave Amanda a bittersweet smile and walked out of the diner.

twenty-six

Keeping an eye on the road, Steve Brandt flicked on the hands-free switch on the cell phone, which was plugged into a socket next to the stick shift of his car. He depressed a button on the dial pad and the phone speed-dialed his office. After three rings, his secretary picked up.

"Julie," said Steve, surprised. "What are you still doing there?"

"Working. . . . Someone's got to do it," Julie answered jokingly. So . . . how's the weather in the Bay Area?"

As he cruised across the Golden Gate Bridge, Steve glanced out of his car window at the clear San Francisco sky. It was getting close to twilight and the sun was sinking slowly beneath the distant horizon. Usually, one could expect to see vastly conflicting weather patterns above the bay, with glorious sunshine on one side and dark rainclouds on the other, but today the weather was even and perfect. It had been bright and breezy all day with hardly a hint of clouds, and the nighttime promised to be cool and clear.

"It's beautiful out here—as always," Steve replied. "Any messages for me?"

He could hear the sound of papers being shuffled and then Julie's voice came back on the line.

"Only two. Robert Darlington called regarding the Phoenix Mobile deal. He said he needed to talk to you about the closing dinner. The second message was from your bank, something about a wire transfer."

Steve frowned. "Wire transfer?"

"That's what they said. They wouldn't tell me anything else. Just that they wanted to inform you about a wire transfer to your account—they left a number."

"Do me a favor and email me the number. I'll call them tomorrow before heading to the airport."

"All right. There were also a bunch of emails for you."

"Anything important?"

Julie rattled off the contents of a half dozen emails to him. When she got to the last one, she stopped.

"There's one here from someone that says 'Urgent Information Regarding Luxor' I opened it, but it seemed to be a private letter for you, so I didn't read it. I thought you would want to do it yourself."

"Who is it from?"

"I don't know. It just says 'a friend,' and it came from a Hotmail account."

Steve pondered this for a second. "All right, Julie. Thanks a lot. I'll be at the office in a couple of hours and will look at it then. See you tomorrow."

"Bye, boss. Have a good evening."

Steve shut off the phone and focused on his driving. He came off the bridge and turned right, heading towards the city. The traffic was mild and he made good time through the steeply angled streets of San Francisco. As he turned into the circular driveway of the hotel, he was thinking about the message from the bank and the seemingly anonymous email about Luxor. He wondered what was in the email and who had sent it. It could be a journalist trying to get a story—he received a lot of such emails when he was working on a deal; the emails were always titled provocatively to ensure they would be opened.

The car stopped at the front entrance and a uniformed valet rushed over. Adjusting his tie and hair in the rear-view mirror, the banker stepped out and handed his keys to the young man with a muttered thanks. Inside the hotel, he crossed the lobby to the house phones next to the reception area. There was only one other person using the phones and Steve sat down a few feet away from her, turning his back to her and dialing the room number on the phone in front of him. The phone rang twice and then an attractive female voice came on the line.

"Hi, darling. I'm downstairs. Are you ready?" asked Steve in a discreet voice.

"I thought we could order in," came the suggestive response.

Steve grinned. "You read my mind. I'll be right up."

"Bye, baby."

He hung up the phone and headed towards the elevator bank, feeling jubilant and excited.

By the time Steve left the hotel, it was dark. As he had predicted, the night had turned out to be clear and a myriad of brilliant stars dotted the heavenly landscape. As he waited for the valet to bring his car up front, he took the time to savor the view.

The hotel overlooked the bay, and from his vantage point, Steve could see brightly lit boats crisscrossing the surface of the water underneath the Golden Gate Bridge. The bridge itself was brilliantly lit and stole the show with its towering red structure and vast length. In a way, the bridge was the heart and soul of San Francisco. Despite the city's other eccentricities, including its tall office towers and undulating streets, nothing compared with the grandeur of the landmark bridge.

When the valet pulled up with his car, Steve tipped him and got in behind the wheel. Shifting the car into gear, the managing director drove off.

He had arrived in San Francisco earlier in the day, after a four-day media conference in Los Angeles that he had attended on behalf of his company. His trip to the Bay Area had been sudden, and he had made the arrangements himself, much to his secretary's surprise. He had simply informed her that he would need access to the San Francisco office that evening, and Julie had taken care of it.

The office of Morgenthal Winters in the Bay Area was a satellite, used primarily for client liaison purposes for companies on the West Coast, and was staffed leanly by ten people, most of whom were administrative staff. When visiting, managing directors and vice presidents were allowed to use a series of conference rooms and makeshift offices that were kept ready for that purpose.

As Steve turned into the parking lot, he could see a lone security guard manning a post in the high-ceilinged lobby of the tower. Getting out of the Mercedes, Steve crossed over the asphalt to the glass doors that formed the entrance to the building. The guard saw him coming and buzzed him in. Steve offered his ID and within a few minutes was headed up to the forty-fifth floor. He was relaxed and happy, and thought back on the evening.

He had made the trip to San Francisco for only one reason—Laura Briggs. He and Laura had seen each other every week since their first night together, and she had even come down to spend a few weekends with him in Westchester, where he maintained a relatively modest but comfortable residence deep inside a ranch-sized wooded enclave. It was the perfect reclusive hideaway for a busy investment banker who spent most of his days in the concrete jungle.

Steve had grown very fond of Laura, and their intimacy had increased beyond just the physical aspect to a more emotional one. She provided him with something that had been glaringly missing in his hectic life—true companionship. On several occasions, he had had the feeling that this could be the one, but he knew that it was too early to jump to such a conclusion. For the moment, they both seemed content to let things coast. There would be plenty of time later to figure out long-term plans.

Tonight had been just as satisfying and wonderful as the previous times, ending with the two lovers embracing each other closely in the pale moonlight sweeping in through the large picture windows of the hotel room. They had spent the evening drinking, talking, laughing, and making love, and Steve felt pleasantly tired. She had been a little cross when he left for the office, but there were things he needed to do. Besides, his curiosity about the email had grown, and he was eager to find out what it contained.

When the elevator doors opened, Steve could tell that everyone had gone home. Since this was just a satellite office, most of the work was usually wrapped by 6:00 P.M. The only exception was when there was a live deal being transacted on the West Coast, at which time there would be a skeleton crew of two people manning the office at all times, in addition to the bankers from New York who were visiting.

Walking into his de facto office, Steve switched on a laptop that had been placed there for him and hooked into the office network earlier in the day—thanks to Julie's efforts. The lights in the office had been dimmed and Steve didn't bother to turn them up. In the semi-darkness of the room, the computer screen flickered eerily as the laptop came to life. The managing director settled himself into an office chair and waited for the system to boot up. A few minutes later, he was able to access his work email via the Internet.

After looking over the emails that he had received since his conversation with Julie, he turned to the one from "a friend." Before accessing it, he quickly checked *Properties* to see who, if anyone, had opened the email before him. Something about the correspondence made him feel vaguely uneasy.

As he already knew, the email had been checked (but not read) by Julie earlier in the day, but that was all. Satisfied, he clicked on the link, and a letter sprang to view.

Steve read it slowly, stopping intermittently to digest the information. The import of the short letter was clear. Along with the text was an attachment, which the banker opened. The screen filled up rapidly with numbers and lists.

His face turned pale as he scrolled through the sheets. He could hardly believe what he was seeing! With his pulse pounding in his head, he reached for the phone on the desk, knocking over a cup of coffee that had been left there that afternoon. As the leftover fluid poured onto the surface of the desk, he clumsily pulled out a handkerchief and threw it over the mess, lifting the cup to stanch the flow of the coffee.

Turning back to the laptop, Steve tried to compose himself. He had been badly rattled by what he had read and couldn't make up his mind how to handle it. He had been about to call Robert Darlington III, the ranking partner at MW, to seek his advice, but now, in a calmer state of mind, he saw the inadvisability of that.

After all, he didn't even know if the email was a hoax. It could be a trap set by one of Luxor's competitors, or even TriNet's rivals, to destroy the merger. It was no secret that some parties were unhappy with the deal and would do anything to stop it from closing.

And even if there was truth to the email, what did it really mean, anyway? As far as Steve knew, no one at TriNet had seen or heard anything about this report. The email simply claimed that the author had been retained by someone to compile the attached information, and it didn't state who that someone was.

Although secretly the banker suspected that it probably *was* someone at TriNet who had commissioned the report, nothing in the email indicated that explicitly, and raising a false alarm could have disastrous consequences for everyone involved. In Steve's position of seniority, he couldn't afford to speculate, and he certainly couldn't afford to call Robert with unconfirmed information and random suspicions. Besides, he didn't even know who had sent him the email—neither its address nor its contents gave any clue to the sender's identity.

The safest option, thought Steve, was to respond to the email and try to elicit more intelligence from the author. Returning to the email, he clicked on *Reply* and typed out his query. After reading it over and making some modifications, he sent it. There was nothing to do now but wait, and Steve tried hard to focus his attention on the other work that was pending. Finally he gave up—there was simply too much on his mind right now to deal with anything else. He wouldn't be able to relax until he had figured out what to do with the email.

It was late and he wanted to get back to Laura, but he decided to check his email one last time before heading out. He logged onto the network and once again accessed his account. The mail icon on the screen was lit, indicating that he had new mail. Feeling a little nervous, Steve hesitated before clicking the mouse. Some part of him hoped that this was all a big, if inappropriate, joke that would get cleared up by the morning; but his instincts told him otherwise.

The message that Steve had sent had bounced back over the Internet, unable to locate the address of "A friend." The managing director stared skeptically at the screen. He couldn't understand it. *Why would someone send him a letter that he could never take at face value—and then block a return reply?* Without a name, it was impossible to confirm the validity of the attached data discreetly, and Steve wasn't about to put his career and reputation on the line to test out a crazy theory.

At the same time, he couldn't just sit on this information either. If there was even a chance that the email was authentic, it was his job to bring it up with the client.

After deliberating on these issues for a while longer, Steve determined that his best course of action was to call Vikram Suri directly. If there was anyone who could check into this, it was the CEO of TriNet. Even if nothing turned up, as Steve hoped would be the case, he would still win high points with Vik for his honesty.

Since New York was three hours ahead of Pacific Time, Steve decided to put off the call till the next day.

As he rode down in the elevator, his mind turned to Laura. She would probably ask him what had taken him so long at the office. He decided not to mention the night's events to her. There was no sense in worrying her and all he wanted was to enjoy their time together.

Getting into his car, he remembered vaguely that he needed to call his bank in the morning about a wire transfer.

───────────twenty-seven

Jack Ward called Amanda five days after their meeting in the diner. He sounded excited on the phone and they fixed up to meet later that day at Serafina, a chic restaurant on Madison Avenue and Seventy-ninth Street. Amanda was hopeful as they sat down at a table in the corner of the crowded room. A waiter came by to take their order and then discreetly retreated into the rear confines of the restaurant.

Jack rubbed his hands confidently and gazed straight into Amanda's hazel eyes. She blushed a little in spite of herself but quickly regained her composure. She waited expectantly.

"Not to put the cart before the horse, but I think we hit pay dirt," he said, grinning broadly. Then, getting serious, he issued a caveat: "—to some extent anyway."

Amanda nodded excitedly, smiling just a little bit. She was afraid to get her hopes up too high.

Obviously interested in impressing her with his own diligence, Jack gave her the details of how he and his private eye friend had unearthed the information. He began his narrative with how the detective had convinced a junior officer of the New York Stock Exchange to run a partial list of the companies and individuals that had conducted large trades in a number of media stocks.

In exchange for the data, he had agreed to help the NYSE officer clear up some outstanding parking tickets with the Department of Motor

Vehicles, where Jack happened to have a friend. With the list of names in hand, Jack had then contacted the SEC, which was usually happy to cooperate with the FBI since occasionally they needed reciprocal favors from the bureau, and asked the clerk there to check the names against an international government database that tracked the provenance of corporate entities globally.

The clerk at the SEC, who was simply a civil servant observing the commission's protocol, complied without wondering or caring about the reason behind the request. Since the two government agencies routinely "helped each other out," there was little risk of raising eyebrows, something that had worried Jack with regards to the NYSE.

While most of the names on the list had no connection with each other, as Amanda had expected, there were five entities that raised red flags. It seemed that all five were the names of dummy corporations that had conducted block trades in TriNet stock through small brokerages scattered around the United States. Two of the companies were in South America, one was based in Tokyo, and the final two were located in Eastern Europe. According to the database, all five of the dummy firms were owned by a holding company based in the Isle of Man, off the coast of the United Kingdom.

Jack had contacted the bureau's London office to get more intelligence on the holding company, and they were checking.

"Of course, you realize this could just be a coincidence—it isn't out of the ordinary for holding companies to conduct business or trading activities through dummy subsidiaries. It's usually done to minimize the tax liabilities in their home country, and is perfectly legal. Besides, we were only able to obtain a subset of the names on the NYSE list, so we could have missed something," Jack pointed out matter-of-factly.

Amanda nodded. "I agree. Until we hear back from London, we don't have much to go on. But I can still run the holding company through the databases at the *Times* and see what turns up. This is really helpful, Jack. Thanks," she said, taking his hand and smiling warmly.

"Don't mention it. Our researcher in London, an Australian guy by the name of Derek, is good. If there's anything out there, he'll find it," promised Jack, reciprocating the smile.

The waiter returned with their food.

They talked generally for another hour and then left the restaurant, promising to call each other if anything turned up.

At the same time that Jack was filling Amanda in on what he had found, Vikram Suri and Steve Brandt were standing on opposite sides of a billiard table on the thirty-ninth floor of TriNet's offices in lower Manhattan.

Steve was dressed conservatively in a black Burberry suit with a cream oxford shirt and a dark green tie. His hair, graying slightly at the temples, was cut short in a clean, corporate look.

Vik wore a bottle-green double-breasted suit from Anderson & Sheppard one of the top names in Savile Row, a powder-blue shirt with French cuffs, and a midnight blue tie with white polka dots. His luxuriant black hair was combed neatly back and seemed to be perfectly in place from every angle. His jacket would stay on until he got home. Rather than the American habit of taking the suit off at work, Vik subscribed to the old-world British custom of staying fully dressed in the office.

The pool table, covered in a rich red baize, was in the center of a large, high-ceilinged room fronted by a wall of windows that looked out over the city. A long dining table sat next to the glass, and directly across, on either side of an elevator, were neat rows of mahogany bookshelves. The rows to the left were broken only by a barely noticeable door that led to a pantry. A buzzer at the center of the dining table could be used to summon help from the kitchen.

This was a private suite and the elevator could only be accessed from the CEO's office a floor above. Except for the kitchen, the rest of the floor was deserted to maximize seclusion. It was the boss's own private Shangri-la.

Vik offered Steve a cue stick from a rack on the wall. The investment banker shook his head.

"Suit yourself," said the CEO, shrugging his shoulders.

He lined up the billiard balls using the triangle and placed the cue ball at the other end of the table. Bending low, he took careful aim. He pulled the cue stick back and propelled it forward gracefully. The white ball whizzed across the table and sent the colored balls flying in every direction. A green-striped ball rolled easily into a corner pocket. Throughout the shot, his motions were fluid and controlled.

Steve watched with pursed lips. He was getting impatient with his client.

He had called Vik almost a week ago about the email and wire transfer, but hadn't gotten a meeting until today. The CEO of TriNet had assured him that everything was all right and that it was all a big misunderstanding. Steve had been tempted to protest, but had reconsidered when he realized that he still had no reasonable cause for suspicion. For all he knew, Vik could be right and this was all just a false alarm. He didn't intend to lose his firm a premier client over his personal paranoia.

Nevertheless, there was still the matter of the wire transfer. Upon his return to New York from San Francisco, he had been informed by his bank that a sum of $500,000 had been deposited to his account the day before—from a numbered account in Switzerland.

Steve had debated whether to transfer the money back to the Swiss bank account, but had decided to wait until he could determine the source. It could all be part of a major (and expensive) hoax, or a frame. He wasn't sure which, or whether the transfer was in any way related to the email that he had received regarding Luxor Satellite, but he hoped that Vik would be able to shed some light on the matter tonight. Regardless, he would wire the money back tomorrow morning.

Having broken up the tightly clustered configuration of balls in his first shot, Vik now concentrated on pocketing them one at a time. He still did not speak, and Steve felt angered at being so blatantly ignored. Finally he decided to say something.

"What's going on, Vik?" he asked in a controlled, but steely voice.

Walking around the table to survey the possible angles, Vik didn't respond right away. He needed to settle on a shot first.

"Pool is a great game, Steve. It tests the ability of your mind and body to work together in an exquisite continuum. The physical shot is just an extension of what the mind conceives. You don't really pocket the ball with your cue stick—you pocket it with your mind. You *see* the ball going into the pocket long before you actually send it there. Once your mind and body get used to working together, the actual shot is just an extension of what you have already done—in your mind's eye."

The banker's face was impassive. He wasn't here to be coached in the Zen of billiards.

As if reading his mind, Vik wandered over to the rack and put away his cue stick. He turned to face his guest.

"The email you received isn't a hoax. The information contained in it is accurate, and was compiled by someone we employed. You could say that it was part of our due diligence process," Vik stated candidly.

"So who's this guy you hired?" asked Steve, surprised.

"Someone on the inside, but that's not important. What's important is that the information was extremely useful to me in securing the Luxor deal."

Steve's eyes widened. "So Craig Michaels is in on it?"

Vik considered his answer carefully.

"Again, that isn't relevant. Things like this occur all the time in a merger of this size, and you and I both know that a lot of deals wouldn't even happen without this sort of investigative work. As CEO and board member, my primary responsibility is to the shareholders of TriNet and I think I did a decent job of living up to that."

Steve was incredulous.

"Your *duty* is to inform shareholders truthfully about the facts, and if you had—"

Vik interrupted him.

"If I had, I would have let the deal of the century slip through TriNet's fingers. I'm paid to exercise my executive judgment and that's what I did." After a brief pause, Vik added: "Just like you . . ."

Steve fell silent. Vik was right. When the CEO had insisted on changing the bid, it was Steve who had arranged for the numbers to be doctored to fit the price. In that respect, he too had violated his ethical obligations. But this was something else. It was one thing to be selective with the truth, quite another to lie.

Steve Brandt felt a rush of anger welling up inside him. "That's bullshit, Vik! You've exposed my bank to a lawsuit and God knows what else."

"Oh, get off it, you bloody twit! Your bank isn't going to take the fall for this. Some schmuck on your team will. I bet you've been setting up your vice president from day one," said Vik with a nasty smile.

Steve went pale. *How the hell did Vik know about that?*

He was about to retort but Vik wasn't finished with his tirade.

"What the hell do you know about being a leader anyway? You're a bloody investment banker, living off the deals of rainmakers like me. Without me, your firm would be out prostituting itself with 200-page pitch books filled with ideas so stupid that even a high-schooler wouldn't show them to anyone!

"I'm a visionary, an industry captain who's accomplished more in his life and career than you can ever aspire to. So don't lecture me on fiduciary responsibility, you jerk."

Steve was stunned. He had known Vikram Suri for a number of years and had always regarded him with professional respect and even awe. What Vik had accomplished with TriNet Communications was the stuff that corporate legends were made of. Up till this moment, Steve had grouped the Indian with the likes of Jack Welch, Bill Gates, and other trailblazers of the twentieth century. But the man he saw in front of him now was little more than a common criminal.

To hell with the fee, thought Steve, *it was time to take off the gloves.*

"I'm going to discuss this with Robert Darlington tonight and I'm sure he'll agree that your prior knowledge of this email's contents constitutes a criminal offense. I'm also certain that he'll report the matter to your board."

Vik walked over to the dining table and sat down. He regarded the investment banker carefully. In the subdued lighting of the room, his dark eyes were penetrating, like a cat's. They were the eyes of an animal contemplating a kill.

"Do you know why marble feels cold to the touch, Steve?" he asked in a level voice.

Steve responded sharply. "Cut the crap, Suri. I have no interest in your stupid little games. All I care about is exposure for Morgenthal Winters. Now, if you—"

Vik didn't let him finish. He repeated his question in the same even tone.

Steve pursed his lips in anger. *What the hell did marble have to do with anything?* He didn't reply.

"I didn't think so," said Vikram Suri, chuckling. "Marble is always eleven degrees cooler than the air that surrounds it. Amazing, isn't it? That's why it's always cold to the touch."

"I'm blown away, now what's your point?" asked Steve, his jaw set impatiently.

"My *point,* my dear Steve," smiled Vik maliciously, "is that there a lot of things you don't know. The world is full of revelations and paradoxes."

He continued, as if addressing an adoring audience. His egomania was in full bloom now.

"Contrary to what you might think due to your Wall Street arrogance, neither you nor your self-important firm add a whit of value to anything. You're merely a pawn in a much bigger game. As any chess player will tell you, a pawn is the most expendable piece on the board. You catch my drift?"

Steve studied his host carefully, not at all sure where he was drifting, but quite certain that his words translated to a thinly veiled threat.

A few seconds ago, he had been ready to stalk out of the room and throw the nuttier-than-a-fruitcake Indian to the wolves. In the preceding half-hour, he had lost all respect or sympathy for the TriNet CEO, and his unfavorable opinion about the man had hardened with each passing second.

Nonetheless, there was something disturbing about Vik's sudden self-assuredness. A few minutes ago, he had been defending his actions to the banker and justifying his vision of corporate responsibility. Now he was sitting comfortably, pontificating about games and strategy—more like his usual self. It was as if the tables had somehow turned in his favor. *Or had they been in his favor all along?*

The only way to find out was to flush out the danger.

"What the hell are you talking about?"

"I'm talking about *destiny,* my dear friend. Fate, providence, whatever you want to call it. That which drives us, inspires us, guides us, and sometimes even forces us, to go down a certain path, to make certain choices, and to accomplish the end that we were born to achieve.

"Just as some people are born to be leaders, others are born to be followers. Now what if one of those followers refused to play his or her part in the grand scheme of things and decided to go down a different path—to disregard their destiny? What do you suppose would happen?"

Steve shrugged disinterestedly. His patience was running out, but he knew that he had little choice but to let the CEO talk. By now, he was quite certain that his host had anticipated this exchange and had set him up in advance. He didn't want to leave this room without knowing how.

"I take it the bank has already contacted you regarding a money transfer from a Swiss account?" asked Vik, as if in answer to his own question. His eyes were hard as granite.

The banker stiffened. He was starting to get it.

"Would it surprise you to learn that the numbered account belongs to me?" continued the CEO.

Steve shook his head dumbly. He wanted to say something but his mouth felt parched and lifeless.

"It's a corporate slush fund," explained Vik. "Even my board doesn't know about it."

Vik scanned Steve's face for a reaction. He would have preferred admiration, but there was only shock. Disappointed, he resumed his monologue.

"Of course, a Swiss bank would never reveal the name of its account holders, but if there was to be any sort of investigation into the merger, I would be only too happy to divulge that information," he finished.

At last Steve found his voice.

"Why would you do that? You would only be incriminating yourself to your board of directors, who would demand to know why they were never told of the slush fund. And besides, what does any of this have to do with the Luxor email?"

Vik chuckled. "What's the matter? It never came up at the country club? The money transfer to your account is our insurance policy. If you unwisely decide to bring the email up with the partners at your firm, we would make it known that you received a payoff from someone at TriNet to keep your mouth shut; someone *else* of course. There are other people who have access to the Swiss account besides me. That person would then be fired, as would you."

"But I haven't accepted the money. I'm sending it back tomorrow morning," Steve objected.

"As I understand it, you have had the money in your account for almost a week. That's about six days too long, genius. After all, it's hard to convince people of good intentions when half a million dollars are involved," observed Vik softly.

"That's utter nonsense! Just because I received some money from an anonymous source doesn't mean I took a bribe. Besides, by the time I read the email, you had already transferred the money into my account. How could I receive a bribe before I knew what I was being bribed for?!"

"Doesn't your secretary read your emails first thing in the morning?" asked Vik meaningfully.

Understanding finally dawned on Steve Brandt.

"Steve, Steve, Steve. The only thing that's going to make a difference is the *appearance* of impropriety on your part. The fact that you *could* have known about the report before the money was wired to your account, the fact that you *could* have known about it while you were advising us on the deal, will be enough to damage your career. Let's face it, you work in a snobbish business—the smallest smear and you're history."

"You know something, Suri?" responded Steve quietly. "You're two bricks shy of a full load."

"Well then, I hope you like *these* bricks," said Vik cheerfully.

Reaching into his inner suit pocket, he pulled out an envelope. Without opening it, he tossed it through the air onto the billiard table. The envelope swished through the empty space, glided across the smooth surface of the table, and came to a halt at the far end. Steve stared momentarily at the ominous brown package, then walked over and picked it up.

He slit open the envelope and pulled out its contents. He studied the photographs wordlessly. In the strong light above the pool table, his complexion paled visibly. He was beginning to feel ill.

"What in heaven's name—" he began, but couldn't think of what else to say.

"Nice artwork, eh?" grinned Vik perversely.

Without responding, Steve looked back down at the photographs. There were six color shots, probably taken from a camera concealed in a wall or closet. The pictures were clear, candid and calculated. They showed Steve Brandt and Laura Briggs completely naked, and in a variety of compromising positions. One photograph in particular was extremely graphic and Steve shuffled it hastily to the bottom of the pile.

His initial panic at seeing the pictures having subsided, he began to relax. In his logical banker's mind, he realized that the shots, albeit racy, were evidence of nothing more than a sick voyeurism on the part of the photographer; after all, both Steve and Laura were single adults who had a right to carry on a sexual affair if they pleased, and it was no one's business but their own. Calmly, he tore up the photographs and let the pieces fall to the floor.

"This is nothing but rubbish, Suri. I really hope you have something better than this to threaten me with," said Steve. "Did you honestly think that I would get intimidated by this filth?! In case you've forgotten, I'm a bachelor. Who I sleep with and what I do in bed are entirely my business. . . ."

Vik, who had been watching his guest with amusement all this time, now reached into his jacket pocket for a leather cigar case. Pulling out a Cohiba, he lit it at a leisurely pace, not bothering to offer one to his guest. After taking a long puff, he exhaled slowly, watching the thick smoke curl up towards the high ceiling. The aroma of luxury excited him. He turned his attention back to the banker.

"She's a hooker, Steve," he said simply, waiting to let the words sink in.

Steve's mouth fell open in amazement. At no time during the last few minutes had it crossed his mind that the photographs might have been taken with the cooperation of Laura. He had automatically assumed that she was an innocent victim.

"Go to hell, Suri! This is just another one of your cons," he growled, refusing to believe.

"That's exactly right—it's a con. You can ask her the next time you see her, or should I say the next time you screw her. . . . She's a high-priced call girl and has been on my payroll for a number of years—you wouldn't believe how adept she can be at changing men's minds."

"Her job as a political consultant?"

"A front. She *does* work with some minor players in Washington, but . . . you know. If you remember, I'm the one that introduced you—at my party in the Hamptons. I asked her to seduce you and sleep with you whenever you wanted—on our dime, of course," answered Vik, turning the cigar around between his thumb and forefinger and watching the bright red glow of the tip with fascination. He continued.

"It was a pretty good deal for you, Steve. For the past few months, you have had the best that money can buy, without having to spend your own money on it. Of course now that you've brought the situation to a head, I don't see how we can keep paying for it. But feel free to call her up on your own."

There was shock in Steve's eyes, but also grief. As he heard the Indian businessman speak, his mind raced with thoughts of his encounters with Laura. The passion, the sincerity, the cozy intimacy, the shared hopes and fears—it was hard to believe that it had all been fake. Making it doubly difficult was the fact that he had entertained the notion of love with this woman. If she was a whore, then he was a fool.

As if reading his mind, Vik said: "What did you think—that she loved you? The only thing that Laura loves is money, which of course isn't much different from you or me."

"I'm nothing like you!" Steve shot back viciously.

The CEO laughed and took a puff of his Cuban.

"All right, so Laura is a whore and I let myself fall for it. I'll survive," resumed Steve, his voice hardening to steel. "It still doesn't explain why you took those pictures. What are you planning to do, send them to the police and get me arrested for using a hooker?"

Vik shook his head. "No, that would never work. For one thing you never solicited or paid her for sex, and for another you could simply deny that you knew she was a hooker, which is the truth anyway. After all, women like her don't exactly advertise in the yellow pages."

"Then what?" asked the banker, genuinely puzzled.

Vik leaned back expansively in his chair, his arms spread regally over the ornate armrests. The cigar protruded jauntily from the side of his mouth.

"You've been sleeping with Laura since the beginning of the Luxor deal. Given the line of work she's in, you can imagine that she loses little sleep over the idea of perjuring herself. If you do anything, I guarantee she will tell *Hard Copy* that you received sexual favors from her in exchange for keeping mum about the Luxor report. Couple it with the wire transfer and your own mother wouldn't believe you. . . ."

"But that brings your name into the picture as well," frowned Steve.

"Oh, for God's sake," shouted Vik, exasperated. "What the hell am I doing here, talking to myself? Laura works for me. She'll only say what I tell her to say, just like everybody else on my team. *Do you get that?* This is *our* picture. We can paint this any way we want."

For the first time that evening, Steve noticed the use of the word "we," which Vik had sprinkled intermittently in his speech. Despite his untenable position, his curiosity was aroused.

"Who is 'we'? You keep referring to yourself in the plural. I don't think even your egomania has reached that level, Suri."

Vik laughed genuinely at the remark. Only this guy, thought Steve wryly, could find such a statement flattering.

"I think we've had enough pithy sayings for the evening, so I'll spare you the 'curiosity killed the cat' routine. But I strongly suggest that you stop worrying about *us* and start worrying about yourself.

"If you blow the whistle and the merger dies, I can still leave TriNet on a golden parachute. At worst I look like I was duped. You, however, are saddled with the honor of having lost your firm a generous seventy-million-dollar fee, and of involving it in a scandal; not to mention the cloud of suspicion that will hang over your head for the rest of your life. . . ."

Steve Brandt stared at his host for a long, painful moment. He could not think of any logical response to all that the CEO had thrown at him. Finally, for lack of anything better he whispered: "This is blackmail . . ."

"No, Steve; this is capitalism—at its textbook best," responded Vik coolly. "As long as everyone works for their personal best interests, the collective good will be served automatically. Now be a smart capitalist and you can keep your job, your reputation, and of course, the five-hundred thousand; we might even do more business in the future. It's not a difficult choice."

Steve turned away with a curse.

Walking over to the window, he stared out over the luminous cityscape through the polished panes of glass, his hands clasped behind his back. The night lights of Manhattan, although bright, seemed distant and impersonal. There was nothing cheery or radiant about them tonight; instead they seemed like a lugubrious testimonial to the greed and corruption that powered the very heart of the city. *Capitalism, or legalized mayhem?*

He addressed the CEO without turning around.

"All right, what do you want?"

"That you keep your eyes and ears open and report to me with any rumors or problems. Think of yourself as my personal grapevine," breathed Vik softly. In the dead silence of the room, it sounded like the hissing of a snake.

Steve nodded his assent.

His face was unemotional and his eyes impersonal as he coolly bade the Indian businessman good night. Five minutes later, he was headed down in the main elevator to the lobby of the tall office tower.

Back in the private suite, Vik resumed his game of billiards.

If he got his way, he mused, one day the colored balls would pocket the white one.

─────────────twenty-eight

While Vik and Steve sparred with each other across a billiard table, Amanda Fleming yawned. She was chafing at the lack of movement with her story and wondering what, if anything, could move it along.

She had decided not to go into the office and instead work out of her apartment. Waking up early, she had poured herself a large cup of black hazelnut coffee, lighted a cigarette, and sat down in her living room to read. Her mind was whirring away with thoughts of the TriNet-Luxor merger. Even though she had other assignments on her plate, and had yet to disclose her investigative efforts to her editor, she found it impossible to concentrate on anything else.

Underneath her sophisticated veneer and mature countenance lurked a terrier mentality and a shrewd common sense. Her instincts told her that this story could be her ticket to fame and fortune, yet she had no new leads or ideas. She had run the holding company in the Isle of Man through *The New York Times'* databases, but had come up with nothing. She couldn't shake the conviction that somehow time was running out and with it, the chance of a lifetime.

To add to her insecurity, Jack Ward hadn't called her back since their last conversation, and Amanda feared the worst. He had promised to speak with his bureau contact in London regarding the suspicious holding company, and if he hadn't called her back that could mean he had either hit a dead end, or simply decided to drop the matter. Either way, it was her only lead and she couldn't afford to lose it. She hoped desperately that her fears were misplaced.

As if in answer to her prayers, the phone rang an hour later.

It was Jack Ward on the line and he conferenced in his London colleague, an Australian by the name of Derek John.

Derek was extremely cordial and helpful. He was a junior researcher in the FBI and seemed to be in awe of the field agents. He addressed Jack in a deferential tone and was excited at the prospect of having his work utilized in a real-life investigation. Jack decided not to burst his bubble.

The results of his search were splotchy. By contacting the office of business registries in the Isle of Man, he had managed to unearth the provenance of the holding company whose subsidiaries had traded actively in the stock of TriNet Communications in the weeks following the news leak.

The holding company, generically named the International Trading Company, was a private entity with a dozen shareholders scattered across Continental Europe. Amanda asked Derek if he had any idea who these people were. His answer surprised her.

The shareholders were low-income people with no business background. Most of them were junior clerks in small companies. *It made no sense,* thought Amanda. *How could these people have the money to trade in stocks when they were little more than office assistants?*

Derek explained. "When I was in Australia, these sorts of scams were fairly common. They are called bottom of the harbor deals. Essentially, a fake company is formed to hold assets in various parts of the world. In order to prevent the authorities from discovering who the real founders are, low-income people are literally picked up from the street and offered a few bucks anonymously to put their name on the charter of the company.

"These blokes receive a small up-front payment in cash and in return become the legal shareholders of the company. The trick here is that on paper, the founders can't be linked to the company; yet behind the scenes, they control everything, including the disbursement of earnings."

When Amanda inquired what "bottom of the harbor" meant, Derek responded patiently that as private entities, the holding companies would pay "consultants" or "advisors" without recording their actual relationship with the company. Similarly, capital would be received from outside as "payment for services" without further details. In this way, money could flow into or out of the company from any source. The laundered profits would then be siphoned off to the real founders, who would receive such payments through numbered bank accounts or third parties.

The net result of all this was that the actual trail of the money would be nearly impossible to trace due to all the intermediaries involved and the lack of paperwork linking the company to its actual founders. Since these were usually one-shot deals, the company itself would be bled dry of any cash after a large business transaction, after which it would be liquidated—or sent to the "bottom of the harbor."

"So who does these kinds of deals, Derek?" inquired Amanda.

"Organized crime and arms dealers use them to launder money. Major corporations, even celebrities, do it to hide their income."

"Why doesn't Interpol or someone try to stop this?" wondered Amanda naively.

"Too complicated. Other than the many jurisdictions involved, there are the issues of proof in law, governmental resources for tracking this sort of thing, and of course political corruption. It's deeper than a kangaroo's pouch," explained Derek cheerfully, the marsupial analogy eliciting a frown from Jack.

The journalist in Amanda was fascinated by all this. Americans were shocked when they discovered that a CEO had re-priced his options after a fall in the market. *How would they react if they knew that billions of American dollars were being laundered and hidden by some of their favorite companies and movie stars through bottom of the harbor deals in the Isle of Man?*

"Couldn't the Brits help us with this?" ventured Amanda.

"Not really. You see, the Isle of Man doesn't belong to the U.K. or the European Union. It has its own parliament and laws. That's why it's a banking haven in the first place," answered Derek.

"So what's the upshot of all this, Derek? Is there a way to find out who's behind this international shell game?" asked Jack.

Derek replied in the negative.

"Not without a major cross-border investigation. And even then it would probably take months to figure out where the money for the holding company came from and where it's going. Also, the shareholders were probably approached anonymously, which means they're not much use.

Unless you have a solid lead, it's like looking for the needle in the haystack, mate."

Once the Australian was off the line, Amanda and Jack discussed next steps.

Based on the conversation with Derek, two things had become evident. One, an insider trading scam was certainly plausible, maybe even likely. Secondly, it would be impossible to go further down this track without the cooperation of law enforcement.

Jack muttered an awkward apology that he couldn't launch an official investigation through the FBI, but Amanda waved it away. She had already asked him to risk his career once. And he had.

"I'll call Tom and see if he has any ideas," she said.

At the mention of Tom's name, Jack signed off, but reluctantly.

Tom Carter wasn't in his office, so Amanda tried his cell. Three rings later he was on the line. She filled him in briskly, leaving out the names. The investment banker was impressed. Amanda had uncovered a lot more than he had expected her to. He recalled doubting that she could unearth the names in the NYSE order book. He would not make that mistake again.

"Sounds to me like we're playing the role of the Securities & Exchange Commission," he observed jokingly. "Maybe we should bring in the real thing."

"Would they do that?" the reporter asked hopefully, taking his words at face value.

Tom groaned inwardly. He had walked into that one. He thought about Suzie Goldwater and her first, and last, foray into the world of corporate law enforcement.

"After the fiasco with the girl, they're going to be extra careful. Unless they're convinced they can nail someone on this, I doubt they will take the chance," he pointed out pragmatically.

"Can't they look into it unofficially, without alerting the press or TriNet?"

"Sure. But it will still take a lot of manpower and time to investigate the holding company, and you said yourself that without international cooperation, this thing is dead on arrival. Official or not, I don't see how the SEC can do this without beating some loud drums, some of which are bound to get picked up by the press in one country or another."

Amanda had an idea.

"I think my editor knows the chairman personally. They used to work at the same bank or something. Maybe he's got a marker that he can call in. Even if the commission can't nail anyone, they might find something that will give the *Times* a story."

Tom caught on to her stream of thought. "And once it comes out in the press, the SEC will have the perfect excuse to launch an inquiry, is that it?"

"Exactly. And without any implication of harassment," she finished.

"But will your editor go along with it?" Tom wondered out loud.

"Leave that to me," answered Amanda determinedly.

─────────────twenty-nine

Hal Reardon, the cigar-chewing CEO of Trademedia Publishers, had liked Tom's acquisition idea very much. He called him on the phone to tell him that they would hire Morgenthal Winters to explore the possible deal. Tom had already forwarded him an engagement letter, which the client signed and faxed to him a few minutes later.

As per protocol, Tom called up the compliance department at MW. The compliance department was in charge of ensuring that the firm met the requirements of the law, and most importantly, didn't get pegged for insider trading. The department was responsible for monitoring trading activities and maintained a watch list of companies that the firm was currently advising. Once a client was put on the list, the employees of the investment bank, except its sales and trading personnel, were restricted from buying or selling stock in that company while the bank was engaged.

It was this list to which Tom added Trademedia's name. The vice president also included the acquisition candidate since their shares too would be affected by a deal. As part of the drill, Tom had to inform the compliance department about the nature of the assignment, the duration of the engagement, and whether any of the bank's personnel would need to be brought over the Chinese Wall.

The Chinese Wall was a set of rules implemented by the investment bank to prevent the unauthorized sharing of inside information within the firm. As a general rule, communication between bankers and traders was restricted, and traders were prohibited from soliciting inside information. The same applied to research analysts. An effective Chinese Wall enabled the firm to carry on sales, trading, and research in the ordinary course of business at the same time that its investment bankers were engaged in a transaction with a client.

Occasionally, a trader or research analyst would need to be brought "over the wall" in order to facilitate a deal. In such cases, the compliance department, along with senior bank officials, needed to approve the crossing.

In the case of Trademedia, Tom had determined that a research analyst was needed to gain a better understanding of the company's financial and strategic standing. For the vice president, it meant a lot of paperwork.

While he chafed at having to deal with the onerous requirements of the compliance department, Tom knew the reason why the procedures existed.

Following the abuses of the '80s, insider trading laws had been tightened and the SEC's oversight activities broadened. Under the current law, anyone who had access to material non-public information regarding a company—either through tips or other means—and traded on it, was considered to be an "insider," regardless of whether they were connected with the company or not. This meant that the SEC could prosecute anyone at an investment bank including mail clerks, as well as the bank itself, for a breach.

The compliance department was a pain in the ass because they had to be. Their stringent policies minimized the firm's legal exposure and ensured deniability for senior officers.

As he was filling out the forms, Tom stopped to think about the implications of the Trademedia assignment for his own career. He had brought in a large client for the firm, and that was a big deal. It was a *coup d'état* for the young vice president that would fast track him to a higher office.

That was, of course, if his own involvement in the TriNet investigation remained a secret.

Suddenly Tom was worried. For the first time since he had so consciously set the ball rolling on Amanda's investigation, he felt a tinge of regret at his decision.

Had he overreacted and made the wrong choice? Could this all blow up in his face?

He prayed to God that it would not.

Anyway, promotion or not, there was little he could do about it now. The process he had started was irreversible, and the only option was to trust it.

The business editor of *The New York Times* was a short, silver-haired man with a round face and an ashen complexion. In a moment of extreme kindness, his closest friends would have termed him "distinguished looking." In reality, however, Alex Taylor's looks left something to be desired.

With features that seemed to have been arranged in a horrendous hurry by the powers that be, he embodied in the flesh what schoolchildren imagine trolls to be like. His eyes were too closely set, leaving one wondering whether two were even necessary; his nose was sharp but displeasingly so; and unusually large lips accounted for at least a quarter of his face. In a dark alley, he would have been a formidable creature. In the light of day, he looked just plain ugly.

As so often happens in life, providence had made up for its cruelty to Alex in the looks department by being generous in other areas. He had an amazing brain for facts and figures, and a business acumen that would have put most of the financial moguls he covered to shame.

With this package of negatives and positives, Alex had made himself a force to be reckoned with. Realizing as early as high school that his displeasing appearance could be a handicap or an asset depending upon which way he used it, he had turned it rapidly to his advantage.

Since most people automatically assumed that an ugly man would also be dumb, Alex found that he could almost always beat expectations and surprise everyone. By adopting his natural countenance, he was able to mislead people into thinking that he had much less talent than he actually did. Then, much like a pool hustler, he would jockey them into a compromising position before moving in for the kill. In the world of finance, this was akin to pulling a rabbit out of a hat, and Alex had soon made himself a rich man on Wall Street at the expense of others' gullibility and propensity to stereotype.

The post at the *Times* had also been offered to him for exactly the same reason that banking firms on Wall Street had wooed Alex two decades earlier—for his uncanny ability to surprise and vanquish. He was the one that no one saw coming. He was the secret weapon in the arsenal of a major newspaper. Although the business beat was decidedly dull compared to its political counterpart, Alex had quickly managed to make it interesting, with exposés and left-field pieces that had made him a formidable figure in the field of financial journalism, and much feared by the business community.

Had Amanda worked under Alex in those early days, she would no doubt have gotten a taste of the guerilla journalism that she so craved. But as the editor grew older and more successful, his jets cooled. With the tacit approval of some conservative executives at the paper, he had gradually lowered the temperature in his department, to the delight of the more faint-hearted journalists.

In a world driven by circulation, Alex's approach had gone over well with the corporate bean counters. The business readership of the *Times* was primarily white-shoe and averse to controversy, and the best way to retain their subscriptions was to give them what they wanted—basically bland business news that didn't give them ulcers. It was a honey trap, and Alex Taylor had sunk right into it. He had soon realized that he couldn't bring the patient back to life if he wanted to.

When Amanda Fleming had first joined the *Times,* she had been apprised of the editor's history, usually in hushed tones that indicated the disapproval of the more intrepid journalists in the crowd. She was bitterly disappointed at the reports, and even more disheartened by the type of assignments that had landed on her desk. But unlike other reporters who were afraid to cross swords with the "old man," Amanda could not stay on the sidelines.

She had eventually made her ambitions known to the aging editor. Not that it had yielded spectacular results, but somewhere in that sharp brain of his, Alex had filed away the information for future use. Even the staid business section needed a controversial piece once in a while, and if Amanda came to him with such a story, he would be willing to listen.

That, and the fact that she had brought in the initial exclusive on the TriNet-Luxor merger, was why he was indulging her now.

Amanda explained briefly why she was there. The editor listened shrewdly to her request, but made no move to respond. His astute mind had already sifted through the facts as she relayed them to him, and determined that there was indeed a story here. In a way, the editorial post at the *Times* had been the consummation of Alex's life's work, the apotheosis of his intellectual talent. The years of financial dealings on Wall Street had honed his senses to razor-sharp condition, and despite his eagerness to please his timid bosses in the corporate office, some part of him was still the tiger waiting to be let loose on the world.

A paradox of Alex's life, and one that his underlings at the *Times* barely recognized or knew about, was that he regarded the present crop of silver-spoon reporters with a sentiment bordering on contempt, even as he sought to emulate their approach for the sake of readership. It was the most private of battles for the man who had learned early on to turn adversity into triumph; listening to Amanda, Alex now found himself once again at a crossroads in his career.

Without saying a word, he stood up from his desk and began to pace the spacious office, his forehead creased in a frown of concentration. His footsteps created a sharp sound against the polished wood floor as he strode forcefully back and forth across the room. Wisely, Amanda remained silent.

She had been right about two things. One, Alex had indeed worked with the chairman of the SEC in their previous lives on Wall Street; being approximately the same age, they had toiled side by side first on the trading floor of Salomon Brothers and subsequently moved into investment banking within the same firm. The two men had cemented a good, if not great, friendship, and often saw each other at business parties and political functions.

Secondly, Alex was aching for a real front-page exclusive. With hardly a year left to his retirement, he wanted to leave the office with a bang rather than a whimper. Although his decision to "run the burners on low" had been a conscious one—and he had few regrets about it, he now desired to change that by pursuing the sort of intrepid journalism that nailed Pulitzers. As his curtain call neared, he was determined to leave behind a legacy of *real* news that he hoped fervently would be remembered by future generations of editors, even if not followed.

It was, however, a risk. As chairman of the SEC, his friend was no longer in the position of handing out favors. Admittedly, Alex would merely be giving him a tip on a possible case of insider trading, but he would also be asking for an exclusive if something turned up, and he wasn't at all sure if the Chairman would go along with that. It bordered on checkbook journalism, and could put both men in an awkward position.

If the commission did investigate, but refused to grant an exclusive, then the *Times* could have handed over a major story to the world without so much as a five-hour lead.

As if reading his mind, Amanda broke the silence.

"I know that it's a risk, Alex. We could lose the story completely by letting the cat out of the bag, but what choice do we have? If we do nothing, we have nothing. I've come to the end of the line with this unless the SEC gets involved."

The editor stopped his pacing to look at her.

"The SEC doesn't just get involved on a whim, Amanda. To be honest, what you have is a lot of extrapolation. If I go to the chairman with this, he might just shrug it off as the insane ramblings of an old journalist."

"Your instincts for news are undeniable, Alex," said Amanda flatteringly. "I know you'll convince him."

Alex smiled. He knew that he was being manipulated, but the truth was he really didn't mind. The reporter was right, and that made all the difference. He decided to test the waters a little more.

"And what if this is just a false lead? What if there was no insider trading? What do you plan to do then?"

Amanda gazed thoughtfully at her boss. After a moment of silence, she replied.

"I believe there's something else. Something to do with the merger itself."

"Meaning?"

Starting at the beginning, Amanda encapsulated the events leading up to the final bid for Luxor Satellite, including the rapid changes in valuation and the analysts' reaction to the purchase price. She never mentioned Tom Carter. At some point, she supposed, she might have to reveal her source to her editor privately, but not yet. If the SEC was able to establish a case, it wouldn't even be necessary. Either way, she would keep her promise to Tom.

"So you think that the merger itself may not stand up to scrutiny?" asked the editor, absorbing the information.

Amanda shrugged. "I can't say that for sure, but something certainly seems to be off. And I have an even stranger feeling that it's linked to the insider trading."

Alex mulled this over. He would need more time to digest the details and sort through the pieces of this puzzle, but Amanda was right—there *could* very well be a smoking gun here. The question was where?

The silver-haired editor finally nodded his affirmation.

"All right, I'll call the commission. In the meantime, pull together as much as you can on this merger and see if you can find an inside source," he instructed.

Amanda stifled a smile. *Already on it, chief,* she thought happily.

It was 1:00 P.M., Day 50.

thirty

At 10:30 the next morning, Vikram Suri was seated at his expansive desk in the downtown headquarters of TriNet Communications, holding court. Attending the session were his personal deputy Helen Mosbacher and Mark Pearson, the CFO of the firm. Helen stood in front of the desk while Mark was perched on the edge of a chair, leaning forward. He proffered a set of papers to the CEO.

"The ESOP plan is being set up now. We received the funds from the loan yesterday from the bank in Boston. As per ESOP rules, the funds will be kept in escrow until the shares are transferred from our treasury, which will happen at the time of the closing. We can break escrow and access the money at that point."

Vik perused the documents quickly and then put them down.

"What about my shares?" he demanded.

Mark shifted uncomfortably in his seat.

"My office will contact your broker to take care of that. It's an awfully large number of shares, so there could be some questions from the board, Vik."

"That's my problem, not yours. You just mind your end of the equation," ordered Vik quietly.

He didn't bother to tell the CFO that he had no intention of informing the board that a portion of the ESOP shares were being purchased from his personal account, at least not until the last second, when it would be too late to modify the arrangements.

Mark fell silent. As CFO, it *was* his concern if an existing shareholder, particularly the CEO, was dumping a large number of shares via an ESOP; but he was also a loyal member of Vik's camp and couldn't afford to antagonize his imperious boss. Additionally, as one of Vik's personal hires, his allegiance to the CEO had been assured early on through a generous compensation package.

Vik now turned his attention to Helen. She had been keeping track of the approval process by the Federal Trade Commission and the Department of Justice, and now delivered her report to the CEO in a crisp, professional tone.

"We should receive approval by the end of this week. Of course, the government could make a second request for information, but my contacts at Justice informed me that it's unlikely. The paperwork will take another couple of days, but come next week we should be in the clear," she assured him.

Vik nodded his approval.

"Good. With a little bit of luck, we should be able to close the merger in a fortnight. Thanks for your help, and now if you'll both excuse me, I have some calls to make."

With old-world courtesy, he stood up when they did and waited till they had left the office before sitting back down. In the privacy of his empty office, he picked up the secure phone on his desk and dialed a number in Maryland.

It was time to give an update to his "silent" partner.

The sweat on Helen's forehead glistened like a sheen of bright cellophane under the powerful white lights of the Sports Club LA. The tall redhead was tired, winded, and sore. Yet she continued to hit at the punching bag with the stamina and ferocity of a jungle cat. It was part of the routine she had practiced three times a week for the past eight years, and by now her body had accepted the reality of its demands.

The routine itself consisted of an hour-long cardio workout on the treadmill, followed by weight training, aerobics, and finally boxing. The last was her favorite, since it allowed her to test the limits of her strength, agility, and willpower. By the time she got to the punching bag, and sometimes a live partner, her muscles were screaming in protest and her lungs begging for a break. But that was when she really pushed it. In the end it felt good, very good.

Her physical workout coming to a close, Helen glanced up at the wall clock high above the room. The next twenty minutes would be spent in the sauna, followed by a hot and cold shower and finally an exquisite massage—all part of the full-service gym that catered to the rich and famous. After a small salad and an Evian, she would get into the chauffeur-driven car waiting for her downstairs and be whisked away to a firing range in New Jersey. There a private instructor would evaluate her marksmanship with a variety of handguns, some of them meant primarily for self-defense, others intended for more heavy use. It was all part of the curriculum at the Vikram Suri school of criminal training.

Helen Mosbacher, born Helen Donatello, had changed her name to facilitate her profession and attitude in life. Hailing from a poor Italian family in Queens, the striking redhead had learnt early on that the world belonged to those who had the muscle to rule it. That included those with money, either from inheritance or empire building; those with exceptional talent and luck, like movie stars; or those who had no qualms about snatching it from the other two. It was that final group that Helen had decided to join, and with her looks and brains, she refashioned herself from the honest but destitute Donatello to the ruthless but successful Mosbacher. In the snobbish world of corporate America Italian names were invariably regarded with suspicion, Helen had noted, and so she had altered it, as well as anything else that could impede her progress in her new life. It was a transformation worthy of an Academy Award and Helen had achieved it at the astonishing age of twenty-seven.

Having observed her hardworking father toil away uselessly as a carpenter till the stress of trying to make ends meet finally did him in with a massive coronary, she was determined never to get caught in the web of ordinary life, where upright citizens trudged through the brutal desert of existence every frigging day, looking for an oasis that didn't exist and breaks that were reserved for those who already had everything. By aligning herself with powerful men and manipulating their greed and lust to satiate her own voracious appetite for the good life, Helen had defeated not just her own humble beginnings, but life itself.

Minor inconveniences like weapons training, which she abhorred because of a virulent distaste for guns, had to be borne simply because they were part of the discipline. Like a soldier who will eat insects just to stay alive, Helen would become a crack shot if it served her interests. Also because Vik had ordered it, and there was no arguing with the man who was her season ticket to the Super Bowl of privilege.

Yes, Helen Donatello would kill if it meant retaining her box seats.

Tom had decided to try his luck with Amanda a second time, and had broached the subject of dinner during one of their routine phone conversations. To his utter surprise and delight, she had answered in the affirmative, even expressing a preference for Moroccan cuisine. After narrowing down the choices with *Zagat's,* they had settled on a quaint little place called Casa La Femme in SoHo.

After walking around the block once, since there was no sign outside proclaiming the name of the restaurant, Tom walked through a straw-covered porch and into the bar which fronted Casa La Femme. The décor was Middle Eastern, and unlike many such restaurants scattered throughout the city, reasonably authentic. Cozy cushions lined the wall opposite the bar and a ceiling fan whirred gently above the room. Directly in front of the bar were half a dozen luxuriant barstools covered with plush red leather.

In the back of the restaurant was the dining room, lined on either side by a row of mesh tents with floor-level tables inside, and regular tables down the middle. Candles and incense burned strategically throughout the dimly lighted room, and the whole atmosphere was one of exoticism and romance.

Tom saw her as soon as he stepped inside. She was seated at the edge of the bar and beamed when he walked in. She was wearing a rust-colored décolleté dress with a faux belt that looked like a ribbon. Her golden hair shimmered ethereally in the sparse lighting of the room, and the candlelight seemed to dance in the reflection from her eyes. Tom's heart didn't skip a beat—it stopped completely.

He had imagined many times what Amanda would look like on a date, but nothing in his dreams had prepared him for the real thing. Composing himself, he stepped forward and kissed her lightly on the cheek.

"Hi," he said, staring straight into her hazel eyes.

"Hi, Tom," she replied, blushing slightly. There was something girlish about her tonight and Tom noticed. It made him feel more masculine.

They talked generally for a few minutes over glasses of Chardonnay, and then the waiter ushered them toward a tent in the dining room.

Being a tall man, Tom had some difficulty fitting his legs underneath the floor-level table, but eventually managed to squeeze himself in. Amanda laughed at the spectacle and settled down across from him, placing her handbag to the side.

"How was your day?" asked the banker, shifting uncomfortably in his position.

"It was hectic, but good. Are you sure you're comfortable?" asked Amanda, gazing amusedly at him.

"Yes, don't worry about it," answered Tom, meaning the exact opposite.

"How are things going with you? You have a new deal?"

"Yes, it's a publishing company. I'm quite proud of it actually, since I brought in the client."

"That's great! Does that mean they'll promote you?"

Tom chose his words carefully. "Maybe. It's definitely not going to hurt my chances, but promotions are always a political affair. All the partners at the firm have to be convinced that it's justified and then approve it. Even if I'm in the running, it could take months before anything actually happens."

Amanda nodded.

"If they're smart, they'll promote you fast. Otherwise, I'm sure there are dozens of other banks that will be happy to oblige," she smiled encouragingly.

The menus arrived and Tom studied the items carefully, being unfamiliar with Moroccan cuisine. Noting his discomfort, Amanda stepped up and offered to order for both of them. Tom made a joke to hide his embarrassment but gratefully conceded.

For the next half hour, they made small talk. It was amazing, reflected Tom, that even though they had known each other for nearly a month and spoken practically every day, here they were—meeting like strangers on a blind date. There was a dramatic line between friendship and romance, and tonight Tom and Amanda were trying to determine the feasibility of crossing it. It might have been easier had they met under different circumstances, but then any context could be good depending on how it turned out.

When the food arrived, Amanda explained patiently what each item was. True to her journalistic nature, she described everything in detail and Tom pretended to pay attention. In truth, the only thing he was paying attention to were her lips, which had just the smallest trace of gloss on them. He was hungry and the food smelled delicious, but he was more interested in what her lips would taste like. He wondered if he would find out tonight.

Amanda, in the meantime, was sizing up the situation from her polar opposite angle. She had debated for weeks whether to accept another invite from Tom, which she was sure would come, and had at last decided to give it a try. Unlike Tom, her attraction was more mental than physical and the physical part would come naturally if she felt comfortable with him.

There was no doubt in her mind that she liked him as a friend. And for a banker, he was a saint. But whether she could see herself dating him was quite another matter. It was a different plane of thought, of life, and only a woman really understood the difference.

What made this such a game of Russian roulette for him, she thought cheerfully, was the fact that her decision could come in a split second, and even she didn't know whether that moment would be tonight or a month or a year from now. It was one of the exquisite prerogatives of being an attractive woman.

As the evening progressed, however, Tom also exercised *his* prerogative—namely, that of charming the beautiful young woman he had asked out. He kept the conversation light and deliberately non-work-related. Outside of banking and his business suit, Tom was relaxed and happy. The edginess that permeated his professional persona was noticeably missing, and Amanda was pleasantly surprised. She had dated investment bankers before and usually they were tight-asses. This one was different.

Between mouthfuls of delectable lamb and red-hot curry, Amanda and Tom chatted about their lives and interests for almost three hours. At one point, Tom reached over and touched her hand. The feeling was electric and Amanda didn't move her hand. In the body language of dating, it was a good sign for him.

After dinner, they walked through SoHo, peering into the restaurants and checking out the dessert menus outside the door. At last they settled on a small corner restaurant near Thompson Street called Café Noir, and walked in. The lounge was crowded and past the bar they could see clusters of young people seated at narrow tables that filled the rear of the restaurant. Ornate rugs and paintings adorned the whitewashed walls and an attractive waitress with a Mediterranean look dovetailed between the tables, delivering bottles of beer and steaming plates of *tapas* to the waiting guests. It was a world within a world.

The reporter and the banker were led to a small alcove table at the far end of the dining area. It was very private. Tom's face lit up at the sight of a regular table with space for his legs. Amanda smiled knowingly. Upon her request, the waitress came back with the dessert card and they ordered the banana flambé.

"So, do you ever regret not becoming an athlete?" quizzed Amanda, unfolding her napkin and placing it on her lap.

Tom thought this over for a while. It had been a decade since he had played football in college, and the memory of his knee injury and forced exit from the sport still pained him. But it was a darkness that he inhabited alone. He preferred it that way.

"I did for a while, but not anymore. I don't see a point in revisiting the past," he said, dropping the reporter a hint.

Amanda refused to take it.

"But that's not how you really feel, is it?" she asked perceptively.

Tom started at that. He was about to retort, then changed his mind. He gave her a crooked smile instead. "Someday that journalistic instinct of yours is going to get you into a lot of trouble, you know that?"

Amanda studied him carefully. One of the reasons she had gone into journalism and what made her so good at it was that she had powerful instincts. Not always, but sometimes, she could read people like a book. She was reading Tom Carter now, and his casual brush-off told her more about his feelings than if he had yelled them from a rooftop. Suddenly, she felt sympathy for him. The only question now was would he tell her himself, or would she need to elicit it from him? Did she even have a right? It didn't matter. She was a friend, and friends always had a right. They had a duty too. She waited.

"It's not so much regret but disappointment, and it passes. I try to redirect my energy into banking, and that's how I get through," he finally confessed, offering more than he usually did to anyone.

Even though he hadn't exactly poured his heart out to her, Amanda realized that he had just told her something very private, and possibly painful. It made her happy that he would confide in her. She looked deeply into his eyes, and glimpsed a man who wanted to open his heart, but didn't know how. She could feel her own heart racing in her chest.

Tom coughed awkwardly, then lowered his eyes. As Amanda suspected, this process was difficult for him. Over the years, the banker had been through a handful of relationships, with varying degrees of seriousness, and his experience with such matters was shaky at best. He had been in love just once—a long time ago—and it had ended badly. The memory of that rarely bothered him, because he seldom allowed himself to get close to women. Though he wanted the connection with Amanda badly, he was also afraid of it.

When his eyes returned to her, they were noncommittal.

"What about you? Do you ever think about what else you could be doing instead of journalism?"

Amanda scrutinized his face, wondering if he was really interested or just deflecting the spotlight from himself. His handsome features offered no clue.

That was all right, she thought. The night was still young.

"I can safely say no. I always wanted to be a journalist, ever since I was a little girl. I suppose it's kind of weird—knowing something like that so early and then having it come true, isn't it?" she replied cheerfully.

"Not really," said Tom, shrugging his shoulders. "It's just a self-fulfilling prophecy."

"I guess that's right," said Amanda, smiling wickedly. She always got a kick out of knowing that she had made her own destiny happen. Tom's smile conveyed his kudos. *So he was interested.*

The dessert arrived. The waitress set it down between Amanda and Tom, and pulling out a box of long wooden matches, carefully set it ablaze. A brilliant flash of orange-blue fire leapt upwards and then subsided, leaving a crisp layer of sugar on top of the fried bananas. A scoop of vanilla ice cream sat on a small plate next to the bowl.

The waitress placed empty plates in front of the guests and retreated silently.

Now that the night was almost over, Amanda's thoughts returned to the merger. She had tactfully avoided the topic all evening, and so had Tom, but it was important and needed to be discussed. She hoped he wouldn't mind.

"Listen, Tom, the merger. What happens now?" she asked carefully, breaking the unspoken pact.

Tom groaned inwardly. He really did not want to discuss this. Not tonight. But he responded anyway.

"We wait to see what the SEC turns up. If there's something to the insider trading theory, then the commission will launch an official inquiry, and our work is done. At least mine."

"What do you mean?" asked Amanda naively.

Tom gave her a bittersweet smile. "In my business, there's no glory in doing the right thing. If they find out that I blew the whistle on the deal, the partners at MW will make sure that my career comes to a dead halt. I'm the invisible man. You get your story and that's it."

The reporter pondered his words. For her it was about the exclusive, for him it was about protecting himself. There was no other reward at the end of it for the banker, no brass ring. The most he could look forward to was not losing his career. It seemed like a raw deal. She should have heeded the warning shot.

Instead, she resumed.

"But what if the SEC can't find anything? After all, the FBI guy in London said that tracing these things is next to impossible."

This wasn't happening, thought Tom. He could feel his head throbbing. "Then I don't know what happens next, okay? You're the journalist," he replied wearily.

But Amanda was in the zone now and the banker's tone hardly registered.

"If nothing turns up with the commission, my editor will pull the plug on the story, Tom," she continued unabated. "We need to find something, anything, to keep this thing alive."

"Yes, of course. Your story . . ." observed Tom bitterly.

This time she heard it.

"I'm sorry, Tom. I didn't mean it that way," she muttered hastily.

But there was a cynical look in his eyes. For the first time, he wondered if he was anything more to this reporter than a source.

For the remainder of the evening he said only a few words. Amanda tried to lure him into a conversation, but he remained reticent. She felt like kicking herself. She had let her terrier mentality get the better of her and it had ruined their evening. She wondered nervously if she had lost his trust.

On the cab ride home, the reporter decided there was only one way to fix what she had broken. Leaning over suddenly, she kissed Tom full on the lips.

He didn't resist, but neither did he respond. Despite his attraction to her, he felt frigid. Although he had calmed down since leaving Café Noir, his irritation and mistrust were still strong, and he couldn't decide whether the kiss felt pleasant or not. Finally Amanda pulled away. She peered at him curiously.

Tom caught the anxious look in her eyes, and began to relent. There was a mixture of confusion and feeling in them that he found very endearing. He could feel his own confusion melting away like butter on a hot stove. The anger of a few minutes ago seemed remote, even alien.

"Is this personal, or business?" he asked her frankly.

After thinking about it, she replied truthfully: "Both."

Tom reached out and touched her hair tentatively. It was the same electrifying feeling that he had when he touched her hand earlier in the evening. It was enough to convince him.

He leaned over and kissed her properly.

In the days following his meeting with Vikram Suri in which he learnt of the elaborate trap that he had fallen into, Steve Brandt found it increasingly difficult to concentrate on work. After the initial shock of the incident had passed, he felt angry, and betrayed. The fact that he was now an accessory to criminal activity paled in comparison to the realization that he had been emotionally duped by a professional hooker. *How could he have been so stupid, and so gullible?*

He knew the answer to that, of course, which bothered him even more.

Steve Brandt was a lonely man. His profession left him with little time to socialize, and even when he did, he usually found himself unable to relate to people on a personal level. His world contained mainly numbers, complex financial deals, and long hours. It was a cold and precise existence that left little to the imagination, and little room for it.

For a select few, the field of investment banking held the allure of corporate ruthlessness, hardball negotiating, brilliant deal-making, and the thrill of the kill. Unfortunately for Steve, he didn't belong to that group. It was true that during his career on Wall Street he had become a rich man, and that few other professions would have afforded him such material gains in such short order, but what good was all that without passion? He woke up every morning not with the smell of the chase in his nostrils or the thrill of creation on his mind, but with the sole desires of flawless execution and exemplary ass-kissing. It was like a bad dream that just kept recurring.

Every year when the top investment banks came to the campuses of the Ivy League, they trumpeted their commitment to excellence, creativity, and the creation of value for their clients. The best-kept secret in investment banking was that this was pure Madison Avenue bunkum. The reality was different.

The reality was that investment banking was a machine, a machine that existed solely for the purpose of making a select few very rich while exploiting a large number of others by selling them dreams that would never come true. These others could then be counted upon to work like slaves in the belief that they too might one day win the brass ring. The only saving grace was that even managing directors were basically overpaid clerks.

Steve was a clerk. A clerk who brought in deals and took a cut of the profits, but only as long as those deals were in keeping with Wall Street's paint-by-numbers approach to investment banking. The net result of all this was that Steve spent most of his time thinking within a tight box, an activity that generated little in the way of fresh ideas, but a hell of a lot of old and tired ones. From the firm's perspective, once in a while one of those old ideas would hit and then Steve would have earned his keep.

Personally, he would have preferred to imagine out of his prescribed limits, but that was like crossing the Grand Canyon on a tightrope. If his ideas didn't succeed, he would be penalized severely for his maverick approach. Rightly or wrongly, his unwillingness to comply with the investment banking code would be blamed for his failure and stamped on his bonus.

The bonus. The brass ring. The annual wet dream. That's what it was all about and that's the one word that got Wall Street salivating like a hungry dog, or cowering like a scared child. Since the majority of investment bankers' compensation came at the back end, firms basically had them on a string. Perform or die, said the sign outside the door and inside the lavatory. But perform according to our rules. Either that or you could figure out some other way of financing that million-dollar apartment and private yacht you just purchased on credit.

The firm reigned supreme.

Steve knew this fact by heart and was not about to rewrite the history of corporate America. Also, unlike some bankers, he did not have the guts to play the game by his own rules. Oh yes, it could be done, it *had* been done. But it required balls of steel to make magic like that happen, and Steve's were decidedly non-metallic.

Besides, by injecting some false gusto into the role, he could always convince himself that he was happy and fulfilled. It was the ultimate banker's trick, and had worked reasonably well—until now.

The incident with Laura Briggs had shattered that façade, and all the intricate self-delusions that went with it.

Ironically, it wasn't the fact that she was a hooker that really distressed him, nor that she had made love to him only because Vikram Suri had paid her to. Those things were disturbing in themselves, but didn't cut close to the bone. What did him in was the reluctant knowledge that he would have been unable to help himself even if he *had* known of her motives. He needed a woman's love so badly that he was willing to entertain hollow fantasies in the absence of the real thing.

That had not happened in this case—he had been betrayed—but the suspicion remained. *What if Laura had told him everything the first time they had slept together? What would he have done then? Probably continued seeing her . . . and hoped that she would learn to love him. Damn his weakness!*

The biggest problem confronting the managing director was that his work was beginning to suffer. His distraction with Laura's treachery had now turned into a full blown exercise in self-recrimination, and Steve seemed unable to stop indulging in it. His personal problems aside, he was creating a professional morass for himself that could jeopardize his future.

The specter of losing his job or at least his prestige in the investment banking community scared Steve far more than the thought of living with a deep-rooted emotional dysfunction.

As he always did, as he knew he always would, Steve Brandt went back to his old mistress.

─────────────── thirty-one

On Day 54 of the TriNet-Luxor merger, it was decided that the princi-
pals of the deal should meet to discuss a timetable and the details of the
closing. The FTC had given a casual indication to both parties that the
merger would be approved and the official announcement was expected
any day.

It would have been a fairly easy matter for the CEOs of TriNet Communications and Luxor Satellite to meet in New York or Los Angeles to
iron out the details, but there were other issues to be addressed, issues
that required the highest secrecy. Moreover, Vikram Suri had additional
plans he needed to put in place, and one of these involved a public figure
whose profile made it impossible for him to meet anywhere in the Western Hemisphere.

It was decided, therefore, to hold the conference outside the United
States.

The British Airways jet descended smoothly through the clouds as it
prepared for landing on the sprawling runway strip below. The plane
banked to line itself up for the approach and the landing apparatus
emerged simultaneously from the underbelly of the aircraft.

The tall, stately American seated in first class gazed through the small
port-hole window next to him in anticipation. Even at sixty, and despite
his extensive traveling, he still got a thrill out of takeoffs and landings. It
gave him pleasure to watch the approaching scenery get closer and closer

till the wheels touched down on the runway and the plane bounced gently on the impact.

His first flight had been as a child with his father, an Air Force pilot, in the P-61 Black Widow, the first U.S. night fighter. As an adult, he had flown himself in Vietnam, and gained a medal out of it. Three decades later, that medal—and a distinguished career in politics—had helped him land his present job.

As the commercial airliner reached ground level, a row of tall palm trees rushed by in a blur of velocity. The American sighed with contentment. Of course, his excitement wasn't just a result of the thrill he got from aviation. He was here in connection with a deal, one that would make him a very rich man and enable him to enjoy the same luxuries as the people he was paid to watch. Now *that* was a very satisfying feeling.

Ten minutes later, the American was walking through the airport terminal toward immigration.

The official at the immigration desk asked for his passport. As an American he did not require a visa, but he would need to leave his passport with the authorities until his departure. This was done to ensure that you couldn't leave the country without checking in with the government. If you were wanted for something, well, you weren't going anywhere until they caught you. In lieu of his travel document, they would give him an entry slip that would be his permit for the stay.

The officer flipped open the passport and stared at the name: Alistair Waxman.

The airport official leafed through the rest of the travel document, stopping at a visa entry for Israel. He looked up quizzically at the passenger and asked him a question. The American responded briefly, and after considering his words for a moment, the immigration officer handed him the entry slip and waved him on.

Alistair Waxman relaxed.

He had been nervous about the Israel visa; not because he would have been refused entry due to it, but because he might have had to present his other identification papers to immigration—something he preferred to avoid since he was counting on his anonymity during this trip. Luckily, that hadn't become necessary.

Since he had only a small carry-on bag with one night's change of clothes, he didn't need to wait at the luggage carousel and proceeded directly to customs.

Customs was a perfunctory affair and within five minutes, he was outside the airport hailing a taxi. A Mercedes cab pulled up to the curb. The American got inside and was whisked away to his hotel. Behind him, the vast, modern complex of Dubai International Airport receded into the distance.

As the car made its way down the highway leading to the city, Alistair surveyed his barren surroundings with wonder. It amazed him how a modern metropolis like Dubai could exist in the middle of the godforsaken desert. Wherever you looked, there was only sand, tons and tons of it. An endless expanse of ocher dust hammered mercilessly by an unforgiving sun. No man's land.

The only relief along the boringly straight road was a single line of palm trees that adorned the cement divider in the middle. In the approaching distance, the road seemed to turn into glinting pools of water, which disappeared only when you got close—the infamous mirages which lured men to their deaths in this mysterious region. The illusion was compelling.

As the Mercedes entered the town of Bur Dubai, Alistair was startled by the sight of trees and flowers everywhere. Flora and fauna lined every street and courtyard around them. The greenery seemed a glaring impossibility in the desert climate. It was one of the many paradoxes of the Middle East.

Due to its proximity to the water, Dubai is extremely humid in the summer, and few people dare to brave the high temperatures and discomfiting moistness by venturing outside. As the cab made its way through the town area, it became obvious from the barren streets that most people were indoors in the comfort of their air-conditioning and would come out only when absolutely necessary. Most of the buildings that lined the streets had been constructed in the past two decades, and had an air of modernity about them. Shops and restaurants were scarce along the streets, but were plentiful inside expansive air-conditioned malls known as *souqs*.

The car turned off Al-Souq Street onto Al-Falah Road and drew up in front of the Ambassador Hotel. The hotel, one of the oldest in Dubai, was a clean if sterile structure, and moderately priced. It hosted mainly economy travelers who wanted a decent place to stay without paying five-star prices.

Although Alistair didn't know all of it, Vikram Suri had arranged for the American and himself to stay there for two reasons: for one, it was low-profile and therefore anonymous; secondly, the Ambassador Hotel was strategically located next to the Dubai Creek, an expanse of water that separates Bur Dubai from its sister-town of Deira. On the Deira side of the creek is a vast covered marketplace, known as the Gold Souq, where local and foreign merchants sell impressive quantities of gold, diamonds, and other precious items to retailers and tourists, at prices which vary from the absurdly cheap to the horrendously high, depending upon the gullibility of the buyer.

The CEO of TriNet had personal business to transact there.

Alistair Waxman checked into the hotel and went straight up to his room. After making a quick phone call, he lay down on the bed and shut his eyes. Vikram Suri had checked in, but wasn't at the hotel. Alistair would meet him later that evening, as planned. In the meantime, the sixteen-hour flight from Washington to London and thence to Dubai had tired him out, and he decided to sleep for a few hours.

While the American slept, a few miles away to the southeast Vikram Suri and Craig Michaels sat facing each other in a plush hotel suite atop the Burj Al Arab Hotel, part of the famed Jumeirah Beach Resort and the definition of luxury and decadence. At 321 meters the Burj was the tallest hotel in the world, and with its soaring sail-shaped structure and surreal offshore location, the most recognizable landmark of the region. Of all the hotel's distinctive features, Vik's favorites were the private reception on every floor and the fleet of Rolls Royce Silver Seraphs that shuttled passengers across the Arabian Gulf to the man-made island over a 920 foot-long road. Even by American standards, the Burj was a marvel of modern architecture and extravagance.

Craig Michaels had flown into the United Arab Emirates earlier in the day on the request of Vikram Suri, who had intimated that he wanted to discuss the final arrangements for the merger. Although unaware of the logic behind it, he had voiced no objection to the transcontinental journey. In the world of ordinary people, such an out-of-the-way trip might have seemed extravagant; in the lives of these people it was business as usual.

Characteristically theatrical, the Indian gestured expansively at the modern cityscape visible through the floor-to-ceiling windows of the suite and gave his guest the ten cent tour.

"The first time I landed here was in the early '70s. Back then Dubai was just a sand-patch. Few cars, plenty of camels. In less than a decade, the city transformed itself into a center of high finance and material decadence that would make your head spin. I'm telling you, Craig, there's no place like it in the world. There are golf courses in the middle of the bloody desert! And behind closed doors, the Arabs are just as perverted as the rest of us . . ."

Craig smiled. Since their unlikely paths had crossed as a result of the merger, he had grown used to Vik's over-the-top personality. Even though he disliked him for both personal and professional reasons, he couldn't help but admire the media baron's zest for life and "damn the torpedoes" approach toward business. It was the way Craig himself liked to function.

All the same, he hadn't come all the way to the Middle East to be tutored by Arthur Frommer, and politely requested that his host get down to business. The CEO of TriNet shrugged his shoulders in a "suit yourself" gesture, and acquiesced.

With FTC approval on the horizon, and with TriNet's own postmerger arrangements almost complete, the deal could conceivably be closed within a week. The short timetable favored both CEOs. Given the countless complications that could arise in a merger of this size, it was best to seal the deal as soon as possible.

At a private meeting, to be held at TriNet's New York headquarters in approximately seven days, Craig Michaels and the other shareholders would receive their payment for Luxor. The cash portion of the purchase price would be wired to shareholders' accounts in real time. The equity portion would be processed later in the day.

Concurrently with that, Craig and the other shareholders would sign documents transferring their ownership of Luxor Satellite to TriNet Communications. All such paperwork had already been executed by attorneys on both sides and was now only awaiting signatures.

All this, of course, was standard operating procedure, and Craig was surprised that Vik should have taken such elaborate security precautions to discuss this. He could have specified these plans just as easily over a phone line. He waited quizzically for Vik to continue.

"After the money is transferred into your account, you will need to leave the U.S. permanently," explained Vik.

Craig frowned. *What the hell was the Indian talking about now?*

"It's pretty simple, Craig. You take the money and run. Go to some city in Russia or Africa, someplace where your money will buy you anonymity. More importantly, someplace where you can bribe the reigning government," continued Vik, reaching for a cashew from a dried fruit tray that the hotel provided in every room.

"Bribe them for what?" asked Craig incredulously.

"So they won't extradite you," answered Vik, shrugging.

"Are you smoking something, Suri?" retorted Craig. "What are you talking about, anyway? I haven't broken any laws!"

Vik ignored the outburst. "The simple fact of the matter is that someone, somewhere, could always uncover the truth. We already had a little glitch that I took care of, but there could be others."

"What sort of glitch?" asked Craig suspiciously.

"Nothing you want to know about. All you need to know is that with you out of the country, we'll both be safer." After a brief pause, Vik delivered his bombshell. "Oh, and you *did* break the law, and I have a report to prove it."

Craig's stomach turned. He had all but forgotten about that. Ever since Vikram Suri's party in the Hamptons, when he had first seen the report, he had made every effort to put it behind him. Since he had met Vik's demands, he had naively assumed that the report was buried and forgotten. After all, it was in both their best interests that the report never came out.

As if reading his mind, Vik continued. "Let me assure you there is no evidence linking me to the report, not a shred. I can live without the merger. Can you live in jail?"

The Californian's blood pressure mounted.

"You Harvard-mouth cocksucker . . ." he whispered menacingly, half-rising from his chair.

Vik didn't flinch. "You're right, cowboy. Harvard grads *are* cocksuckers, but I wouldn't worry about that right now," he said sarcastically. "Right now you need to think about how mad you want to get me, because once I get there, I *will* destroy you."

"I think you're forgetting that I know about the news leak; and then there was the first bid, which I rejected on your request. I don't know how they do business in India, Suri, but in the U.S., market manipulation is illegal!" snarled Craig, suddenly feeling confident of his position. He had something to bargain with.

Vik smiled at the racial overtones in Craig's words. He had dealt with his kind before. He popped another cashew into his mouth as he pondered his response.

"I called this meeting so you and I can be on the same page. Obviously that's not going to happen, so let me spell it out for you. Every deal we made was verbal, which means that the only thing you can do to save yourself is testify against me. But that won't work.

"There's a report out there that implicates you for gross corporate negligence and hiding material information from an acquiror. If it becomes public, what kind of witness do you think you'll make?

"Given the odds of being able to convict me on such shaky evidence, I predict the government will opt for the easier kill—you. So let's recap—either you leave the country or the report goes to the feds!" snapped Vik, his voice rising with every word.

Realization finally dawned on Craig Michaels. *So that was why Vikram Suri had called this meeting!* He was tying up loose ends. With Craig out of the way, the CEO of TriNet could rest easy in the knowledge that his underhand tactics would never be discovered. And if Craig *did* go public, he would only be putting a noose around his own neck.

As these thoughts shot painfully through his head, the broad-shouldered Californian slumped in his chair. He had been outsmarted and outmaneuvered, it was that simple. For now at least, he could be humble enough to realize that it was better to get the money than go to jail. He would figure out how to get back at the brown-skinned son-of-a-bitch another day.

He ran a hand over his jaw and then brought it down to rest on his knee.

"You got yourself a deal," he said quietly.

But the CEO of TriNet wasn't finished. "One last thing. I suppose I should have brought it up with you sooner, but . . ." he trailed off.

Craig glared sullenly. "Go on."

"I want half of your after-tax proceeds from the merger," said Vik, as if ordering pancakes at a diner. "You will wire it to my account right after the closing."

Craig Michaels was past the point of being surprised or angry. Nothing that Vik said or did could shock him anymore. He gazed silently down at the carpeted floor, deciding whether to accept this humiliation or tell his tormentor to get lost—and take his chances. *After all, how bad could jail be?*

It took him less than four seconds to answer that. "Fine," he accepted tonelessly.

After Vik had departed, the CEO of Luxor lit up a cigar and stared out of the window of his hotel suite. Dubai. An ultra-modern city in a dangerously backward land.

The same as Vikram Suri.

thirty-two

In a different time zone, while it was day in Dubai, it was night in Gotham. Tom Carter was leaning over Amanda Fleming and kissing her mouth. The couple was lying on Tom's bed in his apartment on Central Park East. They had spent the evening watching a Broadway show and then returned to his apartment to cook dinner and relax.

Tom reached down and caressed Amanda's firm breasts. She closed her eyes as he kissed her slender neck and shoulders, and hugged him tightly against her. Slowly, he undid the buttons of her blouse and pulled it open. She was wearing a lacy pink bra, and Tom massaged her breasts through the flimsy fabric. She moaned softly in response to his touch. Pushing herself up on her elbows, she reached back and undid the clasp. Tom eased the straps off her shoulders and pulled away the lace.

He took one rose-pink nipple in his mouth and sucked on it gently. It came hard as Amanda's body responded. She arched her back and pushed her breasts into his face. Tom took the message and sucked harder, biting her nipple with his teeth. She cursed softly.

A few seconds later, Tom turned the journalist over on her stomach. Amanda felt a shudder go through her body.

He began to massage her back, luxuriating in the smooth touch of her skin and the warmth of her body. Gradually, his hands made their way below her waist to unfasten her skirt. Now Amanda was completely naked except for her panties, and Tom peeled them slowly off her flesh.

Rubbing his hands over her rounded hips, he lay down on top of her and kissed the nape of her neck.

Amanda moaned in anticipation and begged Tom to enter her. But he was not ready to give her what she wanted—not yet. Inserting his fingers into her moist hole, he teased her. Amanda gasped. An urgent sense of arousal gripped her and she quickly spun around.

"Take off your clothes," she commanded.

When Tom was naked, she slid below his waist and made love to him. Tom shut his eyes and uttered an animal sound. Every part of his body was tingling from the sensation between his legs. He could hardly believe the sheer pleasure of the experience. Amanda's mouth and tongue were driving him over the edge. It was his turn to be teased.

Just as he was about to climax, she pulled away. This was the game, he realized. He could not win, he could only play. He had some power, but hers was beyond comprehension. It was the curse of being a man. He waited for her to get below him, then went to work.

Amanda uttered a scream of delight as he entered her, bucking her hips to meet his thrusts. Her eyes were glazed over from the sex, and she was no longer in control of her own body. Tom intensified his efforts, and she thrashed about wildly, biting and scratching with a forcefulness that surprised and delighted her lover. With a smile, Tom noted that he had been wrong. He had a lot of power. It was the gift of being a man.

The couple soon reached their climax, and when it was over, lay blissfully in each other's arms, feeling spent but happy.

A few minutes later, the reporter disengaged herself and walked out of the bedroom. Tom stared after her, wondering where she was going. She returned a moment later with her pack of Marlboros. Pulling one out of the box, she lit it with a matchstick. The tip of the cigarette erupted momentarily in a flame and then died down to a glowing ember. In the light from the bedside lamp and *sans habile,* she looked like someone out of a '70s porn film. Tom laughed out loud.

"What's so funny?" she asked inquisitively.

"The cigarette after sex—the whole thing. It's very clichéd," he explained, his eyes filled with mirth.

"Well, what would you prefer—a healthy fruit shake? I don't know any place that sells them this time of night," she replied archly.

"Yeah, I guess a shake would kill the romance a bit," he said, propping himself up on his elbow and staring lustfully at her. Amanda caught the look and stifled a chuckle. Men were such pigs. They had just made love and already he was ready for a second round!

"So how many girlfriends have you had, Tom?"

"Hah! That's a loaded question if I ever heard one!"

"I'm not going to be upset. I just want to know."

"The life of an investment banker doesn't leave much time for relationships."

"I don't believe that."

"No? It's hard to spend time with someone when you're working fourteen hours a day."

"But you seem to have time for me."

Tom knew where this was going. He was guarded. "Yeah, I guess I do."

Amanda stared at him, waiting for more. Tom pushed himself up on his elbows. She had been angling for this. He could give her what she wanted, or he could have some fun. He opted for the latter.

"You're a great lay," he finished.

Amanda picked up her pillow and hit him with it. He laughed hysterically as she continued to pummel him with the soft cushion. Finally, he put his arms around her naked body and subdued her. She crouched in the cradle of his arms like a cat.

"It's because I'm crazy about you," he said, stroking her hair. When Amanda looked up at him, her bright eyes had misted over. Tom leaned down and kissed the top of her head. She was about to say something, but he put a gentle finger to her lips.

"I know," he smiled. Amanda laughed.

A moment later, she returned to her playful mood. "I think lovers should confess to each other," she said decisively.

"Confess to what?" asked Tom, confused.

"Something personal. It cements the bond between people."

Tom groaned. "Let's not go there." He was speaking from experience.

To give him some incentive, Amanda reached down and began to rub him. Tom sucked in his breath. She stroked him harder. A powerful blush crept up the banker's face. "Come on, baby. Tell me . . . ," giggled Amanda, exerting her considerable control. But Tom remained silent. He was aroused, not out of his mind.

Amanda realized he was not about to break. It was time to get tough. She stopped rubbing him abruptly and rolled over. "All right then, good night." The male of the species reacted in the only way that he could. He panicked.

"I had sex with a prostitute once," he blurted out, not thinking.

Amanda froze. The color seemed to drain from her pretty features. Like most women, she was staunchly opposed to prostitution and thought ill of the men who used it. She realized too late that this was a bad idea.

"Why did you do it?" she asked.

Tom shifted uncomfortably.

"Look, it's hard when you work all the time—I mean, it's tough when you're a man not to get some sexual gratification. We crave it."

But Amanda already knew that, which was why she had threatened to withhold it from him just a minute ago.

She was still distressed, but the initial shock was wearing off.

"Was the sex any good?"

Tom had no idea how this was going to turn out for him. Right now, he was seeing visions of himself going to bed alone for the remainder of the night. The old hand still worked, but . . .

"It was all right—I mean—it wasn't bad; but it wasn't the same as—"

"—making love to someone you actually care about?" Amanda completed his sentence, with just a trace of sarcasm in her voice.

Tom nodded sheepishly. He had decided that he would plead the fifth on any further questions. This had gone far enough. Luckily, Amanda felt the same way.

"All right, at least you were honest with me. You want to hear my confession?"

Please God, no, thought Tom. Instead he said: "Of course."

"Jack Ward and I used to be a couple. It lasted six months," she admitted.

"Do you still have feelings for him?" he asked cautiously.

Amanda sighed. Once again, she was conscious of having a bad idea. She was on a roll tonight.

"I like Jack. He's a good man." After a pause: "But I don't love him."

"Does he still have feelings for you?"

"I don't know, Tom. He might. Probably. Definitely. But I'm in love with you, and nothing will change that," she said tenderly, leaning forward to give him a quick kiss.

The conversation ended there and Tom seemed satisfied.

Nevertheless, when he finally drifted off to sleep after the second round of lovemaking, he was still wondering. *Why was Jack helping Amanda out with her investigation? What did he expect in return?*

The gin was beginning to take effect. As he swirled the clear liquid around in his glass, he tried to remember which drink this was. Somewhere at the back of his mind it registered that it was his fifth drink, but he couldn't be sure. Steve Brandt had been drinking steadily since early evening, and now it was night. The bar, which had been almost empty when he walked in, was now crowded with patrons sitting around on barstools, standing in clusters, or generally leaning over the counter trying to get the bartender's attention.

A woman seated next to him leaned over and made some inconsequential remark about the crowd.

He didn't respond. He wasn't here to pick up someone. He was here to do some serious drinking, and thinking, in that order. If all went well, he would eventually be too drunk to worry about the thinking. He was getting there.

The woman tried again.

"Do you work in this neighborhood?" she asked, casually tossing her hair to the side. It was a come-hither gesture and Steve noticed it from the corner of his eye. The aroma of a subtle perfume wafted up to his nostrils. It was not unpleasant.

"A few blocks from here," he answered noncommittally, trying to stare at his drink.

"What do you do?" asked the woman, encouraged.

"I'm an investment banker."

"So you sell stocks?"

Steve groaned. *Why did everyone ask the same damn question?* Few people actually knew or understood what an investment banker did. Most simply latched onto the word "investment" and figured that he must be a broker or a trader. That was what they saw on television and so that was their reality.

Not caring to explain the intricacies of his profession to a stranger, he gave a vague answer: "In a way, yes." It wasn't a lie, just an oversimplification.

"Where do you work?"

"Morgenthal Winters—it's a boutique firm," explained Steve, quite sure that the woman wouldn't understand what that meant in the context of Wall Street. She probably thought it was a hairdressing salon.

"I work in advertising," she offered hopefully.

"That must be exciting," said Steve, who couldn't care less. But this time he turned to face her. She was wearing a halter top, and through the alcoholic haze he noticed that she had beautiful shoulders. He felt himself getting aroused.

"It can be—sometimes. It really depends on the account. When you're working with a client that has a lot of money and wants to create a new brand image, it's great. It gives you plenty of elbow room to fool around with new ideas."

"Sort of like the Energizer bunny?" asked Steve, sipping his gin.

The woman smiled. Steve noted that she had a pretty face.

"That's right. But it's not always like that. Sometimes the client just wants to scream BOGO in a late-night television ad."

"BOGO?"

"Buy one get one free," explained the woman, laughing.

Steve smiled.

"How long have you been here?" the woman continued, looking around the bar.

"Since well before it got crowded," said Steve, and immediately regretted it. He didn't want her to think he was a lonely drunk. Tonight, of course, he was.

"Oh," said the woman, not knowing what to make of it.

"I had a long day at work," Steve explained hastily. "I needed to get away."

The woman seemed to accept that, but fell silent. She fingered her glass pointedly. Steve realized that it was empty.

"What were you drinking?"

"A cosmopolitan."

The managing director nodded and leaned over the counter. The bartender was at the other end of the bar, and Steve had to wait a few seconds before he caught his eye. The young man walked over with a polite smile.

"Some more gin, sir?"

Steve grimaced. "No, a cosmopolitan for the lady."

"Sure," replied the bartender. A minute later, he placed a cosmopolitan in a martini glass in front of the woman. She turned and thanked Steve.

"My pleasure," he replied. He drained his gin and waved again to the bartender. This time he didn't need to tell him what he wanted.

"Do you like your work?" asked the woman, lifting her glass to her lips.

That was a silly question, thought Steve. *Why would anyone like work?* He gave a clichéd response: "It pays the bills and keeps me out of trouble."

The woman was confused. She couldn't figure out whether he liked being a broker or not. "Excuse me for saying so, but you don't seem too enthusiastic about your job," she pointed out, hoping he wouldn't take offense.

Steve laughed. *You couldn't be more right, my dear.*

"Then what *are* you passionate about?" asked the woman, looking at him over the rim of her martini glass.

The banker thought about this. He turned to survey the room behind him. The lounge was like a sardine can by now. It was impossible for people to make it to the bar, so a waitress in a black leotard was walking around the room, taking orders and trying not to spill anything on the customers. She seemed harried and hot, and had a strained smile on her face. She seemed to be caught in a web of someone else's making. Steve Brandt knew the feeling.

He returned to his new friend. His vision was getting just a little blurry, but he was still alert. Alert enough to notice the well-rounded breasts staring him in the face. The blouse, which was secured by a thin strap behind her neck, was tight around the front, and Steve imagined that he could see the contour of her nipples. It was a nice sight.

"You know, I honestly don't know," he shrugged. It was a sincere response, and one that delighted the woman.

"At least you have the guts to admit it," she said with a grin, shifting in her seat to face him, and crossing her legs. Once again, Steve felt excited.

"Are you hungry?" he asked her.

"Famished, actually . . ."

"Then let's go to The Carlyle for dinner," the banker suggested.

She nodded. "That will be great, let me just run to the ladies' room." She stood up and made her way to the back of the bar.

Steve pulled out his wallet. He was about to pull out some bills, then changed his mind and put the wallet down on the counter. "Get me another gin and tonic, and make it fast," he said to the bartender.

By the time the woman returned to her seat, Steve had downed two more drinks in rapid succession and was paying the bill. As he stood up, he felt a bit unsteady and held onto the counter for balance. Luckily, the woman didn't notice. Taking a silent breath, he pulled himself together enough to make it out of the bar and onto the street. The woman followed, looking happy and a little flushed.

Steve hailed a cab and opened the door for her. She sat down and he climbed in beside her. As the car made its way to The Carlyle, the managing director stole a long look at his unexpected date for the evening. The woman seemed to be in her mid-thirties, with a firm, slender body that was well kept. In the passing light of the street, Steve could tell that there was some Latin in her. He thought he saw both defiance and lust in those deep black eyes, and it stirred him.

Since the affair with Laura Briggs, Steve hadn't seen any woman socially. He had been too heartbroken to even consider going out with anyone. More than the fear of being hurt again was the fear of having to confront the emotional and psychological issues that had been dredged up by the debacle. Through a mixture of mental discipline and work-related distractions, he had managed to bury the incident so that he could avoid dealing with its implications—namely, his desperate and constant need for companionship. If he had a therapist, he would have been fired as a client.

And now he was seated in a cab with a beautiful stranger who would hopefully make love to him with the passion that her Latin lineage was famous for.

No, he wouldn't allow himself to think of Laura tonight. The demons could wait.

─────────────── thirty-three

A playground for the rich and famous as well as a mecca for enterprising business people, Dubai is one of the richest and most liberal cities in the Middle East. Of course, it hadn't always been that way.

Originally a fishing village inhabited by the Bani Yas tribe, the Emirate of Dubai includes the city of Dubai, its neighbors on the Gulf Coast and the enclave of Hatta in the Hajar Mountains to the east. Contrary to popular misconception, Dubai isn't the capital of the United Arab Emirates (UAE); that mantle is held by the Emirate of Abu Dhabi, which occupies more than three quarters of the land mass of the country. Unlike Abu Dhabi or neighboring Sharjah, Dubai has only one substantial town. However, the city remains unequivocally the center of trade and tourism in the UAE.

Appropriately nicknamed the Hong Kong of the Middle East, Dubai's commercial history really began in the early twentieth century, when Dubai's ruler, Sheikh Maktoum bin Hasher al-Maktoum (descended from the Bani Yas tribe and a member of the dynasty that still rules today) exempted foreign traders from taxes. The facilities for free trade made Dubai a haven for merchants and lured them away from the more expensive trading centers such as Linagh (in Iran). Additionally, Dubai established links with British India and numerous Gulf ports, including Bahrain, Kuwait, and Basra in Iraq. The international trade which flowed in from these sources provided the basis for increasing prosperity in the emirate.

Over the next three decades, the merchants of Dubai became experts at importing goods which were then sold at other ports rather than indigenously. Loosely translated, this meant smuggling. The smuggling of gold to India was a particularly lucrative enterprise and it's a safe statement that the wealth of the region was built upon such activities. The creation of a new breakwater near the mouth of the Dubai Creek in 1963 provided a tremendous boost to smuggling (euphemistically referred to as trading), and even after oil was discovered in the mid '60s, this "trade" continued to fuel the city's growth.

Despite crackdowns on gold smugglers by the Indian government, Dubai's merchants continue to ply their trade successfully and in large volumes. The basis for this is a surprisingly unsophisticated but brilliantly coordinated system that has not changed in nearly a century. *Dhows*, or trading ships, take electronics and precious metals to foreign ports and return laden with money or carpets, cigars, and other luxury items, which are then sold throughout the Gulf for a handsome profit. Some of these items are even reexported to Western nations through a network of dealers.

The fact that makes this system work is that the departure of these goods from Dubai is perfectly legal; it's the countries at the other end that consider it smuggling.

The revenues generated by oil and trade fueled an economic boom in Dubai during the '70s and '80s that was unprecedented. Along with commerce came rapid development, leading to the construction of a major international airport that's one of the busiest in the Middle East, a large dry dock to repair ships and oil tankers, and the ultramodern port of Jebel Ali, which accommodates the largest free-trade zone in the world.

Ironically though, most of the smuggling activities in Dubai don't originate from these ports but rather from the much less ostentatious, but incredibly efficient, harbor which lines the Dubai Creek. It was here that Vikram Suri had headed from the Burj Al Arab Hotel after his meeting with Craig Michaels.

He stood now surveying the *dhows* as they glided in and out of the small port from where millions of dollars of gold and other materials were smuggled every year. Merchants and laborers plied away during the day and into the long hours of the night, loading and unloading their wares from a narrow wooden plank that served for a dock. Snatches of Arabic could be heard over the din of the nearby traffic and the constellation of shops that lined the road parallel to the Creek. The most amazing thing, thought Vik, was that all this happened in plain sight, and for the thousands of merchants that conducted business along the Creek, it was simply a way of life.

Largely because it's so commonplace, smuggling is not at all the glamorous profession that's portrayed in books and movies, where dangerous men clad in dark clothes or Hawaiian shirts and sporting $10,000 Piaget watches conduct their trade under cover of darkness with submachine guns under their shirts. Dubai's version involves ordinary Arabs, Indians, and Pakistanis hoisting plain crates of solid metal onto rickety boats with no guns, rival gangs, or undercover cops to worry about. There's plenty to go around for everyone and the authorities have no reason to interfere since it's all perfectly legal.

Once the *dhows* arrive at their port of destination, however, the story is very different. Since the countries that become the unwitting recipients of the smuggling trade in Dubai don't look favorably upon such activities, the ships have to make their way discreetly toward ports where they are unlikely to be searched, either because of a lack of customs presence or because the officials at those ports have been bribed to allow the shipment. The small size and unassuming appearance of the *dhows* are extremely conducive for the purpose of making their way undetected through international waters.

From there, the goods are transported by land to remote villages, from where they're distributed through an underground network for sale to dealers throughout the country. Once their inbound wares have been unloaded, the *dhows* are filled up with goods or money for their return trip to the Middle East. Since Dubai is a free port, the captains of the *dhows* need not worry about this leg of their journey.

It was almost sundown by the time Vikram Suri's contact arrived. He was a short, dark Arab with a thick beard and moustache, dressed in faded jeans and a T-shirt. In some parts of the region, thought Vik, he could still be stoned for that. They exchanged a brief greeting and then shook hands. Another Western habit.

One way of crossing the Dubai Creek is by *abra*—small, open air water-taxis that ply the waters incessantly through the day and into midnight. The *abras* leave only when they're full. On the Bur Dubai side, the main dock for the *abra* is at the western end of the Dubai Souq. It was here that Vik had been waiting for the last hour, reading a newspaper and smoking a cigar at the waterfront café.

Vik and the Arab now boarded one of the small boats and seated themselves in the rear of the vessel. The seating area, which was mostly just a set of unpainted wooden planks lined up in a row and fastened to the edges of the boat, filled up slowly. Both Vik and his chaperone were fluent in Arabic, English, and Hindi, but stayed discreetly silent in the public environment.

As the boat rocked gently on the surface of the water, still tied to the pier by a thick rope and waiting for its remaining passengers—who could be heard making their way to where the *abra* was moored, Vik had time to reminisce about the events leading up to this moment.

He had conceived the plan on a rainy night eight months ago, while relaxing unsuccessfully in his penthouse apartment and staring at the sheets of water washing down the tall windows with an expression bordering on morose. In his hand was a glass of Bristol Crème sherry and a cigar, but neither helped. From his vantage point, the refracted lights of Midtown Manhattan danced drunkenly in the rainwater, adding to his creeping edginess.

The motivation behind the idea had been a mix of boredom and greed. Despite his numerous successes and high public profile, the CEO of TriNet had reached an impasse in his life. If he had been an ordinary person, it would have been called a mid-life crisis. In his own mind, however, Vikram Suri preferred to view it as a desire to take his life and achievements to "the next level." The next level, of course, had to be climactic—a crowning success that would enable him to feel like the emperor that he always imagined himself to be.

Having struggled against both racial and financial barriers in his life, Vik had learnt that the only real currency of power in this world was money. Not that he wasn't rich, but he wanted the sort of wealth that would make him untouchable. Only then would he feel truly secure, and only then would he be able to realize the full potential of his destiny. As with most people with delusions of grandeur, he didn't actually know what this destiny was, but sensed that it was there, and that was enough.

At first the idea of buying another company seemed inadequate fodder for his vaunted ambitions. With a strong balance sheet and stock, he could certainly grow TriNet into an empire, but his personal ownership of the enterprise was still limited. The history of corporate America was filled with CEOs who had taken their firms to great heights, only to find themselves as hired hands in the end, eventually having to retire and pass on the reins to younger executives. It was true that most of them had amassed considerable wealth by the end of their careers, but Vik didn't want all that when he was sixty-five—he wanted it now.

Even though he was on TriNet's board, and to the public he was a media baron, behind the scenes Vik felt like an underpaid lackey, and that was something he could no longer live with.

As the rain outside had subsided and the night lights of the city had come into distinct relief, so had the plan. After rejecting the idea of a merger initially, Vik had realized that his current position was an asset that he could utilize to achieve his ends. Being the CEO of a rich media company was a passport to indulgence, provided the indulgence was kept secret from the board and the public. A merger with Luxor Satellite, if managed correctly, could become his one-way ticket to a personal fortune.

All great schemes are prepared from the basic formula of one part simplicity to two parts complexity. The first step was to aim for results that were predictable and controllable; the second was to create an arcane web of measures to shield the plan from prying eyes. The idea that Vikram Suri had come up with was of that breed, and it had been executed with clockwork precision.

Immediately following the first bid for Luxor Satellite, Vik had arranged for the news to be leaked to the press through his deputy Helen Mosbacher. The resulting fluctuation in TriNet's stock had provided the first opportunity for profit. Through a holding company based in the Isle of Man—the International Trading Company (or ITC)—and its stable of dummy subsidiaries, Vik had conducted trades in his own company on the New York Stock Exchange. Since the trades had gone through dozens of small brokerages, often in Street Stock; and since most of the transactions had been modest in size, they were virtually undetectable.

As the stock price had soared upwards on the $7 billion purchase price, which was viewed by the analysts as a steal for Luxor's assets, the brokers had sold TriNet shares short by the hundreds of thousands. When the bid was rejected (as per the arrangement with Craig Michaels) and TriNet's stock plummeted in response, those very same brokers had purchased the shares at considerably lower prices to fulfill their short sales, thereby making a clean profit. At the same time, the brokers had purchased additional shares in TriNet on behalf of the ITC, with instructions to hold until further notice.

Since Vik had been assured by Craig Michaels that the revised $10 billion bid for Luxor would be accepted, he knew which direction TriNet's stock would move next. Following an initial period of uncertainty, the price had climbed—as analysts realized the potential for synergies between the two companies and factored incremental growth into their analysis. Within a few weeks following the official announcement of the merger, all the shares held by the International Trading Company had been disposed of at prices much higher than those at which they had been purchased. Vik had estimated his profit from all the transactions to total approximately $200 million.

Impressive, but not enough—not nearly enough. So Vik had decided to gamble.

The one good thing about being Indian, he often mused, was that he had a direct pipeline into the political and economic setup of one of the largest growing economies in the world. The Indian markets had always been hard to crack by the West, either due to self-indulgent ignorance about the region, or due to severe restrictions imposed on foreign businesses by the Indian government, including esoteric trading licenses, foreign currency controls, and marketing censorship. To add to that, corruption was not only rampant, but a virtual way of life in a country that, for one reason or another, had never quite established a stable political and economic structure after the exodus of the British Raj in 1947.

In the midst of this chaos, Vik had seen the opportunity to prosper. As a native Indian with high-level connections in the homeland and a powerful base in the Western world, he had all the tools necessary to make a killing. Through meticulous planning and almost a decade of laying the groundwork for such a coup, he had finally found a way to exploit his background and race to maximum advantage.

Unbeknownst to anyone but himself and a high-ranking official in the Dubai government, the ITC had been founded by two people who had provided all the capital for the stock trades and who had received all the profits from the transactions. The paper shareholders of the company were figureheads who had not been heard from since their receipt of a one-time payment of $1,000 each, and had no connection to the company except for their name on the official records. Even the addresses of the individuals had been fabricated. Neither Vikram Suri nor his Arab colleague were named in the charter, since they had never been on it.

All the money that came in or was disbursed by the ITC was done through a discreet and reliable intermediary in Zurich, and funneled through a chain of dummy corporations scattered across the globe, flowing ultimately into the bank account of a small corporation based in the Middle East by the name of Al-Riyadh Associates. Al-Riyadh Associates, if anyone had been able to trace the money trail through so many smokescreens, was owned jointly by Vik and his Arab partner.

In the event of an inquiry, even the much vaunted Interpol would have a snowball's chance in hell of actually tracing the money to the Middle East, let alone to the Hamptons. Vik felt pretty safe, but then all this was kindergarten stuff. The real game had yet to be played.

It was this latter that had brought Vik to Dubai and because of which he was sitting next to a taciturn Arab in the *abra,* watching the twinkling lights on the opposite shore grow inexorably and enticingly nearer. On the other end of the brief boat ride was a man who could make Vik a handsome profit. The Arab seated next to him was merely a facilitator.

The arrangement was quite simple. The money from the illicit stock trades would be used to buy gold from the merchant on the approaching shore. In exchange for the money, the dealer would not only provide them with the precious metal, but also smuggle it to India on his personal fleet of *dhows.* The shipment would be received on the Indian shore by police officers who were very much on the take. With this "official" convoy, the gold would be transported in trucks to a hidden warehouse, from where it would be distributed over a period of hours to several wholesalers.

The wholesalers, in turn, would offload the shipment to smaller dealers through a perfectly legitimate network; the dealers would utilize the gold to make ornaments which they would sell themselves or vend to other retailers. In return for the precious metal, the wholesalers would pay a local politician, who in this case was functioning as Vik's mule, almost four times the value of the gold in Dubai. This for the fact that they couldn't obtain such large quantities through legal channels.

Most of that money would then be transferred through a network of banks across the Middle East to the waiting coffers of Al-Riyadh Associates. The company's profits from its "trading operations"—a convenient euphemism for smuggling—would be subject to minimal taxes in Dubai. After the transaction, the company would be liquidated and the cash disbursed to the private bank accounts of its owners, all under the official aegis of Vik's local partner.

All said and done, and after all the parties involved had received their respective payoffs, Vik's pocketbook would be thicker by a healthy $350 million.

At the same time, Vik had arranged for TriNet to buy back some of his shares for the ESOP. Since the company was taking a substantial loan against the ESOP to finance the merger, it made it possible for the CEO to monetize a significant portion of his holdings. Of course, TriNet would be saddled with $700 million of additional debt from the repurchase, but Vik felt that he had it coming to him.

Since he had obtained most of his shares through option exercises over the years, Vik would make a tidy profit off the spread. Tidy to the sum of $650 million.

None of that took into account the deal that he had cut with Craig Michaels that afternoon. Since Luxor's shareholders would receive $8 billion for their shares (excluding the net debt of $2 billion which TriNet would assume in the merger), Craig's 62 percent ownership would be worth approximately $5 billion, which after taxes would come to $4 billion. Vik would receive half of that, bringing his total fortune from the merger to a staggering $3 billion—an emperor's ransom.

The *abra* arrived at its destination, and Vikram Suri disembarked along with his Arab chaperone, who extended a hand in the direction of the main market area and bid him follow. The streets were busy at this time of evening and loud Arabic chatter could be heard from all sides as the pair made their way past the myriad of textile shops, fruit stands, and electronics dealers, toward the large indoor market known as the Gold Souq. Inside, they made their way past the ostentatious stalls of gold and jewelry to a small shop in the rear of the arcade. There they were greeted by an attractive olive-skinned woman who recognized Vik's chaperone and led them quickly through a gold-sequined curtain at the back of the store.

Sitting on plush cushions and eating grapes from a large silver bowl filled with fruit was the fattest Arab that Vik had ever seen in his life. The obese man, who was dressed in traditional Arabian garb, seemed disinterested as the woman introduced the visitors. He waved them unsmilingly to some cushions, and resumed his eating. Vik grinned privately at the spectacle. It seemed like a scene from a James Bond movie.

As the guests made themselves comfortable, their host pushed forward the bowl of fruit for their eating pleasure, but other than that made no move to initiate a conversation. He had no need to. It was his land, his shop, his gold. He could afford to wait.

But Vik couldn't. After almost five full minutes of silence, he got exasperated. He decided to jumpstart the discussion.

"Thank you very much for your kind hospitality—" he began, but was cut off abruptly by the merchant.

"Let's cut through the nonsense, eh?" he said in thickly-accented English. He was not happy at having his eating-fest interrupted, but now that the negotiations had begun, he wanted to move it along. "You're here to make a deal, no?"

Vik nodded.

"All right, then let's deal. You have made the arrangements on the other end?"

Again, Vik nodded.

"Good, then give me the information and I'll give you my bank account number. When the money is in the bank, the gold will be on its way."

This time Vik shook his head. "We'll give you part of the money now, but the rest on delivery of the gold."

The ample man seated in front of Vik laughed heartily.

"Do you think I'm a fool? Once the shipment reaches India, how am I to know you won't have my men killed and the gold confiscated? The people picking it up are corrupt police, no?"

Vik winced at the man's lack of subtlety. He wondered briefly what the Western press would have thought of this conversation if they had been here to witness it.

The Arab merchant had lost interest in the grapes and now reached between the cushions to locate a tray of nuts that he had placed there recently. He didn't bother offering it to his guests. He didn't share his victuals with people who were trying to exploit his good nature.

"I understand your concern, but how do *we* know that once we transfer the money to your account, the gold will ever reach India?" countered Vik.

The merchant responded with a weary look, as if he had done this many times before and couldn't fathom the idiocy of these foreigners.

"You have my word about the gold. Your friend, whose man has brought you here today, has done business with me many times. He's a powerful man. Him I would not cheat. Your gold will reach its destination—but not without my money."

Vik knew that the Arab was telling the truth. His partner in Al-Riyadh Associates *was* powerful, and if this merchant planned on double-crossing him, he would best make arrangements to leave the Middle East in a hurry. . . . The deal had already been cut. All this was merely a formality— in the Arab world, a businessman who didn't negotiate was considered untrustworthy, or worthy of being cheated.

Half an hour later, the details had been ironed out and the meeting was over. Vik and his chaperone boarded the *abra* once again, this time headed back to the Bur Dubai side of the creek.

From the dock, the CEO of TriNet Communications walked to the Ambassador Hotel. It was 8:00 P.M., and he had an appointment to keep.

Alistair Waxman had spent the entire afternoon in his room. After waking up from his nap, he had ordered room service, then settled down to read. He couldn't afford to walk around and have some American tourist identify him. The smallest whiff of gossip would be enough to set the media wheels spinning. He could not be put in the position of answering awkward questions by the press, and more importantly, the White House.

To top it all off, he was on this week's cover of *Forbes*. As he leafed through the high-brow magazine that he had picked up absently at Dulles Airport, he prayed that the issue had not reached these shores yet.

At 8:15 P.M., Vikram Suri rang from downstairs and announced that he was coming up. The American shut the magazine and replaced it in his attaché case. Walking over to the window, he pushed it open to let in some air. Desert nights are cool, and he much preferred the natural breeze to the air conditioning.

A few minutes later, Alistair and his guest were seated comfortably on sofa chairs, sipping drinks. Unlike during his meeting with Craig Michaels, Vik was less theatrical, more deferential. He knew how to turn on the charm when it suited his purpose.

After the initial pleasantries, Vik launched into a briefing. He detailed his trip to Deira as well as the conversation with Craig, but left out his side deal with the Luxor CEO. Alistair already knew about the FTC's feedback, so Vik skipped that.

When the CEO concluded, Alistair leaned forward contemplatively. He was still tired from the jet lag, but his gray eyes were sharp. Vik knew from experience that the American's mind was sifting through this new update like a thresher. That was why he was who he was.

"How do you know we can trust this Arab partner of yours?" asked Alistair a moment later. "What's to stop him from keeping all the money? After all, this is his domain."

"In addition to being a high-ranking government official, he is *also* a distant cousin of the royal family," explained Vik. "Everyone here earns money from smuggling in one way or another, but the royal family is never involved. They look the other way for obvious reasons, but getting their own hands dirty is another matter. If it ever came out that one of their own was smuggling gold to India, the punishment would be *severe*."

The American whistled softly.

"Exactly," said Vik. "In this part of the world, the authorities don't screw around."

"All right. What about this chief minister from your own country? Don't tell me they put people to death in India too?" asked Alistair dryly.

Vik laughed.

"Unfortunately no, but I wouldn't worry about it. The chief minister is a joke, a corrupt politician desperate to hold on to his power. His payoff will buy him a hundred elections, so he's got plenty of incentive to play along."

"And what's to stop him from keeping *all* the money?" asked the American incredulously.

Vikram Suri shrugged. "Off the top of my head, I would say a ten-inch knife . . ."

Alistair did not want to hear any more.

"Handle it any way you want. Just make sure I get my cut," he growled.

"Don't worry, you will," answered Vik, staring daggers at him. He didn't like being challenged. The American had already been paid $15 million as an advance and would receive an obscene $45 million "success fee." For that kind of money, the least he could do was show some goddamn trust!

But Alistair Waxman couldn't have cared less. He was putting his head into a lion's mouth for this merger, and for that he would collect his money if it meant bleeding it out of the TriNet CEO. After some more questions, he ended the meeting.

"All right, I'm satisfied," he said obnoxiously.

"I'm so glad," responded Vik dryly.

The next morning, both men headed back to the United States, on different flights.

In the rack in front of Alistair's seat, the stewardess had considerately placed the latest copy of *Forbes*. The American groaned.

———————————— thirty-four

By the time her boss got off the phone, Amanda Fleming had already re-arranged most of his desk from her perch on the corner. It was the way she dealt with waiting, much to the editor's constant chagrin. Alex Taylor sighed as he put down the receiver. The news was not good. He gave it to her straight.

"That was the chairman. He checked into your findings, and there's nothing that he can go on," he stated apologetically.

Amanda waited for him to continue.

"In a nutshell, the holding company in the Isle of Man is no doubt a front for *something*, but for what is anyone's guess. Figuring that out would require a full-scale cross-border investigation, and the SEC isn't thrilled about spending taxpayers' money on our hunches. . . . I'm sorry, Amanda, but that's politics," Alex finished without emotion.

The journalist, who had been hoping for a break, couldn't hide her disappointment.

"But there *is* something here, Alex. You know that," she insisted.

The silver-haired editor sighed once again and carefully folded his hands on the desk in front of him. He had a fondness for Amanda and admired her investigative drive, but there was only so much rope that he could give her. He spoke slowly and thoughtfully.

"Amanda, you know that I used up a big chip with that call, and now I have to tell you to drop this story. I can't have my star reporter chasing a dead end lead. For all we know, the holding company may be just a tax front for some Swiss or British businessman who saw an opportunity to turn a quick profit on the merger. No inside connection, no conspiracy. *The New York Times* won't publish a story on pure speculation. Either way, I need you to turn your attention to the other assignments on your desk."

The aggressive young reporter tried in vain to argue with her editor, but his mind was made up. Eventually, unable to convince him, she reluctantly agreed to drop the investigation. Refusing to meet his fatherly gaze, she left his office sullenly.

Back at her desk, her frustration mounted. She felt like she had been hit. She understood Alex's position, but it still seemed like a copout. It was true that without a break, there was really nothing more to go on, but dropping a story when it got too difficult was like getting divorced because you argued a lot. There *had* to be way. And spending her time doing fluff pieces on electronic publishing or dot-coms was not going to help her find it.

After clenching and unclenching her fists several times, decimating the available paper clips, and generally destroying everything in her cubicle that could be destroyed without getting her fired, she called Tom Carter.

The investment banker listened attentively as she filled him in on her conversation with Alex.

"So what do you think?" she asked him in the end.

At the other end of the line, Tom debated his answer. He would never admit it, but he was actually relieved at the outcome. The truth was he had started to doubt his own judgment in catalyzing the investigation. Not that he doubted the rationale behind his suspicions, or the obvious red flags that foreign holding companies with dummy shareholders raised, but he was just not sure if he had the stomach or the need to go through with this any more.

For one thing, the investigation was Amanda's domain, due to obvious reasons, and therefore completely out of his control. Consequently, the banker felt like a passenger in a car that was going too fast. The brakes were underneath someone else's foot, and that made him nervous.

Secondly, despite all the shell games and conspiracy theories that Amanda and he had conjured in their apartments and countless New York City cafés, so far the feds had *not* come knocking. No RICO violations, no SEC subpoenas, no rumors in the press, nothing. No matter what had transpired in the private boardrooms of TriNet or Luxor, and regardless of what secret deals may have been cut behind shareholders' backs, the fact remained that the merger was proceeding smoothly and there was no imminent threat on the horizon to the deal, Morgenthal Winters, or Tom himself.

Finally, and most importantly, as his own career prospects brightened, not least of all due to the Trademedia deal, the stakes had gotten a lot higher.

For all these reasons, Tom was relieved that the commission had declined to proceed with an inquiry.

"I'm not sure what to think right now," he replied guardedly. "But I just don't see how we can proceed without the SEC's cooperation. Your editor may be right, Amanda."

Amanda frowned. She couldn't see Tom's face, but something in his voice made her uneasy. It was as if he was trying to talk her into something. She needed to test him.

"So you think I should just drop this?" she asked carefully, throwing the bait into the water.

"Not necessarily. Just slow it down a little. You've tried your best and frankly I'm amazed we even got this far. I just don't want you driving yourself crazy over this," answered Tom, unaware of the trap he had just walked into.

"But the FTC approval for the merger is expected any day now. Once the deal closes and cash changes hands, it's pretty much over. The trail is growing colder each day," objected Amanda, waiting nervously for the moment she could feel coming.

Tom sighed. "Look, I know all that, but what are you going to do? All the pressure in the world doesn't make a difference without a lead. Let's take some time off from this, Amanda. We'll go away somewhere, maybe to the Bahamas. Maybe we'll get an idea there," he offered, tasting the shoe leather in his mouth even as he said it.

Time to start reeling in the fish.

"Tom, do *you* want me to give up this investigation?" asked Amanda quietly.

Tom tensed up. He measured his words carefully. "I didn't say that. You're the one who's been running around on this and I'm just thinking of your—"

Amanda cut him off. "No, you're not. You were actually hoping the SEC would refuse to look into this. You have a lot more to lose now that you may be up for a promotion, so suddenly this whole thing is a massive inconvenience," she said dejectedly.

Tom's heart sank. She had decoded his hidden agenda, and now he looked like an insincere jerk.

"Amanda . . ." he began, but it was too late. She had already hung up.

Tom Carter was in shell shock. In the blink of an eye, his relationship with Amanda had gone from fabulous to terrible. By the time he had realized his mistake, too much had already happened. He wondered with trepidation whether the damage he had done was irreparable. Human relationships, particularly romantic ones, were always fragile, and sometimes there were no second chances.

The brutally simple fact was that Amanda did not trust him anymore, and anything he said to explain himself would only be met with more skepticism. It was a slippery slope and he had jumped onto it with both feet. What made it even worse was the recognition that even if she allowed him to make his case, he really had nothing to offer in his defense.

The reporter had put her time, energy, and relationship with her editor on the line, all on the say-so of Tom Carter, and he had repaid her by wishing her failure! It *was* a betrayal and she had every right to hate him. If that was the sum of his character, then he did not deserve her, as a friend or a lover.

As he berated himself for his foolishness, Tom realized that he had a clear choice. Either accept the fact that he had misled and finally betrayed the woman he loved and had lost her forever; or take action to vindicate himself in her eyes. And that did not mean send her flowers.

He had to show her how much she meant to him, and how much he was willing to sacrifice for her. The way she had done for him.

Sure, he had already taken a huge gamble by precipitating the entire drama, but that was for himself and born more out of his fears than his conscience. Now he had to do something that would be for Amanda, and for the truth. So far he had been little more than a spectator, offering encouragement but never really getting his own hands dirty. It was cowardly and selfish.

He had one chance to fix this, and time was running out.

Nervously, Tom reached for the phone on his desk.

────────── thirty-five

One of the benefits of a doorman building is that it's difficult for unauthorized persons to enter the premises without the knowledge of the doorman. The notable exceptions to this occur when the concierge is incompetent or preoccupied, or when the culprit is very, very clever.

For the latter, there are a variety of methods for securing entry to a restricted complex. One of these tricks is the UPS method.

Doormen rarely allow deliverymen to go up to an apartment; they usually just sign for the package themselves and inform the tenant that something is waiting for them at the front desk. If the building is large enough, there's also a separate room in the back where deliveries and dry cleaning are held until they're picked up.

In this instance, the man who showed up at Amanda Fleming's apartment building was carrying a large cardboard box, and announced loudly to the doorman that he had a delivery for Mr. Paul Vallone, who lived in the building. Mr. Vallone, as the messenger had ascertained earlier in the week, was a history professor at Fordham, and lived alone. More importantly, he was vacationing in Oregon this week. This latter fact was critical, since the box contained only packing material, and had Mr. Vallone been around and discovered that fact, he would surely have alerted the doorman, thereby complicating the escape plan.

The messenger, who had a ponytail, mustache, and goatee, was dressed conveniently in a white T-shirt, pants, and a thick brown jacket. Convenient because of what he planned to do that night.

The concierge signed for the package and the deliveryman pretended to walk away. Since the package was unusually large and Mr. Vallone was away, the doorman carried it to the back. He was gone for about fifteen seconds, which was just enough time for the deliveryman to double back and go through a side door a few feet to the left of the front desk, which led down to the basement. Had the building been even more exclusive, it's possible there would have been cameras in the basement and the doorman would have seen the man sneaking down the stairs on his monitor. But there were no such devices, and the messenger slipped into the basement undetected.

Downstairs, he lifted his T-shirt and withdrew a tightly folded woman's dress. He snapped the dress open and spread it over a washing machine. Reaching behind him, he undid his ponytail and shook his long hair so that it cascaded around his shoulders. He took off his two-sided jacket, which was brown on one side and white on the other, and threw it on the floor. Next came the T-shirt and pants. Now bare-chested, he undid a string wrapped around two foam balls taped to the upper part of his chest. The balls, which had been tamped down by the string, now sprang free and assumed their natural shape.

Retrieving the dress, he slipped it carefully over his head so as not to dislodge the foam balls and smoothened the fabric down to his knees. His legs were shaved so the portion showing below the dress wouldn't cause alarm. The foam balls fit snugly under the dress and the illusion of breasts was convincing.

Picking up the oversized jacket, he rummaged around in the pockets for his remaining tools—a lipstick, a compact, and a slightly pregnant laundry bag.

The mustache and goatee were fake, and he peeled them off carefully, rubbing his skin to alleviate the rawness from the adhesive. Within seconds, he had applied the makeup to his face, and to any set of prying eyes, would have appeared to be a woman, albeit a strikingly sad one.

Satisfied, he reached into the laundry bag and pulled out a pair of house slippers, a hairbrush, a baseball cap, and a black T-shirt. He replaced the cap and the T-shirt in the bag—those were for later. Taking off his sneakers, he threw those into the bag as well and donned the slippers instead. Then he brushed his hair rapidly many times to ensure that it hung naturally, and deliberately pulled the sides closer to his face so that as little of his features was visible as possible.

Finally, he stuffed the jacket, white T-shirt and pants, fake facial hair, makeup, and hairbrush into the laundry bag and flicked the bag many times to iron out the wrinkles.

Ready for action, he pressed the button for the elevator. Within a few minutes, he was riding upwards to Amanda Fleming's floor, his face lowered to avoid direct exposure to the camera on the ceiling of the car.

To the doorman who saw him on his monitor, he seemed like one of the female tenants riding up from the basement with a bag of laundry. He gave it no thought, and returned to reading the sports section of a local newspaper.

Tom walked into Steve's office just as Amanda's visitor stepped off the elevator onto her floor. He had called ahead, so the managing director was expecting him. Steve put down the presentation that he was reading and offered Tom a seat. His face betrayed his curiosity.

Tom sat down nervously, his heart racing in his chest. A few minutes ago, the thought of confronting Steve Brandt with his suspicions about the merger seemed like the right thing, a brave thing. But now that he was actually here, sitting across from his boss, about to confront him with a bombshell, he wasn't so sure anymore.

The stakes seemed almost ludicrously high, and Tom knew that his odds of success were abominably low. The tension in his face was obvious, so Steve broke the ice for him.

"You mentioned you wanted to talk about the merger, Tom. Is something bothering you?"

Tom gulped. He had gone over what he wanted to say several times in his head, but now that it was time to do it, he could feel a part of him wanting to run away, forget the whole thing, and just go back to the way things were before . . . *before what? Before the merger? Before he called Amanda? Or before he betrayed her?*

Man's desire for stability is so strong that he'll do almost anything to avoid conflict. But the irony is that sometimes diving into conflict is the only way to find peace. The fabric of Tom Carter's life had already ripped, and there was no other way to fix it now but to follow through on his intent to find the truth, whatever the difficulty, whatever the cost.

Amanda paid the cabdriver and got out. It was evening now, and the sky was beginning to get dark. She entered the lobby of her building and was greeted by the doorman as she walked by his desk.

The reporter smiled politely and proceeded to the elevators. On the ride up to her apartment, she thought back on her argument with Tom a little while ago. After her initial reaction to what she had perceived as a shocking betrayal of her confidence, she had cooled down. Her anger at being manipulated was replaced by simple doubt. She was still unhappy with Tom over his flip-flop behavior, but as the minutes ticked by, she felt that she had overreacted. Her intense desire to trust him mixed with her journalist's paranoia had caused her to be unduly harsh.

In her heart of hearts she didn't really buy that Tom had been secretly waiting for her to fail. No amount of anger could cloud the fact that he had a lot more to lose in this situation than she did. At least until her editor had asked her to drop the story, Amanda had had the full support of her newspaper behind her. Tom, on the other hand, had been at risk from the first moment he called her. Had she turned out to be unreliable or had her investigation caused suspicion in the wrong quarters, he could have wound up in serious trouble.

The bottom line was that he had put his faith in her, and now that he was feeling the heat, she owed him the same courtesy. At the very least, she would give him the chance to explain himself.

She decided to call him as soon as she got upstairs.

Tom told Steve everything, starting from his own first contact with the *Times* reporter to the latest development with the SEC. It was the only way, he reasoned, to flush out any hidden facts. He also hoped that their findings would encourage Steve to do his own due diligence into the merger.

But Steve's face grew increasingly grimmer as Tom's story progressed. It was evident that he was not reacting in the way the vice president had hoped. Tom's nervousness grew in direct proportion to Steve's barely contained anger.

When he had said his piece, Tom took a deep breath. He had put his cards on the table, and now it was up to Steve to decide how to respond. The usually boisterous managing director stayed quiet for a long time, so long in fact that Tom began to wonder if he had heard a word of what had just been relayed. When Steve finally spoke, his voice was gravelly, his gaze icy.

"First of all, I don't know who the hell you think you are, coming in here and implying that Morgenthal Winters might have been involved in something shady—"

Tom corrected him hastily. "I never said that *we* were involved, Steve. The evidence we found indicates possible insider trading, and that some-one could be at TriNet or Luxor."

Steve's response was like a hot poker down the vice president's throat. "And that makes it better?! You're accusing our biggest and best client of criminal behavior! You stupid bastard! Do you have any career ambitions at all or are you *trying* to destroy your future?"

Tom remained silent. Steve continued unabated.

"The fact that you had the temerity, and I would like to add stupidity, to talk to a goddamn journalist regarding the merger is bad enough. But to work with this stupid bitch to compile a wild conspiracy theory—"

It was Tom's turn to get angry. "You want to yell at me about this, that's fine. But keep her out of it!" he said firmly.

Steve smirked. "Or what? You'll object? If I were you, I wouldn't be posturing about anything right now. Your irresponsible actions have put everyone at risk, and I'm disgusted by your tone and attitude towards this firm and our client. So I'll make this quick.

"First off, you're fired. Pack your stuff tonight and don't come back tomorrow—I'm alerting security as soon as you leave this room. Second, if you or your journalist friend reveal anything that we feel was obtained improperly through this bank, we'll sue your asses off till you're both in the poor house, you got that?"

Steve didn't even realize it, but he was beginning to sound more and more like his guiding light, Vikram Suri. Somewhere at the back of his mind, he remembered that he himself had been preparing to set up the unsuspecting vice president in the event of a problem. Now that the call signs of trouble had come knocking, he was doing precisely that. He was preparing to throw an innocent man to the wolves.

Tom was shocked by Steve's invective. He struggled to say something, but was unable to find the words. He had known walking in that the meeting was likely to be incendiary, but had never imagined anything like this!

He rose quietly and left.

. . . .

Amanda entered her apartment. Switching on the foyer light, she dropped her handbag on the credenza next to the door and stepped into the kitchen to get a glass of water. The apartment was completely silent.

She was dressed in a work suit and decided to change into something more comfortable. Placing the empty glass in the sink, she walked down the semi-dark hallway to her bedroom. It was a little stuffy in the apartment, and along the way she stopped to open a corridor window that overlooked a small courtyard in the rear of the building.

The door to her bedroom was ajar and she walked in curiously. Even though it was a mundane detail, she had a sharp memory and could distinctly remember shutting the door behind her when she left for the office. There was no wind in the apartment since all the windows had been closed, *so how had it swung open?*

She was about to switch on the light when out of the darkness, a hand reached out and grabbed her. She spun around in alarm but barely had a chance to view her assailant before a rough hand was clapped over her mouth and she was dragged into the room. The strength of her captor was undeniable, and he lifted her easily by the waist and threw her onto the bed, climbing on top of her.

Amanda struggled furiously but was no match for the brute holding her down. Her screams were muffled by the hand covering her mouth. Only when her assailant placed a knee threateningly against her stomach did she begin to calm down.

In the darkness of the room, she could barely make out the visage of the man in front of her, but whoever it was, she felt sure that he was going to hurt her. Fear coursed through her body like an inferno, and her breathing grew shallow; but she still had the presence of mind to realize that she would never be able to escape the vise-like grip from her prone position. She was like an animal trapped in a net—the harder she tried to get out, the more entangled she would become.

The man waited till he was certain that she wouldn't move, and then eased himself off her. All the same, he kept one knee on her chest just in case she tried something. With his free hand, he picked up something lying on the edge of the bed. As he brought it up to the light streaming in through the window, Amanda could see that it was a carving knife—one of hers. The blade gleamed wickedly in the moonlight, and the reporter found herself unable to blink. Her assailant brought the knife close to her face.

"I'm going to remove my hand, but if you scream I'll cut you into a million pieces—I promise," he snarled menacingly.

Amanda nodded her acknowledgement, and he slowly removed his hand from her mouth. She gulped in the air gratefully, her chest heaving at the exertion. The man kept the knife at her face.

"I have a message for you. You are to stop investigating the TriNet merger immediately. If you don't, you'll die," he said simply, bringing the blade of the cutting knife to rest on her cheek. The metal felt sickeningly cool as it touched Amanda's skin.

The man continued tonelessly.

"If you ask any further questions—of anyone—I will be back to kill you."

Amanda could feel her skin crawl, and stared silently at her captor.

"We're pretty tired of all your snooping around, and believe me when I tell you that you won't die a painless death. This knife is just a toy compared to what I will use on you the next time. . . . If you go to the police, just remember that we *will* be watching you, and then it's bye-bye time for you, honey." He laughed maliciously.

Amanda wanted to nod, but couldn't bring herself to move. Every muscle in her body seemed to have frozen. She felt powerless and afraid, the way she imagined rape victims felt while they were being violated.

Her captor waited. He was looking for some sign that she understood, and wouldn't leave until he got it.

With an effort, Amanda moved her head up and down, a fearful moan escaping her thin lips. Her assailant seemed satisfied and got up from the bed as if to leave.

Then, without warning, he clapped a hand over her mouth again and with his free arm punched her in the stomach with his elbow. It was a violent blow, and before she could even feel the pain, Amanda Fleming blacked out.

A few minutes later, a clean-shaven man in a black T-shirt, white jacket, and baseball cap walked out of the building with a laundry bag clutched under his arm. He looked like one of dozens of people who lived in the building, and the doorman didn't give him a second glance.

Despite Steve's threats, Tom knew that the firm wouldn't prevent him from coming into the office in the morning. There was still a protocol that needed to be observed, and Tom had a right to at least make his case to Robert Darlington III before he was booted unceremoniously from the firm that he had given his best work to.

Sighing, he shut off the light in his office, knowing full well that it would probably be for the last time. He felt a vicious pounding in his head, and quickly popped some aspirin that he always kept inside his briefcase.

He needed to sleep.

When she came to, he was gone.

In the light from the bedside lamp, which her assailant had considerately switched on before he left, Amanda could see the knife lying at the foot of the bed. She tried to get up, but a throbbing pain in her abdomen made it difficult, and she lay back down, breathing heavily.

Even though she had only been out for a few minutes, she could barely remember what had happened. It all seemed distant, as if it had been a bad dream. But the pain in her stomach told her otherwise. She tried taking a deep breath, but it seemed to hurt her lungs. As she stared up at the ceiling, her eyes moist from a light but steady weeping, she began to recollect the incidents of the evening.

With the memories came a sense of dread and frustration. The former was a function of her fear—her assailant had clearly accomplished what he had come for, which was to frighten the wits out of her. Amanda Fleming was a brave woman and an intrepid journalist, but tonight's events had shaken her up badly. It was one thing to read about or watch death threats being made in a book or a movie, and quite another to actually receive one at knife-point. More importantly, she had no doubts that the man meant what he had said about killing her.

Her frustration, however, wasn't with her present predicament, but with her inability to crack the merger investigation. Prior to this attack, she had been disappointed with the results, but now she felt infuriated at the impasse. Unlike most people, who gave up when things really got tough, Amanda's instincts were to redouble her efforts when the situation looked hopeless. As much as she was genuinely in fear for her life, she was also smarting from a sense of violation. *How dare this animal come into her home, her bedroom, and then threaten her life? Whoever had done this to her had to pay—it wasn't just something she wanted but something she needed.*

The fact that the death threat had been ordered by someone probably making millions from the merger, and the fact that they were mocking the journalist's inability to get to them, irked her even more.

Even so, in her current physical state and with the undeniable dead-end in her investigation, she knew that her determination and ire were of little use. For a brief moment, she felt angry at Tom again, but it quickly passed. She wished right now that he was here. Ironically, the utter hopelessness of her situation seemed to dampen her angst somewhat and she began to relax.

She slid carefully over to the side of the bed and gingerly swung her legs over the edge. There was a moment of intense pain when her feet touched the ground, but she steeled herself and it eventually passed. Now able to sit, if not stand, she looked up at the dressing table, which was facing her. Lying on the table was a damp cloth stained with lipstick and rouge, and next to it was a half-empty glass of water. The cloth was Amanda's but the makeup on it was not.

It was then that she saw the message. It was on the mirror above the dressing table, like an obscene piece of graffiti. Scrawled in bright red lipstick and crossing the length of the mirror diagonally were the words DROP IT OR DIE, CUNT!

Without even trying to hold herself back, Amanda began to sob. Putting her head in her hands, she cried like a baby, unable to summon her earlier bravado or even a sense of hope. The young reporter who had once dreamed of uncovering another Watergate now felt nothing but despair and defeat. In the real world there were no happy endings, and Amanda had just learnt this lesson the hard way.

She needed to call Tom.

The banker's face was grim as he inspected Amanda's bruises. A small purple welt had appeared right above her abdomen, but there was no swelling and the bruise seemed to be localized. He looked up at the reporter.

"We should go to the doctor and have you checked up," he said matter-of-factly.

"I'll go tomorrow morning. I think I'm all right."

Tom shook his head. "You need to see one tonight. He hit you pretty hard and you could be hurt internally. The sooner a doctor takes a look at you, the better. I'll take you to the emergency room."

"They'll want to know how it happened. What are we going to tell them?"

Tom stared at her in surprise. "We tell them what happened, of course; and file a police report."

Amanda shook her head. "We can't go to the police, Tom. The guy who threatened—attacked me warned me against doing that. He said he would kill me if I opened my mouth, and I believe him."

Tom considered this for a moment.

"Maybe the cops can figure out who this guy is, and even if they can't, maybe they can shake up someone at TriNet or Luxor to find out who was behind this," he conjectured.

Amanda gave a hollow laugh. "You make it sound like a TV show. The police will never be able to figure it out—you know that. And exactly who at TriNet or Luxor would tell them anything?"

"How about your friend at the FBI? Can you call him?" Tom hated to mention Jack's name, but his primary concern right now was Amanda's safety.

"Jack will go ballistic if I tell him what happened, and he's got a pretty bad temper. Knowing him, he'll go down to TriNet's offices and start browbeating the senior officers. Best case scenario he'll get fired for his troubles . . . and I'll wind up dead," replied Amanda cynically.

"Not if he can get you some protection," Tom pointed out.

"For how long, Tom? A couple of days, a week maybe. The FBI isn't going to waste an agent on me indefinitely. Eventually I'll be on my own again, and I can't live with the specter of coming home one day and having my throat slit. . . ."

Tom gazed at her sympathetically.

"All right, but you have to drop the story immediately. It's not worth this. Nothing is. I wish I could do more," he said with a strange look.

Amanda looked at him quizzically. "What do you mean?"

Tom told her about the evening's events at his office, his explosive discussion with Steve Brandt, and the final outcome. The reporter's face fell at the news.

"Oh, Tom. I'm so sorry. If I hadn't—"

Tom cut her off gently. "You didn't do anything except take a chance on a complete stranger. You were right, I was a jerk."

A tear appeared in Amanda's eye. Notwithstanding Tom's assurance, she felt terribly guilty.

"What are you going to do now?" she asked with concern.

The banker looked grim. "I don't know yet. After all, I basically accused someone at our client company of being a crook, and admitted to speaking with a journalist about a confidential transaction. Not to mention the fact that I gleaned absolutely nothing new from Steve. Any way you cut it, I made a fool of myself."

Amanda shook her head vehemently. In her current state, it hurt.

"No, you didn't. You did the right thing. Few people would have had the guts to put everything on the line the way you did."

Tom smiled. She was the one who had just been attacked, and she was comforting him! At that moment, he loved her more than he could have ever imagined. Pulling closer to her, he kissed her gently on the lips. She reciprocated, feeling the warmth of her body merging with his. It was like a salve for her wounds.

Reluctantly, Tom disengaged himself. He looked deeply into her eyes. "I think we should stop seeing each other for a while. If they're watching you, any contact with me is dangerous. I don't want anything to happen to you. . . ."

Amanda took the investment banker's hands in hers and squeezed them tightly.

"No one is going to scare me away from seeing you."

Tom shook his head. "It's not that simple. These people are dangerous. You need to get that. And I need to hear you say that you'll do everything you can to protect yourself."

Amanda sighed. "I will. But I won't cut you out of my life. *You* need to get that."

Tom grinned. "You're one bull-headed girl, you know that? Let's take you to see a doctor."

As Tom was assisting her into a cab outside the apartment building, the reporter caught sight of a white van parked down the street. It was standing next to a newsstand with its engine idling. From this angle, she could see through the front windshield. The interior was dark, but there was definitely someone behind the wheel. She froze.

Was it her assailant, or maybe one of his cronies, keeping a watch on her like he had promised? Did the driver have a butcher knife or a gun lying on the passenger seat next to him? Maybe there were two of them, and they would first rape and then kill her!

Just then the side doors of the van opened and a young boy jumped out with a stack of newspapers in his hand. He threw the papers down by the newsstand and climbed back inside to bring out another stack.

Amanda glanced at her watch and then gave a short, nervous laugh.

It was tomorrow's edition of *The New York Times*.

As they rode to the hospital, Amanda ruminated on the incident with the van a few minutes ago. *Was she already becoming paranoid? Would she always be looking over her shoulder now that she had been assaulted, and find herself unable to function normally? Was she a victim for life?*

By the time they reached the emergency room, Amanda Fleming knew that the only way for her to resume a normal life was to find out who was behind her attack, which of course meant solving the puzzle of the merger.

Unfortunately for her the investigation was going nowhere. It wasn't so much that the avenues they had explored had been unfruitful, but they were all part of a maze and none of them led to an exit. Without another lead, they were back to square zero.

Moreover, after Tom's discussion with Steve, it was possible that whoever was masterminding this would start covering their tracks—quickly.

To top it all off, Amanda was now under the watchful eye of an assailant, and any moves she made would be discovered and thwarted. As it stood, Amanda Fleming had only one thing to look forward to in her future—fear.

Damn it, she thought. *All we need is one break.*

part 4
endgame

thirty-six

The break came two days later.

While Amanda Fleming had been receiving an update on the SEC's findings from her editor, a young Hispanic man named José Rodriguez was conducting a routine check of the premises that he ran on behalf of his ailing father.

The junkyard, which was situated on the outskirts of Long Island City, was quiet for the most part. The loud crushing noise of the industrial-strength compressor that usually permeated the yard was noticeably missing, and as he walked through the rubbish strewn about the place, the only discernible sound was that of a door creaking.

After about ten minutes of the creaking noise, which in the relative silence of the yard had the same effect as a nail scratching the surface of a blackboard, he got irritated and decided to check on it. Walking past a row of decrepit chairs and tables that he had just this morning bunched into a corner in a fruitless attempt at organizing the messy yard, he made his way towards the rear. He rarely went back there, and had to navigate his way through forgotten piles of junk that had accumulated over the past few weeks.

Several feet directly in front of him, he saw the source of the trouble.

An Oldsmobile that was seriously out of commission stood amidst a group of other similarly distressed cars that looked like they were begging to be put out of their misery. The front door of the car on the driver's side was open and was swinging back and forth in response to the wind whipping through its interior.

José sighed and advanced toward the vehicle. As he drew closer, he spied something inside, wedged between the steering wheel and the front seat. A vague but ominous stench from the Oldsmobile reached his nostrils. José quickened his steps.

When he reached the car, the smell was overpowering. Covering his nose in disgust, he reached forward and pulled the door open all the way. Inside was a large, shapeless mass wrapped in garbage bags. Upon closer inspection, the plastic seemed to have torn in several places and he could see insects crawling through the holes.

José retreated involuntarily, feeling nauseous. He tried taking a deep breath, but the revolting stink made this impossible. Turning away from the car, the Hispanic vomited. As the spasms receded, he felt a little better.

A part of him wanted to run. Whatever lay in that car was not right. Every instinct he had told him so. But his curiosity was strong enough to override his common sense, and he found himself tearing open the garbage bags nervously. What he found made him wish he hadn't been so rash. Inside was a tangled mass of rotting flesh and bone that at one time had been the strong, healthy body of a human being. The only thing left now was a decaying corpse whose face would have been unrecognizable even if it hadn't decomposed—so forcefully had the visage been deconstructed.

Back inside the small office of the junkyard, José picked up the phone with shaking hands and dialed the number for the police. Fifteen minutes later, two uniformed cops showed up who took one look at the body and immediately called in a forensics team. While the car and its environs were being scoured for clues, a bleary-eyed detective took José's statement.

The Hispanic wanted to be as helpful as he could, and led the police to a hole in the chain-link fence surrounding the yard. He had discovered the gap in the metal wiring sometime back and had simply assumed that it was the work of punks trying to sneak into the yard. In the present context, another theory seemed more plausible.

None of this, however, provided a clue as to who had dropped the body off at the junkyard. Indeed, it would be almost twenty-four hours into the investigation before it could even be determined that the corpse was that of an engineer employed by a satellite company—a man by the name of Frank Wachowski.

On the evening of the same day that the body was identified, the name and picture of the dead man were released to the news media, and Frank Wachowski's erstwhile image was dutifully blasted over the tri-state area by all the major news networks.

Two days later, Amanda Fleming and Jack Ward found themselves in the small living room of Uljana Wachowski's Brooklyn apartment.

When news of the murder first hit the wires, Amanda had ignored it. But then she had noticed the name of the deceased's employer, Luxor Satellite, and an alarm bell had gone off in her head. She couldn't tell exactly why, but her journalist's compass had started spinning wildly. And so here she sat, interviewing the family to determine if there was any connection between the engineer's death and the merger. Jack's bureau identification had earned them an invitation into the apartment.

Over the past two days, Uljana had been inundated with questions from the police. Did Frank have any enemies, had he been fooling around with anyone, who were his closest friends, where did he hang out in his free time, did he gamble, had he taken any money from loan sharks, had he ever had any arguments with anyone? The cops had even combed the brownstone for clues and questioned friends, neighbors, and other Luxor employees, all without success. Uljana's earlier missing person's report was strategically forgotten. For the shell-shocked Polish woman, it was the ultimate test of courage.

Beyond her grief, there was also the issue of survival. With no income and a college-bound daughter, she was at her wit's end about how they would make ends meet. Even though Amanda knew nothing about this, her intuition had caught on to the widow's distress, and the reporter found her eyes watering as she questioned Uljana about her husband.

For the most part, Uljana was unable to add anything new to what she had told the police. Since Jack had managed to obtain a copy of the homicide detective's report on the case, Amanda already knew those details. Other than the macabre discovery of the body, there was little of note in the story. Frank Wachowski seemed to have been an honest, hardworking man who loved his family and lived a clean, if unremarkable, life. His friends and colleagues liked him and no one could think of anyone who would want to harm the God-fearing Polish immigrant.

The only interesting thing, thought Amanda, was that the day after Frank was supposed to have been killed (as per the coroner's report), his wife had come home from shopping to find the front door unlocked. She had quickly surveyed the apartment but found nothing amiss—except for a footprint in the room that doubled as the couple's bedroom and Frank's study. Thinking that perhaps Frank had returned home briefly to get something from his computer and forgotten to lock the front door on his way out, she had thought nothing of it and wiped off the footprint.

Amanda asked if they could see the computer. Uljana led them to a small but comfortable bedroom in the rear of the apartment. As she stepped inside, the journalist noted that the room hadn't been cleaned since the NYPD's departure. Books and papers lay in untidy piles on the floor near the window, the bed was unmade and a man's clothes were crammed messily into an open closet by the door. She guessed correctly that the bereaved widow hadn't been able to muster up the desire or courage to come in here since the discovery of her husband's corpse.

She switched on the computer that sat atop a plain-looking office desk on the far side of the room. Moments later, she was scanning through the hard drive with Uljana's permission. Strangely, there were no files at all on the system. Other than the usual software and system files, there were no personal documents of any kind. She turned and asked Uljana a question. The widow answered in the affirmative, looking confused. Amanda turned back to the computer screen, but didn't make any comment. She thought it odd that there was nothing on the machine. If Frank had used the computer often, then there should have been *some* files on the hard drive.

It was as if the machine had been wiped clean.

After a few more questions, Amanda and Jack took their leave and headed for the front door. As they were walking out, Uljana caught the reporter's arm. Amanda turned around quizzically. Waving the guests back in, the Polish woman went back into the bedroom and returned a moment later with a folded newspaper in her hand. She offered it to Amanda, who accepted it silently.

"It was lying in the bathroom the night Frank disappeared. Frank always read in the bathroom," explained the widow. "I forgot to give it to the police."

Amanda unfolded the newspaper and spread it out on the coffee table in the living room. It was an old edition of *The Wall Street Journal.* With Jack staring curiously over her shoulder, she flipped through the pages, glancing quickly at the headlines. Nothing unusual jumped out at her, until she reached the sixth page.

On the top left hand corner of the page was a small news story about the TriNet-Luxor merger. It was basically a follow-up piece that talked about the anti-trust review of the deal and the FTC's expected approval of the merger. By itself, that wasn't so interesting, considering that Frank had worked for Luxor and was probably keeping up with the latest on the merger like everyone else; but in the fourth paragraph, a short section had been highlighted and a notation scribbled next to it in pen. The notation was an email address for someone named Steve Brandt.

The highlighted passage was about Morgenthal Winters and Bradford Associates. It listed the senior bankers who were advising on the transaction. One of them was a "Steve Brandt." Connecting the name to the handwritten note, Amanda committed the email address to memory. She shut the paper and handed it back to Uljana, but the Polish woman just shook her head.

"Keep it. I don't know if it's important, but if it is, maybe it can help the FBI with their investigation," she said, trying to smile.

Jack suddenly felt guilty. He didn't have the heart to tell her that he was here informally and there was no official probe into her husband's death on the part of the bureau. He muttered an awkward thanks, glancing nervously at Amanda.

As they were about to leave, the reporter spied a picture lying on the credenza in the foyer. It was a snapshot of an athletic teenager with long blond hair. She was gorgeous. Amanda picked up the photograph.

"She's very beautiful," she remarked.

The widow smiled gratefully. "Eighteen years old. She's going to Brown in the fall," she proclaimed proudly.

Amanda gave the picture a sad smile, as if Tracey could see her through the glass. *Brown. Her father should have seen her off to college. Every girl deserved that.*

Ten minutes later Amanda and Jack were driving back to the city. Both the passengers were thinking the same thing: Was there a connection between Frank's death and the merger? In a gruesome way, it seemed too good to be true. So far the merger had been about corporate malfeasance and maybe some insider trading, but now the stakes seemed much higher.

Jack broke the silence first.

"If there's a connection here, we may have a tiger by the tail, you realize that?"

Amanda nodded. A guilty blush crept up her face. She hadn't informed Jack of the incident in her apartment.

Since the attack, Amanda had been following a regulated schedule, which involved leaving for the office at 8:30 A.M. every day and returning home at 8:00 P.M. every night. She had given up her habit, at least temporarily, of working out of her apartment during the day, since she felt safer in the more public environs of the *Times'* office. As an added precaution, she had purchased a can of Mace—and was prepared to use it.

Tom Carter had offered to stay with her for a few weeks, and made it a point to check in with her every few hours when she was out. Since Robert Darlington was out of town, Tom had been suspended by MW but not terminated. The final decision would be made by Robert when he returned and once he had spoken with Tom and Steve.

The doormen in Amanda's building had received a stern warning by management after Amanda had reported seeing a stranger lurking in the hallways. She hadn't informed them of the assault, and was content with the knowledge that the doormen had become extra-vigilant in response to the directive.

On the night of the attack, the doctor at the emergency room had performed a thorough checkup on Amanda and concluded that she would be fine with a little bit of rest. Although the engineer's death had rattled her and refreshed her fears, she was hesitant to put Jack in a compromising position. Once he was told, Amanda knew that he would risk everything, including his job, to protect her. She also knew that there was precious little he could do.

"Well, now that we have something to go on, we can jumpstart the investigation again," said Amanda. A feeling of excitement was building up inside her. She felt like a hound who had picked up a lost scent.

"Excuse me?" said Jack.

"This," she said, waving the folded newspaper in front of him.

Jack sighed.

"Ah, yes, that. First of all, you may just have tampered with evidence. Secondly, just because the guy read a news story regarding his company and highlighted some names doesn't mean anything," he stated matter-of-factly.

"I disagree. I don't know if the highlighted name means anything, but the fact that Frank scribbled the email address next to it suggests he intended to correspond with the man. Why would a mid-level engineer do that? What could he possibly have to say to an investment banker representing the other side?"

"Don't you think the cops are in a better position to follow this up than two vigilantes?" asked Jack dryly.

"Three," Amanda corrected him pointedly.

"Whatever," said Jack. Since he had started helping Amanda, he had heard a lot about Tom Carter, and suspected that the reporter's interest in him was more than just professional. Tom was becoming a real pain in the ass, thought the FBI agent. "I still think we should turn this over to the police," he finished.

"And give away my front-page exclusive? You sample something from a drug bust?" said Amanda sarcastically.

Jack glared at her.

"Besides, the police would just screw the whole thing up. If Steve Brandt *is* involved, he'll simply get a sharp lawyer and refuse to answer any questions. Without the evidence that the NYPD will never find, they'll have to let him walk. You still think it's a good idea?" Amanda continued, challenging him.

Jack shook his head. And for this he was giving up tracking down terrorists and serial killers. . . .

"You're absolutely right," he stated. "I should have realized that."

Amanda was too preoccupied to notice he was patronizing her, or all hell would have broken loose. "I should ask Tom. He knows Steve Brandt," she mused, more to herself than for Jack's benefit.

Jack had an idea. It was all he could do to suppress a smile.

"Hold it a second. Look, I know Tom is the one who brought all this to you, but how do you know that *he's* on the up and up?"

"What do you mean?" asked Amanda.

"I mean maybe he's in on the whole scheme, but for some reason didn't get what he wanted out of the deal, and so now he's trying to incriminate everyone else. After all, he knows that his own involvement can be covered up through you."

Amanda's face reddened.

"That's bullshit, Jack! And I don't like your insinuation that I would cover something up . . . for anyone."

Anyone? So she *was* sleeping with Tom! Jack pursed his lips in anger.

Ignoring his jealousy as only a woman can, Amanda dialed a number on her cell. She had dialed it many times before and knew it by heart. On the third ring, Tom Carter came on the line. He seemed both excited and disturbed by Amanda's news.

"I'm glad you have something to go on, but it still doesn't make sense. What could Steve and this Wachowski guy have to talk about?" he argued.

"What if it wasn't a two-way conversation, Tom? Perhaps Frank had something he wanted to tell Steve about, a secret maybe. The question is, how do we find out what happened?"

The banker pondered this. He still remembered his own encounter with the managing director and how viciously he had reacted to Tom's insinuations. "I don't think a direct confrontation will work."

"So what do you suggest?"

Tom hesitated. He couldn't decide whether he wanted to go ahead or not. On one hand there was the prospect of rattling the man who had abused and fired him so unfeelingly, but on the other he had a great deal of professional respect for Steve and that went a long way. *But did he really have a choice anymore? Hadn't he cast the die a while back? Was he looking for a way out, or a way to the end?*

"I have an idea," he said finally.

Since Vikram Suri had first opened Steve's eyes to the reality behind the merger, the investment banker had been forced to keep an ear to the ground for rumors relating to the deal. It was unlikely that anyone could have suspected the truth, but the CEO of TriNet was unwilling to take chances. Steve had complied, reluctantly. At first it seemed to him that he was worsening his own dilemma by continuing to be an accessory in Vik's scheme, but he had soon realized that it was also his best insurance against being exposed. Having rationalized it to himself, he had immersed himself in the role of Vik's watchdog.

As time went by, his initial fury at Vik had subsided, and was gradually replaced by a grudging respect, and finally all-out admiration. He had always idolized the man for his many successes and shrewd corporate instincts, and while it was true that he was also slimy and vindictive, that didn't change the fact that Vik was a master of his game and could control his destiny in a way that Steve could only fantasize about.

In the conservative world of his profession, Steve felt restricted and inadequate; and like any man who's ill, he sought an antidote. By admiring Vikram Suri's power and ruthlessness vicariously, he could at least dull the pain, if not cure it. On a rational level, he knew that he was acting like a teenager who worships the poster of an actor or a rock star, but logic has little allure for a man who finally reaches the limits of his self-imposed world and realizes that it isn't only finite, but curves upon itself.

Vik had been supremely confident that the banker would come around to his way of thinking, and he had been right. As a result, Steve had started to identify with Vik, and imagined that he could see the world through the Indian businessman's eyes. What he didn't understand was that Vik had simply tapped into his stream of consciousness and suggested the perfect illusion. Steve's *own* desires and disappointments had done the rest.

Secretly, Steve harbored the hope that after the merger there would be a spot for him on Vik's team. He would even sacrifice the stability of investment banking for that privilege. He had spent too many years being a trooper for Wall Street, living by the rules and keeping his mouth shut. By hitching his wagon to Vikram Suri, he could finally escape from hell.

Salvation was within his grasp.

──────────────── thirty-seven

Wong Lin was the computer guru of Morgenthal Winters. As head of the information technology division at the investment bank, it was his responsibility to make sure that the intricate computer systems employed by the firm functioned smoothly and without crashing. Given the data-intensive nature of the banking and trading operations of MW, and the time-sensitivity of transactions, it was crucial that the networks be up-to-date and fault-tolerant. Being an MIT graduate and a former systems analyst from Microsoft, Wong was ideally suited for the job and paid handsomely for his troubles.

One of the elements of his job was to ensure that the data stored on MW's computer systems wasn't lost, either due to a hardware glitch, or due to someone's accidental deletion of a file or an email. This he accomplished by periodically backing up all the information on external disks. Even if something was deleted, it could still be found at a future date on these disks. The only exception was when a deal closed; then he would be assigned the unenviable task of finding and deleting all files related to the transaction from the backup disks. This was done to protect the firm from legal exposure in the event of a lawsuit, much like the hard copies of documents.

Since the TriNet-Luxor merger hadn't yet closed, he hadn't purged those files, and was able to help Tom Carter find what he was looking for. Also, since the IT office was located separately from MW's headquarters, Wong was not privy to common office gossip, and had not yet heard of

Tom's suspension. The only time the IT guys ever heard anything was when they were asked to revoke someone's privileges, which in Tom's case would happen only after Robert passed his judgment.

"Are you sure Mr. Brandt has approved this?" asked Wong when Tom made his request.

"Yes, and it's urgent we find it. The client's going nuts about this and Steve needs to call them back within the hour," explained Tom, lying.

The words "urgent" and "client" in the same sentence were enough to convince Wong to shut up and get to work. The easiest way to get fired around here was to ignore those two words, especially when delivered by a banker.

By going back over the chronologically marked disks, and with Tom's guidance on when the email might have been received, the IT expert was able to locate and retrieve all the messages received by Steve Brandt during that period. The volume was large, and Tom had to wade through a ream of printouts, looking for the likely culprit. At last he came to the email from "A friend." There was no mention of Frank Wachowski's name anywhere, but the text made the connection plausible.

Along with the email was an attachment, and Wong happily downloaded both onto a floppy disk for the vice president.

"Say hi to Mr. Brandt for me," said Wong to the departing Tom. He was trying to secure a better bonus for himself this year and kissing up to a managing director was always a good idea. Unfortunately, managing directors seldom knew the names or even the existence of lowly people like Wong.

Tom grinned broadly. "Sure will, Wong. Thanks a lot."

Upon arriving at Amanda Fleming's apartment, he received an unpleasant surprise. Standing with the reporter at the door to greet him was Jack Ward.

The meeting was tense. Tom was still suspicious of Jack's motives for helping his ex-girlfriend, and as the *current* boyfriend, understandably jealous. Trying to muster up some poise, he pretended to be friendly but nonchalant.

Jack, for his part, was equally jealous of Amanda's current beau and unlike him, was unable to hide his feelings with quite so much aplomb. Without bothering to shake Tom's outstretched hand, he simply muttered a hello. Tom withdrew his hand immediately.

Amanda, who could feel a sudden chill in the room as if the temperature had dropped thirty degrees, tried to stimulate some conversation.

"Tom's been wanting to meet you, Jack," she said unconvincingly.

"Is that so?" asked Jack, not so much speaking as growling.

Tom scowled. "Yeah, it's a real pleasure," he said with as much sarcasm as he could muster.

A long, heavy silence followed during which nobody moved towards a chair, and there was certainly no motivation for either man to speak—at least not unless he could vocalize his true feelings. Amanda shifted uncomfortably. But before she could say anything, Jack took the gloves off.

"I'm not sure I trust you, Carter. You could be in on this whole thing, and simply using Amanda as a tool to get back at someone who didn't cut you in on the deal. Besides, what kind of person would try to blow up his own deal? It stinks to high heaven."

Tom's face reddened at the accusation. To hell with civility, he thought!

"That's the biggest load of crap I've ever heard! You've been watching too many cop shows, Ward—I'm sure that's where the FBI learns about law enforcement anyway. . . . Either way, I don't give a damn about your opinion. You're only helping Amanda so you can get back in her pants."

Amanda groaned. She had feared tension between the two men, but nothing like this!

"Are you both nuts?" she exclaimed. "We've got a case to crack here. . . ."

Ignoring her, Jack advanced menacingly towards Tom, balling his hands into fists to pummel this little corporate bastard to a pulp. Tom, in turn, experienced the same rush that he had felt a long time ago on a football field, and moved aggressively forward with shoulders squared, ready to fight. He was aching to use the old muscles again, and this dumb government employee had just given him the perfect excuse.

Amanda stared at them in disbelief. *What a pair of idiots!* Had she not issued her own challenge at that moment, both men would likely have wound up in a hospital with head concussions.

"If you guys don't stop this nonsense right now, you can both get the hell out of my apartment! I mean it," she said, her voice rising sharply.

Both men stopped dead in their tracks, stunned. Hell hath no fury like a woman pissed off, and they knew it. Retreating sheepishly from their fighting positions, Tom and Jack positioned themselves on either side of

Amanda, not wanting to be near each other. It was a reluctant, a very reluctant, détente.

Amanda heaved an audible sigh of relief. She turned to Tom.

"What do we need?" she asked tonelessly.

"A laptop," he replied sullenly, not meeting her icy gaze.

A few minutes later, all three were huddled over Amanda's laptop and reading through the email.

The text was simple:

Dear Mr. Brandt,

I felt that you should know the following:

I was retained to compile the attached information on Luxor Satellite. As you'll see, the data suggests clearly that the assets of Luxor are in very bad shape, due to defective manufacturing, poor maintenance, and outdated equipment. While the information contained in the attachment is highly technical in nature, I've summarized the key statistics for each division and put them in simple terms.

I think you'll agree with me after viewing the attachment that Luxor Satellite is in trouble, and so far the senior management at the company has hidden this information from the public and even its own shareholders and employees. What you choose to do with this information is your business, but I thought that you should have it.

Best wishes,

A friend.

Frowning, Tom opened the attachment. A series of spreadsheets with numbers and statistics sprang up like the lost words of an ancient prophet. As the screen filled up with information, Jack let out a low whistle. There was a lot of data in the file, but most of it seemed meaningless. *It would take a scientist to figure out what all the numbers meant,* he thought.

The author of the email had anticipated just that and true to his letter, had compiled a series of simple statistics on a separate tab, a sort of *Idiot's Guide* to the data. As Tom and Amanda read through the categories and numbers, their eyes widened. In the context of the email, the implication of the statistics became clear.

Luxor's satellites were old and seemed to require constant maintenance and repair. In addition, the rate at which various key components seemed to fail was alarmingly high. It was obvious that the necessary upkeep for the satellites wasn't being provided, since the cost side of the equation indicated that very little money was actually being spent on maintenance. Most of the expenditures seemed to be directed at buying refurbished satellites and replacement parts from small countries around the world at cheap prices. Yet from what Tom knew himself, Luxor was passing these "patched-up" machines off as new.

The final statistic that was disturbing was the rate of satellite failure for Luxor. Since most of the satellites were controlled by the FSS division and their transponder capacity leased to third parties, there was a considerable expenditure on the part of Luxor to correct these anomalies on an ongoing basis.

From his own analysis of Luxor's numbers, Tom knew right away that neither the maintenance costs nor the failure costs had been accurately represented to the acquiror. Moreover, TriNet and its bankers and lawyers had been led to believe that Luxor's fleet of satellites was in top-notch condition and relatively new. There had been no mention of excessive failures or needed repairs.

If this was true, thought Tom, then the purchase price being paid for Luxor was too high. Doing some quick mental math, he estimated that the actual value of Luxor under these circumstances could be south of $3 billion—a far cry from the $10 billion that TriNet was prepared to pay for the satellite operator's assets!

Equally importantly, it meant that Craig Michaels had lied about the condition of his company both to his own shareholders and those of TriNet, and essentially defrauded everyone, including Luxor's creditors.

At the back of his mind, Tom remembered the SBC/Ameritech merger in 1998, in which SBC Communications, a local phone and wireless service provider, had purchased Ameritech, a Bell company, for a hefty sum—only to discover that the assets they had bought were old and disintegrating. After consumer complaints reached a fever pitch, SBC had been forced to expend huge amounts of capital to rapidly upgrade the systems, and had a hard time explaining to its shareholders why the company hadn't discovered the problems before buying Ameritech. The parallels between that incident and the TriNet-Luxor deal were striking.

His rage against Jack having subsided somewhat in deference to more urgent concerns, Tom now decided to deal with the FBI agent as a partner rather than an adversary—at least for the moment. Besides, he suspected that they would need his help.

"If this information is true, then why didn't Steve bring it up with TriNet?" wondered Amanda.

"We don't *know* if it's true," corrected Tom. "But I'm guessing that Steve either didn't bother to read the email, or discovered that the message is a hoax."

"Or he's mixed up in something," added Amanda.

Tom didn't respond. Despite his volatile encounter with Steve, he was saddened at the prospect of his managing director being involved in a criminal act. He had always admired and respected Steve, and the thought of him being a crook was very disillusioning.

"Couldn't the FBI bring him in for questioning?" asked Amanda, looking at Jack. She always phrased her questions in a way that would make refusal seem unreasonable. It was a journalist's skill.

But Jack had dealt with it before. He shook his head.

"Based on what? The receipt of this email isn't evidence of criminal behavior, and besides, we have no idea who really sent it. Chances are the Hotmail address is just a dummy account—you or I could set it up in minutes and no one would be able to trace it."

"But it would be possible to trace the email to the source computer, right?" asked Amanda.

"Only to the host server, which belongs to a third party. The email could have been sent from a Kinko's for all we know," mused Jack. "But even if we could, there's still no link between Steve Brandt and the murder, and without that I can't get the bureau to appropriate the case from the NYPD."

"I'm sure it was Frank Wachowski who sent the email," stated Amanda.

"Prove it," challenged Jack.

"Why don't we just turn over the email to the police and let them follow up on it?" asked Tom, confused.

"Because Nellie Bly here doesn't want to give up her exclusive," replied Jack wearily. Noting the reporter's fierce gaze, he added hastily: "And because she doesn't trust the fuzz."

"All right then, what if *I* confront him?" suggested Amanda.

"You could do that," answered Tom carefully, "but if he *is* guilty he'll just deny reading the email and then start covering his tracks, ruining our chances of finding further evidence. We have to confirm this report first." After a pause, he added: "He could also be innocent."

Amanda felt irritated by Tom's desire to give his boss the benefit of the doubt. In the world of investigative journalism, there was no room for emotions or favoritism. She responded testily.

"So what *do* you propose we do—hope that the confirmation falls out of the sky?"

Tom ignored the remark. After mulling over the options in his head, he settled on a plan. It wasn't the most appealing course of action for him personally, but under the circumstances there was no other way. He would just have to take the risk.

When he had finished relaying the plan verbally, he turned to Jack.

"If the email turns out to be accurate, could you then rope in the bureau?"

Jack hesitated. He was eager to help, but wary of making such a large commitment, even if there was a homicide involved. The FBI's resources, like those of every other government agency, were stretched thin, and he wasn't at all sure that his bosses at the bureau would take kindly to a request for manpower and time on a case that could well be outside of their jurisdiction anyway.

As if reading his mind, Amanda jumped in. "If our theories about the merger are even half right, Jack, this was a corporate shell game, including insider trading, market manipulation, and money laundering. And now someone's dead. Somewhere in that whole mix, the FBI could find a reason to pursue this, no?"

Jack shot the reporter an angry glare. He didn't like her condescending tone. Tom noticed the impasse and moved hurriedly to diffuse the situation.

"Why don't you think about it and let me know?" he addressed Jack. "In the meantime, I'll see what I can find out about this email."

As he was leaving, Tom paused at the door. Amanda looked at him quizzically.

He lowered his voice so Jack couldn't hear. "I'll be back later tonight. I'm sorry about that . . . display . . . earlier," he said nervously.

Amanda rolled her eyes.

"Go," she commanded.

Tom nodded and withdrew. As usual, he found it hard to read Amanda's reactions, and found himself praying fervently that he hadn't damaged their relationship by his earlier display of jealousy.

A few minutes later, as Jack rode down in the elevator, he was thinking the same thing.

It was 3:00 P.M., Day 59.

─────────── thirty-eight

The next day, the Federal Trade Commission and the Department of Justice approved the merger between TriNet Communications and Luxor Satellite.

Helen Mosbacher, who in addition to being the CEO's personal deputy was also the general counsel of TriNet, called him as soon as she heard. Vikram Suri was jubilant and immediately started to rattle off last-minute requirements for the closing of the transaction the next week.

Helen had anticipated most of the arrangements and had been busy coordinating them. The meeting would take place in TriNet's headquarters in lower Manhattan, and would be attended by the CEOs and board members of both companies, the lawyers, and some computer staff to facilitate the transfer of funds into the bank accounts of Craig Michaels and the other shareholders of Luxor. Concurrently with the wire payments, Luxor's shareholders would transfer ownership of their company to TriNet Communications, and the merger would be complete.

The funds from the ESOP loan, which had been placed in escrow by the bank in Boston, would be released simultaneously with the closing of the transaction. The shares of TriNet required to set up the employee stock ownership plan, including the portion being sold by Vik, had already been "purchased" from the company's treasury and the CEO (although no cash had yet changed hands), and at the meeting the shares would be moved into the ESOP account, enabling TriNet to break the escrow.

One of the reasons that Vik was so upbeat was that he would receive the $700 million for his portion of the ESOP shares at the same time that Craig Michaels received his money. Shortly thereafter, Craig Michaels would wire $2 billion from his share of the merger proceeds into Vik's account as per their arrangement.

The coup would be complete.

Pacing back and forth in his office, Tom Carter was going over what he would say to Caroline Brown. He had spent the better part of the day preparing himself for the conversation, which could be tricky.

Caroline and her firm, Rohm, Forrester & Carruthers, were outside counsel for TriNet in the merger. She was also the person who had examined every document from Luxor regarding its assets. If there was anyone who could help Tom determine the truth, it was she.

The problem was that Tom was no longer authorized to speak with Caroline regarding Luxor. If it got back to anyone at MW, Tom could be in very big trouble—legal trouble this time.

From his experience with Caroline, Tom knew that she was a straight shooter. Most lawyers who represented large corporations invariably wound up becoming rubber stamps for the general counsel, in much the same way that investment bankers often parroted the wishes of the CEO. Caroline was different, and that's why Tom trusted her.

Half an hour later he was seated in front of the matronly woman, relating his carefully rehearsed story. The banker had received an email from someone and was concerned about the information that it contained. Could she give him some guidance on the accuracy of the email? All the while, Tom watched for any signs that she knew about his suspension, but Caroline remained inscrutable.

She listened patiently as Tom went through the text of the email, as well as the statistics that were contained in the attachment. He didn't touch upon the possible implications of the email, and she didn't ask. As a corporate attorney, she knew full well what the implications were.

After hearing him out, she paused to collect her thoughts.

Unbeknownst to Tom, she had her own suspicions about the merger. Her unease had been sparked by the contentious liens that she had discovered while doing her due diligence for the deal. The documents had contained language relating to manufacturing dates and satellite maintenance that seemed ambiguous to her. She had, of course, brought the issue to the notice of Helen Mosbacher and forced Luxor to provide stronger reps and warranties on the state of their assets. Nevertheless, the initial incident had planted a kernel of suspicion in her mind and Tom's words had just added water to it.

Without explaining why, Caroline asked Tom if he would excuse her for a second. Tom nodded in surprise and the attorney walked out of her office. He had no idea where she had gone or what she was up to.

Out in the hallway, Caroline turned right and walked briskly towards a cubicle at the far end. When she arrived at her destination, she tapped the young man seated at the narrow desk on his shoulder. She may as well have set off a firecracker. James jumped.

"Another assignment?" he asked dryly when he saw who it was.

"No, nothing like that," laughed Caroline. "I just wanted to ask you a question. Do you remember those documents I asked you to shred a while back? The ones related to Luxor Satellite?"

James gave her a blank look. Then he remembered. He had thrown the documents into a pile and they must have somehow gotten covered up, because he had forgotten to shred them and never thought about them again. Caroline noticed his pale look and spoke kindly.

"Don't worry. I know you're overloaded, so if you forgot to do it I understand. But if you didn't destroy them, where are they?"

James racked his brain for the answer. He never threw anything out without looking at it first, so the documents couldn't have wound up in the trash. His secretary cleaned up his cubicle once a month, and at that time, anything that was lying on the floor and wasn't specifically marked would wind up in the miscellaneous drawer.

Pulling himself out of his chair, he walked over to the filing cabinet and opened the miscellaneous drawer. After rummaging around for a few seconds, he found what he was looking for. He returned to Caroline with the documents. The attorney glanced at them quickly and then handed them back.

"File these away under Luxor Satellite and make sure they stay there."

The associate nodded sheepishly. This time he would do it right away. While Caroline headed back to her office, she debated whether to inform Tom about the documents.

In the context of what he had revealed a few minutes ago, it seemed plausible that her earlier suspicions were correct. Even so, she was TriNet's attorney and couldn't possibly discuss her doubts with an outside party. For a lawyer, breaking confidentiality was the ultimate sin, not to mention malpractice.

At the same time, there was the Enron scandal, in which the independent accountants and company employees had shredded documents relating to the energy giant even after it became known that the SEC was likely to subpoena the records. It had been a flagrant violation which had tainted the entire profession of accounting. As the shocking story had unfolded, the public had first been surprised, then angered, by the degree of corporate malfeasance and legal and financial incest between Enron and its auditors, lawyers, and bankers. Caroline had felt disgust at the whole affair.

The idea of hiding potential evidence, even under the guise of her legal obligations to her client, was anathema to the woman who regarded her profession as noble and dignified. In her eyes, there was nothing more undignified than protecting the guilty.

She recalled clearly her conversation with Helen Mosbacher in which she had warned the company about the risks they were incurring. *Could Helen have known about the problem all along and swept it under the carpet to ensure that the merger went through? Could Vikram Suri have instructed her to do so?*

By the time she reached her office, she had made up her mind. The only question now was how to address Tom's queries truthfully without breaking the law herself. Sitting in front of the investment banker, the only female partner at RF&C chose her words carefully.

"We have in our possession certain documents that *might* indicate that the information contained in the email is true. I have no way of confirming, and in my position can't speculate, whether the documents do indeed prove anything.

"After some discussions with the general counsel at TriNet, we were forwarded a revised set of legal papers that satisfied us as to the state of Luxor's assets. At that time, as per protocol, I ordered the old documents to be shredded. It seems, however, that there was a mix-up and the files are still in our possession."

She was doing this by the book.

"I can't, of course, destroy the documents now that you have brought this matter to my attention, and they're being added to the rest of our files for Luxor Satellite. At the same time, due to attorney-client privilege, I can't discuss the content of the documents with you or anyone else, and won't produce the documents without a court order. Either way, I assure you they will remain safely in our drawers for the foreseeable future."

Tom listened attentively to Caroline's words and understood the import of her remarks perfectly. Based on the contents of the email, he could piece together what was now lying in the law firm's drawers.

The management of Luxor must have manufactured legal documents in order to hide the decrepit state of the company's assets. Even though he wasn't a lawyer, Tom could guess what had been fabricated—dates of manufacture, history of failures, sources of raw materials and replaced parts, capital expenditures and maintenance logs. It would have been a simple matter for those items to be doctored.

If the acquiror didn't look too closely.

Tom was about to walk out when Caroline stopped him.

"I was sorry to hear about your suspension," she said delicately.

Tom's eyes widened in surprise.

Then he smiled.

On the street, he dialed Amanda.

"I think we just found the evidence we need to corroborate the email. I guess now we have to question Steve. . . ." said Tom, feeling glum. "Can you talk to Jack?"

"Right away. This is great, Tom," said Amanda excitedly, failing to notice the disappointment in his voice.

Tom said goodbye and shut the phone. For the second time since the reporter and the banker had embarked on their adventure together, he was afraid of what they might find.

--------- **thirty-nine**

Exactly sixty-four days had passed since Vikram Suri had first called Steve Brandt at his office to tell him that TriNet Communications wanted to buy Luxor Satellite.

On the morning of the sixty-fifth day, the CEO of TriNet and his counterpart at Luxor were busy making vastly different preparations for the day ahead.

Vikram Suri had contacted his bank in Switzerland and instructed them to stand by for a money transfer later in the day for $700 million, which was the amount that would be remitted to him against the shares that he was selling to the ESOP. The money would first go to a bank account in the United States, in order to avoid suspicion, and from there to a discreet establishment in Zurich.

In the meantime, Vik's Arab partner in the Middle East had reported that the money from the smuggling of gold into India had come in and that his share would be deposited into the same account in Switzerland once the shell company in Dubai, Al-Riyadh Associates, was liquidated in a couple of days.

Counting the money that Craig Michaels would pay him under the table, Vik estimated cheerfully that by the end of the week, he would be almost $3 billion richer.

In approximately six months, Vik intended to step down as CEO of the company that he had helped build, and move his place of domicile to a remote island in the Pacific. At that time, he would dispose of his remaining shares in TriNet, and being free and clear of any obligations to the company, plan out the next stage of his king-pin strategy. All the while sipping whatever the hell he wanted on a sunny beach.

Craig Michaels, on the other hand, was planning to leave for Nigeria that afternoon, as per his arrangement with Vik. Characteristically, the Indian had provided him with an ex-Israeli-army "chaperone" who would escort him from TriNet's offices to the airport in a limousine. The man who would only be CEO of Luxor for a few more hours had no doubts whatsoever that the chaperone was not there for his protection. He was Vik's insurance policy in case Craig didn't keep his end of the bargain.

But the rough-hewn Californian hardly cared. From Africa, he could form a plan of revenge that would enable him to get back at the man who had blackmailed and humiliated him so viciously over the preceding months. With nearly $2 billion left in the bank, he had few doubts that one way or another, he would figure out how to teach Vikram Suri a lesson that he would never forget.

Besides, given the horrifying state of Luxor's satellites and the slipshod maintenance of its birds, he was quite content in the knowledge that he personally was receiving the entire *actual* value of the assets. Even though he hated Vik, Craig realized that the Indian was inadvertently doing him a favor by getting him to leave the country.

It was inevitable that his deception would eventually be discovered, and the shareholders of TriNet would then come looking for Craig's hide. Sitting in Nigeria, he would be untouchable by them or even the United States government. Dollars went a very long way in poor dictatorships.

As the time of the meeting neared, both these men put on their best suits and headed for their respective offices. In less than two hours they would meet in Vik's conference room and the merger would close.

It was 9:30 A.M.

At first, Jack Ward had been unable to convince his boss at the bureau to appropriate the investigation into the murder of Frank Wachowski—despite what Tom had discovered from TriNet's law firm. As Jack had expected, the FBI's reticence to take on the case stemmed primarily from the fact that it had many more pressing investigations on its roster; and there seemed no reason to supplant the police at this stage.

But Jack persisted, focusing on the fraud and embezzlement angle and being a general pain in the ass, until his superior relented. He agreed to make it a joint investigation between the NYPD and the bureau. Picking up the phone, he set the ball rolling through the appropriate channels, and within twenty-four hours Jack Ward was officially authorized to pursue the case.

While Vikram Suri was straightening his tie in front of the mirror in preparation for the big closing, Jack decided to pay a visit to Steve Brandt. He called his usual partner but he was out sick and the phone went straight to voicemail. Jack wondered briefly if he should try to requisition another partner, but knew that his boss would throw a fit if he found out. The old man had already used up a chip with the brass to get Jack the case and wasn't about to throw scarce resources at it too. By the time they assigned him another agent, it might be days.

Jack decided to go it alone. Without bothering to call ahead, he simply showed up at the offices of Morgenthal Winters. His credentials secured him an escort up to Steve's office and straight to Julie's desk. Steve's secretary could scarcely hide her curiosity when she saw his badge, but Jack refused to offer any information.

A few minutes later, he was ushered into Steve's office and the door closed behind him. The managing director stood over his desk and offered his hand. Jack shook it noncommittally.

"Mr. Ward, my assistant tells me you're from the FBI. How can I help you?" he asked, motioning him to a chair.

Jack sat down and pulled out a set of printouts from his jacket. He pushed them across the desk towards Steve. "Have you ever seen this email or the attached data?"

The banker accepted the printouts curiously and started reading. A brief flicker of recognition crossed his eyes, but then vanished. His face was expressionless when he returned the papers to Jack. "Never. I must have deleted it without opening it. I get a lot of emails."

The federal agent had caught a glimpse of Steve's eyes and knew that he was lying.

"You realize that we could check with your computer department to see if you opened the email?" Jack asked meaningfully. He had already obtained an official copy of the email with a court order earlier in the day.

Steve nodded. "Sure, but it won't tell you anything. My secretary Julie, whom you just met, opens all my emails, especially when I'm away from the office. By the date on this printout, the email arrived while I was on a trip to San Francisco."

"But she wouldn't delete emails without asking you first, right? So if I call Julie in here right now and ask her if she ever mentioned the email or its contents to you, she'll answer in the negative?"

Steve shifted uncomfortably. He didn't like being painted into a corner.

"All right, I *might* have opened it. But there's nothing in there that seems credible and I probably just ignored it. You have to understand, Mr. Ward—whenever we're working on a large deal, we receive a ton of emails, some of them from reporters trying to trick us into giving them a story, others from crackpots who want to scuttle the merger for fun or because of some grudge. We simply can't pay attention to unsubstantiated stuff like this."

Jack nodded. "I understand that; but you see, in this case we have good reason to believe that the email's contents are accurate. So if you did get the message and ignored it without checking, it constitutes gross negligence on your part."

Steve gave him a skeptical look. "Since when is the corporate responsibility of investment bankers the concern of the FBI?"

Jack explained.

"We don't really care about that. But we do care about the engineer from Luxor whose body was found in a junkyard last week. His name was Frank Wachowski, and he has an eighteen-year-old daughter," finished Jack, anger creeping into his voice.

Steve's face was motionless, but his heart was thumping like a drum.

"Our computer experts have established that this email was sent to you from Frank's home computer the day after he was murdered," lied Jack. "We think the two are linked."

Steve's face turned ashen. *Damn Vikram Suri! The crazy bastard had certainly done it now.*

"I don't quite follow. How is all this connected to me?" he asked nervously.

Jack gave him a cold look. He was convinced now that the banker was up to his neck in something, and treated him like a suspect.

"You're either covering up for someone, or are involved yourself. The fact remains you were probably the last person to hear from Frank Wachowski," he said, indicating the email. "Add to that you're working on a multi-billion dollar merger that could have been 'scuttled' by the information in this email. So until we can establish otherwise, we have to assume that you know something."

Steve thought quickly.

"You say the email was sent the day *after* Frank was killed?"

Jack nodded in affirmation.

"Then how could he have sent it?" asked Steve, lunging at the inconsistency.

"The email was set on a delay timer at the host server. It was programmed to be sent out the next morning," Jack explained, lying again. As far as he was concerned, Steve didn't need to know that the anonymous email account couldn't be traced to anyone, let alone Frank Wachowski; or that the Hotmail server from which the email had originated had sent it instantly in response to a direct command.

Steve digested this information with a grim expression on his face. When Vikram Suri had first confronted him with the truth regarding the email, and then threatened to frame him with the wire transfer and the photographs, he had been infuriated. In time his anger had vanished and was replaced by a paradoxical admiration for the man and his methods. But that was in the ivory-tower world of white collar crime. There were no dead bodies in that world, no sordid murders for profit. In the real world—the world in which he found himself now—there was violence, and casualties, and consequences.

On the one hand, he was horrified by the notion that he might have helped Vik cover up the murder by not going public with his knowledge of the email and its contents. At the same time, he *had* taken a bribe and if Vik was in trouble, he was too. In spite of his qualms about his actions, he had no wish to incriminate himself.

"I'm sorry for this man's death, but I really don't know anything about it. As I said earlier, I probably just dismissed the email as garbage when I first saw it," he tried to explain, hoping that the FBI agent would give him a break.

Jack's face hardened to steel. He had interrogated many men in his time, and had little sympathy for liars.

"Brandt, let me make one thing very clear to you. You're in a dangerous position here. For one thing, I don't believe you. And even if you're telling the truth, I still can't understand how you could let something like this slide. It's bush league, and I don't buy that a guy in your position would make such a mistake.

"That leads me to believe that you're covering up for someone, probably someone who has either paid you off or has some hold over you. If you cooperate, we may be able to help you."

Steve sprang from his chair.

"I want to call my attorney. I'm not prepared to discuss this any further," he stated flatly.

Jack smiled. He had expected this, and under the circumstances, this was probably the surest indicator of guilt on the part of the managing director.

"Sit down, Brandt!" he growled. "If you play games with me, I'm authorized to charge you right now with accessory to murder. Call your attorney if you want, but he'll have to meet you at Police Plaza, because that's where I'm taking you."

He rose to reinforce his words, and pulled out a pair of handcuffs.

Steve backed away reflexively. He looked genuinely scared. Jack grinned. "Change your mind?"

"I'll cooperate with you," Steve said quietly. "What do you want to know?"

"Why don't you start at the beginning and tell me everything?" said Jack, sitting back down in his chair.

Steve Brandt did tell him everything, including the events leading up to the email, the multiple changes in the valuation of Luxor, the rubber-stamp fairness opinions, his affair with Laura Briggs, his discussion with Vikram Suri over a billiard table in the TriNet office tower, the wire transfer of $500,000 to his account, and finally his own detective work for Vik in financial circles to ensure that no one knew about the decrepit state of Luxor's assets.

Since Steve didn't know about the rest of Vik's plans, he was unable to shed any light on the insider trading or the murder. But Jack had already started to piece together a theory with the information that he had, and he knew that eventually they would find the evidence to link it all up.

Now that it was evident that the CEO of TriNet had been aware of Luxor's deception and had still gone ahead with the merger, it was logical to assume that he was behind, or at least connected with, a larger scheme to defraud TriNet's shareholders and possibly the stock market. In addition, it now seemed likely that Frank Wachowski had been killed to cover up the report that he had compiled for Vikram Suri, and that made the TriNet CEO the prime suspect.

"Are you prepared to testify to all this in court?" asked Jack, after Steve had finished telling his story.

"Will you cut me a deal?" asked the banker nervously.

Jack nodded. He had already decided that whatever else Steve was, he was low man on the totem pole, and hence could be cut some slack in exchange for the bigger deal.

"Do you know when they're closing the deal?" asked Jack.

"At eleven A.M."

"Today?"

Steve nodded. Jack looked down at his watch. "Where?" he asked tensely.

"At TriNet's offices downtown."

"Why aren't you there?"

"I have a meeting with another client."

"I would cancel it if I were you," said Jack dryly, and walked out.

As he was leaving the building, Jack called the police detective in charge of the Wachowski case. The detective had already received instructions from the police chief to cooperate with the FBI, and was grudgingly helpful.

Jack rattled off the address of the MW building.

"His name is Steve Brandt, with a 'd' in it. Put a couple of men down here right away and tail him wherever he goes. If he tries to take a plane or train, arrest him," Jack snapped, and shut the phone.

He glanced again at the time. It was 10:25 A.M.

forty

After Jack left his office, Steve called his lawyer. He relayed the conversation that he had just had with the FBI. Even as he spoke, Steve realized that he had made a terrible mistake. He had allowed himself to be badgered by a federal agent and had given what amounted to a full confession. As his counsel informed him wearily, he had just created a huge obstacle to his own defense.

The lawyer advised him to keep his mouth shut from here on in and confirmed that he was on his way to Steve's office. As soon as he got off the line, the banker felt ill. He could see his life crumbling in front of his eyes, and without any hesitation or shame, he started to cry.

While Steve was talking to his lawyer, Corey Meeks—the computer maven on Vikram Suri's payroll—was listening in. Through an intricate network of computers and telephone lines, and with the aid of a small bribe to a phone company official, The Center had set up a tap on Steve Brandt's phone. It was Vik's way of ensuring that his faithful servant was indeed being faithful.

When Steve put the phone down, Corey took off his headset and dialed a number on his land line. After three rings, he was connected to his master.

Five minutes later and one step removed, Vik received a call on his cell phone. He listened attentively to the voice at the other end.

"The agent is headed here?" he asked incredulously after the caller had finished filling him in.

The voice on the phone confirmed it.

"Where's the girl?" asked Vik, referring to Amanda Fleming.

The answer did not please him.

"Well, find her! I told you to keep a tail on her till the deal closed, didn't I?" said Vik furiously. "She could screw this whole thing up, you idiot! *Find her*," he snarled, stretching out the last few words for emphasis. Vik shut the phone.

He checked his watch. It was 10:43.

He pressed the button on his intercom. "Are they here yet?" he asked his secretary.

"Yes sir. Would you like them to wait?"

Vik thought it over. He wasn't going to delay the closing because of this glitch. In fact, he needed to speed it up.

But there was something he needed to do first.

"Tell Helen to get in here now. Send the rest of them in after five minutes," he ordered.

Vikram Suri was seated at the head of the conference table, flanked on his left by Craig Michaels and on his right by George Lomax. He had already informed George that he was selling some of his personal shares to the ESOP, and while the senior board member was critical, he couldn't really object. As Vik had foreseen, he was hesitant to make any last minute changes that could jeopardize the merger.

Since the bank in Boston had already disbursed the funds for the ESOP-backed loan, the number of shares that TriNet had to contribute to the employee benefit plan was locked in. If George had disallowed Vik to unload his shares at this stage, the company would have had to issue new shares from its treasury, increasing the dilution for existing shareholders and possibly endangering the deal.

On either side of Craig and George, lining the periphery of the long conference table, were board members and lawyers from TriNet Communications and Luxor Satellite. Caroline Brown was notably absent, having sent her law partners instead.

Helen Mosbacher was seated at the other end of the table, and would coordinate all the details, including the transfer of funds, the delivery of treasury shares to the ESOP account, and the signing over of Luxor's assets to TriNet. To aid her in all these was a small team of computer experts, who were seated around the table with open laptops connected to a private network. The real-time transfer of funds would be done via these laptops and secure connections had been established earlier in the day with the banks.

Standing up theatrically, Vik issued a brief, but grandiose, introduction to the closing process and then turned the floor over to Helen, who went over the nuts-and-bolts of the process and explained to everyone how the next few hours would work. Of course, most of the critical steps would be consummated within minutes, but afterward the board members would receive an extensive update on the post-merger arrangements from the CEO of TriNet.

By 11:00 A.M., the closing process was well under way.

A few minutes after leaving the offices of Morgenthal Winters, Jack Ward had called Amanda Fleming on her cell. She was walking along Third Avenue past Twenty-ninth Street when her phone rang. She flipped it open and held it to her ear.

"Hi Amanda, this is Jack. We hit pay dirt."

Conscious of the time pressure, he went through his conversation with Steve Brandt quickly, ending with his call to the police detective to "secure the witness." There was an edge to his voice that betrayed his controlled excitement. He loved racing against the clock—it was what he was built for.

Amanda caught his adrenaline-fueled mood. "Are you going to arrest Suri?" she asked breathlessly.

"And Craig Michaels. Brandt's story incriminates him as well, although not directly."

Amanda glanced at her watch. It was 10:38.

"What time did you say the closing was supposed to begin?" she asked.

"Eleven A.M. It's at the TriNet headquarters downtown."

"How soon can you get down there, Jack?"

"If I can get a blue-and-white to drive me, probably twenty-five minutes. I'm on the West Side so it can't be faster than that."

"Can't some other agent get there sooner?" asked Amanda pressingly.

The voice on the other end was tentative. "I'm not sure. I can make the request but they'll probably patch it through to my boss. I'll bet anything the old geezer's made sure that everything goes through him. I can convince him, but it could take some time. I'll call it in now and keep my fingers crossed. It's the best I can do, Amanda."

Amanda bit her lip. It probably *was* the best he could do. This time she couldn't argue.

"All right. I'll take a cab there right now and call Tom on the way. I'll see you at TriNet," she signed off.

Tom Carter wasn't at the apartment when she called, and she tried him on his cell. She got his voicemail. She left him a hurried message and started looking around for a cab. All the taxis seemed to be full. Cursing under her breath, she headed for the subway on Park Avenue South.

Chad Rollins was in a quandary. He had been told by his boss to keep an eye on the girl but had slipped up. Since the attack in her apartment, Amanda had followed a mostly predictable schedule, going from home to work and back. Other than a single trip out to Brooklyn to visit Wachowski's widow, she had stuck to her routine. It had made Chad's life fairly easy, since he could goof off for hours and still know where she was. Her phone taps had revealed that she hadn't really stopped investigating, but nothing in those conversations had caused any alarm.

Not realizing that since the assault, Tom had given her a new cell phone and it was this that she was now using, Chad had led Vik to believe that everything was all right. Not to mention that he had simply stopped tailing her after a while, assuming that he could always track her down on short notice between her apartment and the *Times'* office.

It was a lazy mistake and one that would cost him his life if he couldn't find the bitch now. He called both her apartment and the office, but Amanda Fleming was in neither place. He racked his brain. She could be out shopping and that would be a problem. But if she was out shopping, she couldn't create any trouble so that was all right. Other than that, he had no idea where she could be.

Chad thought hard. Vik's orders were to find her, but his goal was to keep her away from the closing. Regardless of where she was right now, Chad's primary mission was to make sure she didn't get near TriNet's offices. He himself was near Bloomingdale's on Fifty-ninth Street and Lexington.

Hopping onto his motorcycle, Chad kick-started the engine. Feeling at least partially relieved, the thug-for-hire raced downtown. He could fix this thing yet.

Tom Carter was in a meeting with an employment attorney when his cell phone began to vibrate. He was in the middle of learning about his legal rights at MW and didn't bother to answer it. Seven minutes later the conference ended, and Tom walked out of the lawyer's office. He headed to the offices of MW a block away for a meeting with Robert Darlington III, who would make a decision on Tom's future.

When he arrived, he saw two police cruisers parked outside. He wondered what they were doing there but continued walking. Just as he went through the revolving doors, his phone rang again. This time he answered it. It was Amanda.

"Hi, there," he said good-naturedly.

"Listen," she responded brusquely. "I don't have time to talk. Did you get my message?"

Tom frowned quizzically. "What message?"

"I left you a voicemail on your cell ten minutes ago," Amanda said frustratedly.

Then he remembered. He had forgotten to check his messages after the meeting.

"I'm sorry; I was in a meeting. What's going on? You sound nervous."

Amanda explained. She finished with: "I've just come out of the subway station and I'm walking towards TriNet. Jack's headed there too." She didn't ask the banker if he would join them, but it was implied.

Tom was shocked. He had hoped that Jack would get his arrests, but had never imagined that things would move so suddenly or so quickly, and that it would come down to such a thin wire.

By now he had made it to the elevator bank and was waiting for a car to take him up.

He hesitated. He didn't want to cancel his meeting with Robert, not under these circumstances. And it was dangerous for him to show up at TriNet's headquarters. Someone might recognize him and then all hell would break loose.

The elevator arrived. He moved to get on, then halted. Amanda was still on the line waiting for his answer. People glared at him angrily for holding up the door but Tom was too preoccupied to notice. Then abruptly he turned around and headed for the exit.

"I'm probably crazy for doing this, but I'm on my way," he said into the phone, going back out through the revolving doors.

Amanda sprinted most of the way from the train station, fully aware that she wouldn't be allowed up to TriNet's offices without Jack, but hurrying nonetheless. Feeling a bit winded, she slowed down to a walk as soon as her destination came into view. The tower was like most downtown office buildings—tall and businesslike with a jaunty glass and steel exterior. In front of the entrance was a spacious plaza, with a group of benches clustered around a large garden. In the middle of this garden was a tall metal structure polished to a gleam. The familiar logo of TriNet Communications glinted proudly in the bright sunlight and proclaimed the building as the worldwide headquarters of the media giant.

Amanda glanced at her watch. The meeting would be starting any minute now. She looked around in a vain hope of seeing Jack or Tom, but neither of them had arrived yet. Fretting, but relieved at being able to rest, she sat down on a bench in TriNet Plaza and settled down to wait. She wondered what was going on right now on the top floors of the massive building.

In the distance, out of sight behind three city blocks of concrete, steel, and wood, a man on a motorcycle approached.

Vik was tapping the polished surface of the conference room table impatiently. Even though Helen Mosbacher had ensured that all arrangements were in place, and even though the techies were almost ready to begin their digital dance, he was in no mood to wait. To the man whose dreams were about to be realized on an astronomical scale, each passing second felt like a millennium.

Not privy to the CEO's private anxieties, and unaware of the impending arrival of an FBI agent on the premises, George and the others stared at him in amusement. They were all eager to get this done, but this was the process. It took time. The CEO of TriNet had been through it many times before. So why did he look like a teenager afraid that his girlfriend would change her mind about having sex?

Just then Vik's cell phone rang. In the respectful silence of the conference room, it might as well have been the Big Ben tolling twelve. He reached hastily inside his jacket and pulled out the offending device. The digital screen proclaimed that it was a private number. "Excuse me for a second," said Vik to no one in particular, and walked out of the conference room.

In the privacy of his adjoining office, Vik answered the phone.

Chad Rollins sounded breathless. "I have her in my sights, boss."

"Where is she?"

Chad grinned as he stared at Amanda Fleming waiting expectantly on a bench at TriNet Plaza. "Downstairs. I thought she might visit your office, so I took the prec—"

Vik cut him off. "Bring her up."

"What?" asked Chad, surprised.

The door to the conference room opened and Helen stepped inside the CEO's office. She had a quizzical expression on her face.

"You heard me," continued Vik. "Bring her upstairs. Helen will meet you at the elevator and escort you to a private room. Keep her there and watch her," said Vik, glancing meaningfully at Helen.

"What if the bitch resists?" asked Chad, gazing with concern at the dozens of people walking around the public Plaza.

"She won't. Just use your considerable charm," replied the CEO sarcastically.

After he had dispensed with Chad, Vik turned to Helen with an almost adolescent grin. "He found her. She's downstairs."

Helen raised her eyebrows in surprise. "And you asked him to bring her up here?" she asked incredulously.

Vik's smile broadened. "Call it a gift for our friend from the FBI."

Helen frowned. "Meaning what?"

"Meaning we can now kill two birds with one stone," replied Vik with satisfaction.

After a pause, he added: "Literally."

Jack arrived at the tall office tower in which TriNet housed its headquarters exactly five minutes after Amanda was escorted inside at gunpoint.

The feds weren't there yet but he wasn't surprised. As far as the FBI was concerned, they weren't exactly hunting Al Capone.

In keeping with his promise to Amanda, Jack Ward had called the bureau immediately for backup. As he had guessed, the request was shuttled over to his boss's office, albeit faster than he had expected. Two minutes later, his boss had called him back. He listened attentively as Jack made his bid, then delivered his verdict.

"Two men, that's all you get. Take it or leave it."

Jack took it. He knew that if things turned ugly, he could always call on the NYPD for additional backup. Once someone else had already done the legwork, the cops were more than happy to rush in with sirens blaring and guns drawn. He would push that panic button when he needed to, but with a Fortune 500 CEO that didn't seem likely.

Besides, he didn't have high hopes for speed-of-response from the FBI on this one. Whether he liked it or not, his best bet for the moment were the two cops who had escorted him to the TriNet tower and followed him into the lobby. Indicating the dual elevator banks, he stationed them as lookouts while he strode over to the security desk.

The guard watched curiously as Jack approached. The federal officer held out his credentials and demanded to be led to Vikram Suri's office. The guard responded to the peremptory tone by immediately dialing his superior. He listened for a long moment while his boss talked at the other end, then whispered something in return. Jack frowned suspiciously. This was taking too long.

He was about to reach across and grab the phone when the guard put it down. He waved to a single elevator set discreetly at the back of the lobby.

"The fortieth floor. The express elevator is coming down for you now."

Jack stood for a second examining the eyes of the security guard. What did he see in them? Smugness? *Deceit?* He pushed the thought out of his mind and walked back toward the express elevator.

After meeting Chad and Amanda and escorting them to the private room as instructed by Vik, Helen did not return to the conference room. Instead she sat in front of Vik's desk, waiting for his phone to ring—which it did two minutes later. It was the security chief of the TriNet tower with a message for the CEO.

Helen smiled to herself as she put down the receiver. As usual, Vik had all the bases covered. Walking over to the conference room door, she pushed it open casually. The people in the room were busy with their respective commissions and private conversations, and no one noticed her. No one that was, except Vik, who noted the twinkle of her eyes and nodded his head in receipt of the signal.

Helen slipped back into the quiet confines of the CEO's office. She glanced at the clock on Vik's desk and calculated the time it would take the FBI agent to get upstairs and make his way to the office. As the second hand ticked inexorably forward, she realized it would not be long at all.

It was time to lay the bait.

Amanda Fleming had also laid bait, but had no idea whether the fish would even see it.

It was a small item, and while she sat bound and gagged inside the glass and steel prison of TriNet, she prayed to God that it would not be discovered by some teenager who would consider it a freebie and walk away with it.

She was holding the cell in her hand when Chad Rollins approached her, smiling handsomely. At first she thought he was going to hit on her, but the Beretta that had appeared in his hand had shot that theory to hell. Realizing that with a silencer he could kill her and still walk away from the Plaza, Amanda had stood up quietly and done as he said.

Except for gently dropping the cell phone on the bench. So softly had the Motorola device landed on the wood that Chad had heard nothing. Even if he had, he was too preoccupied with not attracting attention to notice it.

In different circumstances, she might have been proud of her presence of mind at leaving behind a clue, but right now she was only petrified. The odds of Tom or Jack discovering her phone or realizing that it *was* hers were as remote as her flapping her arms and being able to fly out of the building.

But it had been all she could do. And now it was her only hope.

The cab carrying Tom Carter pulled up in front of TriNet Plaza at 11:17 A.M. He noticed the police cars right away. There were two NYPD blue-and-whites parked down the block, each with a cop behind the wheel. That meant their partners were somewhere else, probably together.

Tom paid the cabbie and hurried up the steps of the Plaza, towards the main office building. He wondered if the cops were here for Vikram Suri. Amanda had told him Jack was heading down to TriNet's offices, so it was plausible that he had called for backup. At least the press wasn't here.

Then he realized and started laughing. Amanda *was* the press. He was so used to looking at her as a woman and his girlfriend that he hardly associated her with a tough journalist anymore. *Was that what happened when you were in love? You forgot what your significant other did for a living?*

When he was ten yards from the entrance to TriNet tower, Tom pulled out his cell and dialed Amanda's number. He wanted to know what was happening. *Had Jack interrupted the closing? Had he made it down here in time? What was going on up there right now?*

There was no signal. Tom frowned, then realized he was too close to the metallic tower. Some buildings interfered with wireless reception as if they had been designed for that. He walked back towards the street and dialed again. This time the call went through.

Then something odd happened. As Amanda's phone kept ringing, Tom thought he heard an echo. Not over the phone line, but from his other ear. A second later, the voicemail came on and the echo was gone. Tom spoke into the mouthpiece.

"Amanda, this is Tom. I'm outside the TriNet building. No idea where you are but I'm coming up."

As soon as he shut the phone Tom realized his mistake. In his excitement, he had forgotten that he was the invisible man. He was the one person who could not afford to have his name associated with what was about to happen. If he went upstairs now, he would be giving himself away as surely as if he had appeared on national television and proclaimed it on the evening news. He had only intended to be there to support the reporter, not put his neck in a noose.

Besides, he didn't even know if Amanda or Jack were really inside. To go into the building without ascertaining that wasn't just nuts, it was just plain dumb. Tom decided to try the reporter again. Maybe she would pick up this time. The banker wandered over to the benches and sat down.

As he called Amanda for the third time, he heard the echo again. This time it was louder. Tom frowned. He took the phone off his ear to listen. Now he could hear it clearly. It was the sound of a cell phone ringing, and it was somewhere close by. The banker glanced around curiously.

Then he saw it. Five feet away, lying on the benches. Walking over, Tom picked up the Motorola phone. He had a strange feeling. Taking his own phone in his other hand, he pressed "redial."

His stomach turned.

forty-one

Tom spotted them as soon as he stepped through the glass doors.

The police officers were standing at the back of the lobby, close to the elevator banks. Two of them, looking tense. The banker watched them curiously and wondered how long they had been there. He was about to walk over and ask them when a voice called out firmly: "Can I help you, sir?" Tom turned sideways to see a security guard. He was beckoning to the banker.

The guard had a neat crew cut, and was probably ex-marine, mused Tom. It was common for firms to hire ex-army people for this job. They knew how to intimidate. Even though Tom was in a hurry, he had dealt with enough of these people to know that they were not. The quicker he gave them what they wanted, the faster he could move on from the Twilight Zone that was the corporate lobby.

"All visitors need to sign in," the guard stated, pushing the tall ledger book that served as a security register toward him over the marble counter. Tom leaned over and put his name down impatiently. "Who are you going to see?" asked the guard.

Tom thought quickly. "Helen Mosbacher," he said. Worst case scenario, he could always pretend he had some business to discuss with the general counsel. It was safer than asking for Vik.

The guard's indifference suddenly turned to deliberate iciness.

"Ms. Mosbacher is busy in a meeting. She won't be available for the rest of the day."

Tom regarded him with incredulity. "And you know that without even calling her up?" he asked sarcastically.

The guard shrugged coldly. "She left instructions with the desk."

Tom glanced over at the cops. They were still by the elevators. He turned back to the guard. "Listen, I need to speak with those police officers. It's urgent."

The security guard looked like the banker had asked him for nuclear launch codes. "I'm sorry, sir. I can't let you go past the security desk. Please come back with an appointment."

"I'll only be a second," said Tom, trying to reason with him. He watched the cops out of the corner of his eye, as if afraid they would disappear if he blinked.

"I can't do that," came the adamant reply. The guard was getting genuinely annoyed now.

Tom felt Amanda's cell phone in his hand, and squeezed it hard. He had to find out what had happened to her. He decided to forego caution and sprinted towards the rear of the lobby, ignoring the security guard's protestations.

At this, another guard who had been watching the proceedings rushed forward to intercept him. Tom had barely covered four yards before he was tackled by a tall Jamaican with a serious attitude problem. The banker struggled against the powerful grip of his captor, but it was no use. He was lifted from the floor and shoved roughly against the wall. Vaguely, Tom heard the word "intruder" barked into a walkie-talkie somewhere in the vicinity. The guard at the desk came around and joined his partner in subduing the troublemaker.

Now in the custody of a bellicose Islander and a psychotic ex-marine, Tom Carter was hauled to the front doors of the TriNet tower. A food deliveryman waiting at the front of the lobby watched in amusement as the well-dressed banker was paraded past him towards the revolving doors. He grinned happily. Even guys in suits got booted once in a while.

Then Tom saw a familiar face.

Jack Ward was about to blow a gasket. The express elevator was taking forever to arrive, and once again he wondered if the delay was deliberate. The security guard's conversation with his chief should have been crisp and quick, not protracted. It suggested deception and machination.

The irate FBI agent was about to move to the regular elevator banks when he heard a yell. He whirled around and saw a man in a suit being shoved forcibly towards the front entrance. Jack frowned. *What the hell was happening here?*

The elevator pinged its arrival and Jack was about to ignore the commotion when he heard his name shouted by the man being led away. His blood pressure surged. It was Tom Carter! Jack cursed under his breath. The last thing he needed right now was this. He should probably just let the idiot get thrown out. But he knew that wasn't an option. Amanda would never let him hear the end of it.

Jack took a deep breath to calm himself, then walked rapidly back into the main lobby. The security guards had released their grip on Tom, wondering who he was calling. A look of worry crossed the Jamaican's face. If the visitor they had been about to toss out turned out to be someone important, their manhandling could cost them their jobs, even if they were just following orders. The ex-marine was thinking exactly the same thing.

Tom's eyes fixed on Jack's as he approached. He was about to say something but the fed beat him to it. "What in God's name do you think you're doing?" he demanded angrily. Tom was flummoxed by Jack's reaction. This was not what he had expected, but he had to let it slide. There were more urgent things to worry about. In answer to Jack's query, he proffered Amanda's cell phone.

"I found this outside on the bench, Jack" he explained grimly. "It's Amanda's phone—I checked. I think she's inside the building."

Jack Ward froze. The icy hand of danger crept slowly up his spine. He took the telltale cell phone in his hand and turned it over, as if the reverse side held some clue to Amanda's whereabouts. When his eyes moved back up to Tom's, they were uncertain.

"It doesn't necessarily mean she's in danger," he reasoned, not sure who he was trying to convince.

Tom suddenly realized that Amanda had never told Jack about the attack on her life. Bracing himself for an outburst, he filled the FBI agent in as quickly but fully as he could. Jack's face colored with anger, but this time he did not take it out on Tom.

Instead, he strode over to the ex-marine and grabbed him by the lapels of his cheap jacket. "Did you see a blond woman walk in here before me? Tell me the truth or I'll have your ass hauled off for obstruction of justice," he threatened.

"Yeah, there was a woman, but she was with some guy," stammered the guard.

"What kind of guy?" asked Tom nervously.

The guard described Chad Rollins.

"How did they get in?" asked Jack.

The guard shrugged. "He had a building pass. From TriNet."

Jack released the man and shot a worried look at Tom. The banker's suspicions seemed to be correct.

The NYPD officers, who had watched the whole spectacle in amazement, were standing close by, waiting for instructions. Jack addressed them one at a time: "You call for backup and seal off the exits, including the basement. You get me the Con Ed regional chief on the line now!"

Tom followed Jack as he raced to the elevators. The cop calling Con Ed spoke rapidly into his shoulder mike as he ran, keeping pace with the FBI agent. He turned to Jack.

"I got the Con Ed guy on the line. What do you want?"

Jack looked serious. "Tell him to shut down the power in the building."

The cop spoke into his shoulder again. A second later, he shook his head at Jack. "Can't do it. There's a shopping arcade downstairs. Hundreds of people. They need clearance from Police Plaza for something like this."

"How long will that take?" asked Jack wearily.

"At least fifteen to twenty minutes," answered the policeman matter-of-factly.

"We don't have that kind of time," growled Jack. He thought quickly. "Tell them it may be a terrorist situation."

The cop didn't move. "I can't do that," he said quietly.

Jack glared at him, then stepped forward and ripped the shoulder mike off his uniform. Under the disbelieving gaze of the police officer, he delivered his message to Con Ed. Tom swallowed hard.

There was a crackle from the receiver and Jack's face suddenly broke into a Cheshire grin. He handed the mike back to the stunned cop. "They're doing it now. Don't worry—it's my ass, not yours."

Despite his concern for Amanda, Tom was about to argue that this was hardly a national security matter, when the elevator arrived. He piled in behind Jack while the cop stayed in the lobby to finish speaking with the electric company. As the doors closed, the NYPD officer flashed Jack a tentative but impressed smile.

As the two passengers rocketed up the TriNet tower, traveling at the insane speed of 120 floors a minute, the FBI agent's face turned somber. Although the thrill of the chase was racing through his veins at jet-speed, he was wary of an ugly showdown. There were always surprises. Reflexively, he touched the side of his jacket and felt the reassuring presence of the gun in its holster.

"Why cut the power?" asked Tom finally.

Jack turned to the investment banker in surprise. "To freeze the money, why else?"

While Tom and Jack were heading for the fortieth floor, in the basement of the building the chief of security for TriNet Communications was busy reviewing the security tapes for that floor from a few minutes ago. The screen showed Chad Rollins and Amanda Fleming emerging from the elevator banks and Helen Mosbacher stepping forward to meet them. The tall redhead led her guests onto the floor and down the hallway, every step captured by one of the many ceiling cameras in the ultramodern business tower.

Unlike the old system where the footage was stored on physical tapes, the camera images were now saved digitally on a computer, enhancing the ability of the security department to keep a record of the comings and goings in the building for years to come.

They were also much easier to erase.

Looking around to ensure that the security guards whom he had sent on coffee breaks were still out, the security chief seated himself in front of the television monitors and began to type on a keyboard. With the aid of a highly sensitive Forward-Reverse dial on the console, he isolated the segment with Helen and Chad, and pressed *Delete*. There was a whirring sound from the security server and all traces of the meeting were wiped out. The chief of security tapped some more keys and the computer automatically closed the gap left by the deleted sequence by inserting a generic shot from each of the cameras in its place.

When he played it back, fifteen seconds of history had disappeared forever.

The boss would be pleased, thought the beefy man with satisfaction. And that meant a good bonus. Vikram Suri was a very generous man.

Exactly five seconds later the lights went out.

At first no one noticed. Since it was daytime, there were no lights on in the conference room and since the laptops all had auxiliary power, the screens stayed alive. But the networks that served TriNet's headquarters were run by servers based on the twelfth floor, all of which went dead to the machine. The people sitting at the laptops tapped their keys in confusion. They were all plugged into various external sites through the intranet and now those connections were down.

Vikram Suri glanced angrily at Helen, as if blaming her for the screw-up. The CEO's deputy walked hastily around the room examining each of the computers. Shaking her head in disbelief, she reached for a phone on the wall and dialed tech support. The phones, which were managed through a central switching system in the basement and also powered by electricity, were down as well.

It took Vik two more seconds to get paranoid. It was an instinct that had saved his neck many times before. He walked over to Helen and pulled her aside.

"What the hell is going on?" he hissed.

Helen shrugged her shoulders. "A power outage, I guess." It wasn't a great answer, but the only one she could think of.

"How long for the emergency power to kick in?" he snapped.

"Four, maybe five minutes," replied Helen, not very sure herself. "But the emergency power doesn't support the computer network. It's mainly for the lights, phones, and emergency elevators."

"What the hell do we need lights for? Call tech support from your cell and have them reroute the power to the servers," commanded Vik.

"Do you think it's a coincidence?" wondered Helen, referring to the outage.

The CEO felt like laughing. "Are you kidding me? This has the Federal Bureau of Investigation written all over it. It seems our agent is more determined than we thought." He paused, then: "Did you set the trap?"

Helen nodded.

"Well, it's not going to do much good if he can't actually walk into it, now will it?" Vik followed up with sarcasm. "Get that damn elevator running, Helen. I want this agent dead."

"But what if he comes with backup?"

Vik shook his head. "The security desk reported just him, with two cops in the lobby. He doesn't know we have the reporter, remember? As far as he's concerned, he's on his way to arrest a businessman."

Helen nodded noncommittally. "All right, Vik. I'll see what I can do."

In a swift, discreet motion, Vik suddenly grasped her arm and dug his fingertips into her flesh. In spite of her own physical strength, the pressure hurt like hell. Helen was too smart to cry out in pain, but tears welled up in her eyes.

"You know what I will do to you if you screw this up, Ms. Donatello?" he asked, reminding her of a past she was desperate to forget and the power that she didn't have.

Helen shivered inwardly. She knew only too well.

It was pure luck that their elevator reached its destination before it stalled. Tom and Jack stepped out of the wood-paneled car and into the dim elevator bank. In the absence of the hum of air conditioning and all other electronics, they could hear the secretaries talking inside the office, wondering what had caused the blackout.

They made an odd couple—the investment banker and the FBI agent. One was dressed in an immaculately creased Armani suit and the other in a wrinkled Eddie Bauer jacket. Sure, Jack had better clothes, but not a lot better. It suggested more than just a style of dress. For the moment, however, the cop felt superior. He knew what he was doing.

Jack strode purposefully to the sliding glass doors leading to the reception area and waited. Nothing happened. He cursed under his breath. Of course the damn doors wouldn't open—there was no power! He could wait for the emergency generator to come on, but that would defeat the purpose of cutting the juice in the first place.

"What now, genius?" asked Tom, walking up coolly behind him. He had been up to TriNet's offices before and had expected this.

Jack spared him an annoyed look. "Shut up."

While Tom was glad of the chance to embarrass his arch rival, and would have liked to prolong the experience, there really wasn't time for that. A clock was ticking, and so he dropped the sarcasm.

"The glass isn't bulletproof, you know," he said, gazing meaningfully at Jack.

The FBI agent sighed, pulled out his Colt, and delivered his own payback. "All right, but you pay for the new doors. You're the rich banker after all. . . ."

forty-two

The two men stepped over the shattered glass and onto the top floor of the TriNet building. There were people huddled in the hallway on both sides, staring with unabashed curiosity at the intruders. Ignoring them, Jack headed straight for the reception desk, where a young woman watched him approach with deer-in-the-headlights eyes.

He flashed his identification in front of the awestruck receptionist and demanded to know where the CEO's office was. The woman, who was just a temp, rose nervously from behind her desk and headed down the hallway, motioning for the visitors to follow. When they came within sight of the grandiose entrance to Vik's chambers, Jack dismissed her, much to her relief.

The nearest office to Vik's was the CFO's—a good twenty feet away, and Jack pointed it out to Tom. "We'll start at that door over there, and work our way around the floor," he stated. The lines on his face grew deep with concentration.

There was no one inside Mark Pearson's office and Jack shut the door softly. He moved on to the next one, again repeating the ritual. As he walked, he pulled his gun silently out of its holster and slipped it into his waistband.

Tom looked on curiously, and impatiently.

"Why don't we just arrest Vikram Suri?" he asked. "He'll lead us to Amanda."

Jack shook his head, trying the handle on a locked door. He hesitated for a second, then took a step back and kicked at it. The wood around the lock splintered loudly and Jack winced at the sound, but the door swung open. The office was empty.

"He's too clever for that," responded the FBI agent, advancing to the next room. Now that the advantage of stealth had been lost, he sped up the search. "Knowledge of the crime incriminates him. He'll just deny the whole thing and we'll lose precious time. At best it will be a bargaining chip he can hold over our heads. If she's in here, we've got to find her first. *Then* he's ours . . ."

"You don't think security told him we were coming up?" argued Tom skeptically.

"Of course they did, but it doesn't make a difference. He can't leave via the lobby or the basement. And with the power down he can't complete the money transfers. If there's one thing a CEO won't leave without, it's his money," remarked Jack contemptuously.

"And if she's not on this floor?" said Tom, asking the dreaded question that was on both their minds.

"The NYPD will have called for backup by now to seal off the shopping tunnels in the basement. After I've arrested Suri and Michaels, I'll get them to strip down the building," explained Jack. After a brief hesitation, he completed his answer: "But by then it might be too late."

Tom went pale at the thought. "How long can Con Ed keep the lights off?" he asked nervously.

"Not long," answered Jack bitterly. "Even now a report's being called into Police Plaza and from there it will make its way to the bureau. Once they discover I lied about the terrorist threat, they'll turn the juice back on. Probably have my hide over it too."

"Welcome to the club," rejoined Tom cynically.

The search proceeded fruitlessly and with each room they checked, they were drawing closer to the CEO's office from the other side of the rectangular floor.

In the background, the two men drew anxious stares. The secretaries huddled around the bullpens could see a man with a gun crashing open doors, and had already started gossiping. Only one of them had the presence of mind to wonder whether they were themselves in any physical danger. At that, the assistant pool shut up, suddenly panicked.

They were still ten yards away from their final, and inevitable, destination when the power came back on. The federal agent glanced up at the glare of the overheads and quickened his pace. With the networks back up, the cash transfers could be over in seconds and crucial leverage would be lost.

There was now only one room left to inspect between them and Vik's office. Bubbles of sweat appeared on Jack's forehead and were immediately replicated on Tom's. They had no idea whether Amanda was behind that door and what the consequences of their actions would be if she was. With the violent criminals who had killed Frank Wachowski involved, the risks were evident and surprises were assured. The only thing they knew with absolute certitude was that the reporter's life hung in the balance.

Next door and in the privacy of Vik's office, Helen had been arguing with the building management on her cell phone. She was getting exasperated, which was unusual. Helen Mosbacher was the living epitome of an ice queen, and it took a lot to rattle her steely nerves. But the menace in Vikram's grasp and his reference to her destitute past a few minutes ago had chilled her to the marrow. There are pecking orders even among the ruthless and the brutal, and Vikram Suri stood at the top of both pyramids. As a consequence, Helen needed an outlet for her edginess.

"What the hell do you mean you can't activate the elevator? It's one frigging car! Cut one of the emergency elevators and route the power to this one, for Chrissakes!" she fumed into the microphone.

The building supervisor on the other end tried to explain but Helen was in no mood to listen. She resumed her toxic diatribe, feeling better as she passed on the fear of God to someone else.

Just then, as if in answer to her prayers, the lights came back on and the private elevator in the CEO's office, leading to the exclusive suite one floor below, hummed to life. Without bothering to sign off, Helen snapped the phone shut. Relief washed over her like a cool shower.

Taking a deep breath, she pressed the button on the wall. Three seconds later the smooth steel doors slid open like the entrance to Aladdin's cave.

Jack pushed open the door and looked inside.

A grotesquely empty office stared back at him.

This was it, he realized. He had run out of options. The only thing he could do now was arrest Vikram Suri and let the chips fall. It was a dangerous move, but what was the alternative? He glanced over at Tom, who looked equally perturbed. If Vik could be brazen enough to abduct a journalist in broad daylight and have her brought into his own offices, there was no telling how far the crazy son-of-a-bitch would go.

"Come on," muttered Jack hastily. "Maybe we'll get something out of him."

The agent and the banker strode to the mahogany double doors with a heavy heart. As Jack pushed down on the gilded handles with his clammy hands, it felt like he was opening the doors to a morgue. He shuddered at the thought of Amanda with these animals, then purposely shoved the image from his mind. He had to think clearly and react fast. There was no room for distraction.

Even as they entered the cavernous environs of the CEO's office, a stern voice from behind stopped them. "Where do you think you're going?" asked Vik's assistant, an older woman with an officious air. She had seen them coming and had walked over from her desk, like a mother hen protecting her young.

"Official business," replied Jack calmly. "Please return to your desk and stay there."

The secretary was visibly flustered by Jack's manner. As the chief's assistant, she was usually treated with respect, even reverence, at the firm. Her voice was polite but steely. "I'm sorry, sir, but Mr. Suri is in an important meeting and cannot be disturbed. If you like, I can set up an appointment—"

Jack's patience ran out like an hourglass running out of sand. He addressed the woman harshly.

"Do I look like I'm asking for an appointment?! I already told you—this is official business. So get lost, kapeesh?"

With a superciliousness that only executive secretaries can muster, the assistant withdrew. Retreating resentfully to her desk, she picked up the telephone and dialed the extension in the conference room.

Tom and Jack resumed their tour of Vik's office. Tom had been in the building several times during the merger, but it was always to a conference room on a lower floor. Unlike Steve Brandt, he had never been invited into the inner sanctums of TriNet Communications. The room was everything he had expected it to be—efficient but luxurious, businesslike but decadent. A perfect blend of modern technology and antique furniture, like an ad for HP.

Jack was less impressed. To him the decadence seemed criminal, and shameful. The fact that the office was bigger than his whole apartment and probably worth ten thousand times as much did nothing to endear the owner to him. In his experience as an officer of the law, there was only one way someone could make enough money to enjoy these privileges, and that was by screwing everyone else.

There was a single door at the far end of the room and Jack pointed to it. "That must be the conference room where they're closing the deal."

He was moving toward it when he heard a discreet but audible ping. He swiveled toward the sound and spied an elevator set in a corner of the room. As he watched, the doors yawned open with a metallic swish.

On the floor of the elevator, propped up against the back wall of the car were two items: that day's edition of *The New York Times,* and a leather handbag. The bag looked familiar, thought Jack, as he walked up and lifted it from the floor to inspect its contents. Inside was Amanda's pocketbook. His mouth went dry.

"What is it?" asked Tom, appearing outside the elevator.

Jack didn't reply. He just looked over his shoulder at the conference room, and back to the pocketbook in his hand. Then he made a split-second decision.

"Go into that conference room and do what you can to delay the closing," he instructed the banker.

Tom began to protest. "Me? But how can I—"

Jack reached down and withdrew something from under the cuff of his pants. He handed it to Tom. "Use this."

The banker's eyes widened. "You must be kidding me."

"You'll be fine. Just get in there," insisted Jack, pressing the single button on the elevator console.

"Where are *you* going?" asked a flabbergasted Tom.

"No idea," replied Jack truthfully, as the doors shut in front of him.

On the other side of the closed conference room door, Vikram Suri had taken over the supervision of the closing process.

He had waited impatiently for the power to come back up and now that the network was functional again, he barked orders to the computer staff like a military general planning an imminent attack. The war room was filled with the sounds of nervous fingers tapping frantically on keyboards as the tech personnel scrambled to execute the money transfers.

Craig Michaels was stoic. He had hardly reacted to the blackout and even now seemed indifferent to the sense of urgency radiated by his counterpart. This was Vik's problem, not his. As far as he was concerned, a few more minutes would hardly make a difference to his fortunes. There was plenty of time in which to make it to the airport, so in the interim he would enjoy watching his nemesis squirm in discomfort.

High above them, a massive bird turned its wings a full thirty degrees. It had received a signal from the ground and slowly but surely positioned itself to transmit one back to a spot 10,000 miles to the east. Four other satellites did the same thing for a variety of distances from TriNet's headquarters. All of them carried the sleek logo of "Luxor Satellite," and all of them had been specially commissioned for the closing of the merger. It was the ultimate dedicated network.

Vik watched as one of the tech staff logged into a bank's computer using an access code created expressly for a single transfer. This would be the first payment of the day and set the ball rolling for the rest. The Indian businessman leaned over the shoulder of the young man to inspect the screen.

His back was to the door and so he did not notice the grim-faced banker who stepped into the conference room, shutting the door softly behind him.

To Jack the elevator ride seemed unusually long. He had no idea where it was going and nor did he care. His task right now was to make sure his feelings for Amanda didn't paralyze him when the action came. In his line of work, kidnappings and physical threats were commonplace, and conventional wisdom dictated that law enforcement did not mix with emotion. But when it was personal, it was never so simple. When it was someone you loved, the risks were exponential.

To clear his head, he ruminated on the irony of the situation. Vikram Suri, the poster child for the free market and living proof of the American dream, was also the prime example of the triumph of commerce over law. He could do whatever he wished to whomever he wished, and not even the FBI could stop him. Why? Because he had a megaphone and Jack Ward did not. It was that disturbingly simple.

In a world where money was the chief currency of power, those with it could do what they wanted with impunity. As long as the smokescreen of legal equality was maintained, the average Joe would go to sleep at night believing that his interests were being genuinely looked after. He was safe—as long as he didn't look under the hood. Americans were living in the Matrix and they didn't even know it, thought Jack.

But not today. Today the Matrix would be penetrated, the code broken and the reality behind the illusion revealed. At least temporarily. At least for one criminal mastermind. The muscles of Jack's hand coiled firmly around the handle of his gun like a taut steel spring. Every nerve in his body switched to a state of heightened alert as the elevator stopped moving.

Showtime.

George Lomax was the first to take note of the anxious-looking man who had slipped into the conference room and now stood directly behind Vikram Suri. He had never actually seen Tom Carter and only knew of him by name. Board members seldom interacted with anyone under the managing director level. As often happens in large corporate meetings, most people in the room simply assumed that Tom was a latecomer. One of the lawyers indicated an open chair next to him, hinting that he should take it. Tom ignored him.

George coughed awkwardly. "Hi, can I help you?"

Tom stared momentarily at George, equally unaware of who he was. He did not respond. His gaze returned to the back of the man standing in front of him.

Vik was still engrossed in the computer screen but something inside him stirred. It was a sixth sense, a feeling of impending danger. He swiveled around on his feet like a ballet dancer.

He *did* recognize Tom Carter, having seen him at a due diligence meeting. Most investment bankers did not attend closings even though they had worked on the deal. They had no reason to. The analytical work was over, the numbers were locked down, so the only remaining tasks were legal and technical in nature. *So why was he here?*

Tom felt the piercing eyes of the Indian boring into him like a high-powered drill. He shifted uncomfortably. Standing there, he could remember how uncertain he had felt when he voiced his suspicions to Steve Brandt. The risks had been high then. Now they were stratospheric.

Vik spoke first. After all, this was his conference room. "What are you doing here, Tom?" he began. He was polite as always, deadly polite. "I thought Steve said you guys didn't need to be at the closing."

Tom gulped. He thought he knew what he was doing, but now that he was actually here, he felt like a lamb who had presented himself willingly to the slaughter. He couldn't answer.

Vik spread his hands in an impatient, incredulous gesture. The truth was he was just as nervous. The fact that the banker had shown up here at this critical moment was to him as good as an alarm bell. He had a vague recollection of Chad telling him that the reporter was dating "some banker." *Could it be Tom Carter? Had this little snotnose sold out his own deal to the press? And why had Steve Brandt not mentioned anything?* Probably to cover his own carelessness, he mused. He couldn't be sure, but his instincts told him that something was very wrong.

"Well?" he drawled angrily. "What do you want?" The faces in the room assumed a curious look.

George cut in with a question, directed at Tom. "I'm sorry, but who *are* you?"

Vik answered the question for the banker. "He works at Morgenthal Winters."

Several faces frowned. *Why was the CEO berating his own banker?*

Their question was answered a second later, when Tom finally found his voice. "I'm sorry, gentlemen," he addressed the room without taking his eyes off his adversary, "but this merger is a sham. The CEOs have been hiding material information from their board members and lawyers."

Vik's fears were confirmed. He looked around hurriedly for Helen. *Where the hell was she? What could be taking her so long?* He would have to handle this himself. Striding over to the wall phone, the CEO dialed a number. Security came on the line. The Indian identified himself and issued an order. Satisfied with the response, he replaced the phone with a flourish.

Walking back past the banker, Vik returned to the techie who was waiting to execute the kickoff transfer.

"Do it," he ordered. George Lomax was about to say something but Vik interrupted him. "Gentlemen, we are running late as it is. Amusing though all this might be, you've all heard the old maxim time is money. The banks are waiting, so without further delay, let the closing begin."

The finger hovering over the *Enter* key on the laptop hesitated. The computer expert that Helen had recruited from TriNet's information technology department stared around the room, looking for confirmation of Vik's orders. He was not about to second-guess the CEO, but he had caught George's glance and it made him nervous. Before he had a chance to decide, however, the option was taken away from him.

Vik pushed the young man roughly aside and commandeered his laptop. Ignoring the embarrassed murmurs from around the room, he prepared to crown himself.

Then he heard the click. Even in his distracted state, the sound was unmistakable.

The first thing that Jack saw upon exiting the elevator onto the thirty-ninth floor of TriNet tower was a full-sized billiard table in the center of a gigantic room with high windows. His weapon cocked and held on the ready, his eyes made a quick sweep of the private parlor, taking in everything they could in three seconds, including the cue-rack and bookcases. Then his gaze settled on the lone figure seated miserably by the window, at a dining table. By the brilliant shaft of sunlight that fell on her face, Jack could see that Amanda was scared. Her arms and legs were tied to her chair with what looked like the cord from copy-paper boxes, and her beautiful mouth was invisible behind an ugly strip of masking tape.

Angrily, the FBI agent advanced towards her, swearing to himself that he would make Vikram Suri pay for what he had done to the reporter. But before he had taken two steps, a fist whipped out of the side and slammed into his jaw with staggering force. Jack reeled diagonally at the blow, struggling to keep his balance. Almost immediately the hard leather tip of a shoe plunged into his abdomen and the agent doubled over in pain. With the pain, however, came awareness and before his attacker could land another blow, Jack scrambled reflexively to his right, narrowly escaping another kick that emerged from the left. He straightened his body despite the throbbing in his stomach and prepared to square off with his opponent.

Chad Rollins moved swiftly forward, trying to find an opening through which to deliver his attack, but now that Jack was alert, it wasn't so easy. The federal agent swerved with the speed and agility of a boxer to avoid another fist, which found nothing but air where his face had been a moment ago. At the same time, Jack lunged upwards at the thug's arm, grasping it on either side of the elbow and twisting down and around. Chad howled in agony, but quickly reacted by swinging his free arm toward Jack, this time delivering the punch on the side of the agent's neck. Jack released his grip and backed away, grinning.

So this is one of Vik's goons, thought Jack. Large and brutal, but also lazy and dumb. Near Chad's left armpit hung an empty holster, but where was the gun? Jack's own weapon had fallen to the floor and he could see it out of the corner of his eye.

Chad saw it too. Walking vengefully over to the gun, he kicked it behind the billiard table—and out of Jack's reach. Jack was about to go for his backup weapon, then realized he had given it to Tom. He cursed himself for his carelessness.

The two men circled each other like wild animals fighting for survival. Neither of them was armed, and neither of them was inexperienced enough to give the other an opening. So this would be a street fight, won or lost not on technique or weaponry but on sheer willpower.

Jack struck first. In one violent riposte of motion, he dived at the exposed torso of his opponent, his full body weight going into the attack. Chad saw him coming and sidestepped deftly, but not fast enough. The FBI agent's right shoulder struck him full on the stomach and he was propelled backwards and onto the wooden edge of the billiard table. He pushed himself up off his elbows to plow back, but Jack was too quick, slamming him back into the table. The vicious force of the assault lifted Chad's feet off the ground and boosted him onto the red baize surface, where his hands crabbed desperately for the opposite edge, trying to gain some leverage to hit back. One hand found the wooden frame and Chad pulled his legs back for a kick.

Jack, who had clambered up after him, saw the meaty palm grasp the angled edge and heaved to the side, missing the flying feet by inches. But Chad was prepared and before the agent had the chance to counterattack, he twisted and leapt onto him, punching wildly at the prone figure. Jack was at a disadvantage and the sheer ferocity of the blows took his breath away. The thug grasped his throat with both hands and started squeezing. Jack began to feel faint.

He scratched desperately at the powerful hands strangling him, but the iron fists wouldn't budge. Finally, acutely conscious of the remaining oxygen in his lungs running out, Jack let go of his hold and reached instead for the face of his attacker. In the throes of certain death, he did not have to calculate or even hope. He just lunged forward like a madman, pushing his screaming muscles to the limit and stretching his arms to a length that under normal circumstances he would not have considered biologically possible.

Jack's hands found Chad's face blindly, and his fingers crabbed their way toward the eyes. Placing a thumb firmly against each eye, the FBI agent pushed with all his might.

There was a short yell from Chad as the pressure became unbearable and a tiny bolt of pain shot through his head. Reflexively, he relaxed his grip on Jack's throat. That was all the agent needed. Prying his assailant's hands from his neck, he used the muscles of his back and arms to reflect himself off the surface of the table and onto his temporarily disabled opponent. Jack's head connected with Chad's like a soccer player and the thug staggered backwards.

With his legs finally freed from the man's weight, Jack rose to his knees and crawled behind Chad. Grasping the brawny neck in a wrestler's grip, he commanded him not to move. At the same time, he used his free hand to reach inside his jacket for handcuffs. He need not have bothered.

Like a cornered animal, Chad struck back as hard as he could with his elbows. It was a natural reaction, but also a mistake.

Reacting instinctively and without the luxury of time to think, Jack twisted—hard.

There was a sickening crunch and Chad Rollins's neck went limp. He writhed for a few seconds inside Jack's hold and then his body settled into the stillness of death.

Jack let go and pushed the body away in disgust. He felt nauseous. A few feet away, he could hear Amanda whimpering. He looked up and saw the terrified look in her eyes. He smiled grimly to himself. *How's that for a romantic moment, baby? Want to get back together with a guy who breaks people's necks for a living? Sometimes he's got to kill 'em just to stay alive. Maybe we can grab a drink after this.* He almost laughed out loud at the sick joke.

Distracted by his morbid thoughts, Jack failed to notice that Amanda's terror was induced not just by the snapping of Chad Rollins's neck but by what she was looking at behind her former boyfriend's back. By the time he caught her gaze and whirled around, Helen Mosbacher already had him in the sights of a sleek Beretta. Somewhere at the back of his mind, Jack guessed that it was the missing weapon from the dead man's holster. Well, at least now he knew where it was.

Questions flooded Jack's mind. *Who was this woman and how had she gotten in here? For that matter, where had the thug emerged from so suddenly?* It couldn't have been in the elevator or he would have heard it. A hidden door perhaps?

Then he saw it, a discreet outline concealed between neat rows of bookshelves. Given the dining table across the room, it was probably the entrance to a pantry. It had all transpired so quickly that he hadn't been able to reconnoiter the room properly.

"Who are you?" demanded Jack, not sure whether he was dealing with friend or foe. After all, if this woman had walked in accidentally, she might only be protecting herself.

"Let's skip the introductions, all right?" answered Helen, watching him carefully. Jack noticed that she held the gun like an expert, her hands steady as a rock, one finger poised menacingly over the trigger. He didn't know of any woman in the business world who knew how to hold a weapon like that. The notion that she might be a "friendly" began to evaporate.

Nevertheless, he explored some more. "I'm an FBI agent," he said, creeping slowly off the billiard table and settling his feet on the floor. He leaned back casually against the edge, his hands planted for balance on the smooth baize.

"I know who you are," replied Helen, then realized her mistake.

A cloud descended over Jack's rugged face. The fingers of one hand began to crab their way closer to his body.

"What do you plan to do?" he asked, eyeing Helen cleverly. He had to keep her talking, and preoccupied, while he positioned himself.

"Kill you, of course," stated Helen simply.

"You'll never get away with it. There are cops in the lobby and backup is on the way. You've run out of time," said the FBI agent, trying to sound confident. "Killing a reporter is one thing, murdering an FBI agent is another."

Helen laughed shortly. "And who will testify? Three corpses? As far as the police will be able to tell, a gangster abducted your friend, brought her up here and murdered her. You discovered the kidnapping, barged in and a struggle broke out. You killed the kidnapper but not before he fired his gun." She waved the Beretta in the air briefly. "*This* gun."

"And you disappear back upstairs," finished Jack, understanding. The hand that he had moved surreptitiously behind him now closed firmly over a hard object.

Helen nodded. "Precisely. As you can see there are no cameras in this room, the elevator, or the CEO's office. The kitchen's closed. No one knows that I am here. By the time your backup arrives, the only witnesses will be dead."

"But why kidnap her?" asked Jack, glancing casually over at Amanda. He was actually scanning the floor on the other side of the billiard table, looking for his own firearm, which the thug had kicked there during the fight. "You could have just refused her entrance into the building."

"She's a loose cannon. And eventually she might have identified me," explained Helen frankly.

"Identify you for what?" asked Jack, genuinely confused. Once again he wondered who this woman was and what exactly she did at TriNet.

Amanda was also confused. In spite of her fear, her mind was alert and she was listening intently to every word that Helen uttered. She had an intense feeling of déjà vu. *Where had she heard that confident voice before?*

Helen noticed the reporter's stare and smiled slyly. There was a hint of pleasure in those blue eyes. "You don't know who I am, do you?" she asked Amanda, even though the gagged reporter couldn't answer even if she wanted to. Instead, Amanda shook her head in confirmation of Helen's guess.

"We spoke once," explained Helen. "I was your 'source' for the news leak."

Now it connected. The woman on the phone! The one who had known so many details about the merger and was almost certainly someone on the deal team, but who had refused to divulge her identity. At the time, Amanda had pictured Helen to be some disgruntled employee who had leaked the story to hurt the merger. This was corroboration that the leak had been a setup all along, just as she and Tom had figured out.

The brief distraction that Amanda had provided for Helen was a boon for Jack. In the few seconds that it had taken Vik's second-in-command to spot and address Amanda's unspoken question, the watchful agent had twisted his body to be parallel to the edge of the table, and flexed his hand with the billiard ball backwards like a catapult. By the time Helen's attention reverted back to him, he was ready.

In a single, powerful movement, Jack flung the billiard ball in the direction of the redhead, while simultaneously throwing himself onto the table and rolling over the surface to the other side. The projectile shot through the air like a mini cannonball and struck Helen on the shoulder, eliciting a gasp of surprise. She fired involuntarily, the tubular hood of the silencer muffling the sound. The bullet thwacked into the rim of the pool table and send splinters of wood flying in every direction.

Jack spun himself off the opposite edge and landed clumsily on the floor. Having recovered from the momentary shock, Helen circled carefully around the table, looking for another shot and watching for a threat. Unwilling to rise to his feet and provide her with an easy target, the FBI agent crawled on his stomach toward his gun, which was almost four feet away.

The second bullet ripped through the floor an inch from Jack's head. The agent winced but continued his horizontal march towards his gun. To falter now would have been fatal. His only chance was to reach his weapon, and if she got him before he made it, there was nothing he could do to prevent it. Before Helen could fire off a third shot, his hand closed around the handle of the Colt Series 70 pistol and he lifted it without a thought. The aluminum trigger felt like a panic button to the beleaguered agent.

The boom of the gun reverberated around the room like an earthquake, sending ripples of vibration through the windows and rolling thunder through the walls and floor. Even before the subterranean rumblings beneath Jack's body had subsided, Helen froze like a mannequin in a wax museum, a single button of red appearing and expanding on her high forehead. As if in slow motion, Helen Donatello pitched forward like a lamppost keeling over, landing on the carpeted floor with a dull thud.

A pool of blood began to form around her head as she lay face down on the thick rug, the viscous fluid seeping quickly into the soft beige fiber and forming a deep red stain. Jack raised himself to his knees and carefully crept toward the body. He leant over it, put a finger on her neck to feel the pulse, confirmed that there wasn't one and stood up. For the third time since entering the suite, his thoughts returned to the one person who mattered more to him than his own life.

Amanda, who had borne mute witness to the entire scene, looked spent and colorless. Jack hurried over to her and undid her bonds. Her hands freed, the reporter peeled the tape from her mouth and spat in disgust. The saliva that rushed to her mouth felt acidic, rancid.

Leaning down, Jack rubbed Amanda's wrists to restore the blood circulation. Slowly the life started to return. A sense of liberation flooded her body and the stress on her face ebbed away. Standing up to stretch her cramped legs, she caught Jack's concerned gaze, and smiled grate-fully.

"Thanks," was all she could say. But the warmth in her voice conveyed the strength of her feelings.

Jack felt a stirring inside him, like a schoolboy who had received a kiss on the cheek from the girl of his dreams. It wasn't much, but it was enough to send him to cloud nine. "I almost lost you there," he offered clumsily.

It was a promisingly awkward moment, and Amanda realized intu-itively that it had to be ended before it went too far. Under these circum-stances, another word or gesture could easily send her flying back into the waiting arms of Jack Ward, leaving Tom Carter in the lurch and her in a state of hopeless turmoil. It was a bad idea, made worse by the inexpli-cable guilt creeping over her heart right now. If she would ever be able to choose between them, as she must, it was now or never.

"Where's Tom?" she asked cautiously.

So that was it, Jack thought bitterly. That was her answer. An irrational sense of betrayal rose inside him and flashed outwards through his eyes like the rays of an angry sun. Amanda could feel his resentment burning into her, and felt terrible at being the cause of it. *Why did life have to be so complicated? Why did someone have to get hurt for someone else to be happy?*

"He's downstairs. In the conference room," Jack replied after a long moment, looking away from the reporter. His rage was subsiding, but in its place came a dull, throbbing ache. Subconsciously he touched his shoulder and felt the contours of a scar. It was where a bullet had grazed him early on in his career. This new wound, too, would leave a mark.

"What's he doing there?" asked Amanda, confused.

"Hopefully throwing a monkey wrench into the merger."

"How?" she asked curiously.

A perverse grin erupted on Jack's face.

One floor above no one was smiling. Most of the people seated around the conference room table had their mouths hanging open. They were all staring at Vikram Suri, whose face was suffused with rage, and a lone in-vestment banker who seemed to be at a standoff with the imperious CEO. What caused their amazement was not the presence of the inter-loper, but the metallic object that extended from his hand.

The silver eye of Jack's backup weapon sneered at the Indian with fury and intent, but it was just an act. In truth, Tom had no idea what to do with it. In a dark alley in a remote corner of the world with a guarantee of escape he still would not have been able to pull the trigger. In broad daylight and in a packed conference room in Manhattan, it was unthinkable.

Vikram Suri knew this, of course, and was not afraid of the banker. The problem was the other people in the room. While he was used to pushing employees and even CEOs and politicians around with the force of his position and wealth, there was a limit to how far he could go in public. The presence of the ever-vigilant and scrupulously honest George Lomax in the room didn't make things any easier. If Vik wasn't careful, he could wind up losing the benefit of the doubt, as well as the merger. What a lack of proof by the feds wouldn't accomplish, a spectacle right now might. The chief of TriNet Communications had to back down—and think.

He quietly returned to his chair and sat down, trying to look relaxed, unconcerned.

"You realize that security will arrest you, right?" he asked the investment banker, hoping to put him on the defensive.

Tom stood his ground wordlessly. Vikram Suri had backed down, at least for now, and that was enough. It wasn't his job to arrest the man. Jack had sent him merely as a sentry to guard the closing process, and he had accomplished that. Now all he had to do was wait till the cavalry arrived.

Vik studied the man like a vulture circling the corpse of an animal, trying to ascertain if it was really dead. What he saw did not comfort him. Tom Carter looked too sure of himself, as if he had concluded his role in the affair and was simply waiting for the curtain to fall. *Was Vik letting his chance to close the merger slip irrevocably out of his fingers? Should he chance it with George and the others and simply go ahead and initiate the transfers himself?* Once the cash was wired and moved around, it would be too late for the deal to be aborted. With the *Times* reporter and the FBI agent dead downstairs, there would be no one to testify except for Steve Brandt and maybe this lowlife, but those testimonies could be defended against. Vik had already laid the groundwork for that.

The only question then was how serious was this banker about stopping him? In his experience with these lily-livered bastards, they did not have the guts to attack anyone, much less kill a man in cold blood. A banker was not a fighter. He would huff and puff, but ultimately be unable to pull the trigger.

Vik issued a tight-lipped smile, and rose from his seat. Holding Tom's eyes in his own, he marched confidently to the laptop on the other side of the table. Tom's eyes narrowed perceptibly—what the hell was the guy doing? Didn't he see the gun pointed at his heart?

The baby-faced techie who Vik had pushed roughly out of his way earlier this time backed off of his own accord. This was none of his business, or his problem. If these guys who dealt in billions of dollars wanted to play chicken with each other, more power to them. But he had no intention of getting caught in the crossfire.

From the other side of the room George Lomax spoke more loudly than usual. "Vik, we should wait till security arrives and then we can settle this. Please take your seat," he enjoined politely but firmly.

Vik ignored the senior director.

"Don't do it," Tom warned, guessing what the CEO had in mind.

"So shoot me," answered Vik arrogantly, preparing to transfer the money.

The voice which answered him did not belong to Tom, or even to George. In fact, it didn't belong to anyone in the room. It came from the doorway.

"I'll be happy to oblige, Suri. In fact I was hoping for the chance, especially after that reception you arranged for me downstairs," growled Jack Ward, stepping into the room, followed closely by a wide-eyed Amanda Fleming. The muzzle of the Colt stared straight at Vikram Suri and something about the man that held it told the CEO that it was not aimed at his arm.

Vik had no choice but to cease and desist. This man *would* shoot, he knew. Reluctantly, he removed his hands from the keyboard and let them drop innocuously to his sides. He glowered at his captor. "All right. So what now?"

"Now," replied Jack, taking one hand off the pistol and using it to pull out the handcuffs that he hadn't needed for Chad, "you have the right to shut up."

As Jack had predicted, the NYPD was waiting in force when they arrived downstairs. Their instructions were to escort the prisoners back to Police Plaza, where Vikram Suri and Craig Michaels would be booked.

Since this was a joint investigation and part of the charges related to SEC violations and now kidnapping, federal prosecutors would eventually move in and handle the case.

The two FBI agents who Jack's boss had assigned to be his backup arrived just as the cops were wrapping up. They seemed amazed at the sight. Contrary to what they had expected, this was a real arrest with real criminals. Not Al Capone, but real enough. Jack greeted them dryly. Under the circumstances, he didn't feel obliged to update them.

During the walk to the waiting squad car, he studied Vikram Suri. He had only met the man a few minutes ago but already knew what to expect. This guy was a cool customer. The Indian was icy calm even as he was being led out in handcuffs, and Jack had no doubts that the prosecutors would have their job cut out for them. If he had learnt anything at all about men like these, it was that they didn't crack under pressure.

All the way from the elevator doors to his official ride, Vikram Suri strode confidently forward, at times outpacing the arresting entourage. Even in defeat, he was the one leading, not following. Craig Michaels, on the other hand, looked severely depressed.

When they reached the car that would take Vik back to Police Plaza, he paused for a moment before getting in. "Could you give me a second?" he asked Jack.

The agent stared quizzically. "What for?"

"I want to speak with the woman who's ruined my merger," replied Vik coolly.

"Forget it," responded Jack, wanting to laugh.

"I just want to meet the woman you've accused me of kidnapping," stated Vik. "I believe I have a right to do that."

"Yeah, in court. Now get inside and let's go," said Jack decisively, pushing Vik towards the open car door.

A voice stopped him. "Hold it, Jack." It was Amanda.

Both men turned simultaneously. A broad grin appeared on the Indian's face. "Ah, the amazing Ms. Fleming. I've heard so much about you. It's a pleasure."

Jack thought the CEO sounded sincere, which amazed him.

Amanda stepped forward from the crowd which had started to gather around TriNet Plaza. Next to her was Tom Carter. A faint smile crept across the reporter's mouth. This was the moment she had been waiting for. She moved closer to the deposed emperor.

"You're finished, Vik," she said, her eyes glittering with triumph.

"Do you really believe that?" asked Vik, still smiling.

A flicker of uncertainty crossed Amanda's eyes, and then slowly her gaze turned steady. She measured her words with care. "Somewhere, somehow, justice will find its way to you," she promised. "So yes. I do."

The media mogul laughed briefly, then bowed low in front of Amanda, as if acknowledging an equal. His theatrical performance over, he slipped wordlessly into the back seat of the police car and was gone.

The forensics team from the NYPD had to go through the billiard cum dining room on the thirty-ninth floor despite Jack Ward's statement of what had transpired. In the event there was an inquiry, the shooting would have to be reconstructed to confirm or disprove the FBI agent's story.

It was routine procedure and the scientists in police jackets went over the suite with a bored efficiency. Their interest factor was rendered even lower by the fact that no innocent people had been hurt or killed. And even if this wasn't a clean shoot, it still wasn't one of their own on the hook.

In the midst of this tepid investigation, the only thing which drew some amused attention was a billiard ball lying on the carpet near the pantry door. It was the one the FBI agent claimed he had thrown at the woman to distract her. A rookie named Eddie picked it up with gloved hands and chuckled.

It was the eight ball.

forty-three

The four people seated around an interrogation table at the FBI office were at an impasse. On one side sat Vikram Suri and his attorney, facing Jack Ward and the federal prosecutor, a woman named Patricia Noble, on the other.

The FBI agent and the prosecutor had been grilling the corporate titan for hours, but with limited success. For one thing, Vik was too sharp to reveal anything that would incriminate him. Additionally, his counsel was one of the top criminal defense lawyers in the country and kept interjecting with objections to their queries. Outwardly Jack and Patricia remained calm, but secretly they were getting frustrated.

Since the CEO of TriNet wasn't an average citizen, they had to tread carefully. He was too smart to be intimidated and his lawyer would take the bureau to the cleaners if they so much as initiated a conversation the wrong way. That was one of the challenges of prosecuting a public figure, especially a rich one.

But then so far neither Jack nor Patricia had really told him what they had.

"Look, Vik, this will go a lot easier if you cooperate," said Patricia, trying to reason with the taciturn corporate chief. "I know you're a smart man, but the fact remains you're over a barrel on this one. The evidence against you is overwhelming, so unless you start talking we've got no option but to go to court."

The defense attorney sighed wearily. "Spare us the lecture, counselor . . ."

"On the other hand, if you work with us, we may be able to work out a plea," she finished evenly.

Even though she was getting weary of sparring with him, she was too much of a professional to lose her temper, or her patience. In the world of real-world law enforcement, the most important qualities to possess weren't aggression or speed, but meticulousness and perseverance. In her experience, the more high-profile and intelligent the criminal, the harder they eventually fell. It was all a matter of finding the right pressure point, and the government had yet to lay their cards on the table.

Neither Vik nor his lawyer made any move to conciliate with the prosecutor, which didn't surprise her. This is how it had been going for a while. It was time to change tactics.

"So why did you have Frank killed, Vik?" she asked softly.

"Oh, come on! We've been over this a hundred times. Are you guys hard of hearing? My client did not have anyone killed, period. So what do you say you stop wasting our time with these cheap jabs?" answered the defense attorney, scowling.

"Is that what you think this is, Vik," asked Patricia, ignoring counsel, "just a lot of lawyer tricks? Well, let me assure you that with or without your confession, we're going to nail your hide, so your best chance of surviving is to be nice to me. Real nice."

Vikram Suri didn't respond. He gazed directly in front of him with a practiced indifference. There were no traces of fear or remorse on that handsome face, and Patricia found herself feeling a grudging respect for the cockiness of the man. Her frustration began to show.

"All right, fine. We've been here three hours now and I'm getting awfully tired of this nonsense. Let me spell it out for you.

"We have a credible witness who is going to testify that you had a confidential report in your possession delivered to you by Frank Wachowski, which detailed the true condition of Luxor's satellite assets, prior to your making a bid for the company. Based on what we've gained from our financial experts, you were willing to pay nearly *three* times the value of those assets—for your personal gain. That in itself amounts to fraud against TriNet's shareholders. But that's just the tip of the iceberg.

"We believe that Frank was about to go to the police or the press with the report and tell them everything; and when you found out about it, you had him murdered. So you have some very serious thinking to do, Vik. Either you help us with our case or we'll hang the whole thing around your neck . . . like an anchor," said Patricia ominously.

"Who's the witness?" demanded the defense attorney. Of course, thanks to his client, he already knew.

"Steve Brandt, a managing director at Morgenthal Winters who worked on the merger with your client," replied Patricia, staring fixedly at Vik to watch for any reaction. Not a flicker. He was a master of the game.

"You're grasping at straws, Ms. Noble," warned the defense attorney. "Mr. Brandt has nothing to back up his wild statements, and we both know it. You'll never get a conviction based on one witness."

"How about three then?" shot back Patricia.

The defense lawyer raised an eyebrow. He waited for her to continue.

"Craig Michaels claims your client confronted him with the report at a party earlier this year, and threatened to release it to the press unless he agreed to sell Luxor for less than its market value. Add to that, your client wanted to share in the proceeds from the merger. That's blackmail.

"He'll also testify that your client informed him that he intended to make an initial bid of seven billion, with the understanding that the bid would be rejected by the board of Luxor Satellite. Following the initial bid, your client orchestrated a news leak to the press.

"Our third witness, Amanda Fleming, will attest to the fact that TriNet's general counsel, Helen Mosbacher, leaked the story to her on your client's instructions. The idea of the leak, as we see it, was to manipulate TriNet's stock price so your client could make a profit."

"How?" sneered Vik's counsel.

"By trading his shares," replied Patricia simply.

"And I suppose you have proof of that?" challenged the defense lawyer, comfortable in the knowledge that Vik had covered his tracks.

The prosecutor leafed through her folder and pulled out a sheet of paper. On it was the FBI report, compiled since the arrest, detailing the numerous and large-scale transactions carried out on the New York Stock Exchange by the International Trading Company—the holding company based in the Isle of Man. She handed the paper over to defense counsel.

Vik and his attorney reviewed the page quickly. Leaning over, the CEO whispered something into the lawyer's ear.

The attorney handed the FBI report back to Patricia. "My client knows nothing about the International Trading Company or any of the transactions contained in this report. For all you know, Helen was the one trading the shares."

"Very convenient for you, seeing as how she's dead," retorted Patricia sarcastically.

Vik's attorney spread his hands. "It's your guy who shot her. Which I might add also makes your kidnapping charge unprovable. If Helen Mosbacher did anything illegal, she was doing it on her own. My client had no knowledge of it, including how and why the reporter wound up in his private dining room. Bottom line, Ms. Noble, you have nothing."

Jack glared at Vikram Suri, who maintained a poker face.

Patricia sighed inwardly with disappointment. Although the FBI report did show that someone had traded extensively in TriNet stock in the weeks following the news leak, there was still no real proof linking the holding company to Vikram Suri. As they had expected, the company's dummy shareholders had no idea who the real founders of the company were and it could take months to trace the money, if at all. Her bluff had failed.

If the federal prosecutor was lucky, she might be able to convince the court that there were enough coincidences and smoldering, if not smoking, guns in the mix to link Vikram Suri to *some* kind of fraud. But there was still no evidence to connect him to the death of Frank Wachowski or the kidnapping, and even less to make a case for the master scheme that Patricia sensed in all this. Without the murder and kidnapping charges, all the arrogant CEO would get was a slap on the wrist.

She needed to gamble again.

"Steve Brandt will also testify that Frank Wachowski contacted him a few days before his death. He told Mr. Brandt of your client's threat to kill him if he went public with the Luxor report."

Vik frowned. He knew that the federal prosecutor was lying since he was sure that Steve had never heard of the engineer prior to his conversation with Vik, which had been *after* the Polack was killed. All the same, he couldn't come out and say that. Without consulting his lawyer, he addressed Patricia.

"Steve Brandt isn't a credible witness. As an investment banker it was his duty to bring the report to my notice and he didn't. He never told me about the email and now he's lying to cover his own ass. It's my word against his."

There was dead silence in the room. Patricia sat bolt upright.

Jack Ward spoke first. *"How did you know about the email?* We never mentioned an email in our interrogation."

For the first time since the interview began, Vikram Suri seemed to lose his nerve. As he digested the implication of Jack's words, his face went pale. His lawyer, who was watching him, rebounded quickly to his client's defense.

"It was a slip of the tongue. You can't pin anything on my client on the basis of an errant word, counselor."

Patricia, who was just as shocked with this incident as everyone else, now recovered her composure. Ignoring the defense attorney, she addressed the corporate titan directly.

"You're in this deep, Vik, and everyone in this room knows it. You know about the email because *you* sent it. We contacted Frank's email service provider and apparently someone hacked into their mainframe to change the settings on Frank's account. He had rigged it so that if he disappeared, the host server would send off an email automatically—the same email that Steve Brandt ultimately received, under Frank's own name.

"Whoever broke into the system removed the triggering mechanism and canceled the setup. The next morning, the same email was sent from a different provider and a different server, this time from an anonymous address. So you see, the only way you could have known about the email without our mentioning it was if you sent it—or *had* it sent, which also corroborates Steve's statement that you were already familiar with the report when he confronted you with it."

Vikram Suri, who prided himself on being unflappable and an expert at dealing with contingencies, now found himself in unfamiliar territory. Slowly but surely his confidence was eroding, and he could feel the noose that he had created for himself tightening inexorably around his neck. At no point since he first conceived this plan had he ever imagined that he would be defeated by his own blunder.

As the fight began to leave him, he slumped down in his chair and stared mournfully at the cheap conference table in the FBI office. More than his legal predicament, it was the prospect of losing the game that really pained him. The fact that a mastermind like himself could be brought down by ordinary mortals was too much for him to bear.

No, he couldn't give up. Not now. He had to get up off the mat and show these buggers what Vikram Suri was really made of. He still had one last card left and it was time to play it.

Leaning over again, he held a whispered conference with his lawyer. The attorney's face showed genuine surprise, then shameless admiration. Patricia, who was studying Vik like a hawk, imagined she saw a spark of triumph in the dark eyes. The defense attorney turned to the prosecutor.

"We're prepared to make a deal. My client will tell you everything he knows and plead guilty to some degree of corporate fraud, but the murder and kidnapping charges must be dropped."

Patricia's face was impassive.

"Forget it. Your client is a murderer, even if he didn't pull the trigger himself; and I intend to make sure he goes to jail for a very long time."

"My client has a *name* for you, one that will make it worth your while to accept his plea. It's the name of a very powerful and high-profile man, and without my client's help you will never get him."

The prosecutor and the FBI agent exchanged glances, wondering what to do.

On one hand, they both wanted desperately to make Vikram Suri pay for his crimes, particularly for the brutal murder of Frank Wachowski, but this new development gave them pause. If there was a bigger mastermind involved in this whole scheme, then he too was as culpable as the Indian sitting in front of them. Even though Patricia was loath to drop the murder charge, she was all the more repulsed at the notion of someone else walking away from under their nose.

Excusing themselves from the room, Patricia and Jack held a hurried conference in the hallway. They returned momentarily.

"The federal government is prepared to lower the murder charge to manslaughter in the first degree and drop the kidnapping charge. The charges related to fraud and insider trading will remain. Your client will have to plead guilty to all the charges," said Patricia, sitting back down.

The defense counsel shook his head. "No deal. As I said, my client wants any charges related to the killing dropped. Only then will he give you the name. Otherwise you're welcome to go to trial and try your case based on purely circumstantial evidence and tainted witnesses. The court will never convict him on murder anyway."

"I don't think you understand. Your client is risking going to prison for the rest of his *life*," pointed out Patricia.

The defense attorney looked at his client. Vik shook his head.

Jack stared in amazement. *Even now, with his neck in a wringer, he was playing his game. The crazy bastard!*

Ordinarily, Patricia would have ended the discussion right there and gone to trial. But despite her fancy theories and stable of witnesses, she knew that there was truth to the defense's argument. In a trial, the insider trading would be difficult enough to prove, but homicide nearly impossible. Despite her outward confidence, she knew that he would walk on the murder charge.

If she agreed to the deal, at least he would plead guilty to the other charges, and give them a name. Given how well Vikram Suri had covered his tracks, she reflected, it was unlikely they would ever be able to catch the other man. In the sum of things, being a prosecutor was about making choices, even if sometimes the choices were distasteful.

Patricia stood up. "I need to make a phone call. I'll be right back."

When she returned a few minutes later, her face was set in stone. Without a flicker of emotion, she addressed defense counsel.

"You got your deal. Now we want the name, and it better be good. If your client is playing games, I promise you I'll personally make sure he spends the rest of his life in a concrete cell the size of a bathroom stall, you got it?"

The attorney simply nodded and turned expectantly towards his client. Vik jotted down a name on a piece of paper and handed it to the federal prosecutor.

Patricia Noble stared down at the sheet.

"Jesus Christ," she muttered.

At the hour when Vikram Suri was offering his testimony to a federal judge in exchange for his plea bargain, Craig Michaels returned home from yet another grueling trip to the U.S. Attorney's office. Things had gone from bad to worse for the arrogant businessman whose only bargaining chip had melted away in front of his eyes when the TriNet CEO had pled guilty to several of the charges which Craig would otherwise have substantiated. Without the need for his testimony, the feds had withdrawn their offer of clemency and promised him the fullest punishment available under the law.

After the taxing ordeal of the day, he was exhausted and sleep-deprived, and upon arrival at his house in Connecticut, went straight up his bedroom and went to sleep. Outside, fifty yards down the road, two police officers held vigil in an unmarked car, one of many such shifts that would be applied to the house around the clock to ensure that the CEO of Luxor didn't skip town while on bail. The assignment was strictly unofficial, of course.

About an hour later, Craig woke up with a start. He listened intently. There was no sound in the large house except for the irregular thumping of his own heart. Even though he was in comfortable environs, his own domain, a powerful fear gripped him. He realized suddenly that he was afraid in a way that he had never been before. It wasn't simply the fear of exposure and incarceration, it was the dread of a life lived aggressively coming to a shattering halt.

Moving his feet over the edge of the bed, he lowered them carefully to the carpeted floor, as if afraid that any sudden movements would damage them. He sat that way for a while, staring blankly at the wall, not at all sure what his thoughts were, just acutely aware of a trepidation that seemed to originate deep inside him. He touched his chest and wondered if he was having a heart attack. *Nope. Just heartburn.*

Even as Craig's momentary panic subsided, depression started to set in. It was slow at first, excessively sweet—like saccharine. Then it began to burgeon, undulating in circular waves around his mind in ever-widening orbs. He could feel his thoughts, his emotions, getting eclipsed by an inexplicable feeling of numbness mixed with an overpowering sensation of dismay. Although he knew that depression was only a time-expanded form of panic, he was powerless to stop it. Inexorably, the most insidious killer known to man drew its fatal tentacles around Craig Michaels, and the old familiar feeling of falling—which he so detested in his dreams—gripped him like a fever.

The ground slipped away from under his feet and the walls receded into the distance. The room was swirling around him now in a cocktail of colors, and the tough Californian mused that it was mocking him, mocking his size, his strength, even his beliefs, by its lewd display of kaleidoscopic madness. The room and the world simply had no respect for him. Despite the vertigo, Craig managed to get to his feet, although he swayed a little and had to spread his arms for balance. Once upright, he stood still for a long moment, trying to determine whether he was steady enough to make it to the dresser.

The dresser was approximately five feet away and at any other time he could have reached it in a single stride. But today was different—today

Craig was in the penalty box, and there were no freebies for someone in that position. He would have to make an effort to reach the dresser, and run the risk of falling.

In point of fact, he didn't fall and only wavered off course by a couple of inches. Grasping the handle of the topmost drawer, he pulled it with all his might. It was unlocked and slid back easily on its tracks, coming to a jarring halt at its extremity. He reached inside and fumbled around blindly, for by now his vision was hopelessly blurred and he saw everything as through a translucent dark screen—the veil of fear. Eventually he found what he was looking for and pulled it out.

It was loaded, the way he usually kept it.

Most men would have wasted their time dwelling on fantastic notions like their life flashing in front of their eyes, but Craig Michaels wasn't interested in such rubbish. Although he had led his entire life his own way, there was precious little about it that seemed worthwhile now that it was about to come to an abrupt end; there seemed little purpose in belaboring the point.

He put the barrel of the gun into his mouth, grimacing at the taste of the metal, and bent it upwards to point towards the brain.

In death, there is nothing but honesty.

Alistair Waxman wished that he had committed suicide.

The peremptory knocking on his office door had come without warning. Before he could react, the officers had marched in and taken over the room. Alistair looked up quizzically at the burly suit-clad men towering above his desk, wondering what the hell they wanted. He knew who they were of course. Their suits would have given them away in a *GQ* convention.

One of them, a youngish man with slicked-back hair and who seemed to be in command, walked stiffly around the desk and stood facing him. Even his body movements were standard issue.

"Mr. Waxman. I'm agent Frank Larosse from the FBI. Would you please stand up?" he asked in a suspiciously polite tone. It was the type of tone one might use for children, before punishing them for a terrible transgression.

"What's this about?" thundered Alistair Waxman, making no move to comply with the federal agent's request. He was a powerful man and not used to being ordered about.

Frank Larosse explained.

There was a moment of dead silence in the room as the FBI agents stared immovably at the silver-haired man in the leather chair, while the government aide who had led them in fidgeted nervously in the doorway.

Alistair didn't budge. He gave the officer standing over him a withering glare, and then turned his icy gaze to the others. It wasn't really a standoff since there was nothing that he could do, but somehow his body wouldn't move. His mind had taken the impact of Frank's words like a cheap Japanese car taking a hit from a Mack truck, and his legs received no instructions from his brain whatsoever. It was as if the machine had simply shut down.

Frank touched Alistair's arm. He did it gently, so as to be non-threatening, but in its damning simplicity the gesture was enough to jolt the recipient to his core. Alistair felt an electric shock pass between the agent's fingers and his bones. Suddenly, his motor impulses seemed to return and his mind was back in the here and now.

The chairman of the Securities and Exchange Commission rose from his desk for the last time.

forty-four

Jack Ward was already into his second drink by the time Tom Carter and Amanda Fleming wandered into the small uptown lounge. He waved cheerfully to them, but if they had been closer they would have seen the sudden expression of pain that flitted across his eyes. By the time they reached the bar, Jack had composed himself and greeted them with as much poise as he could muster.

Amanda kissed him affectionately on the cheek and took the barstool next to him. Tom sat on her other side.

"How are you, Jack?" asked Amanda, studying him with concern. Jack had avoided talking to her for months after saving her life, and it took a dozen phone calls and a personal visit by Tom to coax him out of his self-imposed exile. She knew, of course, the reason for his strange behavior, and was determined to heal his wounds as best she could. It was the least she could do.

"I'm doing fine," replied Jack, lying. "The bureau was thrilled at the SEC collar, so now I get to choose my own assignments, and I have my own junior agents to boss around. Can you believe that?"

Amanda smiled sweetly. "That's great, Jack. I'm very happy for you."

Tom leaned over and shook Jack's hand. "Congratulations, man. You deserve it. You're the bravest son of a bitch I've ever met," he said, meaning it.

"You weren't bad yourself. For a banker, anyway," said Jack, grinning. It was a genuine, refreshing smile and Amanda felt relieved. He looked like the old Jack again.

His gaze moved to Amanda. "So, is the next installment out yet?"

Amanda nodded. A blush of embarrassment crept up her high cheek-bones. Reaching inside her handbag, she pulled out a folded page from a newspaper. She opened it up and laid it on the bar counter. Jack leaned over and started reading.

It was a front-page story from *The New York Times*. The byline read "Amanda Fleming."

After months of investigations and court proceedings, the FBI and SEC have finally released details of the story that has come to be known in Wall Street circles as "Merger-gate."

Ever since the suicide of Luxor CEO Craig Michaels and the bizarre arrest of the chairman of the SEC under the provisions of the RICO Act, the government has been trying to piece together the disparate pieces of a complex scheme that would put a thriller writer to shame.

Meanwhile, Vikram Suri, the charismatic mastermind of the whole affair, continues to play tennis daily in a country-club prison, no doubt planning his memoirs and hoping to benefit from the Supreme Court's ill-advised ruling declaring the "Son of Sam" law unconstitutional. Vikram Suri is also suspected of being involved in the murder of an engineer from Luxor, although those charges were eventually dropped by the U.S. Attorney.

The holding company in the Isle of Man that was the conduit for Vikram Suri's insider trading in his own company, TriNet Com-munications, has been linked to a gold-smuggling operation in the Middle East. The Arab government official who was Vikram Suri's partner in the smuggling venture is under arrest and is likely to face the firing squad. The authorities in Dubai have declined to comment on the case. The gold, which was transferred to India in local boats called "dhows," was subsequently sold on the open market by a consortium run by a corrupt chief minister. The chief minister is currently running for re-election from prison and con-tinues to maintain his innocence.

The White House issued an apology today to the Isle of Man,

the Emirate of Dubai, and India, for the actions of its top corporate policeman, Alistair Waxman. While there has been no direct reference to monetary remunerations, it is rumored that certain World Bank loans may be forgiven in the coming year.

The rest of the article detailed the events and investigation that had led to the final confrontation at TriNet tower and the termination of the merger. Amanda had written and published several such stories since the arrest of Vikram Suri and Craig Michaels almost four months ago. This was the last of the pieces, but Amanda was now a bonafide "above-the-fold" journalist and could write her own ticket at the prestigious newspaper.

When Jack had finished reading, he looked up proudly. His eyes congratulated the intrepid reporter, and Amanda felt another blush coming on. Tom watched the exchange with slight concern, but only slight. Since their adventure together, the three of them had developed a deep bond which could never be broken, even by jealousy. Jack had performed a brave act for the woman he loved and Tom respected him greatly for that. For his part, he had allowed Amanda to make her choice without pressuring her in any way, and in the end she had gone where her heart lay.

As she folded the newspaper and put it away, the hottest journalist in town shook her head in disbelief. "I was up at the Hill two days ago and they *still* haven't recovered from what happened. I don't understand it. How could someone in such a high position have been so stupid?"

Tom shrugged his shoulders. "Greed is a powerful force. With sixty million in the balance, I guess he thought it was worth it."

"But he was already rich," protested Amanda.

"You know the old saying—you can never be rich enough. Besides, it was easy money, particularly since someone else did the dirty work for him," Jack pointed out pragmatically.

"He was the one who informed Vik that *The New York Times* was snooping around. He even fooled my editor into believing that he had conducted an unofficial inquiry into the insider trading. He almost killed our investigation—not to mention me!" added Amanda.

Tom smiled cynically. "Vikram Suri had calculated this down to the last detail. By bribing the chairman of the SEC, he couldn't be blindsided by the authorities. With Craig Michaels on board, and with Helen

Mosbacher running the merger as Vik's deputy while also approving legal documents as the general counsel, it was a sure thing—*if* Vik had been smart enough to pay off Frank Wachowski instead of killing him. . . ."

Amanda nodded absently. She had a far-away look in her eye, and Tom recognized the expression. It meant that something didn't click in the story and her journalist's mind had already locked in on the inconsistency.

"Why did Vik send the email to Steve Brandt in the first place? If his people had already neutralized the system that Wachowski had rigged, why not just dispose of the Brandt email as well? That way the managing director would never have found out," she wondered out loud.

Tom stared at her, genuinely surprised. Somehow the thought hadn't crossed his mind. Now that the reporter had brought it up, it did seem odd. . . .

At length, Amanda answered her own question. "Steve was one of Vik's insurance policies. He figured that once the investment banker became privy to the Luxor report, he would be in danger himself and so could be trusted to watch Vik's back. If the contents of the report *had* come out, Steve would have corroborated Vik's story that he had no prior knowledge of it."

"Vikram Suri's uncontrollable ego made him think he was invincible," said Jack harshly. "He was wrong."

"Was he?" asked Amanda, a trace of bitterness in her voice. "He'll be out in a couple of years and become a celebrity again. Sometimes I hate our culture."

Jack looked away awkwardly. He had no answer for that. It was a question that many Americans asked every day, but no one knew how to fix it. The Matrix reigned supreme.

"So what's happening in your world?" he asked Tom, trying to change the subject.

Tom laughed. "I was saved by a client—a cigar-chewing CEO named Hal Reardon. Just before my meeting with Robert, Hal called to tell him what a great banker I was and how he looked forward to working with me on future deals. With *that* carrot dangling in front of the firm, Robert agreed to stand by me. Nothing talks like money."

Even as he said it, Tom thought of his father. He wondered how Harry would have felt about the outcome of all this. The old man had been a banker of exceptional integrity. Had his son followed in his footsteps, or merely survived on someone else's guts and a good dose of luck?

There was no doubt that Tom had taken risks, but always at dagger-point and always when there seemed to be no other choice. First, the fear of being framed had given him the impetus to approach Amanda Fleming. Then, the prospect of losing the woman he loved had driven him to confront Steve Brandt. Finally, the adrenaline-fueled competition with Jack Ward had forced him to walk into that conference room with a gun. Always the right result, but never of his own accord. Never pre-emptive, always reactive. And now he had skirted a professional landmine because of a generous client.

Harry's kind of man, or Harry's shame?

Then he got it.

Everyone was imperfect, and that was all right. In this morass of madness, Tom Carter had negotiated his path the only way he could—inch by inch. He had kept his eyes on the road and taken the turns that he could. Maybe not always for the right reasons, but certainly with the right intentions. He had wanted to please his father's memory, and the act of wanting it was good enough. It had to be. There was nothing else.

"What do you think will happen to that idiot Brandt?" asked Jack, remembering his encounter with the sniveling banker.

"Steve was shown the door by the partners at my firm for accepting a bribe. He's pretty much finished. Wall Street is a very small world," answered Tom tonelessly. After what had happened, he couldn't care less what happened to the son-of-a-bitch.

Half an hour later, Tom and Amanda took their leave. Jack was sad to see them go.

He would have to drink a lot tonight. A lot to forget. Even more to start afresh.

At the same time that the scandal surfaced, Uljana Wachowski, who had suffered both financially and emotionally from her husband's death and who was at her wit's end about how to provide for herself and her daughter, received a wire transfer from an anonymous source. The amount was one million dollars.

On a short handwritten note that arrived in the mail a few days later were the words *"I'm sorry for what happened. It was a terrible injustice."*

From George Lomax's perspective, it was the only decent thing to do.

. . . .

Amanda had been right.

At the swank country club that doubled as an incarceration facility, known to lawyers and prosecutors as "Club Fed," Vikram Suri found others like him, and gradually became something of a celebrity within its luxurious confines. Not since the heady days of Michael Milken had a criminal come so close to successfully duping the public and Wall Street, and with such *style*. Even though Vik had failed at his attempt to fool the world and still didn't consider himself a real criminal, he basked in the acclaim that he received from his peers.

Nor was his fame limited to his immediate environment.

Within a few months of the scandal going public, Vikram Suri was on the cover of every business magazine and his story on every television news show in America. The former CEO went rapidly from being the butt of jokes at cocktail parties to a revered "expert" in the fields of international finance and securities trading. So sought-after was his business acumen that he was offered book deals to detail his exploits, and even approached by a Hollywood studio to license his story for a screenplay.

After discussing it with his agent, Vik decided on a title for his book: *The Emperor.*

—————————epilogue

The blonde in the Prada shop reared sharply around a corner, bumped into a handsome, suntanned man who was inspecting a handbag for his latest carnal conquest, and caused him to drop the merchandise. She apologized profusely and blushed a deep crimson at her carelessness. The man smiled forgivingly and assured her that it wasn't a problem. As far as he was concerned, nothing was ever a problem where a pretty woman was involved. The young woman, who was tantalizingly beautiful, nevertheless issued a closing apology and walked off hurriedly.

Vikram Suri followed her. He caught up to her just as she reached the checkout counter, and asked if she would have dinner with him. The woman hesitated for a brief moment, but then accepted the invitation. After all, she had almost knocked the man off his feet—the least she could do was dine with him. The date was set and the girl proceeded with completing her purchase, trying to ignore the admiring stare of the Indian. At the last second, as she exited the store, she turned and flashed him a brilliant smile.

Vik loved the islands.

Although minus the obscene wealth that he had envisioned, Vikram Suri had indeed wound up in a Pacific paradise, quite comfortable with the money that he had made from the book and movie deals, and of course the lecture circuit. It wasn't a bad life, he reasoned. He had achieved the level of fame that he desired and celebrity could always be parlayed into more money. Besides, with his business responsibilities minimized he had little to worry about other than which incredible beauty on the beaches and in the bars of the island to bed that night.

He could now add the one from the Prada shop to that list.

The dinner was expensive, delicious, and quick. Neither guest, as the waiter noted with amused perspicacity, was the least bit interested in the food. The blonde and the Indian had started touching each other early on in the meal and by the end of it, were quite obviously in agreement about what dish would come next.

On the drive over to his villa on the beach, Vik tried to engage the girl in a conversation about herself—where was she from, what did she do? But just as over dinner, she evaded the questions teasingly, as if playing a flirtatious game of hide-and-seek. To the man who hoped to become her lover, her coyness was an aphrodisiac. She was what all men secretly desired—an enigma. The voluptuous body, the sensual lips, the coquettish eyes, had all captivated the Indian so much that he couldn't have cared less if she was from Mars. All he wanted was to have her. She also seemed to be independently wealthy, which put her in the category of horny, not calculating.

The cool spring breeze from the sea rustled sexily through her hair as she allowed Vik to escort her from the car through the glass doors of the patio and into the interior of the sprawling cottage where the media baron had lived ever since his brief sojourn in a five-star prison. After giving her a short tour of the Mediterranean-themed home, Vik guided the young beauty back to the living room, where they settled down on a soft leather loveseat with glasses of champagne.

Vik had dimmed the lights, and through the picture windows across the room, they could look far into the moonlit sea. Tides of silver reared up like giant shark fins in the distance, only to ebb into harmless sheets of mercury by the time the water reached the shore, ending in tiny flecks of cream at the waterline. A soft moan of contentment escaped the woman's lips, and Vik felt triumphant. This was the type of relaxation that only money could buy, and it was a testament to his own lavish tastes that even a rich woman would respond to it.

The bottle of Veuve Clicquot disappeared quickly and he was about to open another when a delicate pink hand dropped gently on his bronzed arm. The mystery woman kissed him softly on the mouth and whispered something in his ear. Vik smiled and took her glass.

While his future paramour undressed in the bathroom, Vik pulled down the covers on his king-sized bed and peeled off his own clothes, his excitement at fever pitch. Since their fateful meeting in the Prada store earlier in the day, he had spent every minute imagining what she would be like in bed. *Would she want him to make love to her slowly? Or rape her unapologetically? Was she looking for a knight, or a king?* He couldn't wait to find out.

As Vik was reveling in his perverted thoughts, the object of his desire was staring at herself in the mirror above the sink, and feeling ill. She was seductively beautiful, with piercing eyes whose gaze was the optical version of the sirens' song, a passionate mouth suggestive of sexual promise, and firm, full breasts that had the power to both soothe and arouse. In the world of mortals, at least, she could bewitch any man she wanted. All this should have made her happy, but in reality the realization of her power only sickened her. She was abusing that which nature had gifted her so generously, and that made her feel like a whore.

Fighting desperately against the onslaught of nausea, she breathed deeply until the danger passed. Then she sat down on the edge of the Jacuzzi and tried to focus herself, vaguely aware that she had been in here for too long. Finally, after an urgent entreaty from the bedroom, she knew that the time had come. There could be no more delays. No more pretending to be "freshening herself up." If she couldn't freshen herself up in ten minutes, she probably wasn't worth making love to.

Reaching inside her handbag, she felt for the flat metallic object that she had placed there before dinner. It was wedged inside a zippered compartment and took her a few seconds to pries out. She withdrew it carefully.

Turning off the light, she walked back into the bedroom completely naked and approached the bed with deliberate slowness. Vik's eyes were alight with desire and the delay maddened him. He reached out to touch her. She pulled back slightly, then glided unhurriedly onto the bed, her right hand folded behind her back. In her chest, her heart pounded crazily.

Vik climbed on top of her and parted her legs with his knees. A lascivious look crept into his predatory eyes. He had changed his mind. He didn't care what she wanted. He would hurt her anyway.

But before he could have his way with her, the girl turned the tables by reaching down and rubbing him in an extremely sensitive part of his anatomy. The woman's astonishingly soft touch and the slow, expert motion of the slender fingers sent a mild electric current coursing through the Indian's body. He began to moan helplessly—like a woman in heat. The pleasure of being manipulated so completely by a gorgeous young blonde was far superior to the temporary lust-filled assault that he had been contemplating.

"You're so incredibly beautiful. Don't stop," he implored, nuzzling his unshaven face into the girl's creamy breasts.

In response, the young woman took Vik's testicles in her hand and with the other withdrew the switchblade from behind her back. There was an audible click as the blade flicked into place.

Vik's euphoria was momentarily interrupted by the ominous sound. In the split second following that, he had a strange thought. *The soft, hypnotic eyes of the woman had been watching him at the Prada store even before she bumped into him. It was as if she had* intended *for the accident to happen, and counted on his picking her up.*

He barely had time to ponder the implications of this when there came an abrupt, sharp pain between his legs. There was the instant sensation of wetness and Vik sprang from the bed, staring down in disbelief. His eyes widened beyond their natural boundaries and in the light from the bedside lamp, he looked like a cartoon character. Thousands of miles away, a young computer geek named Corey Meeks suddenly felt the impulse to smile—and couldn't explain it.

A profound sense of satisfaction slipped over the young woman's heart like a warm blanket as she witnessed Vik's shock and dismay. She calmly swiveled off the bed and on to her feet, the blood-soaked switchblade dangling casually from her hand like a cigarette in the mouth of Humphrey Bogart. She faced the former CEO with quiet fury.

Even as the dizziness began to wash over him, Vikram Suri gazed at the woman who had just castrated him, and needed to know the truth.

"Why?" he asked hoarsely, the words barely making it out of his rapidly drying mouth.

"Because you killed my father," came the chilling reply.

Fear gripped Vik like a vise. Then he realized that the girl had never told him her last name. With a doom-filled heart, he finally asked: "Who are you?"

The blade flashed angrily in the light and before Vikram Suri could react he had begun his painful descent to hell. As he lay dying on his own carpet next to his own bed, the woman leaned over him and smiled. Her lips moved in the red haze gathering in front of his eyes and two words emerged. They floated downwards slowly, like feathers, taking forever to reach his ears. They were the last two words he ever heard.

"Tracey Wachowski."

about the author

Sanjay Sanghoee has an MBA from Columbia Business School and was an investment banker with Lazard Frères & Co. and subsequently with Dresdner Kleinwort Wasserstein. At Lazard, he was part of an eight-person team headed by Steven Rattner and had the opportunity of working on banking transactions for major media companies such as Time Warner, Comcast, and Pearson.

He is currently a consultant for LLJ Capital, a special situations fund focused on the media and telecom sectors.

In 1992–1995, Sanjay worked with Strategic Intelligence Network, Inc., a spinoff from Kroll Associates. During his time with SINI, he was involved in all facets of corporate investigative work, including liaising with ex–law enforcement officers to conduct due diligence on business transactions.

In addition to the above, he has also written spec episodes for the TV shows *Law & Order* and *Without a Trace,* and is the Chairman of the Media & Entertainment Committee of Columbia Business School's Alumni Club.

Sanjay is based in New York City.